Judge
of Israel

Timothy S. Wilkinson

Volume Two of the
Eternal Throne Chronicles

Judge of Israel

http://www.timothywilkinson.net

Lulu Publishing, Inc.
860 Aviation Parkway
Suite 300
Morrisville, NC 27560
U.S.A.

First Edition
June 2010

ISBN: 978-0-557-52061-9

PRINTED IN THE UNITED STATES OF AMERICA

-Acknowledgements-

Writing is one of the most solitary of tasks. Banished to the shadowy world of my own thoughts, I find solace in the bridge between that secret place and the rest of the universe: my readers. To them and to the following, I give my thanks:

- To my students: after all these years, still I remember every one of you
- To Cindy Avery, for understanding me and my writing better than almost anyone
- To Holly Wickersham, for not being able to finish earlier drafts because they made her too emotional
- To Corey and Rebecca Wilkinson, who are never far from me, no matter what the map may say
- To Daniel and Cora Bauguess, true friends who have been there from the beginning, and will be to the end
- To Jordan Avery, a true literary conneseuir, who knows the beauty and peril of the writer's world
- To my mother, for guaranteeing me an audience
- To my selfless editor Kate Goschen, whose alchemy helps transform my leaden writing
- To Isaac and Amira Gloor, for devouring *Prophet*
- To my father, who took history from books and put it into my hands
- To my brothers who, taken together, can finish any journey, create any beauty, and defeat any enemy;
- To Circe, Colin, Tavish, and Finian, for giving me twenty years to look forward to
- To Chelsey, who did not know she married a man who lives always in two worlds, but who courageously holds my hand in both

For the lost children of
the House of Wilkinson:
Tiths, Lincoln, and Legend

New chapters in our story

-Priests of Israel-

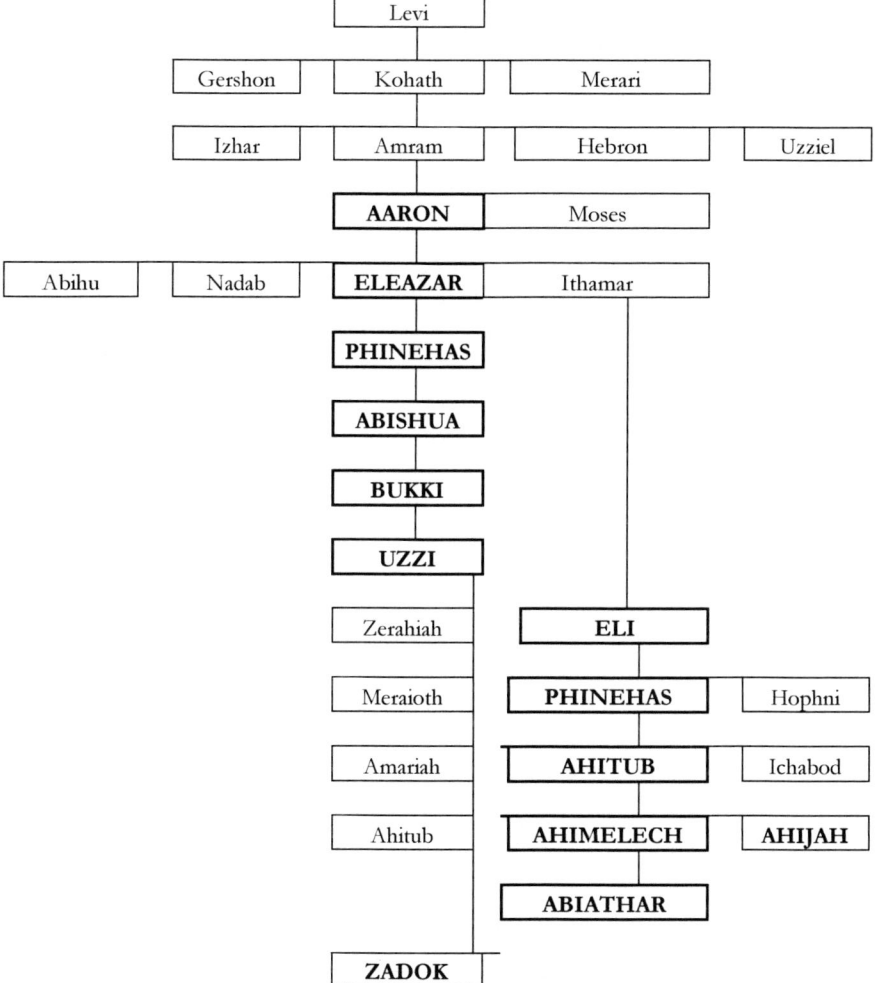

*Names in bold capitals served as High Priest

-The Tribes of Israel-

ASHER
BENJAMIN
DAN
EPHRAIM
GAD
ISSACHAR
JUDAH
MANASSEH
NAPHTALI
REUBEN
SIMEON
ZEBULUN

LEVI, THE PRIESTLY TRIBE

-Author's Note-

This first printing is being printed before my editor, Kate Goschen, has worked her magic on it. I take full responsibility for all errors, grammatical and otherwise, in the text.

The following book is a work of fiction. The historical account from which it is drawn, found in the Holy Bible in the book of 1 Samuel, Chapter 7, is factual. Any similarities between the two are intentional.

As Appendix E will explain in greater detail, this story is written on the premise that the Biblical account of Israel's transformation to a monarchy in the days of Samuel and David is the origin of the famous stories of King Arthur and the Knights of the Round Table. If the story of King David did transmogrify into the story of King Arthur, it might have gone through many gradual changes in the centuries between the writing of the two accounts. This book does not claim to tell the story of what really happened in Palestine in the 10th century, but to present what the author imagines could have been one of those early renditions of the account as it slowly changed from history to literature. Therefore, while I have tried to never contradict any known Biblical fact, the details with which I fleshed out the story came from historical research, the demands of the story, and the tone, themes, and narrative elements of the Arthurian tales.

This is the story of a war fought in Palestine at the dawn of the Iron Age. In describing this war, I have attempted, for the edification of my readers, to capture the grisly reality of Iron Age warfare without resorting to the inclusion of gratuitous violence or gruesome descriptions. It has been my intent to use as a guideline for my own writing the descriptions of battle, war, and violence in the Bible itself (such as Deuteronomy 28 and 32, Numbers 25, Judges 3, 4, 9:53, 16:21, 19, 1 Samuel 15:33, 2 Samuel 2:23, 3:22-30, 8:2, 16:22, 18:14-17, 20:10-13, 2 Chronicles 21, or Acts 1:18). Such details are meant to educate and illuminate.

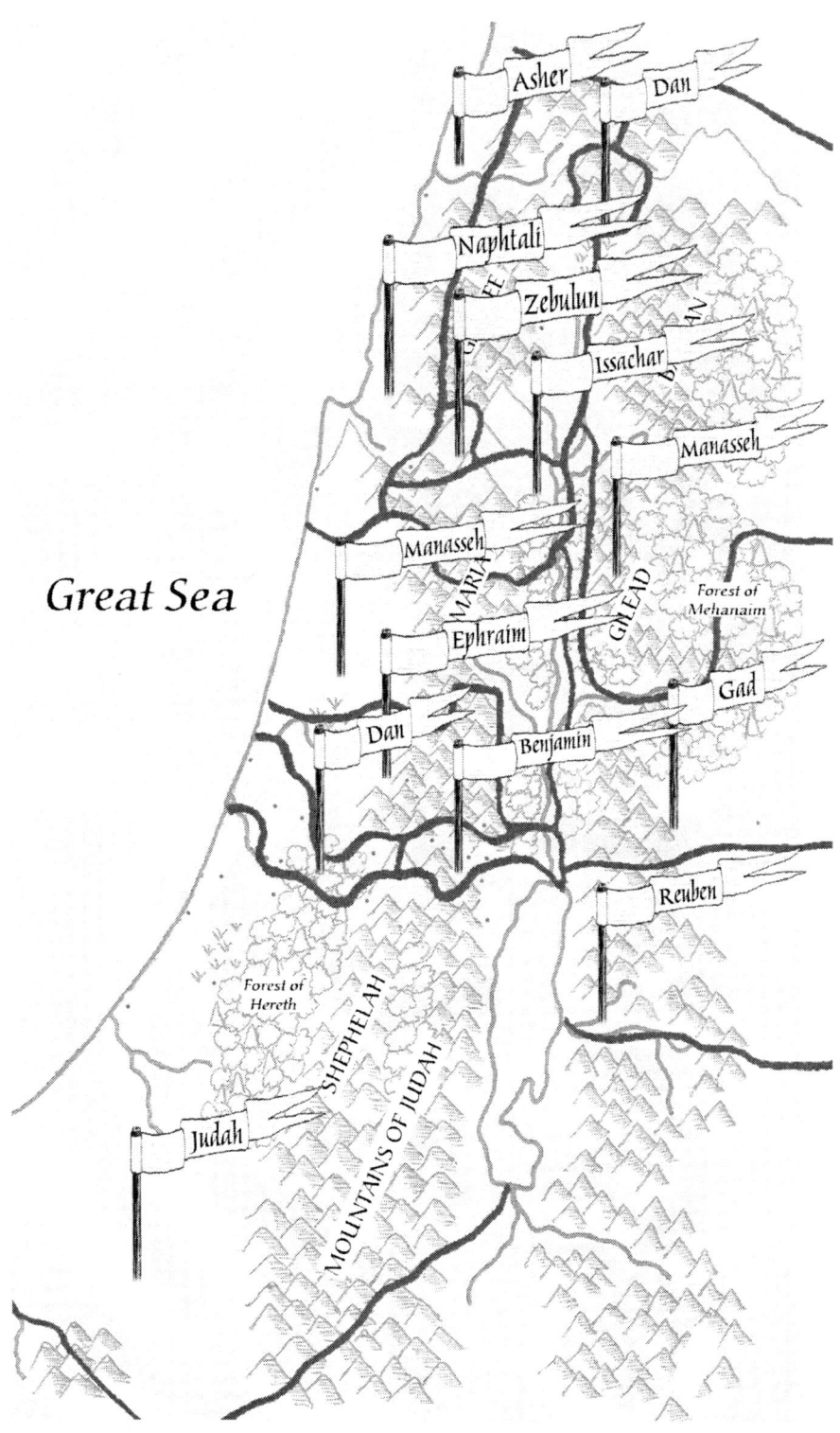

Great Sea

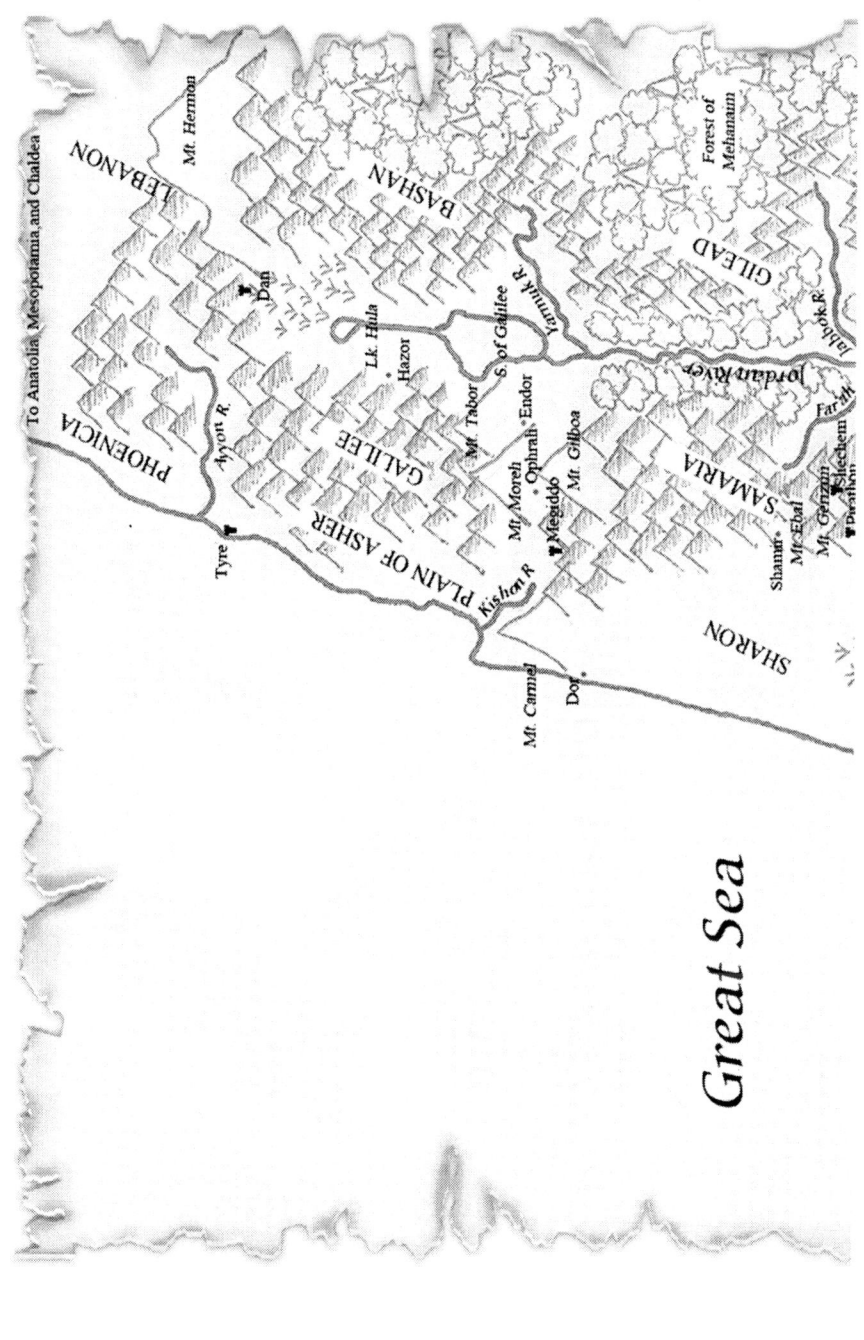

Great Sea

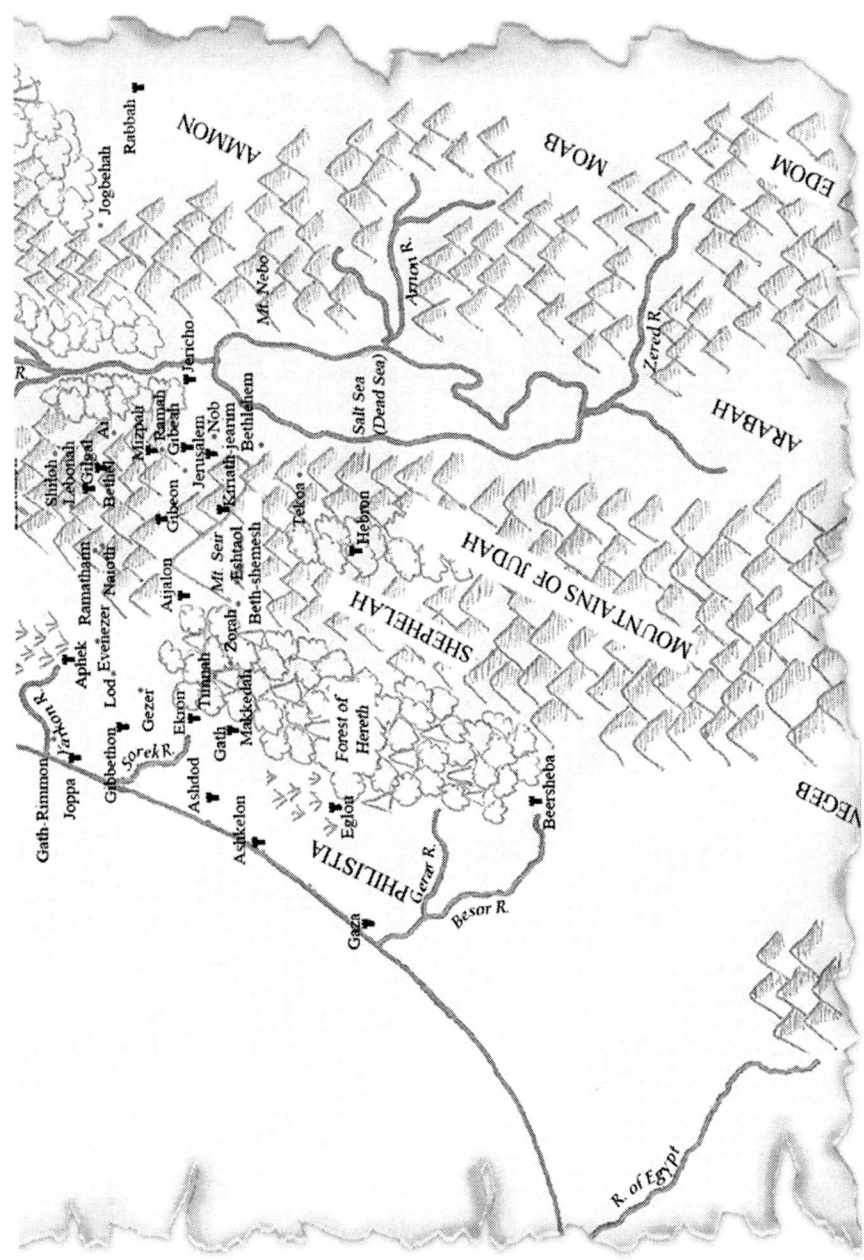

1

"Now after these things it happened that God put Abraham to the test." – The Scroll of Bereshith

Samuel was already awake when the dogs began to bark, but he remained motionless, eyes closed, until he felt Liora sit up beside him.

"Samuel?" she whispered.

He slid one leg out from under the warmth of the wool blanket and rolled out of bed. "I hear them."

The cold of the floor seemed to sap the heat from his feet. He lifted his prophet's *me'il*, the sleeveless coat of his office, from a peg on the wall, wrapped it around his thin tunic and slipped his feet into his sandals. There was still sand in them, gritty against his bare soles. He was reaching for the curtain when it was limned by orange light from without, and then pushed open from the next room, and he was blinded for a moment by the glare of an oil lamp.

The silhouetted shape holding the burning vessel spoke: "My lord— I think you should come."

Samuel shielded his eyes against the flickering light. "I am coming, Reuel. What is it?"

The young man did not answer, but turned abruptly in the darkness and strode toward the dwelling's front door. Samuel glanced over to the corner of the room where his sons normally slept, then remembered that they had built a makeshift tent on the roof to stay in for the night. He turned back toward Liora, a vague anxiety prickling the back of his neck. "Look in on the boys," he said, and her lithe form slipped from bed as he turned through the doorway.

Samuel stepped down from the raised floor of the bedchamber and followed the wavering circle of lamplight that slid across half-hidden furnishings, the fog of sleep lifting from his mind until he distinguished both the barking of the local shepherds' dogs and the distant baying of hounds.

Hunting hounds.

"Philistines," Samuel breathed.

He followed Reuel out into the courtyard, inhaling the crisp, clean smell of heavy dew. Stars pierced the blue-blackness overhead. At the open gate, Reuel took another lamp from an alcove in the earthen wall, lit it and handed it to Samuel; it hissed and spat as the sweet, sharp smell of burning olive oil filled his nostrils. Samuel raised the light as high above his head as he could, his eyes adjusting as he peered into the night.

Drumming hoof-beats rumbled off the nearby hills, and Samuel saw a line of torches wending down toward Naioth, an approaching serpent drawn of intermittent flames. The light and its implications transfixed his eyes, and without turning, he said, "Gather every man who can hold a weapon."

Reuel disappeared around Samuel's house, his sandals clapping in the still air. Samuel walked past the outbuildings and stables to the intersection of the main road and the entrance to the little hamlet known as Naioth. *Where is the sentry?* he asked himself. He held the lamp aloft again, his eyes straining to make out any detail beyond the flames of a dozen torches streaming backwards as their bearers galloped toward him. All but invisible, a pack of low, dark forms stretched ahead of the chariots, baying, their eyes reflecting red torchlight.

Suddenly, two figures stumbled from a tangle of juniper, camphor, and mallow bushes and fell in a heap on the roadway just beyond where Samuel stood. Samuel started back, glancing over his shoulder to see if Reuel was returning yet with reinforcements. The two figures, barely visible against the darkness, clambered to their feet and began lurching toward him.

"Help us!" one of them called, breathless.

"Who comes to the School of the Prophets?" Samuel responded.

The two figures continued approaching; Samuel could now make out that the taller one seemed to be supporting the shorter.

"My lord—help me!" The voice was thin and high-pitched, like Samuel's own sons, but ragged with pain.

At that moment, the Philistines thundered into view over a rise in the road, torches streaming as they drove their chariots forward in mad pursuit. Amber firelight flickered off the crown-like helmets of three warriors in each chariot: driver, archer, and spearman, and the *cracks* of the driver's whips cut the air.

Samuel was already moving. In ten steps he closed the distance between himself and the man and boy approaching, their faces streaked with tears and their eyes wide with terror. "Help us!" begged the man, the boy's right arm draped over his own shoulders.

The boy leaned heavily on a makeshift staff. Samuel took its place, getting under the child's arm, and heard his muffled whimper of pain as the staff clattered to the rocky ground. He smelled of juniper pitch, camphor oil, and sweat. A black-fletched arrow transfixed the boy's thigh, and blood covered his bare knee and shin. Even in the torchlight, Samuel could see that the boy's face was wan, and his eyelids fluttered as he struggled to maintain consciousness.

"Sons of Belial!" Samuel hissed.

Shouts sounded; torches flared and, one by one, golden light spilled from windows in the homes and dormitories all around them. As Samuel helped the injured boy hobble forward, Reuel emerged from the dark with two dozen men and boys, dressed in their *me'ils*: the *Beneh Hannevi'im*, the Sons of the Prophets. Their torches glittered dully against the bronze blades of bills, sickles and knives and the polished, wooden tines of pitchforks. One man carried a simple, patinated short sword; Samuel remembered seeing it propping up a trellis the day before.

The baying of the hounds reached a crescendo. Glancing over his shoulder Samuel saw their lean forms leaping toward him. The *Beneh* charged forward, farm tools outstretched as Samuel half-dragged the injured boy to safety. Philistine arrows hissed out of the darkness; one ricocheted off the ground at Samuel's feet and skidded across the road and into a courtyard wall.

The father was still trying to support the boy's other arm, but limping so exhaustedly that Samuel wondered if he wasn't adding to the burden.

The hounds yelped and snarled in pain, and Samuel knew the *Beneh* had stopped them for the moment. Then a horn sounded, a single, short blat, and the dogs whirled in response and leapt back towards the chariots. The arrows stopped flying as well, and Liora and Reuel rushed from the darkness to help Samuel. Reuel tried at first to carry the boy in his arms, but stopped when the touch of his hand to the boy's leg brought a yelp of agony. As Liora and Reuel aided him and his father toward Samuel's home, the Prophet turned back to the road where the chariots were reining to a halt in a cloud of their own dust.

Samuel immediately recognized the man driving the lead chariot, a lean, rawboned Philistine commander named Glaucus. Beneath his short-cropped grey hair, his right ear was all but enveloped by a purple-veined, bulbous growth that bulged from one side of his head. Sawing the reins, he struggled to bring his lathered stallions under control.

"I am the garrison commander of Aphek in the service of the Axis Lord of Ekron," Glaucus announced, his voice distorted by some resonant effect of the tumor. The horses shook their heads, gnawing the bits, and the chariot shifted forward; Glaucus hauled back on the reins again. The hounds poised on their haunches near the wheels, red tongues lolling.

"By the authority of Lord Ekron I order you to turn over the boy and his father," Glaucus said. "They have violated curfew in an occupied city and traveled beyond their territory without permission from the garrison."

Samuel glanced around. The archers in the other chariots stood poised, their arrows aimed at him. He felt his heart pounding against his ribs and heard it in his ears. The *Beneh* stood on either side of him, "weapons" at the ready, but it was obvious that they were no match for the heavily armed and armored Philistines.

He still held the bloodied staff that the boy had been leaning on, and he planted it in front of him in an effort to appear determined. His first attempt to speak failed and he felt a fool as he coughed and tried to clear the dryness from his throat. "I am a servant of the Sovereign Lord Jehovah of Armies," he finally got out, "the God of the Ark of the Covenant. Leave this place or risk the wrath of Jehovah, who brought Philistia to its knees with plague, who sank the armies of Egypt into the depths of the sea, who brought the walls of Jericho down around its inhabitant's ears!"

Glaucus eased the reins and allowed his horses to lunge forward to within a few paces of where Samuel stood. His scowl etched by shadow, he gathered the reins in his left hand, drew his sword and pointed it at Samuel.

"Jehovah may or may not have been responsible for the plague on Philistia. Who can claim to know the ways of the gods? But today, Seer, this is between you and me."

Samuel said a silent prayer for courage and wisdom. Without looking he felt the *Beneh* gathering behind him, their torches brightening the pool of light on the ground all around his feet. He heard some of them murmuring prayers or psalms, a swelling ritual of chanted sound.

"You have no authority here," he said, forcing his voice to remain steady. "We do not recognize your title or your law—especially when you use it to attack innocent children."

Glaucus shouted at the horses and pulled the reins simultaneously. The stallions reared and thrashed their hooves.

Samuel told himself that his feet had sent down roots into the dry soil of the road, and that he could not move even if he wanted to. He told himself that he was part of the ancient stone that lay somewhere beneath his feet. The *Beneh* eased forward on either side of him, their voices building into the chant of ecstatics, their faces eerily lit by lamps and torchlight, masks to shroud all but their intensity. Some were still children, but they faced the armed soldiers unhesitatingly. It was because of their trust in him, Samuel knew—their confidence that he, the Prophet of Israel, would protect them from all harm.

Glaucus let the rearing horses lurch the chariot forward until Samuel could feel the wind from their pawing hooves brushing his hair. He could see the whites of their wild eyes, shining wetly in the torchlight.

I am an ancient tree, Samuel thought. *I am immovable.*

Then the stallions were stepping backwards, pulling away in response to Glaucus' pressure on the reins. The Philistine sheathed his sword.

"I have no desire to kill children, or women," Glaucus shouted over Samuel's head, as if to assure that all gathered could hear his largesse. "But whether you wish to acknowledge it or not, even the School of the Prophets is subject to the laws of the Axis Lords!"

He wheeled the chariot around dramatically, and the other vehicles followed suit. But Glaucus turned in the car and smiled back at Samuel with fierce and fearless confidence. "We will return, Sorcerer! We have left you and your little hamlet of rabble-rousers alone for too long, it seems. We will come back for the boy and his father. Make certain that these women and children are gone when we do, because you will receive no more mercy at Lord Ekron's hands. What happens then will be on your head!"

He turned back and cracked the whip; the chariots lurched away in a cloud of torch-lit dust, hounds loping alongside them. As fear gave way to relief and Samuel felt himself begin to shake uncontrollably, he heard Glaucus' voice over the crunching of wheels on gravel: "The boy and his father or your precious School, Samuel! Choose!"

2

*"Take, please, your son Isaac, your only son whom you so love,
and...offer him as a burnt offering on the mountain that I show
you." – The Scroll of Bereshith*

Inside Samuel's house, Liora had thrown a blanket of reddish-brown
wool on the floor, and Reuel and the boy's father had lain the injured
boy atop it. He whimpered, but faintly, as though he was asleep and
some terror haunted his dreams. As Liora lit lamps from one of the torches
and placed them all around the blanket, Reuel knelt and examined the
wound.

"They meant to kill him!" the man said, his voice cracking. "A son
of only eight years!"

Samuel's sons had come down from the roof and stood next to the
blanket, lamplight reflecting in their wide eyes as they stared at the dark pool

of blood diffusing slowly across the wool. "What happened, Papa?" Joel asked.

"Stand back, Joel—you, too, Abijah," Samuel said, moving around the blanket to usher them into a corner, out of Reuel's way. "Reuel is going to help this boy get better."

The boys huddled next to their mother. "What happen, Papa?" Abijah repeated the question. Two years younger than Joel, he was rapidly catching up to him in his ability to talk—primarily because he mimicked his brother's every word.

"He is hurt, Abijah. But he is going to be alright."

"Why?" Abijah asked.

Liora knelt and put her arms around the boys, pulling them close and whispering in their ears.

Samuel put one hand on the father's shoulder. "Reuel is the best healer I know. Your son is in capable hands."

The man nodded, his shoulders shaking with barely-controlled weeping.

Reuel lifted a worn, wooden case, its polished sides stained red with vermilion. He placed it on the floor next to the boy and opened it, revealing a jumbled collection of bottles, jars, rolled bandages, and dried leaves. A swirl of aromas wafted across the room: herbs, spices, and the sharp smell of terebinth oil.

Samuel took the father's arm and drew him farther from the boy. "Who are you, and from where do you come?"

"I am Cheran ben Jochabed, of Gath-Rimmon. This is Gavriel, my firstborn. He told us he was having visions. He begged us to bring him here, to the School. We did not know what to do...We were not sure if he even knew..."

"It is hard to accept that one so young could be a prophet," Samuel said, trying to be comforting. He fought back the anger that rose, unbidden, within him. He knew the pain, and the loneliness, of living with a gift like Gavriel's. He knew how desperately such children needed the support and trust of those they loved.

"Yesterday, after the evening meal, he disappeared," Cheran continued. "We are under a curfew—the sons of Philistia will kill anyone they find outside the city walls after sunset. I caught up to him just beyond the garrison. He said he was coming here."

"And then Glaucus found you?" Samuel asked.

Cheran nodded. "As soon as they saw us, I knew...They shot at us in the dark! We have been running ever since."

"And sent a garrison army after you?" Samuel asked incredulously.

"We escaped into the forest," Cheran said. "There were only a few chasing us then. But they must have realized we were coming here. Their feelings toward you are well known, my lord. They will find any excuse to bring an army to your door."

"You are safe now," Samuel said. He tried to think of something else to say, but Gavriel cried out in pain and Samuel and Cheran turned to watch Reuel at work. The healer had mixed balm of Gilead, myrrh, verdigris, terebinth and olive oils, honey, and dried figs into a poultice and was packing it gently around the wound, where the arrow shaft disappeared into Gavriel's leg.

"Liora—fetch me wine, please," the healer said.

She returned a moment later with a half-filled skin, and Reuel poured a splash of the contents into a small, fired-earthenware cup. Grinding golden nuggets of myrrh to fine powder in a stone mortar, he sprinkled it into the wine and held the cup to Gavriel's lips. "Drink," he whispered.

The boy did not respond, but when Reuel tipped the cup Gavriel's lips opened and he let the liquid trickle down his throat, coughing once, weakly. A moment later he blinked several times and his eyes seemed to focus again. He turned his head to look at Samuel. "Are you really the Prophet?" he asked, his voice slurred like a child who speaks even as they fall asleep. "They say that you struck all the land of Philistia with plague, and forced them to return the Ark of the Covenant."

Samuel saw the pooling blood running off the blanket's edge onto the packed-earth floor. He forced himself to smile. "It was Jehovah who struck them. But I did see the Ark returned."

Reuel slid his hand under Gavriel's thigh, and the boy arched his back and shouted with pain. Jaw locked, Reuel kept his hand there a moment longer. Samuel heard the *snap* of the arrow shaft breaking, and Gavriel began to cry.

Samuel was about to say something to him, but the boy spoke first, through his sobbing. "They say that you carried the flame of the Altar in your bare hands from Shiloh to Nob, and were not burned by it!"

Reuel laid the bloody arrowhead on the floor. "We have to get the shaft out now," he whispered, looking from Samuel to Cheran. "We have to clear the wound, and staunch the blood."

Cheran nodded. "Just pull. Make it quick."

"They say that when the sons of Philistia attacked," Gavriel said, almost shouting through his pain, "Jehovah sent a giant to protect you!"

Reuel turned and wrapped his hand around the shaft, crushing the black fletching in his fist. "Hold his arms," he said.

Cheran grabbed one of Gavriel's arms and Samuel the other. "They say that you know the hour of your own death!" Gavriel shouted, sobbing.

Reuel removed his hand from the arrow, wiped his palm on the front of his tunic, and gripped the shaft again.

Gavriel looked down at Reuel's hand, tears streaking his cheeks. "Father?" he pleaded.

Liora placed herself between Joel and Abijah and the blanket, and hid their faces in the front of her dress. Reuel looked at Cheran again.

"Just pull," Cheran whispered. "Just pull."

"They say that you—" Gavriel yelled again, but he did not finish. In one swift, smooth movement, Reuel slid the arrow from his thigh. The boy screamed and his back arched up from the blanket. Then he collapsed, limp, eyes closed, his head lolling to one side. Bright blood, streaked with black, bubbled up from the wound.

"Oh, my son..." Cheran groaned.

Reuel leaned over until his ear was just above Gavriel's open mouth. "He is asleep. It is best that way." He washed the wound with rue and frankincense in terebinth oil, and then packed it gently with the poultice he had made. Unrolling a narrow strip of dark linen from his red box, he wrapped it around and around the boy's leg.

"When will he wake?" Cheran asked.

Reuel shook his head. "I do not know. Sooner is not necessarily better. But he is strong. We will pray for him, that Jehovah's healing Spirit might make him well."

Samuel raised his eyes toward the shadowed ceiling, where lamplight played off of the smoke-darkened sycamore beams. "Sovereign Lord Jehovah," he implored, "heal this boy. Hear our prayer, and heal him."

"He is so young..." Cheran said, resting his palm briefly on the boy's sweat-streaked forehead.

"Many here at the School were called when still very young," Samuel said. "He disclosed to your ears the vision he was granted?"

Cheran nodded, finally tearing his eyes from his son to look at Samuel's face. "He said he saw a cloud of darkness traveling up the lip of the

Great Sea, from the south. It swept across the land, swallowing it up...there was more, but I do not remember..."

Samuel put a hand on his shoulder. "It is alright. I will speak to him about it after he has rested."

"What do you think it means?" Cheran asked.

Samuel shook his head. "I cannot be sure yet." *But the Philistines are to the south,* he thought silently. He could not help but remember the warning vision granted to Rohgah over two decades earlier, a vision that included a cloud of darkness sweeping over Israel...

He glanced at his sons. Abijah was still clinging to Liora's skirt, but Joel, two years older, had stepped closer to the injured boy.

"Can I help him, Papa?" Joel asked.

"Do you have room for one more in your tent on the roof?"

Joel turned toward him solemnly. "We have room, Papa."

Abijah nodded. "We have woom, Papa."

"Good," Samuel said. "Reuel will carry Gavriel up to join you there."

Liora frowned. "Should he be moved so soon? To sleep with two rambunctious boys?"

"Whatever damage could be done by movement is already done," said Cheran. "We walked for almost half the night after he was injured."

Reuel had one palm placed to Gavriel's brow. "It is cooler on the roof," he said. "The fresh night air—or what is left of it—will be good for him."

Liora knelt in front of both boys, tucking her hair behind her delicate ears. Samuel had always thought they looked like the ears of a a child. "You must let him sleep! Right now, he cannot feel the hurt to his leg. But if he wakes up, he will be in great pain again."

Joel nodded and Abijah, watching his older brother, nodded as well.

Reuel lifted Gavriel and began gently carrying him outside to the steps that led to the roof. Joel and Abijah followed, silenced by the seriousness of the task that had been entrusted to them.

"Come and tell us immediately if he wakes or cries out in his sleep," Samuel called after them.

"We will, Papa," Joel answered, and they disappeared into the darkness outside.

An instant later, Abijah peered back around the corner of the door. "Papa?"

"Yes?"

"We will," he said, nodding solemnly, and followed his brother up the stairs.

"You boys have been very brave," Samuel said as they left.

Cheran was slumped against one wall. "You need to rest as well, my brother," Samuel said. "Let us make you a bed here, in our home."

"What of the vision?" Cheran asked.

"I am already scheduled to meet with the Elders of Ramathaim in the morning," said Samuel. "I will share this warning with them then. They will decide what action we should take."

"There is a threat to the nation, then?" Cheran asked.

Samuel shrugged. "I cannot be sure, but that is one thing the vision could mean. We will know more when I can hear the details from Gavriel. Until then, again I tell you—sleep! Remain tonight under our roof."

Cheran was silent for a moment, but that moment told Samuel all he needed to know. *Eyes looking to the left. Hands balled into fists. Shoulders and neck tight.*

"I appreciate your hospitality, my lord..." Cheran began.

"There is some other concern that urges you to leave here at once?"

"My family. No doubt Philistine soldiers were sent to our home after Gavriel's escape was discovered. I do not know what has become of them."

"I cannot persuade you to put off this journey until morning?"

Cheran's chin dropped further. "I would not disobey your instructions, my lord..."

"But your desire is to go." Samuel finished the sentence for him. "Very well. Then I shall provide you with a donkey and provisions—and an escort, if you want one."

Cheran lowered his head. "My lord...my gratitude exceeds my skill with words. My debt to you...the expense of the frankincense alone..."

"Do not mention it again," said Samuel. "Return to your family. Put your heart at ease."

"You do not mind watching over my son?"

"Reuel!" Samuel called, and the healer came immediately to his side.

"Here I am," he said.

"Have one of the *Beneh* find this man a donkey to ride, and someone who can travel with him."

"No escort is necessary, my lord," Cheran said. "You will need every man here if Glaucus returns."

"I can spare one man..." Samuel began.

Cheran shook his head. "It is better that I journey alone. You have done more than enough already."

"Even as you have said, my lord," answered Reuel, and disappeared into the waning night.

"May Jehovah shower your household with blessings," said Cheran.

"Israel is my household. We will keep Gavriel safe until your return," said Samuel. "Now go! May Jehovah be with you."

"And may He grant you peace, and length of days," said Cheran, and ducked through the doorway after Reuel.

The house was finally silent again. Samuel looked over at Liora, sitting now on a low, earthen bench built against one wall. The ruddy lamplight brought out the rich, auburn tones in her skin and hair. "Do you think there is any point in going back to bed now?" he asked.

She smiled the gentle, dazzling smile that made his heart ache. In that smile was a peace that Samuel clung to as the world spun madly all around them, an anchor for his soul. "We could watch the sun rise over the mountains," she said softly, holding his eyes with her own.

"From my parents' rooftop, perhaps," Samuel said. "Ours is a little crowded at the moment."

He walked to her and, taking her hands, lifted her to his embrace. She rested her cheek against his shoulder, and her soft, brown hair tickled his nose, smelling of olive oil, myrrh and a hint of aloe. "On any rooftop you wish," she whispered.

He pictured the first time they had met, when he had been captivated by the inner peace with which she seemed to face the world, a quietness of spirit that he envied. The second thing he had noticed was that everything about her was soft: her black hair, her olive skin—even the dress she had been wearing had been made of flower-soft lamb's wool. The same softness had been in her eyes on the day that her father had held both of their hands at Ramathaim's gate and pronounced: "You shall be my son-in-law."

Their front door opened again, and Reuel poked his head inside. He hesitated for only a second. "My lord—I am sorry to interrupt..."

Samuel had already let Liora go, looking at Reuel's youthful face. *Brow knitted. Lips tight. Eyes glancing from Samuel to Liora and back again.*

"What is it?" Samuel asked.

Reuel glanced again at Liora. "My lord, I think you should come..."

Liora smiled at Samuel and brushed at the air with the back of her hand as though shooing him away. "Go."

He turned, slid his sandals back on, and followed Reuel out the door and through the courtyard gate to the roadway. Low clouds shrouded the first light of the sunrise over the distant mountains, but it was bright enough to see without torches. Reuel led him to the place where Samuel had faced Glaucus just a short time before; Samuel saw the scars in the light, sandy soil, torn by the hooves of their horses and the iron-bound wheels of their chariots.

He followed Reuel to a cluster of plane trees, their roots hidden in a thick swath of grass and spindly mustard plants, the trees' strange russet bark peeling off in strips and chunks to reveal the blonde trunk beneath.

Atop those roots was one of the *Beneh*, a bright, happy young man named Zimri. He lay with his body turned at a strange angle, his prophet's *me'il* twisted around him. A pool of blood spread out from his head, soaking into the earth and smeared across the roots of the plane trees.

"I assigned him sentry duty last night," said Reuel, his voice cracking.

For a long time, Samuel could not speak. Bitterness filled his mouth, and he fell to his knees next to the corpse.

"No," he whispered, feeling hot tears on his cheeks.

"An arrow..." Reuel gestured vaguely at his own throat, but could not finish the sentence.

"O Jehovah," Samuel said, lifting his eyes heavenward. "Strengthen the hearts of his family. Strengthen our hearts."

"The bloodguilt of those uncircumcised dogs keeps growing," Reuel said, rare bitterness in his voice.

"Jehovah will see it, and ask it back from their hands," Samuel whispered.

"May we live to see that day," Reuel said.

3

When Samuel returned home, sparrows had woken with the dawn, singing and darting wildly through the chill morning air. The clouds and fog were burning off with the rising of the sun, and swaths of blue sky were visible across the mountaintops to the east. Somewhere in the distance, Samuel heard a man's voice raised in song, probably a farmer walking to the fields to begin his day's work. He thought of Cheran, riding as quickly as he could back to his family, burdened now by fears and worries that the farmer could not begin to understand.

Samuel allowed himself a sigh and shook his head wearily. He had seen so many fathers and mothers come to Naioth over the past several years, all of them haunted by the same disbelief. *Our son says he is having visions. Our son dreams about what will be.*

As difficult as it was for the parents, Samuel reflected, it marked the dawn of a new age for the nation. Jehovah was again speaking to His people, and not just through Samuel. Seers arrived at Naioth, blessed with an extraordinary insight, granted the ability to discern the divine will. Visionaries came, men whose gift carried them briefly to another world wherein they saw and experienced events taking place far away or that might happen in the future. Prophets, like Samuel, were given inspired messages spoken by God himself or by means of Seers or Visionaries and filled with an irresistible urge to declare them.

Since Rohgah, Visionaries were becoming more common, and Samuel and the others at the School struggled to adjust to this method of revelation. Isaac, Jacob, and Joseph had been given visions many centuries before, but it was not something that anyone thoroughly understood. It was one of the reasons that Samuel had decided to found the School of the Prophets, so that young men who were chosen for these privileges by Jehovah could be surrounded by others who, to some degree, understood their experiences and feelings. All too often parents of Prophets discounted or dismissed what their children tried to tell them. More than once young men or boys had arrived at Samuel's door on their own, only to have their frantic parents appear days later to ask for Samuel's help in finding their "lost" son.

Samuel invited these families to move to Naioth and join him at the School. It was a difficult decision for them. The land non-Levite families lived on in Israel had been apportioned to them by Jehovah himself in the days of Joshua. It was a hereditary possession that could not be sold or given away to another family, and it was their responsibility to care for it and to see that it gave its yield to the nation. Some fathers chose to move to Naioth and allow their relatives to care for their land in their absence. Most, though, reluctantly left their children in Samuel's care. Every time he watched a father and mother say their tearful goodbyes to their son, he was carried back to his own childhood, to the day his parents had left him in the care of High Priest Eli at the Tabernacle in Shiloh. He knew at least what these children were feeling. He would do everything in his power to give them the care he had at times lacked.

His musings made him think of Rohgah, and how much he missed the old man since he had disappeared some years before. The last time he had visited Samuel, Rohgah had all but told him that he was about to die. No one had seen the ancient prophet since; no one had even found a body. Samuel liked to imagine that the old man had chosen some secret place to lay himself down, to rest there undisturbed until time had reduced him to dust.

When Samuel entered his house again Liora had removed the blood-soaked blanket; her circlet of dowry coins tinkled softly as she moved.

A clay vessel sat against the wall, water she had drawn from the cistern behind their home. Having their own private cistern was an extravagance that Samuel was uncomfortable with, but Reuel and the *Beneh* had insisted on building him one and on keeping it filled for his use.

Liora was gathering the pottery fragments and rolling the vellum scrolls that he had been writing on the evening before. She looked up and held out one of the scrolls. "How is your writing progressing?"

He had been working for the past couple of years on a history of Israel since the days of Joshua. It focused so far on the acts of the Judges that had led the nation during those years: Othniel's defeat of the Mesopotamian king Cushan; Ehud's assassination of the obese Moabite King Eglon; heroic Shamgar, alone and armed with only a cattle goad, battling 600 Philistine soldiers; Barak's defeat of the Canaanite army under General Sisera, and the assassination of Sisera by Jael, the wife of Heber the Kenite metalworker; Gideon's defeat of the Midianite hordes with only 300 men armed with torches, horns, and earthenware jars.

"I am nearly finished with the account of Judge Jephthah," Samuel said. "I think I want to have Tirzah read it over before I decide it is done."

"And after Jephthah?" Liora asked.

Samuel shrugged. In the last twenty-five years, since Jephthah's death, three judges had ruled in Israel: Ibzan, Elon, and the current judge, Avdon. Samuel had appointed all of them at Jehovah's direction. The years since had seen no major conflicts—just border skirmishes, cattle raids in Gilead, and the unending struggle to keep the nation from sliding into the degradation of Canaanite religion and culture.

He did not tell her that he had been writing psalms, because he did not plan on showing her any of them. Some of them were an attempt to capture his feelings for her, but it just was not possible. In spite of his best efforts, his feelings were simply too deep, too strong, and too complex for his skill with words. He worried that people—including her—who admired his talent as a writer would not understand his inability to write about that which mattered most to him.

"I haven't decided," he answered finally.

She noticed something in his voice, or his hesitation. "What is wrong?"

"Zimri is dead."

She sank slowly into a stool, brow knit, full lips parting slightly in shock. "How?"

"Murdered," Samuel said. "Sometime last night, while he was on sentry duty. Sometime before the Philistines arrived."

"Oh, Samuel," she said, standing and wrapping her arms around him. "I am so sorry."

He rubbed her back with his left hand. "Something is going on—something that has to do with little Gavriel's vision."

She pulled away, slipping her hands into his own. "You should go and check on him."

"Have you heard any noise from up there?" he asked, gesturing toward the ceiling with his chin.

She shook her head. "Silent as mice."

It was a private joke: in the dry season, mice were forever rustling through holes they had dug in the walls or roof.

"I'll go look," Samuel said, and ducking outside tiptoed up the earthen stairway that ascended one exterior wall to the roof.

Dew had collected on the ends of the sycamore roof beams—Reuel would have had Samuel's home built with cedar, or cypress beams, but Samuel refused to live a lifestyle that might be seen as more exalted than others in Naioth or Ramathaim.

Atop the roof, near the granite roller left there to re-compact the packed clay after rain, Joel and Gavriel had built a framework of green willow sticks and draped a blanket over the top of it to form a little tent. Samuel saw immediately that all three boys were sleeping soundly. Gavriel's chest rose and fell steadily, almost in time to Joel and Abijah's; apparently, he had succumbed completely to the combination of his pain and the myrrh and wine that Reuel had given him.

Samuel finished ascending the steps and stood looking down at the three boys, letting the heat from the rising sun seep through his tunic to his back and shoulders. He remembered the day Liora had looked up at him, her hands resting on either side of her belly, swollen with pregnancy, and said, "Let him be called Joel."

The name meant 'Jehovah is God,' and it was the name of one of their ancestors, a Kohathite Levite, the son of Azariah. Two years later, when their second was born, they had named him Abijah, 'My father is Jehovah,' after a brother of Liora's who had been killed in an accident when he was just a boy. Both sons had been circumcised with a knife of obsidian on the eighth day of their lives, as proscribed in the Law of Moses.

Joel stirred in his sleep, turning slightly and putting his arm around his younger brother's shoulders. Samuel tried to think back to that time in his life, not long after his parents had sent him to live in the Tabernacle in Shiloh. He remembered his parents' visits, and what they had meant to him.

Liora came softly up the steps behind him. He tiptoed to the parapet at the roof's edge, and they stood together, watching the boys sleep. The morning's mist softened the light of dawn around them.

"When you are a child," Samuel whispered, "you believe that growing up means becoming what your father is. Even though it is never said aloud, you know that, in some ways, you are born to take his place in this world."

Liora looked at him, probing his thoughts with her gaze.

Samuel lost himself in the light of her brown eyes for a moment; in the reflection of the morning sun in the gold of her nose ring and the circlet of coins resting on her brow. Then he turned away, staring across the buildings of Naioth spread out before him, rooftops touched with the orange light of dawn. "But growing sometimes means redefining expectations," he said at last. "Going beyond what your parents would ever have dared."

A wisp of wind played with Liora's hair, and she tucked it behind one ear.

"There is an anguish that comes with this understanding," Samuel continued. "An anguish that comes with becoming more than your father, with that moment when you know that you will continue to grow in knowledge and ability while your father shrinks into the irresistible corrosion of old age."

"It is a part of life," Liora whispered.

"But it is wrong!" He looked down again at his sons sleeping, surprised at his own anger. He wondered what they would become when he, himself, grew old. He wondered if they would one day look on him as he now looked on them—as one in constant need of help and guidance.

They stood in stillness a moment longer before Liora took his hand. "It is time to get ready. You cannot keep the Elders waiting."

He nodded and they descended the stairs. Samuel washed his face and arms in a basin of water that Reuel had brought from the well, scrubbing them with soap made from the ashes of soapwort roots combined with congealed olive oil. Liora combed the knots from his hair, grown now past his waist, oiled it, and tied it back with a green headband.

"Do you know what you will say to the Elders?" she asked.

"About their accusations? They are ridiculous," he said.

"That does not mean you will not have to respond to them."

He nodded. "I will be appropriately apologetic and humble."

She raised one eyebrow, but changed the subject. "And about Zimri?"

"I do not know. I wish I could blame it on the sons of Philistia, but they only arrived after I went out, and Zimri must already have been dead."

"The Philistines could have sent someone earlier," Liora said.

"Maybe. But that is not like them. They are direct; they use force to overwhelm their enemies. This was a cowardly act."

"Perhaps you should disclose this to Judge Avdon's ears."

Samuel smiled. "That I will do. If the Philistines are planning some action against us, things will not happen as they did in my childhood. Between Avdon and all his sons and the wisdom of High Priest Ahitub, Israel is as ready as they can be for...for whatever is coming."

"If the Elders will give ear to your words," Liora said.

"If Ahitub or Avdon speak, they will be forced to have their ears opened."

"Will they?"

Samuel pulled her to him again, wrapping his arms around her ribs. "If they do not, I will just send you to convince them. No one could ever refuse those eyes, those pomegranate lips..."

She rolled her eyes and shook her head in mock disgust. Footsteps thundered from outside, and Samuel glanced through the open doorway to see Joel, Abijah, and Gavriel running across the courtyard. Gavriel was hopping, assisted by a crutch that was fashioned from one of the sticks the boys had used to hold up their tent.

"Boys! You have work to do this morning!" Samuel called after them.

"We know Papa!" Joel yelled over his shoulder. "We will be right back!"

"Gavriel needs to rest!" Liora called.

"I am feeling much better!" Gavriel answered, as the boys disappeared out the courtyard gate.

From beyond the wall, they heard Abijah's high, thin voice: "He is feewing much betta, Papa!"

JUDGE OF ISRAEL

4

Later that morning, Samuel and Reuel made the short walk from Naioth across the grassy hillside to the town of Ramathaim. The sun blazed from a sky decorated only by scattered white pillows of cloud drifting over the mountains to the west. Sparrows and finches hopped in the long grass, calling brightly to each other as they picked invisible seeds from the carpet of spring weeds, and swifts darted through the air overhead, forked tails twitching with their abrupt turns.

Just outside the entrance to the School, where the Philistine's chariot tracks scarred the land, they found Joel, Abijah, and Gavriel.

The boys were standing in a circle, their eyes on something at their feet. Abijah was crying.

It took Samuel only an instant to realize what was wrong. He stepped in to look over their shoulders. Amidst a patch of scraggly anise, mustard and fitches, a chariot wheel's swath of churned earth had cut across a tiny almond tree that the boys had planted the year before. The little tree was smashed down into the track, crushed and broken.

Samuel squatted beside the boys. "I am so sorry."

Joel looked at him. *Eyes squinted. Fists clenched.* "I hate Philistines."

"Yeah," echoed Abijah. "Hate Fil-steens."

"We do not hate even our enemies, my sons," Samuel said. "Did not Moses write in the Torah: 'If you come upon your enemy's ox or donkey wandering off, you must return it to him?' We hate the ways of the Philistines, and the evils of their worship, but we do not hate them."

Samuel leaned in and tried to lift the little trunk from the dirt; it broke in his hands just above a white thread of exposed root. Remembering what had produced that little root made Samuel's heart ache.

A trader had passed through Ramathaim the previous year and given the boys a handful of fresh almonds as a gift. They had planted them in an earthenware pot near the southeastern corner of the house. All fall and winter they had watered and fed them, racing most mornings as soon as they woke to see if anything had pushed up through the soil.

Early in the spring something did: a tiny, green stem. Samuel had fed their enthusiasm, eventually taking them to this spot at the edge of the School to transfer the little plant into native soil. Liora worried about how hurt the boys would be if it died, and she had warned Samuel not to get their hopes too high.

But he had, and the boys continued to check on the tree every day, keeping a record of its growth by marking its height each Sabbath with notches cut into the bark of a willow wand. They talked about the giant clusters of almonds it would grow, about climbing in its branches and the games they would play under its leaves. Watching their joy, Samuel had felt justified in encouraging their excitement. Now, he wondered if Liora had been right.

"Is it dead?" Joel asked.

"I do not know, Joel. The best thing we can do for it is to pack the soil back around the roots and keep caring for it. Jehovah has made trees in a wonderful way. Perhaps it will heal, and grow."

"Will it gwow?" asked Abijah.

"I hope so," Samuel answered. "Replant it very carefully and pour some water on it. Then we will have to wait and see."

"We'll hafta wait and see, Joel," echoed Abijah.

Joel and Gavriel knelt and began to do as he had instructed. "Be careful with that leg," Samuel warned. Gavriel nodded, but Samuel saw a flash of emotion across his features: *a tightening of neck and back; a slight lowering of his head; arms unconsciously crossing in front of his body.*

He knelt down next to the boy. "We will talk when you are ready, Gavriel, and not before. Be at peace."

Gavriel exhaled and blinked slowly, nodding.

"Samuel." Reuel cast a look over his shoulder in the direction of the town. "The Elders will be waiting."

Samuel nodded and stood, and they continued toward Ramathaim. The rolling hills around them were the green-yellow of barley that was lightening to the gold of harvest time; in the valleys the grain was already ripe and light flashed off of sweeping sickles. The rhythmic songs of the harvesters hung, indistinctly sonorous, in the still air. On more distant hills, where pale rocks showed through grass and shallow soil, shepherds watched their flocks, svelte from their recent shearing, wandering over hillsides terraced with white walls of stacked stone. Gnarled, ancient olive trees grew on either side of the path Samuel and Reuel followed, and rows of roping grapevines skirted it like a delicate fence.

As they neared the outskirts of Ramathaim, a gap between two hills to the west revealed a glimpse of the city's limestone quarry. The report of hammers striking chisels echoed sharply from the heights as workers shaped the stone into ashlars. From the quarry itself a great shoulder of grey-green rock thrust its way up through the soil, a bone of the land protruding through its thin layer of flesh.

They ascended the rounded hill upon which Ramathaim proper was built and the sharp, musty smell of decomposing flax drifted with them as they walked. Harvesters dried stalks on rooftops, seeded them, and then left them in rain troughs or weighed down with stones in streambeds. The outer stems decayed, releasing the white, interior fibers. After they were removed from the water and dried the fibers were threshed and combed, and then made into precious linen thread.

Blending with this aroma was the pungency of raw wool; as they walked through the gate, in the square and on the rooftops around them, women worked behind mounds of newly shorn wool, washing, carding, and spinning it.

Just inside the gate, a long pitched-roof hall of stacked stone cast its shadow across the square. Standing stiffly around it's open double doors and along its sides were four dozen Phoenician mercenaries, spears in their hands and scimitars hanging at their sides. Samuel and Reuel paused, exchanged a knowing glance, slipped their sandals off, and passed into the shadowed interior.

The murmur of voices in the hall went silent. They stood in the open end of a half-circle of risers illuminated by shafts of light spearing in through high windows that pierced the thick walls on two sides of the hall. Two dozen of the Elders of Ramathaim sat on the risers facing them. Each Elder held the vermilion staff of his office before him or cradled it in his lap.

Samuel glanced quickly around the room. At his far left, on the lowest riser, his father Elkanah sat, his own staff held upright beside him. Samuel nodded in his direction and received a curt nod in response.

The rest of the room, that which was not covered by the risers, was filled with a small crowd of standing spectators: a few *Beneh*, farmers, craftsmen, shepherds—a sampling of the population of the town. Samuel's brothers were there as well, standing in the background against one wall.

Almost as soon as Samuel and Reuel entered one of the Elders stood up from the center of the front riser. He was richly dressed in embroidered linen dyed with stripes of blue and scarlet, and gold glittered on his fingers and at his throat. In sharp contrast to his expensive dress, his face was disfigured by clusters of lesions and pustules that extended down his neck and covered arms. Samuel felt his face flush with anger, and he heard Reuel's hiss of inhalation.

They knew this man.

"At last—the Seer graces us with his presence," the man said. He was thick and stodgy, and intricate gold and silver filigree snaked around his vermilion staff. Scarab seals in the Egyptian style adorned the heavy rings on his fat, blistered fingers. His head nodded constantly, as if keeping time with his heartbeat, and his eyes never stopped glancing around the room, even when he was addressing someone. He smelled vaguely like meat left too long in the sun.

Samuel bowed, noticing that guards in a mixture of Israelite and Philistine armor stood near the wealthy man. "Forgive me if I am late, my lords. I was attending to the needs of my sons." He looked the lesioned man in the eye. "What brings Baghadh of the tribe of Manasseh to a meeting of the Elders of Ramathaim, in Ephraim?"

Baghadh stopped chewing a nail and raised one bushy eyebrow. "I have a house in Ramathaim, as you yourself well know. I have come to stay for a time. Some saw the value of my experience in dealing with these matters. In any case, it is not your place, my son, to question the decisions of the Elders."

Baghadh waited for Samuel to respond, but Samuel knew it was pointless to pursue the matter any further. If Baghadh had somehow convinced the Elders of Ramathaim to allow him to preside here, there was nothing Samuel could do about it now.

After a moment Baghadh turned and gestured expansively toward the Elders, shuffling slowly and wincing with the effort. "My brothers, most of you are already aware that a boy—one of the so-called Sons of the Prophets—was found murdered outside the School this morning. Our anguish over this is deep. But we will deal with that in a moment. First, we must address the actions of Samuel ben Elkanah, a son of fewer than two score years who has tried to usurp the authority of the Elders in a matter as serious as attendance at the festivals!"

He was breathless by the end of the sentence, and Samuel struggled to keep his disgust from showing on his face. Baghadh was grandstanding. For years, he had been campaigning to become the next Judge of Israel. He knew that Samuel would never support him, and was determined to discredit Samuel in whatever way he could. Samuel had told him more than once that it was Jehovah who appointed Judges, but Baghadh was convinced Samuel was somehow manipulating the process for his own insidious purposes. He was infuriated by Samuel's campaign to turn the people away from Ba'als, Ashtoreth, and other Canaanite gods and goddesses. Baghadh had long been an advocate of false worship in Ramathaim—and his business flourished on trade with the Canaanites. No one wanted to admit it, but the main reason he had the influence he did in Israel was his enormous wealth and his favored position with the Philistines.

Baghadh jabbed one finger in Samuel's direction. The lesions around his mouth were red and inflamed. "Well? What do you have to say for yourself?"

"Before we discuss this issue," Samuel said, "I have urgent news for this assembly."

"What?" Baghadh looked slowly around the room, brow knitted in disbelief. He turned his entire body as he did so, as though the neck that bobbed constantly up and down refused to move side to side. "Do you think this is your personal forum, Samuel? You are here today to answer for your actions—nothing else."

"And if this were any less serious a matter, I would not beg your patience while I disclose to your ears what I have learned." He paused, looking around to make sure he had everyone's attention. "I believe that Israel is in imminent danger of an attack from the sons of Philistia."

"Yes, I heard about your foolish confrontation with a Philistine commander," Baghadh said.

"Word travels quickly in Ramathaim," Samuel said.

"Indeed," said Baghadh. "But this is not a matter for the Elders to consider. Give over the lawbreakers to the Philistines, or do not and suffer the consequences. That is your choice."

"I do not refer to some threat from the local garrison," Samuel said. "I have reason to believe a major campaign is about to be mounted against our nation."

For just an instant, Samuel saw something pass, like the shadow of a cloud, across Baghadh's face: *eyes widening; pocked brow slightly furrowed; breath held a moment longer than normal.* He recovered almost immediately. "Not this old song again!" he scoffed. "It seems that every other Sabbath you are telling us the Philistines are coming!"

"You exaggerate, my lord," said Samuel.

"Do I?" countered Baghadh.

"The Philistine numbers have not recovered since the scourge following the battle of Aphek," another Elder said.

"Have they not?" Samuel asked. "Certainly for many years they have held back because the plague that followed the Ark decimated their population. But a new generation of Philistines has arisen, a generation that has forgotten what happened to their fathers. It is time to alert Judge Avdon, that he may rouse the armies of Israel."

"I think we are a long way from needing to alarm my colleague," said Baghadh.

Colleague? Samuel thought. *Since when is the nation's Judge a colleague to an Elder from one of the thousands of Israel?*

"I have heard nothing from my spies about any plans for an attack," Baghadh continued.

Samuel decided to try ignoring Baghadh and talking instead to the other Elders present. "Jehovah has been preparing Avdon for just such a day. With a divinely appointed Judge and—."

"Do you not mean a Samuel-appointed Judge?" Baghadh asked, and was rewarded with a smattering of laughter.

Samuel ignored him. "With a divinely appointed Judge and a faithful High Priest in Nob, we will be victorious."

Another Elder stood. "We have not won a battle against the sons of Philistia since the days of Judge Shamgar, almost two centuries ago."

"Have faith in Jehovah and the men He has appointed as leaders in Israel!" Samuel said.

"Are you questioning our faith?" Baghadh asked. "Is that your accusation, Samuel? That we, the Elders of Ephraim and Manasseh, do not have as much faith as you?"

Samuel held up one hand. "You yourself well know that is not what I meant."

"Is it not? I think that you believe that we, the Elders who serve as leaders under Jehovah's arrangement, should subject ourselves to the whims of the *Beneh Hannevi'im* and to Samuel, their personal priest."

Some in the crowd murmured at his harsh words.

"I only ask that you give consideration to what Jehovah is revealing through His Prophets," Samuel said.

"And how can you be so sure of this...revelation? Did Jehovah disclose to your ears, or to anyone's, that the Philistines are about to attack? Did He give you a day? A time?"

Samuel said nothing, knowing where Baghadh's questions were leading.

Baghadh looked at the crowds standing on either side of Samuel along the walls of the hall. "Who is the source of this intelligence, Samuel?"

"A Prophet of God!" Samuel said. "A Visionary whom Jehovah has led to the School!"

"What Prophet? Can we speak with him?"

"His name is Gavriel, from the city of Joppa."

Baghadh raised his eyebrows and his arms, lesioned palms up, in exaggerated confusion. "I have spent many days in Joppa. I do not remember any Prophet there named...Gavriel, was it?"

"He has only recently been called. This is his first vision from Jehovah."

"Wait—wait, let me guess. He is a child!"

"His age is not relevant to his message."

"Is it not?" asked Baghadh again. "So you ask us to march our sons off to death in battle on the word of a child? What makes you believe this child's...vision is true?"

"I have said nothing about marching to war. And the things his father described from the vision—."

"Wait!" interrupted Baghadh. "His father said? Have you not heard the child yourself?"

Samuel hesitated. "He came to Naioth only early this morning, severely injured..."

Baghadh rolled his eyes, head bobbing slowly. "Samuel here has not even heard this supposed vision from its source—who is a child, whose trustworthiness has yet to be proved! He wants us to start a war against the mightiest nation in Canaan based on the second-hand rantings of a panicked father—who has no doubt been sped away so that he cannot be questioned!"

"I am not asking you to start a war..." Samuel began.

"Samuel," an Elder of Ramathaim interrupted. "We respect your position as a Prophet, and anyone can see that what you are trying to do with the School is a noble thing."

Samuel waited in silence for the inevitable caveat.

"When it comes to matters of national importance," the Elder continued, "such as how the festivals are celebrated and whether or not to go to war...well, it is the Elders of Israel, as a group, who must make these decisions. And we have to weigh these matters very carefully."

Samuel felt rage burning in his nose in response to the man's patronizing tone.

Another Elder added, "Do not think that we do not value what you have disclosed to our ears."

"The time for action is now," said Samuel. "Now, when we have time to prepare *before* the sons of Philistia descend on us."

"You are quick to march our people off to war, Samuel," said Baghadh, his glance darting around the room, refusing to look Samuel in the eye. "But I suppose that is easier for you, since you are a Levite, and so exempt from military service yourself. 'It is easier to stand behind the plow than to pull it,' as they say."

"My lord, you misjudge me."

"Not so anxious to martyr yourself for this cause, eh?" Baghadh asked.

An Elder at the back of the risers stood. "Samuel has served his nation faithfully as a Prophet for many years now. Let us give him the respect his position deserves."

Baghadh shuffled back and forth in front of the audience standing along the walls of the hall. "Samuel has served as a Prophet for many years, and not without compensation. But I am not the first to question the way he uses his authority."

The crowd murmured angrily, and Samuel felt the embarrassing stirrings of pride at hearing their objection to Baghadh's accusations.

Baghadh waved one hand dismissively. "Is Samuel's way always the only valid way? Where in the Torah does it describe a School of the Prophets like the one he has started? Where does it instruct us to keep the Ark of the Covenant in one place but the Tabernacle in another?"

"I have ever been a servant of the Torah," Samuel objected.

Baghadh spun slowly to face him, lips curling back in a snarl that emphasized the clusters of pustules around his mouth. "You have been a servant of your own ambitions!" He stared at Samuel a moment, then, calming himself, turned back to the crowd. "Samuel has set himself up as a leader of the nation! Not content with appointing his friends as the Judges of Israel, he tries to act as the wind driving Avdon's sails and the rudder steering his course."

The grumble of the crowd grew louder, but Baghadh seemed not to notice. "Do you think we do not see what you are doing, Samuel? The common people," he gestured dismissively toward the crowd, "may be awed into submission by the displays of your ecstatic Prophets, roaming the countryside dancing, chanting, and falling into trances—but do not expect the Elders of Israel to be so easily swayed!"

"Are not the Elders also common people?" asked Samuel.

He heard a few chortles from the crowd, but Baghadh's scowl just deepened.

"Do you dare speak so to a Prophet of the True God?" someone called, and Samuel felt the glow of pride once again, cooled immediately by the chill of guilt. Reuel and the other *Beneh* did not react; Samuel had always told them that their work was not to defend one another, but to defend Jehovah's reputation and the sanctity of His words. They had, it seemed, learned the lesson well.

Samuel's brothers did not speak either. He was not surprised to see that they did not appear to share the crowd's friendly sentiments toward him. Their doubt and their unspoken criticisms ate at him, but he could do nothing about it. Sometime—often—he felt that the *Beneh* were more his family than those of his flesh and blood.

"The *Beneh* speak only what Jehovah gives them to speak," Samuel said, thinking of his brothers' feelings as well as answering Baghadh's accusation. "And it was not I who appointed Avdon, but Jehovah!"

"Or is it what Samuel gives them to speak?" Baghadh asked. "Everyone knows that you are on a personal campaign against anything *you* interpret as deviating from *your* ideas of how Jehovah should be worshipped."

"It is the Torah that tells us——."

"Tells us what?" Baghadh interrupted. "That the Ark of the Covenant should be kept these twenty years in Abinadab's back room, guarded by his over-zealous sons? That Samuel should dictate to the Elders of Israel from a so-called School of the Prophets? The High Priest is the highest authority in Israel, and the High Priest, as I recall, appointed you as a gatekeeper in Shiloh, and nothing more—a job that you have now forsaken, I might add! Since you began to call yourself Prophet, our ancient way of worship has become all but unrecognizable!"

For a moment the room fell silent as Baghadh and Samuel faced each other. Another Elder shifted in his seat. "For all these years, Samuel, we have kept quiet, and the Philistines have left us alone. Now that their numbers are increasing, we have to think about how any action against them could affect us. They still hold the trade road from Tyre; we still pay a premium for tin imported by the Phoenicians—for anything that comes through Aphek. We dare not do anything rash that might provoke an attack or cut off our access to the caravans from the north and south."

"We are getting reports that the Amorites are making forays into Gilead again," another Elder said. "The Amorite laborers in cities throughout Israel are getting restless, as though they know that something is about to happen. Some have already mounted insurrections and fled from their cities."

"The Philistines have spread their trade network all the way to the Dead Sea," another said. "They are taking over the harvest and sale of bitumen—money that should be coming to Israel!"

"Judge Avdon is a great man," Samuel said, frustrated that he could hear a pleading tone in his own voice. "With Jehovah's guidance he can lead our nation to victory."

"Avdon has no experience in battle," Baghadh said. "The heroes of Aphek are gone, Samuel. Elon-tohr—vanished long ago into the east; Arod—lain down with his fathers."

"Even without experience," Samuel said, "Avdon is the greatest leader Israel has now. The people will follow him. Jehovah can empower him."

"Even if this child's prophecy is true," Baghadh said, "the men of Dan are watching the border. They will alert us if there is any cause for concern."

"My brothers," Samuel said. "At least let me go and speak to Avdon to get the Judge's thoughts on this matter."

"So that you can whisper your own counsels in his ear?" Baghadh scoffed. "I think not."

"It is unthinkable that I should do nothing," Samuel said.

"Unthinkable?" Baghadh said. "You are telling the Elders of your tribe what you should and should not do? Once again, you forget your place, Samuel!" He turned back to the Elders. "Not satisfied with being a self-appointed Judge-maker, this boy wants to be Judge himself, and general, and Prophet! The next thing we know, he will be building an altar at Naioth and taking over the duties of the Priests!"

Samuel's mind raced, trying desperately to come up with a response that could extinguish the claims Baghadh was making. But before he could think of anything, he was surprised to see Elkanah rise and thump his staff on the risers.

"I apologize for my son," he said. "I beg you, my brothers; let us put our hands to other work. I will speak to my son and he will, as you have said, let the matter go."

Samuel felt the floor drop out from under him and, for a moment, it felt as if he were in a nightmare struggling to wake. He stared at his father in shock, then turned on his heel and marched back out the open door.

"Samuel!" he heard Baghadh calling after him. "We are not done with you! You have more yet to answer for!"

He kept walking, taking the longest strides he could manage, his face burning with shame. He was vaguely aware of Reuel behind him scurrying to keep up. He marched back to his own home without pause, and it was only when his hand was on his courtyard gate that he turned back to Reuel.

"Find Gavriel. Bring him to me immediately."

Reuel nodded, his brow knit with concern. "Jehovah will take care of this, my lord."

"Jehovah uses us to accomplish His will! He will not force fools to become wise, or the stupid to act with insight!"

Reuel nodded. *Head sunk to his shoulders. Eyes downcast. Squeezing his left thumb with his right hand.*

Samuel felt a twinge of guilt, but not enough to overcome his anger. "Reuel—bring Gavriel. Now."

5

Reuel carried Gavriel into the house. The boy had lost his makeshift crutch somewhere. The healer eased him onto a stool in Samuel's common room, then knelt and began to examine the bandages that wrapped the wounded leg. A red-brown spot had appeared on the linen and flies buzzed around it curiously. Joel and Abijah had followed Reuel back; they stood outside the door, only their heads visible as they peered through the opening, one to a jamb.

Samuel knelt next to Reuel. He could smell the herbs of the poultice beneath the bandage. "How are you feeling?" he asked.

Gavriel did not answer. *Eyes wide. Corners of lips pulled back and down. Knuckles white.*

Samuel took one of the boy's hands in his own. "Do you know why your father brought you to me, Gavriel?"

Gavriel nodded.

"Why?" Samuel pressed.

"You are the Prophet."

"Do you know when I first heard the Voice of Jehovah?"

"When you were a little boy."

Samuel nodded. "Not much older than you. I was asleep in my bed in Shiloh—the city where the Tabernacle used to be before you were born. The Voice woke me, calling my name. My skin tingled, my mouth went dry, and my hands and knees shook. Hearing that Voice changes you, does it not?"

Gavriel still stared, silent. Samuel could hear him breathing through his nose. Liora came up behind Samuel and handed an earthen basin of water to Reuel; he began cleaning the boy's wound.

"You understand what I am saying do you not, Gavriel?" Samuel asked.

The boy nodded, almost imperceptibly. "But you didn't see a dream."

"Not that first time," Samuel answered. "But since then, I have. Many of the boys here at the School have."

Gavriel winced and pulled back from Reuel's efforts to bathe the wound.

"Be still," Reuel whispered.

"But these words and images are not for us to keep to ourselves," Samuel said. "We are only messengers. It is time now to deliver the message He entrusted to you."

Tears appeared in the corners of Gavriel's eyes. "Why?"

"Jehovah would not have given you this vision if it were not very important, Gavriel. I need you to disclose to my ears what you saw."

"I do not remember."

"Yes you do." Samuel squeezed his hand a little. "You remember every detail. Tell me what you saw."

Gavriel put his head down and for a long time made neither movement nor sound. Samuel had decided that a new method would be needed to get him to reveal the vision when, still facing his lap, the boy spoke.

"I was like a bird flying over the land. It was the best flying dream I have ever had—so real! I could see everything. Then—I saw these clouds, these black clouds, start moving up."

"When you were flying could you see the Sea?" Samuel asked.

Gavriel nodded.

"Where was it—on your right, or on your left?

Gavriel stuck out his left arm.

"And the black clouds—where did they come from?"

"From the bottom," Gavriel said.

"Good, my son," Samuel said, patting his hand. *From the south.* "What happened then?"

"The black clouds got scarier. They kept coming up until I couldn't see the land anymore—just clouds. There was only one place I could see—a city where people were dumping water on the ground."

"These people—were they dressed like Israelites?"

"They were dressed like us."

"And then what happened?"

"The water they were dumping turned into a big river. It crashed into the black clouds—the river did. Then it all went down."

"What went down?"

"Everything," Gavriel said. "The river, the clouds, the people—everything. It all just went down and it was over."

"Went down where?"

Gavriel started to cry. "I do not know. Just down. Just down!"

Samuel embraced him, laying the boy's head against his chest. "It is all right, Gavriel. You have done well. Jehovah will bless you for what you have done. He will give you the strength to bear this burden."

Gavriel pulled away and looked up, his face red and streaked with tears. "But what do I do now?"

Samuel felt an aching hollowness yawn within his chest. He remembered all too well what the boy was feeling—the sense of suddenly not knowing your own identity, your place in the world; the sense that nothing in your life would ever be the same again. He stroked Gavriel's soft hair and thought of what he wished someone had told him all those years ago in Shiloh.

"You wait for Reuel to finish bandaging your leg, and you go outside and play with Joel and Abijah. Your task is completed, my son. You have done well, and Jehovah is pleased. Be at peace."

Gavriel smiled a little, through his tears, and nodded. *Shoulders relaxed. Eyes clear and bright.* Joel and Abijah shuffled closer. "It's alright, Gavriel," Joel said.

"Yeah, it's a'right," echoed Abijah, patting Gavriel on the head with his little hand. Reuel disappeared outside briefly and returned with a crutch, its top padded with a bundle of linen bandages. He helped Gavriel to stand and hobble out the door, Joel and Abijah on either side.

"I will keep an eye on him for a while," Reuel said.

"Can you arrange for the *Beneh's* lessons also?" Samuel asked. "I doubt I will be able to meet with them today."

"Of course, my lord," Reuel said. "And what of Zimri's death?"

Samuel raised his arms in a silent plea to the heavens. "I had nearly forgotten. The sacrifice must be made this evening."

"I will make the arrangements, my lord," said Reuel. "Think no more on it."

"May Jehovah bless you, Reuel. May He give to you a perfect wage for your loyal service."

"It is nothing, my lord." Reuel bobbed his head in a curt bow and followed the boys outside.

Samuel stood and saw Liora watching him, her brown eyes soft with emotion. "What?" he asked.

"This School. It is what you wish you had had, when you were called as a Prophet."

"A place where I was understood?" Samuel asked, almost in a whisper.

"A place where, when your assignment filled you with fear and self-doubt, a man you loved and respected told you that it would be alright," Liora said.

"I suppose it is."

She smiled and took his hands in her own. "To give to others what you wish you had; to make their lives truly better in some way than your own has been—it is the highest form of love."

"'You must love your neighbor as yourself,'" Samuel recited, and she nodded.

He changed the subject abruptly, no longer comfortable with the direction of the conversation. "Keep your distance from Baghadh, Liora. He is a dangerous man, and I do not know if there are any limits to what he would do to get to me."

The sound of footsteps in the courtyard drew their attention and, a moment later, Elkanah stepped through the door. Samuel met his eyes, feeling even as he did so that he was violating some law so ancient it had existed before there were words to write it.

Liora must have seen something in their guarded stares; she bowed to Elkanah and walked past him out the door. "Excuse me, Father."

Elkanah let her pass and then filled the doorway, one calloused hand gripping the worn, weathered jamb. His once black beard was almost completely grey now, but still bushy and thick. "Are you going to invite me in?"

"You have never needed an invitation to enter my home," Samuel answered, feeling a perverse sense of pride at the tone he managed in his voice: angry and defiant, but so subtle as to be completely deniable.

Elkanah didn't enter and his deep-set eyes narrowed. "I know you are angry at me, my son."

"I am not angry," Samuel answered, telling himself that it was true. "I am frightened—frightened for what might happen to our people."

"Then allow my heart to feel faint for what might happen to my son," Elkanah said, "who seems determined to alienate the Elders of Rama-thaim!"

"And the Elders of Manasseh, apparently," Samuel said.

Elkanah took a step into the room and stood directly across from Samuel, his long arms hanging at his sides, unconsciously aligning his body to face Samuel's exactly. *Open. Unguarded. Honest. Unafraid.* Samuel wished there was some subtle taint of subterfuge in his father's posture—anything that Samuel could use to convince himself that Elkanah did not truly have his best interests at heart.

"Many Elders do not like Baghadh's personality, Samuel, but they recognize truth in what he says."

"Truth?" Samuel said. "The man is a liar. If it was not for the army with which he surrounds himself..."

"Though a man lie once, that does not make all his words false," said Elkanah. "Baghadh is very popular among his people—in part because of his outspokenness. And you cannot deny that, as he says, you are asking us to take a great deal on trust in your words. You have not even talked to the boy—."

"I have now," Samuel said. "And my conclusions are exactly the same." Even as he said the words, he knew that they were not true. He was less sure of the meaning of the vision now than he had been before he had heard the details for himself. The truth was that, although it seemed that it might predict the coming of the Philistines, there was no part of it about which he was certain.

"Even so," Elkanah said, nodding, "there is a procedure, a way for handling such things. The Elders of Ramathaim are not going to take well to being dictated to by a young man—even if they trust that he *is* a Prophet of God. They wish to be consulted, cooperated with—not ordered about like slaves."

"I did not mean to sound like I was ordering anyone! Of course I am not trying to dictate to them—that is why I brought the news to them in the first place!"

"No, my son," said Elkanah. "You brought it to them in the second place."

"What?"

"Before you consulted the Elders, you consulted yourself—and you decided alone on a course of action. Whatever words you may have used in presenting this message to them, you never even considered the possibility that the Elders would not do exactly as you asked."

Samuel shook his head as though in frustration. In reality it was to disguise the fact that he had no response.

"We are an organized people," Elkanah continued. "It is an arrangement set up by Moses centuries ago: fathers to decide for their families, patriarchs to speak for their clans, Elders and princes to speak for their tribes. Who are we to question or work against that arrangement?"

Samuel threw up his hands. "Can we trust an arrangement, though it is Moses', which is ignoring both the threat to our people and the words of the Torah? If I follow that arrangemen, and those Jehovah has appointed to make the decisions do nothing, what then? Am I to lower my hands and watch our people destroyed?"

"You do not yet know if there *is* such a threat," Elkanah pointed out. "I know that you only want to protect those you love, but you are asking men to march to war!"

"I am not! I am only asking that the man whom Jehovah appointed as Judge be given the same information that we have been given, so that he may use it however he sees fit."

Elkanah said nothing for a moment, but in that silence Samuel read many scrolls' worth of words. Elkanah had always had his doubts about Avdon. The last two Judges Samuel had appointed had done nothing noteworthy for their people. And now Avdon had not only failed to lead an army to victory over their enemies, but he had grown wealthy and fat, presiding over a huge, spoiled brood of children and grandchildren. Samuel liked him—he was a man who could be trusted to do what was right in any given situation no matter what the cost to himself. He was a kind and happy man, generous to a fault, and this made him very popular among many of the people. But it was no secret that he was known throughout the land as "Samuel's Judge."

Elkanah sighed. "We must trust that Jehovah will take care of this in His own way and time."

"But Jehovah takes care of things by teaching his people to think and act as He would! If I have learned one thing by becoming a Prophet, it is that divine intervention is rare indeed. In the Torah Jehovah has given us all that we need to know how to deal with whatever challenges we may face. He expects us to use what He has provided, and not wait for Him to supply a law or a vision to guide every step we take."

Elkanah nodded, chewing on one cheek; it made his beard on that side of his face bristle. Samuel felt an awful shame sweeping through him that he should be addressing his own father in such a way. But he had said too much already; there was no going back.

Nevertheless, he softened his tone. "It is only with the value of hindsight that we look back and write in our histories: 'Jehovah did such-and-such for His people.' Most of the time, while the events were happening, the men of those days were wracked with just as many doubts as we face now."

Elkanah nodded again. "Perhaps that is the case. But those men also never lost their faith that Jehovah would prove worthy of their trust and would save them from the hand of their enemies."

"I do trust in Jehovah," Samuel said. "But my heart melts with fear that we are stopping up our ears to what He is trying to tell us."

"Just do not mistake your fears for the truth, my son," Elkanah said. "The men whom you walked out on this morning have, every one of them, been serving Jehovah faithfully for many years longer than you have."

"Then why can they not recognize a threat to the nation when it presents itself?" Samuel asked.

"Show them some trust, Samuel," Elkanah said. "Give the Elders of Ramathaim a chance to think about what you have said. Do not they want to protect their children and grandchildren from harm? Wait for them to decide on a course of action, and show them your support. They are good men, and they want to believe you."

"I do not think they do," Samuel said.

Elkanah was very still for a moment. "You are your own man, Samuel. I trust you, and your judgment. So does Jehovah, or He would not have chosen you as His Prophet. But think about what I have said, and about the way you may appear to other people. We are all of us just men."

He ducked back out the door. "May Jehovah grant you peace, my son."

Samuel sank heavily to the floor, leaned his head back against the cool, earthen wall and closed his eyes. He felt as though anger and sorrow were fighting each other in his mind and that, as long as the battle raged, he could feel neither. He wished he were the kind of person who did not care what others thought about him—the kind of person who was so confident that he was right that nothing anyone said could shake that belief.

But he wasn't. And he knew in his heart that he would not be happy as that kind of person. Uncertainty—a constant questioning of oneself and one's views and ideas—was the only cure for the corrupting disease of arrogance. Once, years before, in a conversation with Rohgah he had told the old Prophet his opinion on some topic they were discussing—Samuel could not remember what anymore. But he would never forget Rohgah's response: "Don't believe everything you think!" the Prophet had snapped at him.

It was advice he tried to live by. But it was made more difficult by the trust others put in him and by their reliance on him for guidance and instruction. He was a teacher; he was the Prophet of Israel. Every day he was expected to tell others what he thought and his words were treated as something valuable. And his unique life experiences—growing up in the Tabernacle, the instruction of Eli and Ahitub and Rohgah, his association with so many men and women of great faith and wisdom—all of it combined to make him wiser than many around him.

Not make him wiser, he corrected himself. They had given him access to the wisdom of Jehovah in a way that few people had it. His obligation as a Prophet was to share that wisdom with others, and that unavoidably changed the way they viewed him.

He was doing his best to fulfill the assignment that had been given to him, but he was all too aware of his failings. And at times that awareness made him overcompensate by pretending to be more confident than he was. Was he, in fact, misusing his position? Is that what people thought of him?

He let his forehead rest on his palm, and felt the wet heat of sweat against his skin. In spite of the position he now had, in spite of the fact that so many people respected and looked up to him, he had never fully freed himself of the feeling that he was only pretending to be the person people thought he was. He lived as though in constant fear of discovery.

He could ignore it most of the time. But when people began to question his motives—when he was accused of forsaking the Law he had sworn to uphold—then the fears and doubts came bubbling up again. They forced him to re-examine everything he did, to search in panic for evidence in himself that they might be right about him.

He wished they would do the same to themselves. Why couldn't Baghadh, or his brothers, or any of the people who attacked his motives and choices—why could they not turn the same critical eye on themselves? How could they be so confident that their ideas and opinions were right, when men like Ahitub constantly questioned themselves?

He replayed the events of the morning over and over again in his mind. He kept picturing the faces of his brothers, his father, and Baghadh. The more he pictured them, the more he seemed to discover clues in their expressions that revealed their hidden hatred of—or at least disgust with—him. Why could his family, at least, not stand up for him? Should he not be able to count on them even when all others abandoned him?

He tried to free himself of his dark thoughts, standing and walking to the open window. Ants were crawling on the sill, carrying crumbs of bread they had collected from some corner of the house. The worn wood was warm from the sun and the light was warm on his face. He breathed deeply of the smells of spring and tried to let go of his anger and frustration.

Perhaps if he was successful in rousing Avdon and if Avdon, in turn, was successful in turning back a Philistine attack…If so, his father and the Elders would have to acknowledge that he had been right. The thought forced him to confront the fact that being right—or rather, being seen to be right—was important to him. More than important, in fact. He felt the weight of others' disapproval as though it were the mark of Cain on his forehead, declaring to everyone that he had been judged and found wanting. Beyond their acceptance he craved their approval, and that craving at times became a crippling weakness.

He knew, in the way that the mind knows what the heart refuses to accept, that the sense of worth that he longed for could come only from within himself. Ahitub had told him so many times, the High Priest's anxious eyes conveying his fear that Samuel would not accept the lesson. But the voice of his own heart spoke more loudly than even his mentor's, and it warned him that to grant himself that approval was an act of unconscionable pride, a sin that would negate the very qualities that would give him reason to feel good about himself.

He had just turned from the window when Reuel put his head in the door. "My lord—there is someone here to see you."

Samuel thought it might be his father again and was about to tell Reuel to send whomever his visitor was on his way. Something in the young man's expression that made him curious, though. "Who is it?"

Reuel's smile broadened and he stepped out of the way to admit two men into the room. The first was almost as old as Elkanah, a huge bear of a man whose every movement caused thick cords of muscle in his arms, neck, and legs, dark and weathered from years of working outside, to writhe and flex. A Philistine-style coat of hammered bronze scale-mail encased his thick chest, and bronze greaves were tied around his bulging calves. Weapons hung from his massive frame: an iron sword, with gold filigree and inset sapphires glittering from the hilt and sheath; a finely wrought bronze-headed spear, carried like a staff; a well-worn sling tucked into his broad, leather belt. On each bare scarred arm, above the bicep, was a band of polished iron, as valuable as silver.

Behind him was a man a dozen years Samuel's junior. Dark-skinned and handsome, his striking blue eyes twinkled mischievously over a rakish grin. No one could miss the similarities in appearance between him and the older man—their eyes, noses, hairlines, and builds all proclaimed that they were father and son. He, too, was armed—a finely crafted sword and long knife at his belt, and a buckler of wood and boiled leather strapped to his back. But it was his hair that drew Samuel's eyes. Though his neatly groomed beard was streaked with red, the hair of his head hung in dozens of slender, black braids, shiny with oil, all the way down to his hips.

Unconsciously Samuel fingered the end of his own long braid and, in spite of himself, smiled.

"Welcome, Manoah of Dan," he said to the older man.

"Seer." Manoah acknowledged him with a nod. "I think my son and I have waited long enough."

"My lord?" Samuel asked.

"Do not pretend you do not know what I mean," Manoah growled. "It is time for you to empower my son to fulfill his destiny. It is time for you to make Samson into the hero of Israel."

6

Liora greeted Manoah with a kiss to each cheek, and set about preparing him and Samson a meal in spite of their half-hearted protestations. They sat with Samuel in a circle on the floor while the room filled with the smell of spiced lentils, warmed from the night before, and of flatbread baking in the courtyard oven.

Samson leaned against the wall, well-muscled arms crossed over his chest and long legs stretched out in front of him. After a moment, one of the *Beneh* came in with a towel draped over one arm and an earthenware basin of water in his hands, sloshing with each slow step. Kneeling before Manoah and Samson, he removed their sandals and began to wash the road-dust from their feet.

Samuel was struck by the fact that Manoah seemed to become more powerful looking, more imposing as he aged. The years had only hardened his massive arms and shoulders, criss-crossed with a script of fine, white scars recording the stories of battles past.

"How are Na'amah, and your sons?" Samuel asked.

"They are well," Manoah said. "As well as can be expected in times like these, living a few bowshots from Philistine garrisons."

"And you, Samson? How are you, my brother?"

The young man grinned rakishly, a flash of white teeth. "Still normal."

Manoah glared at his son, and Samuel could not help but smile even as he felt pity for the young man. From the first time they had met, years before, they had shared a bond that few others could understand. Both of them were Nazirites for life, living out someone else's vow. Both of them bore the conspicous sign of their separateness: their unmistakable long hair. Both of them lived everyday with the burden of their parents' and the nation's expectations. But for Samson, Samuel reflected, those expectations had yet to be fulfilled in any way. The young man took a very sarcastic view of the situation, while his father seemed to live in breathless anticipation of the day his son's power would be revealed.

The *Beneh* finished washing the guest's feet and moved to pour scented olive oil from a narrow-necked flask onto their hair; Manoah gestured him away. "Save it to grease your shield with, boy," he growled.

Bowing, the young man went back out the door.

"He does not have a shield, Manoah," Samuel said, smiling.

"Well maybe he should!" Manoah said. "Rumors of Philistine warships landing south of Ashkelon are filtering into Zorah."

"More than rumors?" Samuel asked.

Manoah shrugged. "Why? Do we need a reason to kill Philistines?"

"To risk Israelite lives, yes—." Samuel began.

Manoah batted his hand at the Prophet. "I was joking, Seer. But I saw with my own eyes hundreds of Rephaim marching south from Gath just days ago."

"There are many possible explanations for that," Samuel said, wondering why he was suddenly hesitant to believe what he himself had been avowing just hours before.

"They were in full battle gear," Manoah said. "Something is happening—or about to happen—in Philistia."

Scuffling sounds from the doorway announced the breathless arrival of Joel, Abijah, and Gavriel. They rushed into the room and stood next to the door, abruptly frozen, staring silently at Samson with wide eyes. They had heard the story of his birth. They knew the promise of who he would someday become.

Samson flashed his grin at them. "Good morning, boys."

"Samson, take the children outside," Manoah said.

"That is not necessary, my friend," Samuel said. "Boys—go and play—."

"It is fine," Manoah interrupted. "Samson—take them outside while the Seer and I talk."

Samson's smile was tight-lipped, but he pushed himself up from the floor. "I wonder if you boys know where there might be any saplings. I have this sword, you see…"

"I know," Joel said breathlessly. "I know where there are some!"

"Excellent!" Samson said, leading them all outside again.

Samuel waited until the sound of their footsteps had faded. "As I have told you before, Manoah—I would love to have you and Na'amah and your sons come here and stay with us at Naioth."

"Me? Among your Sons of the Prophets?" Manoah scoffed.

"You, too, are a Prophet, Manoah—whether you see yourself as one or not. Jehovah's angel spoke to you face to face, and revealed to you the future. It is possible that He will do so again. Here is where you belong— you and Samson, whose destiny was foretold in prophecy."

Manoah waved his hand dismissively. "Your boys do good work here, Samuel. But my son is going to be a man of action, not of words. He has been trained as a warrior since the day he learned to walk. He will not be a Seer, but a doer. He will be a killer of the sons of Philistia. It is the purpose for which he was born."

Samuel watched Manoah's face change as he spoke the words: *Eyes narrowing, going cold. Jaw bulging as he gritted his teeth. Muscles around his lips tightening.*

He wanted to say something to him, something about the futility of chasing vengeance or the danger of allowing hatred and anger take over one's personality. But he felt like a child in the presence of the grizzled warrior and remained silent.

After a moment, Manoah's expression softened again. "It is time, Samuel. Time for you to empower my son to fulfill his destiny. He can take the lead in delivering us from this new threat!"

"Neither you nor I can decide when that time has arrived, Manoah," Samuel said. "We must wait on Jehovah."

Manoah scowled. "Those dogs crawl over the land our God gave to us! They pollute it with their very presence. Have we not done enough waiting?"

"Apparently not," Samuel said.

"No? How long have you been telling us that Jehovah would drive out the Philistines? How long? Twenty years I have waited for that promise to come true, Prophet. Twenty long years of waiting for justice for my murdered family."

"Do you think I can change God's timetable?"

"If you could, would you?"

"Think about what you are saying, Manoah."

After a moment's pause, Manoah shook his head and frowned. "I came here to warn the Seer of Israel. Are you telling me now that you are going to do nothing about this threat?"

"No. I have been considering visiting Avdon in Pirathon. He is Judge of Israel. Let him decide what to do."

"Passing off the decision to someone else?"

"It is not my decision to make!"

Manoah sighed. "It is better than nothing, I suppose. Samson and I will come with you."

"No—no, you should not. I have no idea what will result from this visit, Manoah. In fact, I am going without the blessing of the Elders of Ephraim."

"I am a Danite," Manoah said. "The opinions of the Elders of Ephraim are not my concern. What I know is that wherever you go, trouble with the Philistines seems to follow. I want my son's sword to be there the next time that trouble arrives."

Samuel was spared coming up with a response by Liora's arrival with a copper pot of lentils wrapped in a bit of wool to protect her hands from its heat; the smell of garlic, onions, cinnamon and cumin filled the room. A moment later she carried in a steaming stack of bread. After setting it on a mat in the center of the floor, she leaned out the door and called for her sons.

They entered in a flurry of noise and moving limbs. "Papa," Joel said, "Samson chopped down a tree with his sword!"

Abijah mimed a vicious chop, grimacing, his little fist clenched on an invisible sword.

"Did he now?" Samuel asked. "Not a fruit tree, I hope."

"No," Samson answered, grinning. "Just a row of grape vines."

Joel turned toward him, his brow furrowed. "No—those weren't grapevines. They were just little broom trees."

Samson gave him an exaggerated nod. "Ahhh! Now I understand why there were no grapes on them."

"We're going to the sea with Samson, mother," Joel said. "For a few days."

"Really?" Liora asked.

"Just for a few days," Joel repeated.

"Jus' a few days," echoed Abijah. "He—he has a sword!"

Samuel pulled Abijah onto his lap. "And what will you eat on this trip to the sea?"

"Eggs!" Abijah said.

"Of course," Samuel said, laughing with Liora. Abijah loved eggs. He was constantly finding quail's nests while playing around Naioth and bringing their eggs back to his mother to cook. Liora lived in dread of opening one and finding a half-formed bird inside.

"And fish," said Joel. "Samson said we can catch fish in the sea."

"Well, for now, let's eat lentils," Liora said.

Samuel raised his eyes and arms heavenward. "Blessed are You, Jehovah our God, King of the world, who causes to come forth bread from the earth."

They tore the bread and used it to dip lentils out of the pot. Joel and Abijah sat as close as they could to Samson, and Samuel was impressed at the good-natured way that the young man tolerated them.

Manoah covered his mouth with a fist and burped. "Have I ever told you boys about the day my wife and I learned that Samson was going to be born?"

Joel glanced at his father, then looked back to Manoah and shook his head. Samuel felt the warmth of fatherly pride—Joel had, of course, heard the account from Samuel before, but he had the good sense not to say so.

"Well!" Manoah smoothed his mustache and leaned farther back. "Then I have a story for you!"

Samuel looked at Samson's face: *features frozen; jaw tight; neck stiff and chin pointed slightly down. Lips locked in a joyless half-smile.* He had heard this story too many times. He lived with its implications every day. Every time it was told it reiterated the expectation and hope that the people of the tribe of Dan, and of all Israel, hung around his neck.

"Have you any milk, Liora?" Manoah asked. "This tale can dry the throat."

Liora brought out a skin of sour milk and handed it to him, and Manoah took a long swig, lowering it to reveal droplets of white in his beard and mustache. Deep-set eyes peering down at Joel and Abijah, he began his tale.

7

MANOAH'S TALE

The sun had just eased past its zenith, and I had been since dawn with my hand to the plow, following the lurching, mud-spattered haunches of my ox. Back then, just after we settled in Zorah, I had only one ox—and a scrawny one at that. The Philistine dogs had taken or destroyed everything when they sacked Gibbethon, and we had come practically as paupers and without family to our new home.

The rain had been falling since the middle of the night, and the soil had finally softened enough for the copper-sheathed plow to break it up. Even though I had wrapped myself in a heavy cloak the rain had soaked me to the skin, and my legs were growing heavy with a buildup of clay on my sandals.

In spite of the damp my throat ached with thirst, and I stopped the ox with the thought of going for a drink at the well. When I turned I was surprised to see Na'amah running toward me across the furrows, her sandaled feet leaving contrasting dimples where they punched through the rain-darkened top layer of soil. I left the plow stuck in the ground and walked to meet her.

When I was close enough, I saw that her hooded face was pale beneath a sheen of sweat, and her eyes wide with wonder.

"Manoah!' she said. "A man—a man has just come to me!"

"What are you doing out here?" I asked.

"A man just visited me," she repeated, and her eyes went distant for a moment, as though caught in some rapturous memory. "A man like an angel of God!"

Now some have called me a jealous man, but I think words such as these might have caused any husband concern. Perhaps my…my consternation showed on my face, because she seemed in a hurry to explain herself.

"Oh, Manoah—all our hopes are, at last, come true! Jehovah has heard our prayers and accepted the smoke of our offerings!"

"What are you talking about? Who was this man?" I asked.

"I did not ask him where he was from, and he did not disclose to me his name, but…"

She threw her arms around me and I held her as well, waiting for what I knew must be extraordinary news. After a moment, she looked up at me, eyes swimming with tears. "He told me: 'Look! You are barren and have borne no child.'"

The very mention of her barrenness made something tighten within me, as though I were injured somewhere beneath my skin, and someone had just pressed his fingers to the wound. "Well," I said, trying to disguise my feelings, "it is perhaps surprising that this stranger would know this, but he could easily have learned it from someone in the village—."

"No, no—unstop your ears!" Na'amah said. "He said to me: 'And you will certainly become pregnant and give birth to a son.'"

I admit that, in the first moments after hearing those words. my heart ached within me, for I was sure that Na'amah's mind had broken at last, fallen victim to the years she had spent in fruitless longing for a child. My thoughts began to race along these frightening pathways as I tried to devise some plan to free her of her delusion without causing her even more pain. For this reason I did not pay close attention to what she said next.

"The man further told me," she continued, "'And now watch yourself, please, and do not drink wine or any alcohol, and do not eat anything that the Torah proclaims unclean. For look! You will become pregnant, and you will for a certainty give birth to a son. And no razor should come upon his head, because he is to be a Nazirite of God from the day he leaves your womb until the day he is gathered to his fathers."

If my mind wandered while my wife spoke these words, it was captured again by what she said next. "'And he it is who will take the lead in delivering Israel out of the hand of the Philistines.'"

My feelings about the sons of Philistia is no secret. They destroyed my home and the city of my birth; they slaughtered my family and friends, and to this day their filthy feet walk the streets of towns that God promised to the children of Israel. They are lower than the dogs that crawl the cursed alleys of their cities and whose flesh they eat. But Na'amah has always been less affected by this than I have. She seemed willing to forget what the sons of Philistia had done to us in the past as long as they left us alone in Zorah. So when she said that this son would save Israel from the hand of the Philistines—well, that was something I knew that she would not have made up.

A chill crawled up my spine to my scalp. Who had brought this message? A Prophet, surely. I took Na'amah's soft hands in my own and knelt on the freshly-plowed earth, sitting on my heels; she faced me, rested her knees atop my thighs, wrapped her arms around my shoulders, and put her forehead against mine.

With the warmth of her breath against my face, I prayed, "Excuse me, Jehovah. This man that You sent to my wife—let him, please, come to us again and teach us how we are to raise this son that will be born. Let him, please, return to us that I may speak to him and learn all that is Your will for us in regard to the one that You have promised."

I went back to the fields, but only to collect the ox and put him into the manger for the rest of the day—my mind was too awash with questions to do anything but go home and wait with Na'amah. We prayed again and again that afternoon and into the evening, and Na'amah—for the first time since Gibbethon—began to talk about the dreams of motherhood she had kept locked away in her heart. She fell asleep that night weeping, but the tears were a release of emotion and not the dew of sorrow.

The following morning, again while I was plowing, Na'amah came running to me across the field, and I knew immediately by the look on her face that the man had returned.

I followed her back to our home. He was waiting for us there, and his very presence filled me with an inexplicable awe. He turned as we approached, and I saw that he was, indeed, a beautiful man: tall, broad of shoulder and well-muscled, with azure eyes as piercing as a hawk's and dark skin as smooth as polished marble. Neither scar nor blemish nor wrinkle marred the perfection of his face. Thick, black hair fell, unbound, in waves down to his shoulders. The rain had stopped and the sun was just beginning to pierce the clouds; its light gleamed almost blindingly from his long robe, belted at the waist, as white as new snow. He held a simple shepherd's staff in his right hand. It took me a moment to realize that there was no spot of dust or dirt upon him, as though he had dressed in clothes taken straight from the laundryman's lye vats and dried in the brightest sun.

I admit that I felt a little unsettled, so otherworldly did he seem. "Welcome, my lord," I said. "Are you the man who spoke yesterday to my wife?"

"I am a messenger from the True God," he answered, and his voice rolled from his tongue like honey wine pours from the edge of a jar.

"Then may all your words prove to be true," I said. "Please—we wish to do in accord with all that you tell us. What will be the boy's way of life? To what task will he set his hand?"

He paused a moment before speaking, and his eyes flickered toward the sky above our heads. When he spoke, it was in the careful, deliberate tone of a man intent on exactly repeating the words of another. "Just as Jehovah has instructed your wife, so must she do. She must not drink any product of the vine or any kind of liquor at all. She must not even eat the grapes of the vine, and make sure that she touches nothing that Jehovah has proclaimed unclean. She must keep herself holy while she bears this child, for he has been set apart as one for special service to Jehovah, a Nazirite from birth. And so no razor should come to be upon his head. Everything that Jehovah has commanded her—she must obey it without fail."

"And the Philistines?" I asked eagerly. "He will, as you said, take the lead in delivering us from their hand?"

The man nodded. "So Jehovah has spoken."

My heart pounded against my ribs—I could feel its rhythm with every breath I took. Jehovah had, indeed, given ear to our prayers—our request for a son, and my longing to drive the Philistine dogs from the Land of Promise. After so many years of waiting, in one hour He had answered all the requests of my heart.

"My lord." I bowed low before the man, and Na'amah did so as well. "Please—stay with us here long enough that I may prepare a tender kid of the goats for you, and you must share bread with us before your long journey to...to the place from which you have come."

The man raised his eyebrows (perfect, even arcs of jet-black), and a hint of a smile curled up his lips. "If I do stay, it will not be to partake of your hospitality. We will not break bread together today, Manoah. But if you wish to take that kid of the goats and offer it up as a burnt offering to my Lord and King, Jehovah—then I will stay to smell the smoke of your sacrifice."

I opened my mouth to object, and managed to stop myself before the words came out. My shock was now complete. Here a messenger of the True God stood and asked me, a Danite and a man of war, to build an altar at my home and offer up a sacrifice to God upon it—as though I were a Priest! But there was no jest in his words and, though I knew that I was wholly unworthy of the task, I felt that I dare not deny him his request.

Just outside our home, I pulled flat stones from the edge of the field and stacked them into an altar about the height of my knee. With every clink of stone against stone my sense of wonder deepened. I, to offer a sacrifice to God? I, who was not approved to touch the Altar of Burnt Offering in Nob, to build my own altar as though I were Abraham, Isaac, or Jacob?

When the altar was finished I stacked dry brushwood upon it, and Na'amah brought me a kid of the goats born just a few Sabbaths earlier. He bleated a little, pleadingly, and kicked as I pulled him close. I drew the obsidian blade across his throat and felt the rush of warm blood running through his soft wool and over my hand; in moments the kid collapsed limply to the ground. With the blood that dripped from my hand, I sprinkled the ground all around the altar. As the man of God watched, I skinned the kid and butchered it, removing the offal and washing the intestines and shanks in water Na'amah brought in an earthenware laver. Then I laid the rest of the body upon the altar, atop the wood.

The man of God nodded as he looked over my labors. "You have done well, Manoah of Dan."

I held the flint in my hand to light the offering when I realized that, in my awe at his appearance, I had neglected even to ask his name. "Please, my lord—what is your name, that when all the words that you have spoken prove to be true we may honor you as a prophet?"

He turned and his brilliant eyes bored into me. Though he was smiling, in the light of those eyes my heart melted. "And just why should you ask about my name," he whispered, "when it is a wonderful one?"

With that, he leapt atop the altar with the effortless grace of a hind bounding through the forest. Turning back toward me, he slammed the butt of his staff down among the bundled brushwood. A deafening *crack* started me backward, echoing from the hills, and a great gout of blue flame burst up around him.

Though I saw the flames writhing about his legs, I knew somehow that he was in no danger. He looked once more at Na'amah and me, his face distorted by the waves of heat between us, and to my utter amazement his feet lifted from the altar and he began to ascend with the flames. Spiraling gently as he rose, as though he weighed no more than a bit of ash and the smoke were bearing him aloft, he grew smaller and smaller to our eyes. We watched until he disappeared into the clouds above us, struck dumb with awe.

When nine times the moon had turned full, Samson was born.

Then it was that I knew for a certainty that Jehovah had sent him, that all his words were true, and that my son would become the hero of Israel.

So Abraham rose early in the morning, saddled his ass and took two of his servants and Isaac his son with him, along with the wood that he had split for the burnt offering. And he traveled to the place that the true God showed him" - The Scroll of Bereshith

As Manoah finished his story, Samuel saw that Joel and Abijah were staring at him, wide-eyed. As soon as he concluded, Abijah turned to Samuel, smiling from ear to ear. "Papa—he went up with the flames an' smoke!"

Samuel nodded and smiled back. "Do you know who that man was?"

"An angel," answered Joel.

"It *was* an angel," confirmed Manoah.

Joel looked up at his father. "Have you ever seen an angel, Papa?"

"No," Samuel laughed. "No, I have not.

Samuel glanced at the rigid, half-smile frozen on Samson's face. There was pride in the look—pride in the role he had been prophesied to fulfill; pride in his father's confidence in him. But there was also an abiding discomfort, a fear that he would not be able to live up to all that people hoped for him.

Samson glanced his way and for a moment he and Samuel's eyes met. An understanding passed between them in that glance: only Samuel could truly comprehend being set apart as a Nazirite for life by one's parents and living everyday since his birth with the high expectations of others.

"Well, Prophet?" Manoah growled.

"Well?" Samuel responded.

"Samson's destiny is to save Israel from the Philistines," Manoah said. "If you will not empower him now, then I will haunt your steps until you do."

Samuel glanced at Liora. "Can you take the boys and put them down for a nap?"

"Please—not yet Papa!" Joel pleaded. Abijah began to cry.

"Come along—give ear to your father," Liora said, herding them toward the back of the house.

When they had left the room (although Abijah's crying was still clearly audible), Samuel turned back to Manoah. "Manoah, I know how you must feel..."

"Do you?" the big Danite asked. "Do you really?"

"I did not mean..."

"I know what you meant," Manoah said. "But if you really knew how I felt, if you really understood, a day would not dawn in which you would not wear a sword strapped to your hip. From the moment of your waking to the moment you passed into the land of dreams a single prayer would pass your lips in an unending litany: that you could see the sons of Philistia rotting and bloated in the sun, and the birds feasting on their flesh."

"You are right," Samuel said. "I cannot summon that kind of anger, or hatred."

Manoah snorted dismissively. "I suppose I should not be surprised. A Prophet and son of Levi does not live the life of a warrior, and you have spent your days far from the pounding of the surf on the shores of Philistia. But I did not come here for your sword arm. I came for you to empower my son."

Samuel shook his head. "Jehovah has given me no instruction on when or in what manner Samson is to take up the task for which he has been born. But God will reveal it in His due time."

"And you do not think that now, when we are on the brink of another war with Philistia—you do not think that now is a good time?" Manoah asked.

"What we think is not important," Samuel said. "As Job said, 'Do You have eyes of flesh, O Jehovah, or do You see the way a mortal man sees?' We must be patient, and wait for Jehovah's will to become clear."

"I am a man of action, not subtlety," Manoah said. "I must have tasks to set my hands to."

"There is one thing you can do," Samuel said. "Go to the Elders of Ramathaim with the news of what you have seen. In particular, make sure that a Manassite named Baghadh hears it."

Manoah's brows knitted. "I know Baghadh. What is he doing here?"

"That is a good question," Samuel said.

Manoah left for Ramathaim, while Samuel spent the rest of the afternoon packing for his journey to Pirathon to see Avdon. Samson worked with a group of the *Beneh* who were building an addition onto one of the storage buildings not far from Samuel's home, stacking rough clay bricks within a frame of peeled poles.

Manoah returned before much time had passed, fuming. "Those fools would not even meet with me! Apparently marching contingents of armored Rephaim and Philistines sailing up the coast are not sufficient reason to interrupt the leisure activities of the lofty Elders of Ramathaim!"

"That would be Baghadh's influence," Samuel said.

"They asked me if I had been sent by the Elders of Dan," Manoah said. "The fact that I *am* one of the Elders of Dan is apparently irrelevant."

Samuel leaned heavily against the wall. "They do not want to hear the truth."

"They will not believe until the sons of Philistia are marching through their gates."

Manoah left to help Samson and the *Beneh*. As the sun melted toward the horizon and a cooling breeze blew in from the direction of the sea, Reuel found Samuel and told him that all had been made ready for the sacrifice required by the Torah for the victim of the unknown murderer.

Samuel followed him outside the boundaries of Naioth and toward Ramathaim. Ahead of them and behind, Elders of city, *Beneh,* and other people who had known Zimri walked the same path, somber and quiet.

Reuel led Samuel to a narrow torrent valley a short distance from the city gates. The trail was treacherous, descending the valley's steep sides amidst scattered mustard plants and fragrant rock rose, becoming in some places nothing more than a few footholds kicked into the steep hillside. Their progress was slowed as younger men guided and supported elderly men and women who were determined to witness the sacrifice.

When Samuel and Reuel finally arrived, a group was already assembled at the bottom of the valley. A rivulet of stream trickled among the rocks and the sun-scorched rushes—all that would grow in the stony soil. A thick-leaved myrtle tree on the brown bank, its roots slithering through bright red poppies, cast its shadow across the rocks.

At the crowd's head stood a Priest and a handful of Levites who had come from the city for the ritual. One of the Levites held the lead rope of a dun-colored yearling calf. The valley's walls shielded the evening breeze from reaching its floor, where the rocks radiated the heat they had absorbed through the day. The still air was a little stifling and the calf languished in the heat, motionless except for her swishing tail and when she tossed her arcing horns to jostle flies from her nose.

When the group was assembled the Priest stepped forward and placed his hand upon the forehead of the calf. "Has this calf borne fruit?" he asked.

"No!" responded the crowd, "For she is too young."

"Has this land borne fruit?"

"No! For it is too hard."

"Will Zimri ben Ibrahim bear fruit?"

"No! For his blood has been spilled."

The Priest nodded to one of the Levites who stepped forward, raising a bronze, broad-bladed axe over his head; the orange light of the setting sun gleamed off of its whetted edge. "For atonement, for our brother, who will nevermore bear fruit in Israel," the Priest said.

The Levite holding the calf's lead rope pulled, stretching its head forward. The other swung the axe downward with all his strength and struck the back of the calf's neck, just below the skull. The beast's head snapped unnaturally upward even as her front legs gave out beneath her. She fell forward onto the rocky soil and then rolled slowly onto her side. The axe flashed again, and the Levite severed her head completely; scarlet rivulets flowed between the rounded, grey stones and slipped into the trickling water like wisps of reddish-brown smoke.

The Elders knelt alongside the stream and washed their hands and forearms with the water. As they did so, they intoned in unison: "Our hands did not shed this blood; neither did our eyes see it shed."

The Priest raised his arms toward a sky that burned orange and amber. "Do not set it to the account of Your people Israel, whom You redeemed, O Jehovah, and do not put the guilt of the innocent blood in the midst of Your people Israel."

The Elders clambered to their feet, and the crowd stood for a moment in silence, listening to the chuckling of the stream among the rocks. With that, the ceremony was over, and all began to file slowly back up out of the valley, the elderly clinging to the arms of the younger as they ascended the steep slope.

Samuel stayed a few moments longer, watching as a group of Levites butchered the calf and bundled the pieces into woolen bags to be carted that night to the Tabernacle at Nob. He realized that Baghadh had not been there, and wondered why the ambitious Manassite would have missed the opportunity to participate and be seen as a leader by so many.

Samuel returned home to try and finish packing; he worked at it until darkness fell, and then collapsed into sleep.

— —•— — —•— — —•— — —•— — —•— — —•— — —•— — —•— — —•— — —•— — —•— — —•— — —•—

The lightening blue of an early-morning sky roused him the next morning. By the time he stepped out of his door the morning fog had already evaporated, and crested larks and yellow-browed warblers were praising the warm sunlight that splashed down on Naioth and the land all around it. He found Reuel waiting for him at the gate of Samuel's courtyard. "I have a few things I wish you to do for me while I am gone," Samuel said.

Reuel shook his head. "I am coming with you."

"That is not necessary, Reuel. Manoah and Samson have already agreed to accompany me."

"As am I," Reuel said. "I am already packed. I am not going to let you travel unprotected through the countryside with Philistine warriors riding everywhere."

"And are you going to protect me? Have you been secretly training with the Zebulunite weapons masters?"

"Even my untrained body can serve as a shield for my master," said Reuel seriously.

"There are many duties here I hoped you would look after."

"Duties that cannot be handled by Liora, or Hannah, or Elkanah, or any of a dozen other older prophets who live here? I have already talked to them and they assured me that they could manage without me for a few days."

Samuel hesitated, trying to think of how to dissuade his self-appointed personal servant.

"It is no use, my lord," Reuel said. "Nothing you say can change my mind. I am coming."

Samuel sighed and laughed. "Very well. Better this way than you following us secretly."

Reuel dashed off to gather his traveling gear just as Manoah and Samson appeared at the gate, bags slung over their shoulders and staves in their hands.

When Reuel returned, he also was carrying two staves. He handed one to Samuel.

It was stained vermilion.

Samuel looked at him, puzzled. "It is unthinkable that I should take this!"

"What man or woman in Ramathaim—or in all Israel—would question it?" Reuel asked. "You received your appointment at God's hands—the Prophet of Israel, spokesman of the Most High. You should, without a doubt, be able to bear the staff of an Elder of your tribe. It is madness that the men of Ramathaim have not formally appointed you already."

"The lad has a point," Manoah said. "I assumed you were an Elder."

Samuel wrapped his fingers around the staff. It was polished acacia, almost as long as he was tall, its butt end hardened in coals. It felt good to hold it. Familiar feelings of pride at who he was and what he had accomplished with his life stirred inside him. At the same time, he flushed with the shame of what he was feeling. *You are nothing!* he told himself. *You are less than a speck of dust in the eyes of the Most High! And what would you be if the world around you knew you entertained such arrogant thoughts?*

He glanced again at Reuel. "Such an appointment must come from an Elder—."

"By all that is holy!" Manoah reached out and grabbed the vermilion staff from Samuel's hands. "I, as an Elder of the tribe of Dan, do hereby present you with this staff. Take it, and walk as one appointed among the Elders of Israel."

He thrust the staff back into Samuel's hands. "There. It is done. Can we leave now?"

Liora came out into the courtyard with Gavriel, Joel and Abijah, their eyes still heavy with sleep. Samuel saw Liora's glance move to the staff in his hands. "I didn't want to accept it..." he stammered.

She did not answer, knowing that he had not said what was in his heart, knowing he needed time to come to grips with his own feelings.

Samuel kissed the boys, embraced his wife, and then took her hands in his own. "I should be back in a few days."

She nodded, her eyes holding his own. "May Jehovah watch over you, my love."

Samuel shouldered his bag and followed Reuel, Manoah and Samson out the courtyard gate, through the buildings of Naioth, and onto the road. He paused a moment next to his sons' almond tree, a wilted stem and half a dozen tiny, curled leaves pushing up from a scar of freshly turned earth. The sight awoke a wave of emotion in him, and he turned to look at the shadowed School behind him, its highest roof parapets just touched by the orange of the rising sun.

"My lord?" Reuel asked from behind him.

"I have the strangest feeling," Samuel said, "that I will not see this place again for a very long time."

Shaking his head to clear away his morose thoughts, he turned back and, swinging his vermilion staff beside him, headed down the road to the east.

9

Later that afternoon Liora left the children in Hannah's care and took a walk into the forests that bordered Naioth to the west. She knew that Joel and Abijah would begin to miss their father that night at the evening meal, and that their sadness would grow even stronger when they had to climb into bed without him. A few days before she had seen a carob tree when she was collecting bay leaves in the forest, and she thought she would gather some of the pods as sweetmeats for a dessert to distract the boys when the realization of their father's absence hit them.

The afternoon air was cooler beneath the sycamore branches, and scented by the perfume of scattered pine and cinnamon trees. The forest's gnarled oaks and myrtles, its stately walnut trees and its dark-needled junipers always gave her a sense of peace, as though reminding her that the events of today were only a passing moment in the endless march of time. The wrinkled bark of the trunks all around her was as communicative as a scroll on which was recorded the history of countless ages past, and that would still be telling their tale when the fears and concerns of the present were swallowed up like leaves decaying into the dark forest soil.

The carob tree was farther into the wood than she remembered. As she walked, her concerns about Samuel bubbled up from the dark recesses of her mind where they seemed constantly to simmer. She pictured his face, the shadow cast by his dark thoughts reflected in his green eyes; she saw the way that his anxieties seemed to strangle the optimistic energy and youthful creativity of the man she had married.

He was so hard on himself, and so convinced that if he did not expend every grain of his energy in the constant pursuit of some noble goal that he would vanish in a puff of insignificance, or disappoint and alienate everyone around him. He bore the expectations of others with the anguished certainty that he would one day let them down, or that they would someday discover that he was not the man they thought him to be.

Liora knew that many relied on him and looked up to him—the *Beneh* lived and died by his words. The man Liora knew as an anxious and angst-ridden father was seen by people from Dan to Be'ersheba as a kind of hero and mystic rolled into one. People were in awe of what he did, but they did not understand it, and that ignorance elevated him in their eyes to something more than a man. Samuel—though he did not like to admit it—craved that affirmation of his worth and, in spite of himself. thrived on being able to inspire such feelings of admiration and respect.

But the same qualities that raised him to the level of a living legend in Israel also lifted him beyond the reach of the people who might otherwise have been close to him. He had lived his entire life cultivating qualities that would cause people to respect and admire—even to be in awe of—him, and it was only now that he was discovering that that level of respect came at a very high cost: the unassailable isolation of the man who seemed to be more than what other men even dreamed of being. The struggle to impress the world around him was exhausting him, and Liora knew that he could not continue it indefinitely. His determination to be someone great was only a mask that hid his fear of being no one at all.

Movement to her left caught her eye, and she turned to see three fallow deer, a doe and two yearling fawns, silently picking their way through the trees. Beyond them, a dark-leaved vine was unhurriedly strangling a sprawling plane tree—the tree's branches had already become twisted and stunted, and its leaves covered the ground beneath it in a somber, brittle blanket of grey and dull brown. She recognized the spot, and remembered that the carob tree was not far beyond it.

Samuel tried to be a good father—tried so hard, she worried, that his sons were learning more about the endless pursuit of unattainable goals than they were about enjoying the life that Jehovah had given them. He wanted to handle every situation, every aspect of parenting, perfectly, and he sometimes wept for fear he had done something that would scar his children for the rest of their life. She wanted to tell him that his resilience in the face of his fears, his ability to handle the challenges of life—and even to fail to handle them—and still find joy was the greatest lesson he could teach. But she did not have his gift with words. She had not yet found a way to make him understand.

A pair of partridges glided past her right shoulder and she stopped a moment to watch their wheeling descent through the tree trunks. In the sudden silence, she heard nearby two men, talking in lowered voices. Lifting her skirt to avoid catching it on the underbrush, she crept toward the sound.

A few steps took her to a line of young cedar shoots, splayed up like impatient children from a massive fallen trunk. She ducked behind them, peering between their needled branches at a small clearing twenty steps away. The smell of freshly crushed herbs beneath her feet drifted in the air around her.

Two men stood close together, one shrouded in a cowled cloak, the other unmistakably Philistine in his pleated kilt and feather-crested helmet. The latter turned toward her for a moment and she froze, thinking he had somehow heard her approach. A veined growth that bulged from the soldier's neck immediately identified him: Glaucus, the garrison commander who had pursued Gavriel and Cheran into Naioth two nights before.

Glaucus paced the clearing impatiently; he had not seen her. The hooded figure remained turned away from her, but she could hear his voice, muffled slightly by his cowl, in the forest's stillness. "He left this morning, following the easy roads toward Pirathon."

Liora's heart beat faster. They were talking about Samuel? Or Manoah?

"Why Pirathon?" Glaucus asked.

"It is the home of a man called Avdon, who is the de facto commander of Israel's fighting men."

"Leader or no leader, Israel is no match for the growing military might of Philistia," said Glaucus.

"Maybe not," said the hooded one. "But would you rather march into the land against farmers scattered in their fields, or face an organized force under a charismatic leader?"

Glaucus scowled at him, jabbing one index finger in his direction. "We wouldn't be in this situation if you had done as you promised and delivered the boy to us!"

"I did everything I could!" the hooded one said. "How was I to know that that busybody Reuel would be up at that hour?"

Glaucus spat and wiped his mouth with the back of his hand. "It does not matter now. My lord and master will deal with the Sorcerer of Ramathaim when he arrives—and with this Avdon, if he needs to."

"He is coming? Here, to Ramathaim?" Even from a distance, Liora could hear the fear in the hooded man's voice.

Glaucus sneered down at him. "He has not forgotten the little seer who caused him such trouble all those years ago. He remembers the name of Samuel."

"And what of my request?"

"You know that we Philistines reward loyalty above all. Do as my master commands, and you will have what you desire."

"You will not regret it!" said the hooded one. "When I am Judge of Israel, I will give Philistia access to all the wealth of Canaan, and—."

"Save your assurances for someone who cares about them," said Glaucus.

"Then give me some guarantee that your master will deliver what he has promised," the hooded figure whined.

"Guarantee? There are no guarantees, except the utter certainty of our deaths," Glaucus said.

"I am risking my life for you!"

"And you are being handsomely rewarded. If your service continues to please my master, you can be sure he will find a place for you in the empire that will soon rule Canaan."

Glaucus turned and strode westward through the trees. "Just do not disappoint him! He is not a forgiving man!"

Liora's heart was beating so hard that she felt sure that the hooded figure must be able to hear it in the sudden stillness. She watched him a moment longer before he turned toward her and she could see beneath the shadows of his cowl.

It was Baghadh. Muttering to himself and casting daggered glances back toward where Glaucus had disappeared, he began shuffling through the trees toward Ramathaim.

Liora stepped back involuntarily at the sight of his lesioned face, and a branch beneath her foot cracked.

Baghadh stopped and slowly turned toward her hiding place, head bobbing at an even more rapid pace than usual. "Who is there?"

He lurched slowly in her direction and Liora put one hand over her mouth and tried futilely to shrink into the ground.

"Is someone there?" Baghadh asked, and though she could not see him, Liora could tell that his voice was getting nearer.

"Whoever you may be, I fear for your safety," he said, his words punctuated by his uneven footsteps.

Liora risked a sidelong glance in his direction, through the leaves of the cedars. She saw him reach one blistered hand into his cloak. With a rasping whisper, he drew forth a sharply curved iron knife.

"Come on out!" Baghadh hissed. "At least give me the opportunity to show you mercy."

He lurched a few paces closer. "If I come upon you by surprise, who knows what may happen?"

She knew she could outrun him, but if he saw her, if he recognized her…Samuel had warned her before to stay away from him. He had said that Baghadh was a man for whom no act was unconscionable. If he saw her, she would not be safe even if she got away. If he thought she was a threat, that she knew some secret he wanted to keep concealed, he would find her, wherever she went.

She glanced at him again, trying to calm her pounding heart. She saw the light gleam from the polished edge of the curved knife in his hand.

Then a snap sounded from somewhere to her left and she turned instinctively, starting at the sound.

The three fallow deer she had seen earlier edged into the opposite side of the clearing and stopped when they saw Baghadh, heads lifting sharply, nostrils flared as they waited to see what he would do.

From the corner of her eye Liora saw Baghadh look at them a moment, then make a noise that was somewhere between a laugh and a cough. "Fool!" he said, and Liora was unsure if he was talking to himself or to the deer.

"Get out of here!" he yelled, and the deer bounded off into the forest, vanishing into the rows of trunks as gracefully as they had arrived. Baghadh watched them go, then shook his head and shuffled out of the clearing. The knife disappeared back beneath the folds of his robe.

Liora waited until she could no longer hear the sound of his limping steps before she stood, her legs cramped and stiff from crouching in one place for so long. She leaned against the cedar log and waited for her breathing to slow while she tried to figure out what to do.

For some reason the entire surreal experience made her suddenly anxious about her sons, and she began to make her way back toward Naioth as quickly as she could, her desire to find the carobs forgotten. In the short time that it took her to reach Elkanah and Hannah's house, she had made up her mind as to what she had to do.

The boys were playing in the courtyard of their house with their grandmother, building miniature palaces from pebbles, twigs, and mud. She knelt next to them for a few moments and hugged them both. Hannah looked at her quizzically when Liora told her that she was leaving again, but did not ask her for an explanation.

She left her in-laws' house and made her way toward Ramathaim. She had heard rumors from the women in town about the house that Baghadh had purchased from Gabbai—some said that the purchase was, in fact, the collection of a debt that Gabbai had owed to Baghadh. Liora had never been able to find out the truth of the matter, but when Baghadh had bought the house Gabbai and his family had disappeared, and had not been seen in the tribal lands of Ephraim since.

The house was large but not impressive, although it was apparent that already Baghadh was having its outer wall rebuilt and its simple parapet replaced with a heavier, intricately carved railing. At the courtyard gate four purple-cloaked Phoenician soldiers stood, spears in hand. She did not recognize them. The weapons they carried were of Philistine-forged iron.

"May you have peace," she said to them, bowing. "I have come to speak to Lord Baghadh."

The eldest guardsman looked her over and, as though assessing that she was no threat, opened the courtyard gate. Liora slipped inside.

In the courtyard itself, another three dozen Phoenicians lounged, tossing dice, drinking wine, and sharpening iron weapons with oiled whetstones. Most ignored Liora, but a few followed her with their eyes in a way that reminded her of hunting cats.

The tall double doors of the house itself were closed. "May you have peace!" she called out, and waited for someone to respond. Her eyes followed the dark Passover bloodstains that ran from the lintel down the doorposts and around the mezuzah. Next to the scroll's box a jade amulet hung: a figurine of a Canaanite god she did not recognize; she guessed that was a charm for good luck.

The door swung abruptly open and Liora was startled to be greeted by a tall, beautiful woman. "Who calls on the house of Lord Baghadh?"

It took a moment for Liora to regain her composure. She had never seen the woman before—she would have remembered someone of her striking beauty. She was wearing the adornments of a Canaanite concubine: gold and carnelian beads on golden chains around her neck and wrists, brooches of electrum inset with gems, her eyelids darkened with bands of black kohl and green malachite. Intricate henna designs writhed around her wrists and ankles. Her hair was uncovered, and fell across her shoulders in thick, black ringlets—like a prostitute, Liora thought. Strangest of all, she stared at something behind and above Liora, as though deigning her visitor as being below her dignity even to look upon.

"May I announce you to my lord?" the woman asked, annoyance at Liora's silence apparent in her tone.

"I...I wish to speak to Baghadh," Liora said.

The concubine tossed back her hair in a seemingly unconscious gesture, and a thick wave of perfume wafted past Liora—an odor that did not quite mask a rotten smell from within the house. "I must give him your name," the concubine said.

The woman would still not meet Liora's eyes, and with a shock Liora realized why.

She was blind.

"I am Liora, the wife of Samuel ben Elkanah, of the School of the Prophets."

The blind concubine nodded once. "Please wait here."

She disappeared back into the courtyard, closing the door behind her. Beneath any other lintel, Liora would have felt deeply insulted that she had not been invited inside. In this case, she was glad. Something about the house bothered her, something she could not put her finger on that raised the hair on the back of her neck and made her stomach slightly queasy.

A moment later the door swung open again and Baghadh stood before her, staring down his bulbous nose as though she were a dead rodent he had uncovered. She had never been so close to him before, and the nausea in her stomach increased at the sight of the translucent pustules clustered across his face and neck. It did not take her long to realize that he was, at least in part, the source of the house's rank smell.

"So." His head bobbed rhythmically. "Here is the woman who belongs to the...to the founder of the infamous 'school.'" His eyes slowly crawled over her body, and she felt their focus like insects on her skin. "I wish you had come for some...pleasurable reason. If you gave my Egyptian handmaidens a little time, they could make you into a woman no man could take his eyes off of."

She stiffened, but kept her eyes on the ground and said nothing.

"Very well," Baghadh said. "I suppose both of us know that is not likely to happen. What, then, brings you to the door of Lord Baghadh?"

"Forgive me, my lord. I was walking in the forest today—."

"Indeed?" he interrupted her, stepping abruptly from the doorway toward her. His voice was suddenly harsh and menacing. "And what did you see there?"

She took two steps back into the courtyard, wondering suddenly if coming there had been a very bad idea. Behind her the soldiers turned to see what was happening.

"Please, my lord...I saw the Philistine garrison commander, Glaucus."

"Doing what?"

"Walking, my lord—very close to Naioth. I know you of all the men in Ramathaim are knowledgeable about what is happening from Dan to Be'ersheba, and from the Great Desert to the Great Sea."

She felt, rather than saw, him relax. "Yes?"

"I wondered if perhaps you knew anything about what the sons of Philistia might be planning—if his presence here indicates that we should be concerned about some threat. With my husband gone..."

Baghadh was silent for a long time, and Liora risked a glance from beneath her lowered brows. He was staring at her, eyes squinted as though they had not adjusted to the light. The look was cold, and knowing.

"You have nothing to worry about," he said at last. "But I am sure your husband has already disclosed that to your ears, has he not?"

She knew he suspected something; it was obvious in his tone. But she refused to be intimidated. "I have not spoken to him."

"Ah, yes. He has left town, has he not?"

She wondered if his statement was am implied threat. "I only wish to know anything that might help us to protect our family."

He laughed then, a mirthless sound. "Go home, Liora."

He turned and began to close the door. At the last moment, he turned back one more time. "And the next time you want to spy on me, incline your ears to the voice in your head that is even now telling you that you should never have come here."

10

The Philistine Axis Lords sat in chairs of oak inlaid with richly engraved ivory harvested from Aramaic elephants. Their chairs spread along a long, polished oak table that nearly spanned one end of the banquet hall, awash in music and the noise of revelers. Light speared into the hall from rows of deep windows high along either wall, or glowed in shadowed corners from smoking olive-oil lamps, burnishing the skin of those seated nearest them.

Tables stretched down the two long sides of the hall as well, and seated at them were all the nobles of Ashkelon and visiting lords and generals from other cities of the Pentapolis. Every right hand clutched a jug of barley beer, husks caught in its strainer top like the trapped carcasses of pale insects. Servers and tasters scurried among the dignitaries, trying to avoid the wild, drunken gestures and cuffs of displeasure from their masters. Two-handled copper kraters were piled with roast pork and bread; taller pitchers adorned with preening swans and spirals held olive oil and wine.

At the far end of the hall, human-sized statues of a lightning-wielding Ba'al and wide-hipped Asherah, cupping her bare breasts in her hands, stood atop a dais of cut stone. A priestess poured a wine offering from a black and red glazed pitcher onto a four-horned altar at Ba'al's feet, while a priest arrayed sheaves of grain around the mounded cone of russet-colored incense smoldering at its center. Smoke rose in writhing spirals, and the scent of frankincense blended with the aroma of roast meat, lamp smoke, and human sweat.

At the center of the hall, priests of Ba'al led the most beautiful women from the crowd, robed in translucent linen, in a licentious dance, its eroticism marred only by the unsteady steps of the intoxicated participants. They whirled and writhed in time to the music of harps, pipes, timbrels and drums.

Only a single pair of double doors entered the hall, and at each side of them stood a pair of heavily muscled guards, armed with iron swords, spears, and circular shields of wood and boiled leather.

A presiding *baru*-priest, stripped to the waist, raised his arms and swept the room with his eyes, taking in the Axis Lords and their tasters and attendants, the seated noblemen, and the dancing throng. "Ba'al, Rider of the Clouds, Lord of Heaven: hear our plea! O Slayer of Yotan, the seven-headed dragon—your voice is thunder; your ship is a snow-bearing cloud!"

The *baru*-priest clutched an iron dagger, blade downward, in one hand and with it slashed a crimson cross into his chest. As blood flowed from the wounds, the Axis Lords pounded the tables in approval, rattling their spouted mugs and the platters of roasted pork, boiled dog, and spring vegetables spread before them.

The dancers lifted olive branches from the floor and waved them overhead. "Bless us, Lord Ba'al!" the *baru*-priest intoned. "Steer your ship of cloud over our fields. Be pleased with our offerings to you, and grant us the wealth of harvest."

Servers entered the room bearing platters of steaming, black mussels on their shoulders. The Axis Lords and other seated guests tossed their meat scraps to the floor to make way for this new delight, and the dogs rushed around their legs, snapping up the refuse.

"Asherah, our lady of the sea and the eternal mistress of the gods: Let your fertility awaken the earth that she may produce with the endless bounty of your womb!"

JUDGE OF ISRAEL

Two dozen muscular men loped from a side door into the long hall, their faces hidden behind almond-eyed, tight-lipped masks of earthenware, their olive-skinned bodies oiled and gleaming. The audience burst into applause. As the masked men rushed to the center, the inebriated dancers stumbled aside to make way for them. Silver-hilted swords hung across the black, pleated kilts of the newcomers; their sandals cross-laced to their knees. Lining up in two parallel rows, they drew their swords in unison and pointed them at the ceiling.

"For the honor of Philistia and the Axis Lords of the Pentapolis!" said one of them, his voice muffled behind his mask.

The Axis Lords cheered, their words slurred and ragged from overindulgence. The masked men leapt into the air and began to dance, an intricate, whirling madness, their swords flashing as they swung them in precise patterns over, around, under each other, sharp iron whisking past oiled flesh, and missing it by the thickness of vellum.

The audience clapped and called out encouragement, and the dancers whirled on, their steps and turns unbelievably complex, seeming every moment to be in danger of slicing each other to ribbons, but coming away again and again unscathed.

Servers refilled bird- and horn-shaped vessels with thick, red, lamb gravy and olive oil. The dancers slipped nearer and nearer to the table of the Axis Lords, and the five men and their attendants flinched exaggeratedly back, laughing their approval at the display of skill and precision.

The servers reappeared once more, this time bearing huge, silver platters on their heads. Pushing other dishes aside, they set their burdens down to reveal a whole barracuda on each platter, three quarters the length of a man, their open mouths seeming to grin at the awed revelers. The dancers grew wilder, and the hiss and ring of blade sliding against blade shrilled through the cacophony of the crowd.

A crash sounded from the doorways, and in that instant of interruption, the servers reached with serpent swiftness into the mouths of the barracudas and pulled out long, slender iron blades. Before anyone could react, they slit the throats of all five Axis Lords.

As blood sprayed onto the table, the crowd erupted in turmoil. Arrows hissed across the hall, felling the dancers with the speed of a thought; their whirling swords clattered onto the flagstones. A struggle broke out at the door, but within seconds the guards had been slaughtered and a knot of men pushed past their bodies. They were feral looking, dressed in loose-fitting black and carrying simple, efficient iron blades. At their head was a tall, elderly man with dark, weathered skin and short-cropped grey hair. He was flanked on one side by a hunched, lurching figure whose face was shrouded within the shadows of a deep, black cowl; on the other by a massive, heavily-muscled warrior with a shock of blonde hair and a mass of inflamed scar tissue where his nose should have been.

A few men in the crowd of revelers leapt toward the intruders, scrambling for weapons. The battle lasted only a moment: the black-clad warriors moved through them with chilling efficiency, dispatching anyone who dared to lift a blade against them.

The scarred warrior gestured, and four more men pushed through the crowded doorway, all of them in their sixties or seventies, hardened men with a fell light in their eyes. They took up their places on either side of Sarnam, standing in front of the table where the bodies of the Axis Lords now slumped in pools of their own blood.

"I am Sarnam, Axis Lord of Ashkelon," the grey-haired man said. "And these—." He gestured toward the men to his right and left "These are the new Axis Lords of Philistia."

The crowd stirred angrily. Gedhudhra archers took their places around the hall, arrows fitted to their bowstrings.

A Philistine captain stepped forward from among the revelers. "You will die before the sun sets. Do you dare to think that you—."

"The city will be ours within the hour," Sarnam interrupted him. "By now, every man of rank and station who has refused to accept our authority has been killed. Three centuries of Rephaim march through the streets of Ashkelon. Within two days, the other cities of the Pentapolis will be ours as well. You, the nobles of Ashkelon, can choose to accept our leadership now or..." He paused meaningfully. "I do not wish to kill any of you. I, too, am a son of Philistia. I do not wish to take your ranks, your titles, or your property. Choose to join with me, and live."

He waited a moment, staring at the crowd as if daring anyone to respond. Then he gestured to Phicol again and the scarred warrior ducked out the door. When he returned he was followed by a Rephaim so huge he could only come through the door by ducking and turning sideways. The giant dragged a black stone idol, scraping, across the flagstones to the dais. Its top was in the form of a bare-chested, bearded man, its bottom sculpted into a fish's tail. Muscles rippling, the Rephaim heaved the statue onto the dais, standing it behind the idols of Ba'al and Asherah. It stood a full head higher than either of them.

"Philistines!" Sarnam said, gesturing dramatically at the idol. "Have you forgotten Dagon, father of Ba'al? Have you forgotten the god who gave this land into our hands?"

He strode forward toward the crowd of nobles. "I am not here to kill Philistines. I am here to save you. You have deviated from our ancient traditions, from the ways of our forefathers. Philistia has neglected Dagon, Lord of all the gods, who made lords of this land we have claimed."

He took two steps to the nearest table and lifted a loaf of bread in one hand and a mug of wine in the other. Turning back to the nobles, he proffered the bread. "You have satisfied yourself with grain…"

He threw the bread to the floor and raised his mug. "…when you could have been drinking the blood of your enemies." He tipped the mug and drained it, then paced in front of the tables. "These men," he said, gesturing back toward the slumped bodies of the Axis Lords, "worshipped Ba'al with the strength of their little fingers. We will give to Dagon, the greatest of the gods, the sinews of our arms and the blood in our veins! And he will make us great again!

"I invite you to join me and the other Axis Lords of Philistia in a great ceremony to Dagon tomorrow. Let us show you the military might we have built during our time away from the lands Dagon gave to our people. Let us show you the spoils and the glory that wait for the new armies of the Philistines."

11

S arnam spent the rest of the day confirming that his hold on the city was complete. He had prepared for every contingency, but in the end very little of his planning was needed. The people, including the soldiers of the army, wanted leadership; when they learned that the Axis Lords and some generals and captains had been executed, they more or less willingly followed whomever they were told had taken their place. No doubt the transition had been helped by the presence of the Rephaim and the summary execution of anyone who defied the authority of Sarnam's men—and by the promise of great wealth for those who proved their loyalty to the new regime. Showing chests of gold and silver to the right people was a powerfully convincing technique.

Sarnam regretted having to kill his own people, but blood was the coin of rulership, the only currency universally accepted in politics. A few scattered attempts at rebellion broke out in the city, but the Gedhudhra and the Rephaim quickly quelled them, and then killed the perpetrators publicly and very slowly. After that, the populace seemed ready and willing to accept their new rulers without question. For the most part.

It had to be so, Sarnam knew—he had never doubted. He was the fist of Dagon, the god's chosen servant. With Dagon backing him, he could not, ultimately, fail to accomplish whatever the god asked him to do.

He had thought for a time that he would never return to Philistia. He had dreamed of starting his own empire, a mobile army of his Gedhudhra and the warriors that had joined them for the promise of a share in the never-ending flow of spoils. He would not have come back if he had not had to. If his father had not demanded it.

His father had come to Sarnam in a dream, and told him what was expected of him. He had told him about the work that Sarnam needed to finish, a work that began with the conquest of the land of Canaan. Dagon was with him, his father had assured him. Dagon would not let him fail.

The next day, walking to the theater in Ashkelon for the celebration he had arranged, Sarnam reflected on the power of the father of the gods, and how fortunate he was to have a true priest of Dagon like Sihphil at his side. Of course, the little magus had changed since they were last in Philistia. He looked considerably better than when Sarnam and Phicol had dragged him from an Egyptian dungeon, though his face still bore the scars and pocking of the disease that had ravaged him while he was imprisoned. He was quieter now than the man Sarnam had known two decades before, and not just because he had grown old. His movements were slower and more deliberate, his sibilant voice less powerful. The soles of his feet were crisscrossed with scars; it looked to Sarnam as though they were cuts that had been repeatedly opened to keep them from healing. But whatever had been done to him in Egypt after they had been banished from Canaan had scarred him far more deeply than what could be seen on his skin. The hatred that smoldered in his eyes, his longing for vengeance against the god Jehovah and the Hebrews who had thwarted their plans—that had grown beyond all bounds or measure.

The city passed by on either side of Sarnam as he walked, quiet since the community leaders had been summoned to the festival: the dark, pungent tanneries with supple leather goods and sleek, otter-skin mantles draped over window ledges; wine sellers with tall, voluptuous clay vessels sealed with beeswax plugs stacked along the street; potters' stalls covered in a layer of white dust thrown wet from the wheels; rows of jars, bottles, and skins stacked on shelves in the shadowed alcoves of an ointment-maker's shop, swarming with the smell of spices.

But Sarnam saw something entirely different. He was disgusted with what had become of the great seaport since his banishment. The citizenry had spread their devotion among the countless gods of Canaan, with the result that none of those gods were receiving their due. Amulets and charms hung from necks and over doors; spells appealing to lesser spirits were scrawled on shards of pottery and dangled in front of the shops. He had seen people crossing themselves with the sign of Tammuz and murmuring whispered spells as they went about their daily business—the signs of a populace that had fallen victim to the petty conflicts and discord that raged among the servants and underlings of the deities on Mount Zephon. Ashkelon had denigrated to a place of demons, a haunt of lesser gods. In the face of such indifference, Dagon had drawn back to his palace, allowing the demons free run in the city, and in Philistia as a whole.

Even the late Axis Lords' political and commercial decisions had been marked by shortsightedness and apathy. The fools had allowed Sarnam's carefully constructed chain of slaves, merchants, and transporters organized for bringing Black Sea sand into the country to disintegrate. The one great advantage that Philistia had over its enemies in Canaan, their ability to produce iron weapons, had almost come to a nothing.

He had also learned that a garrison of Philistines had recently been ordered north to Joppa and to a village called Ramathaim to subdue some kind of insurrection among the Hebrews—and that this kind of disturbance was not uncommon. Joppa was not, technically, a Philistine city, but the Axis Lords carefully monitored the trade that passed through it. As the only seaport along the coast besides Ashkelon, Joppa was a gateway to import goods from all over the world—goods that Philistia was entitled to a share of. It seemed that the late Axis Lords had proven themselves incapable of maintaining order even in the most important cities of western Canaan.

He glanced over at Sihphil shuffling along beside him, keeping pace with a dogged determination that defied his age and the crippling effects of the torture the Egyptian physicians had inflicted on him. The little priest had told him the night before that the news about the Joppa insurrection was a sign from Dagon. Joppa was to be the starting point of their campaign against Israel. Sarnam had been pleased to learn that Dagon favored this action—Joppa made sense for strategic and economic reasons as well. The capture of the seaport would give Philistia greater control of the trade route through Canaan, and would provide a springboard from which his forces could penetrate the nation's interior.

He realized he was approaching the amphitheatre to which he had summoned the nobles of the city and of surrounding communities. Gedhudhra, bolstered now by soldiers from the army of Ashkelon, paced near the entrance, alert for any subtle signs of malcontents.

Phicol and a dozen Gedhudhra stepped in beside him as he passed; the shock troops carried several large chests supported by poles threaded through rings at their bases. The weight of their contents was obvious by the ponderous swaying of the chests.

As they entered the stage end of the amphitheatre through a narrow tunnel in the high, circular wall that surrounded it, they were plunged for a moment into cool shadow. He paused in the darkness and turned to Sihphil; the little wizard's eyes shone like a cat's.

"This is a mighty crowd," Sarnam said.

"Sssss!" Sihphil responded. "But you will forge them into one mind. When you do, my sspell will finish the task."

Sarnam paused a moment, battling a rare feeling of self-doubt. The strange, little man was powerful, but to control such a crowd...

Sihphil turned away abruptly and squatted on the dirt floor of the tunnel. His clawed hands disappeared into the folds of his robe and emerged with several dark-stained, leather pouches with drawstring closures. Hissing softly, he swept a patch of dirt clear with the edge of his hand, and then spat twice onto the exposed, packed soil.

Sarnam took a single step away; without turning around, Sihphil held his dirtied palm out toward him. "Do not move until I ssay!"

Sarnam froze, and Sihphil bent over his work, sprinkling dark powders onto his sputum and stirring it with one thick, yellowed nail. The little man gestured to one of the nearby Philistine guards who carried a plain wooden box. The guard opened the box and handed Sihphil two doves from inside it.

Sihphil snapped the necks of the doves and, reaching into their beaks with a long pair of wooden tongs, slowly pulled out their tongues, muttering words in a language Sarnam did not recognize. The priest then split the doves and spilled their entrails into the dirt. Drawing three flasks from the pockets in his robes, he poured wine, powdered incense, and honey onto the steaming pile.

Under his breath, he chanted the words of his spell, drawing indecipherable sigils in a circle on the ground. After a moment, he turned back toward Sarnam and spattered the Axis Lord's tunic with some of the mixture. "Go!"

As Sarnam, still flanked by Phicol and the Gedhudhra, continued toward the amphitheatre, he could hear the sound of the little priest's mutters and hisses reverberating in the tunnel behind him.

A dozen more steps brought them back into the sunlight, and at their appearance the crowd came to their feet with a deafening roar of welcome. Sarnam raised his arms beneficently toward them, the brightness of his smile dampened by the knowledge that paid men had been stationed throughout the audience to instigate the cheering.

The other Axis Lords were already on stage—Sarnam had instructed Phicol to have them enter first, well in advance of Sarnam's own appearance. The crowd had cheered for each of them, as he knew they would, and the delay before his own entry had built anticipation and restless energy in the waiting audience; they released it now in a roar of welcome.

Sarnam took his place at the front of the stage, just a few steps forward of a stone altar filled with sullenly glowing coals.

"Lords and Princes of Philistia!" Sarnam gestured toward the nobles seated in the front rows. "Citizens of our mighty nation!" He indicated the mass of the crowds higher in the stadium, and they responded with another roar.

"All of you know the promises made to us by the gods—by Dagon himself! It was he who gave this land to our forefathers! Pharaoh Ramses himself confirmed our rights to it. It is our destiny to eat and drink of it!

"But we look across the mountains only to find Hebrew squatters on our inheritance! We must take it back from them!"

There was some rumbling among his audience; he knew that they had not yet been sold on the prospect of going to war. He pressed forward: "The men who were ruling you as Axis Lords had forgotten what it means to be Philistine, and if they had been allowed to continue in their course they would have seen to it that you forgot as well. They ran from the farmers and shepherds of the Hebrews! They retreated in fear from the will of the mountain-god whom the Hebrews brought with them into Canaan! Is that the course of a Philistine? Is that the course of the beloved of Dagon, father of all?"

"No!" the crowd responded, some of them coming to their feet.

"No!" Sarnam shouted back when they had quieted. "This is why Dagon, and Ba'al, Anat and Ashtoreth, Chousor and even Mot have turned their backs on our people. We can be mighty again! If we demonstrate our loyalty and devotion, the gods of Mount Zephon will give us the strength to crush our enemies like the grasshoppers that they are!"

The people cheered again, and this time Sarnam could tell that it was not just a response to his planted enthusiasts.

"But Dagon demands sacrifice," Sarnam shouted, "if we are to win their favor again!"

Sihphil appeared from the darkness of the entrance tunnel and a group of Ashkelon's priests came from near the stage and joined him. As they neared the crowd, some of them began to chant and dance. Seeing their religious fervor infecting the crowd, Sarnam whispered a prayer to Dagon. "Father of the gods—please see our devotion! See our willingness to serve you, and accept our offerings. Give us power over our enemies and success in all our ways."

Ashipu priests and their novices climbed the steps onto the stage carrying large baskets of woven rushes. Sarnam reflected on the insatiable appetites of the gods. Blood, sex, animals, crops—these were stones that paved the way for mortals to approach Mount Zephon.

At the sight of the *Ashipu* priests, the crowd realized what was about to happen. A man pushed forward from the front rows, worming his way through the seated nobles. Sarnam saw that he left behind in the crowd two beautiful wives, both of whom were holding infants in their arms. "Why should we listen to you?" the man screamed as he neared the stage, turning then to face the crowd. "What has this man brought us, except for years of hardship, famine, and plague? Dare we challenge the god of the Hebrews again? We have been happy, up until now. Let us live our lives in peace and enjoy the prosperity that is finally returning to Philistia."

"Do you think this prosperity will last?" Sarnam shouted back. "Do you believe for one instant that the Hebrews are not plotting right now to take this land back from us? That they are not right now imagining raping your wives, slaughtering your children, stealing your flocks and herds, and taking their houses for their own?"

"The Hebrews have left us in peace since this madman was banished!" the man said. "Do we really want war?"

Sarnam turned to Phicol. "The people cannot hear the voice of the gods when the dogs bark so loudly."

Phicol smirked, twisting his scarred face like a sick parody of a smile. He vaulted from the stage to the ground, simultaneously drawing his sword and cutting off the man's head.

The crowd fell silent, except for the man's wives, who began to scream; one fainted almost immediately and was lowered to the ground by the people around her. The severed head rolled to the feet of an elderly nobleman seated in the front row. He looked up, eyes narrowed and bony jaw set. "Is this how you would lead us? With fear?"

"If we must," Phicol said, chuckling as he wiped his sword on the dead man's torso.

Sarnam raised his arms. "You need not fear me, but to fear that which is already destroying us! For twenty years I have been gone from Philistia, banished by those short-sighted men who ruled before me. In those twenty years, what has this nation, the pride of Caphtor, accomplished? Did the Axis Lords acquire for you more land? Greater wealth? More children? An increase of your crops and your herds?"

Sarnam waited for them to think about the answer. "But I was a prisoner, I and my men, of the greatest military power in the world. And look! I escaped from Egypt. I left their generals bleeding on the sands of Karnack. I became the right hand of Queen Tiy, and buried my blade into their god, into Pharaoh Ramses himself!"

The crowd rumbled with shock. The attack on the Pharaoh had been only a rumor whispered by traders from the south—until now. Sarnam knew that both their fear and their respect of him would grow with the news. He did not tell them what he himself had just learned: that Ramses had finally died from his wounds, and that Sarnam dare not come within reach of Egypt's long arm again. He did not tell them that if he failed to establish his authority in Philistia quickly, Ramses' successor would have him hunted down. The new Pharaoh would not forget his role in the assassination unless he knew Sarnam to be beyond his reach.

"I gathered our people, scattered throughout Egypt in the wake of Queen Tiy's rebellion," he continued. "Even now, hundreds of Gedhudhra and thousands of other Philistine troops, once prisoners, wait in ships on the sea, and in convoys making their way up the coast."

Sarnam gestured to the Gedhudhra that had followed him into the amphitheatre. They heaved the heavy chests they had carried onto the stage at his feet; Phicol knelt and swung their lids open.

"While the men who called themselves Axis Lords were allowing Philistia to fade into just another petty Canaanite nation, I was laying the foundation for our future greatness!" Sarnam said. "Behold—a taste of what awaits us!"

Reaching into the chests he withdrew fistfuls of treasure: necklaces of gold and silver, colored glass beads and amulets of gold and turquoise; exquisitely carved figurines of delicately veined, translucent calcite; anklets of gold inlaid with lacing ebony figures; lifelike scarabs with bodies of pure silver and carapaces of lapis lazuli and carnelian; elephant-ivory headrests carved into intricate household scenes and brought to life in brilliant color by cut peridot, emerald, amethyst, and quartz; bowls, goblets, platters, and decanters of shining gold with geometric borders of quartz crystal; senet game pieces of agate fashioned into hippopotami and crocodiles. With every handful he lifted, gold and silver coins dripped from between his fingers like oversized grains of sand tinkling back into the treasure chests below him.

"Gedhudhra!" he commanded, and the black-clad soldiers stepped forward and began to toss double handfuls of treasure into the crowd. For several moments mayhem ruled as people climbed over each other in an effort to get at the wealth raining down on them. Two Gedhudhra lifted one of the chests and followed Sarnam as he descended from and slowly circled the platform, tossing handfuls of valuables to people all around him. "This is what comes from the hands of the new Axis Lords of Philistia! I will bring back the glory of our people, and lead our nation on to glories greater than we have imagined!"

He allowed time for all the treasure to be distributed, and for the crowd to stop cheering before he ascended the steps to the stage and spoke again. "We will defeat the Hebrews, and drive them from this land or make them our slaves. For every man who will fight in my army, I will fill his hands with a talent of Egyptian gold. For those who prove themselves leaders among soldiers, five talents. And to every loyal Philistine, I will give Hebrew slaves, Hebrew fields, Hebrew flocks and herds—the inheritance that Dagon intended for us when he guided us from Caphtor!"

The roar of the crowd drowned him out and he held up his hands again for quiet. "Let it begin today. Before tomorrow's sunset the rest of my troops will arrive on Ashkelon's beaches, and we will journey by ship to

Joppa. We will take that seaport for our own, and from that great gateway of commerce we will place a stranglehold on the Hebrews—one that not even their mountain god can free them from!"

Sihphil shuffled over to a group of priests and they led the people in a hymn to Dagon. Sarnam watched and listened, and silently thanked his god for their success in capturing the hearts of the crowd—at least for today. Of course, Sarnam knew that Dagon would lead him to success this time in his efforts to destroy the Hebrews. He had been given assurances by his father in his dreams.

But beyond that, he had other reasons for his confidence. In Egypt, they had a saying: Put your trust in the gods, but do not fail to plant seed in spring. While he knew that Dagon was going to give him the desires of his heart, he had taken steps himself to strengthen his position even before his enemies knew that an attack was coming.

His men had a spy among the Hebrews. A spy who would help him to find every vulnerability, every opportunity that he could exploit to destroy his foes.

With or without the favor of the gods, he was not going to leave Canaan again while there was breath in his lungs.

12

For several hours, Samuel, Manoah, Samson, and Reuel traveled the road in silence, content to keep their thoughts to themselves and to allow the quiet calm of the morning to remain undisturbed by anything but the warbling of bulbuls and the buzzing of cicadas.

The rough track from Ramathaim traveled east through the forest, winding for a time under the shade of pines, oaks, terebinth, and laurels, the chill of night still hiding in the shadows of their branches. Before the sun had fully crested the hills to the east, the travelers emerged from the forest's pillars, where the road descended beneath clear, open skies to a valley bottom filled with orchards and goldening fields. They paused for a moment at the edge of the wood, taking in the view of wrinkled hills and valleys flowing westward to the distant Sea, a haze of blue on the far horizon. One corner of the Ramathaim quarry was visible from where they rested, and weathered grey slabs and fingers of rock jutted out of the green turf like the bones of the land, bared by the tireless efforts of wind and rain.

As they descended, the track widened, bordered now by scattered scrub and clumps of thorny burnet, a few age-darkened, yellow blossoms still clinging to their spiny branches. In the valley their path turned sharply north, then northeast, following the rocky shoulder of a wooded ridge where goats clambered among the white stones and roots; shepherds waved and called out greetings to the travelers as they passed. The road dropped into another valley, its smooth, green bottom spotted by dozens of long-horned cattle and, to the southeast, they could see a cluster of homes and a stacked-stone tower that made up a nameless village of shepherds and cattlemen who were counted with the inhabitants of Ramathaim.

The track's course flattened for a time, as the sun climbed higher in the sky over his right shoulder, Samuel realized he felt increasingly confident in his decision to go to Judge Avdon's. The challenge Israel faced was one of leadership and the threat of war, and it was for just such tasks that Jehovah had appointed the Judges in Israel. Samuel felt in some ways that many things had conspired to bring the nation to the situation in which it now found itself. Philistia had finally regained its military strength sufficiently to challenge them once again. Israel's people were living daily with faint hearts, and looking for a promise of deliverance. They needed a leader in whom could be found the qualities of a seasoned warrior and a diplomat, a charismatic rallying point and a loyal servant of the True God. And at just such a time, Avdon was serving as their Judge.

Samuel hated leaving his family, though, especially during such uncertain times. He told himself he was making a decision for the long term, trading his immediate ability to directly watch over and protect them for the chance at an enduring peace that could serve to safeguard them for many years. His relationship with Avdon was special; Samuel knew that whatever he asked the Judge for, Avdon would do everything in his considerable power to fulfill. In addition, while many Elders might ignore Samuel the child-Prophet (as some of them were still fond of calling him), they were much less likely to ignore the words and leadership of the doughty Judge of Israel and his army of sons and grandsons.

His thoughts were interrupted as they crested another rise in the winding road and came upon a herd of gazelle tentatively crossing their path. At the approach of the four men, the elegant animals stotted away into the hills, tails stiff, ears back. Birds feeding in the garigue scattered before them.

They continued following the rough track northeast, up and down over the wrinkled land before descending deeply into a narrow valley bottom where the path they were on met up with the main road that ran through the region.

As they came once again under the shadow of the scattered oaks and sycamores that grew along the road, Manoah slowed until he was walking at Samuel's side. "You look like one who is traveling in his own thoughts."

Samuel shrugged. "I was thinking about the sacrifices that might be required of all of us if it turns out that Gavriel's vision is fulfilled in the way I think it might be. "

"True." Manoah swung his spear casually at his side as he strode forward, toward the north. "But we are a people who are not unfamiliar with sacrifice."

"Indeed," said Samuel. Images flashed through his mind of the ancient stories he had learned at Eli's knee as a child: the original martyr, Abel, spilling the blood of lambs on the stones of the first altar ever built, and then having his own blood unjustly added to the earth's cruel libation. Only a little more than a day's journey to the southeast, Mount Moriah brooded alongside the Jebusite city of Jerusalem. Atop that famous peak, a stack of stones still marked the spot where their forefather Abraham had laid his son, Isaac, on an altar in a demonstration of their willingness to give anything in service to their God.

"Indeed," Samuel repeated. "Sacrifice is in our blood."

Manoah nodded, but was quiet for a few moments before responding. "It is our willingness even to martyr ourselves in the service of our God that is our greatest power. It is not on stone altars alone that sacrifices are made, but also on green fields under the light of the sun."

"Spoken with the voice of experience—of all the men I know, you are the only one who has firsthand knowledge of both the offerings of the battlefield, and those of the altar."

"What do you mean?" Manoah asked.

"You belong to a very exclusive group among those who walk the land of Israel today," Samuel said. "You have with your own hands built an altar to the true God and offered sacrifices to Him upon it."

Manoah's brow furrowed. "Every son of Abraham places offerings upon an altar during their lifetime."

Samuel shook his head. "But they do not build those altars from stones that they have pulled from the flesh of their own land. They do not act as both Priest and supplicant. Did not Moses write, 'Only in the place that Jehovah your God chooses to have his name reside may you bring your burnt offerings and your sacrifices.'?"

"It was one time only," Manoah said, shaking his head. "I tore down the altar the same day on which I built it."

"Nevertheless," said Samuel, "it is a privilege that very few men enjoy. I am of the tribe of Levi. I served at the Altar of the true God in Shiloh all the days of my youth; I was appointed by the mouth of Jehovah as the Prophet of Israel, but I have neither built an altar nor officiated at one as you have. I have often wondered what it would feel like to do so."

"For me, it was both terrifying and...and *wrong*—or so it felt. Stacking up stone after stone before the burning eyes of the Messenger of God; slaughtering, cleaning, and burning the flesh of my sacrifice as though I was a Priest...It is not something I wish ever to do again."

Samuel smiled. "It is those privileges that we are not granted that we most long for; and the blessings we live with every day that we fail to value."

"Not always." Manoah glanced back over his shoulder, where Samson and Reuel were following far enough behind that they could not hear their conversation. "That boy is a privilege that I have prayed for all my life, and one that I hope will fulfill my every wish."

"He has grown into a fine young man," Samuel said, knowing it was not what Manoah wanted to hear.

Manoah shook his head. "He is a task with no end in sight! When will he take up the cause for which he was born, Samuel? When will he step into the sandals that he is meant to fill?"

"Manoah..." Samuel began, but the big Danite was not waiting for an answer.

"I have done all I can to prepare him. I have had him trained by the very best fighters of the tribe of Dan from the time he was strong enough to hold a wooden practice sword. When he became a son of fifteen years, we lived for an entire year in Zebulun, where he received instruction from the weapons masters there. The boy can use sword, spear, axe and shield as well as anyone his age, and even without his promised miraculous strength he can outwrestle anyone in Zorah—or anyone who lives within a day's travel in any direction. Is there some aspect of his training that I have overlooked? Is there something else Jehovah wants me to do?"

"We must wait," Samuel said. "Nothing we do can change Jehovah's timetable, nor alter His purpose for your son."

"Samson is ready now," Manoah growled.

"But ready for what?" Samuel asked. "To go to battle with a weapon in his hand, certainly. But what if that is not what Jehovah has in mind for Samson?"

"What are you talking about, Prophet? The Messenger of God said that Samson would take the lead in delivering Israel from the hand of the Philistine dogs."

Samuel shrugged. "I certainly do not claim to know any more than you do about it. But consider the lives of Barak, or Gideon, or Jephthah—all of them men appointed to be deliverers of the children of Israel. Their role was that of leaders, organizers. They were used by Jehovah to guide and to rally our people to obedience and to victory in battle."

Manoah's scowl deepened and he turned the expression on some point in the road ahead of them. "That is not my son's destiny."

"We do not yet know that."

"I do," Manoah growled. "He will be a killer of the sons of Philistia! His hands will collect their debt to us in blood."

Samuel glanced at the big Danite's face: *jaw muscles tightened into knots below his ears; eyes narrowed; nostrils flared.* He was genuinely angry. "As I said, I do not claim to know anything more than you do..." Samuel began.

"I have not trained Samson as a warrior to have him become a standard bearer for other men!" Manoah interrupted. "When Jehovah's time finally comes to empower my son, the plains of Philistia will run red with blood that has been ripped from them by Samson's hands!"

Samuel had no chance to respond, even had he known what to say. Manoah stormed off down the road without a backward glance, his long legs carrying him far ahead in moments.

Samuel considered going after him, but quickly decided against it. *Let him stew for a while,* he thought, and could not help but smile as he recognized his old mentor Ahitub's influence in his own personality.

Samson and Reuel still trailed by two dozen paces, and the four men continued down the main road for a short distance, enjoying the shade provided by the oaks and sycamores on either side. A smaller track left the road beyond the grove, heading north-northwest over the rolling hills, winding snake-like among them as they gradually grew steeper. Some were terraced with walls of white, native rock and planted with groves or vines.

Then the road emerged abruptly from the hills to an expansive valley of flat, open farmland. In the distance, across the golden fields, the city of Pirathon blanketed the western side of a hill, steeply sided to the north and the east; gradually sloping to the west. Houses spilled down the western slope and into the terraced groves and farmland that filled the valley bottom, shaped like a great, shallow bowl to the northwest of the city. The soil was rich here, and the hill was surrounded by terraced groves and ripening fields. Samuel could see the snaking line of the road until it disappeared beneath the shadow of an ancient grove of cedars not far from the gates of the city.

"It does not take much," said a voice from immediately behind Samuel, and he jumped.

Samson laughed. "Sorry—I didn't mean to startle you."

"What do you mean, 'It does not take much'?" Samuel asked.

"To get my father upset," Samson responded, looking away down the road at Manoah's dwindling silhouette. "Not if the subject is me, anyway."

"Well, look at you! Didn't your mother teach you to groom yourself? At least I have the gift of prophecy as an excuse for my long hair," Samuel said, pulling one braid emphatically.

Samson laughed again, with the hearty abandon of someone who loves to do so. "Ah, yes," he mocked, "I have been spared the trouble of dozens of haircuts by simply claiming that God disclosed to my ear that it was forbidden."

"You cannot allow your father's…feelings to get to you, Samson," Samuel said. "His feelings are neither your fault nor your responsibility."

Samson shrugged. "I know. But when an angel awakens the ears of your parents by telling them that you will become a hero who will save your entire nation from their greatest enemy, you grow up under the weight of certain expectations."

"You will be set to your task soon enough," Samuel said. "I have a feeling that when that day comes you will wish you had had a little more time without that responsibility."

"I already feel the responsibility every day," said Samson. He grabbed one of his own braids in his fist. "I cannot forget it. I am reminded every time I eat a meal, every time I wash my hair. And the people in Zorah will not let me forget it, either."

His eyes narrowed as the said the words, and the muscles of his neck and shoulders tightened. "What do you mean?" Samuel asked.

"Now that I am an adult, people in the community have begun to mock my family when they think we cannot hear. They say that my parents have been struck with madness and that they made up the whole story of my birth, or that Jehovah has rejected me because of some wrongdoing, and that is why I have not…"

He stopped himself and finally looked Samuel in the eyes. "It does not help that my father brings up the prophecy to our neighbors every chance he gets."

"I am sorry, Samson," Samuel said.

"Even my brothers would rather pretend that mother and father were mistaken—it would certainly make their lives less complicated."

"And you?" Samuel asked. "Do you think they were mistaken?"

Samson stopped and turned to face Samuel. "Do I think my parents are lying? No." He spread his arms wide. "But look at me. Am I any different from any other man, from Dan to Be'ersheba? Can you find any evidence that what my parents say about me is true?"

"Your father and mother believe it," Samuel said. "That is enough for me. They are good people, Samson, and even suggesting that they are either dishonest or mad is beneath you."

Samson let his arms fall to his sides and looked at his sandals, nodding. "I know…I am just a little confused as to what I am supposed to do…in the meantime, while I wait for whatever is supposed to happen to me…to happen."

Samuel began to walk again, and Samson trailed him, following the road around a sharp bend that circled a mound of jagged boulders clustered amidst a grove of tall oaks. "Well," Samuel said, "your father was right about one thing: this trip may very well provide opportunities for Jehovah to use you. My heart grows faint with the thought that we may be riding into danger greater than any of us expect."

"Because of that child's visions?" Samson asked.

"Because of Gavriel's visions," Samuel said.

He would have said more, but Manoah abruptly burst from around the bend in front of them, his naked sword in his hand. "Philistines!" he panted, pointing over their shoulders.

Samuel turned. The hills they had been traveling over hid all but the last few dozen paces of the road from sight, but beyond those hills a camel-colored cloud of dust was billowing, and he was suddenly aware of the drumming of hoof beats.

Samson's sword hissed from its sheath.

"Run!" he said.

13

Hearts pounding, the sound of their breathing harsh in their own ears, Samuel, Samson, Manoah, and Reuel raced toward the grove of ancient cedars that swallowed the road just ahead. Shouts rang out now over the sound of horses' hooves drumming against the road—and over the sound of Samuel's heartbeat in his ears. His *me'il* seemed suddenly terrifyingly constrictive to the movement of his legs and he grabbed at it with his free hand, trying unsuccessfully to pull it up as he ran while clutching the vermilion staff in his other sweaty fist.

The road ahead curved slightly in advance of the cedar grove, and the four men, as if following some predetermined plan, turned from the road and raced across the open country. Jagged boulders and clustered batha bushes and broom trees broke up the landscape just enough to prevent the chariots from following their course.

An arrow whispered past Samuel's head and, as though it were moving at exactly his own speed, he saw its polished reed shaft, the dull shine of its bronze tip, heard the sigh of its tar-black fletching. It glanced off the rocky ground ahead of him and ricocheted into the shadows of the forest.

Then they were among the trunks of the trees, leaping over decaying logs and grasping at the rough bark of young sycamores and cedars to steady themselves. For a moment, the sound of the pursuing chariots was muffled by the still air of the wood, and Samuel could hear only the crunching of their feet on the forest floor and the rasping of low branches brushing against his *me'il*.

They pushed through a huddle of young mallow and rock rose bushes. On the other side, the land dropped sharply and they stumbled and slid down the slope, where a copse of young cedars grew like children clustered nervously amidst a crowd of towering adults.

Manoah stopped abruptly, extending one palm toward them. "Quiet!" he hissed.

They listened while the camphire and mallow bushes they had pushed through quivered themselves into stillness. Back in the direction from which they had come, rhythmic thumps and strokes told them that the Philistines had entered the forest and were beating their way through the underbrush, searching for them.

"This is my fault," Samuel whispered, recalling Glaucus' threat, but Manoah put a finger to his lips.

The big Danite glanced to the right and left. "If we are quiet and quick, we can slip out of the grove to the north of the city, not far from the gate."

Voices echoed from above them, calling out to each other.

Samson raised his eyebrows. "We will have to be *very* quick."

Manoah led them forward through the lacy branches of the young cedars; they crouched as they padded across a bed of decaying, red needles. Samuel held his staff out in front of him, using it to deflect the sweeping branches from his face. Nothing moved in the forest save they and their pursuers, known to them only by the sound of their iron-bladed swords ringing as they cut their way through the underbrush, searching. Reuel's *me'il* caught on a half-rotten branch jutting up from the duff, and he tumbled to the ground. Manoah scowled, but kept moving. Samson helped the young man to his feet, white teeth flashing in a broad smile.

Samuel thought back to the night he had turned Glaucus away from Naioth, and silently berated himself for not finding some way to protect Gavriel without further angering the Philistines.

An arrow glanced from a tree trunk off to Samuel's left, vanishing in the forest shadows. For a second they all froze. Samuel saw Samson's hands, white-knuckled where they gripped the jeweled hilt of his iron sword; the veined muscles of his bare arms rippled with every movement.

"Sshh!" Manoah hissed, waiting in silence. No shouts of discovery followed the arrow, nor did any more black-fletched shafts. After a moment Manoah shook his head, and Samuel understood: the arrow had been an attempt to get them to panic and reveal their position to the Philistines.

Samuel counted eight slow breaths before Manoah began moving again. Slipping down the hill, they circled a massive column of ash-grey rock jutting up and out of the trees—sunlight rouged its moss and fern-topped pinnacle far above them. When they reached the other side, the open fields outside Pirathon's gates were visible through the trees. Mount Lanak rose behind the city, its steep southern face pocked with burial caves.

Manoah crouched next to the splayed, wiry root wad of a wind-fallen cedar. "If we can get close enough to the city walls to raise an alarm," he whispered, turning to Samuel, "will the Judge send out men to aid us?"

"He will. I will risk my life on it," Samuel said. "The instant Avdon knows we are threatened, he will rouse an army if needed."

Manoah nodded. "Very well. We will, as you say, risk our lives on your trust. But we will still have to cross the open country as fast as possible." He looked Samuel in the eyes. "Are you up for it?"

"Nothing you could say or do at this point could make me able to run faster—or motivate me more than the spears of the men who pursue us!" Samuel said.

Manoah nodded. "Samson—stick close to Reuel. I will watch over the Prophet."

Samson's only answer was his rakish grin.

Manoah scowled at him. "Do not take this lightly, my son! Today your sword may feast on Philistine blood."

"Then let us hope for all our sakes that my sword is hungry," Samson responded.

Manoah gritted his teeth and shook his head in irritation at the word-play.

They stood again and slipped through the last of the trees, pausing for a moment behind the trunks that marked the edge of the forest. Samuel scanned the landscape: no one was in sight. A few people milled near the city gate, two hundred long paces from where they hid. If they ran in a straight line toward that gate, they would reach the road halfway there. Samuel prayed that Jehovah would make someone from the city see them before that and send out help.

"Now!" said Manoah, and they burst from the shadow of the trees.

Samuel's legs already ached from the rough clambering through the forest, but his fear energized him and he ran next to the big Danite, matching him pace for pace. The ground was rough, the short grass broken by jumbled, sun-bleached rocks. Samuel forced himself not to look behind them; he kept his eyes glued to the ground, hoping to avoid twisting an ankle in some hyrax hole or on some round stone.

Then unmistakable shouting broke out from the forest, and before he could even think about it, he turned and looked.

A dozen and a half Philistine soldiers emerged from the cedar trunks, swords in hand, already running across the open country. But it was not these pursuing warriors that caught Samuel's eye.

A chariot was hurtling down the road toward them, bearing three Philistines, swords and spears at the ready.

"Sons of Belial!" Manoah shouted, and all of them redoubled their efforts.

Then Samuel went down in a heap, landing on his elbows in the dry grass. He looked back, panicked, and saw that the blue fringe of his robe had caught on the long thorns of a burnet bush. He felt strong hands grab him beneath the arms, and then Manoah was half-dragging, half-lifting him; he heard the sound of tearing cloth as his *me'il* ripped, leaving blue threads clinging to the thorns.

He struggled to his feet and they ran on. Samuel's lungs burned now, and he felt every step as a jolt in his knees and jaw. They surmounted a low rise and raced down the other side of it to the road.

Their pace quickened on the roadway, but the chariot was still closing. An arrow flew wildly past. Samuel locked his eyes on the gate of Pirathon, still a hundred strides distant, and prayed that they would reach it before the Philistines caught up with them.

The thundering of the horses' hooves grew louder even than the sound of Samuel's heartbeat in his ears. He glanced to his right for the briefest of moments and saw Reuel's red-cheeked, wide-eyed face.

The road descended into the edge of the great bowl outside Pirathon's walls, plunging through rows of ancient, gnarled olive trees that reached up from the grass like a crone's knobby hands.

"Samson!" yelled Manoah, and the two of them abruptly stopped running and turned to face their attackers, faces grim.

Samuel stopped as well, confused. "Go!" Samson yelled, and Samuel and Reuel started again toward the gate.

They had barely turned with the scream of stallions spun them around again, just in time to see the oncoming chariot careening on one wheel off of the road, spilling its riders into the grass. They were on their feet in an instant, swords and shields at the ready; behind them, the horses thrashed, legs tangled in their crimson-streaked harness.

"Dan and Jehovah!" Samuel heard Manoah roar, and father and son hurled themselves at the three Philistine soldiers.

Reuel put himself between Samuel and the battle. "My lord! Quickly!"

Samson wielded his long, straight-bladed sword with uncanny precision, slashing and parrying as though the weapon weighed no more than a reed. Then the eighteen Philistines that had emerged from the forest swarmed down the hill to their companions, and Manoah and Samson were surrounded.

Reuel was tugging on Samuel's arm. "My lord!"

A cloud of dust announced the arrival of another chariot, descending the last stretch of road toward the battle. Samuel pulled free of Reuel's grasp.

"We cannot leave them!" he said, tightening his grip on his vermilion staff. Taking a deep breath, he steeled himself and ran back towards the melee.

"My lord!" he heard Reuel yell after him.

Samson and Manoah were surrounded now, standing back to back in the midst of a dozen warriors. A crimson line ran across Manoah's right forearm, and a splash of blood painted half of Samson's forehead. For a moment they paused as the two sides faced each other, the Philistines waiting to be sure of their attack in spite of their advantage of numbers.

Samuel forced his legs to keep moving, but he had no idea what he thought he would do when he reached them.

A Philistine leapt forward then, and Manoah cut him nearly in half, but the rest of the warriors followed him and closed on the two Danites, howling.

"No!" Samuel shouted as Manoah and Samson vanished in the mob.

Then horns sounded from the city behind them, the spine-tickling *blat* of a *shofar*, and Samuel spun to see the gates of the city burst open. Dozens of men flooded out of the opening, a third of them mounted on mules, all of them armed with swords, shields and spears, and armored in purple and green. Banners fluttered at lance tips above their heads: a single grape plucked from a heavy cluster on a vine.

It was the banner of the House of Avdon.

The Judge himself rode at the forefront, a huge man perched atop the biggest mule Samuel had ever seen, his nose and cheeks even redder than his bushy beard. "For Jehovah and the tribe of Ephraim!" he bellowed, his voice rumbling like river-tumbled rocks, his bronze sickle-sword held high above his head.

The troop thundered toward them and Samuel and Reuel barely had time to dive off the roadway before Avdon and his men plowed into the melee.

Another rider, younger than Samuel but richly dressed, trotted up to him and Reuel, pulling two more mules. "I am Tahash! Mount, quickly! I will lead you to safety."

Samuel and Reuel grabbed handfuls of coarse mane and pulled themselves awkwardly onto the mules' backs; their mounts began moving toward the gate even before they were seated.

Judge Avdon was not far away, shouting orders and encouragement, his men responding with unhesitating trust. A coat of bronze scales sheathed his ample torso, and a bronze helmet perched over his bushy, red eyebrows. Samuel saw a tall Philistine with a shaved head driving his long-legged stallion toward the judge, spear clutched in one hand. Samuel cringed as the two men reached each other, but Avdon grabbed the Philistine's spear just below the head and shoved it aside, swinging his own sword with such strength that he nearly split the enemy soldier in two.

Samuel clutched the reins of his own mount, tucking his vermilion staff tightly under one arm. A beardless Philistine galloped toward them from the midst of the melee, his horse still draped with pieces of the chariot harness.

"Go!" Tahash yelled at Samuel and Reuel, kicking his mule's flanks and leaping to meet the enemy.

Their mounts almost collided. Tahash lay back across the mule's withers as the Philistine's black blade whipped over him, missing the tip of his nose by a hairsbreadth.

He sat back up, his own blade gripped tightly, but to Samuel's shock did not attack. The Philistine hacked at him again and Tahash shifted his weight so that his mount deftly sidestepped the blow. The next attack was a vicious, two-handed chop toward Tahash's head; he parried with his own blade, but again did not attack.

The Philistine paused a moment, forehead wrinkled in puzzlement. Spurring his horse forward, he raised his sword over his head with both hands, snarling.

Like a viper striking, Tahash's sword shot forward and transfixed the Philistine through his midsection.

The young man's sword was sheathed before Samuel could even grasp what had just happened. Tahash glanced back at him. "Quickly now!"

They began cantering toward the gate. Moments later, the bulk of Avdon's men caught up with them, Manoah and Samson mounted behind other riders. Arrows fell around them; Samuel flinched and ducked as a javelin whipped past his head and stuck in the flank of a mule just ahead of him. The animal's hind legs collapsed, spilling its rider onto the dusty road. Mules all around reared and wheeled away to keep from trampling the man as he struggled to his feet.

Then Avdon was beside the fallen warrior, reaching down with one massive arm and pulling him easily onto the Judge's mule. Avdon laughed loudly, and turned toward Samuel and Reuel, blooded bronze blade clutched in one meaty fist. Grinning broadly through his thick beard, looking as calm as if he had just risen from a satisfying meal, he rumbled, "Prophet! Welcome to Pirathon!"

He glanced over his shoulder, not even flinching as a black-fletched arrow hissed past his head. "Let's leave these dogs outside, shall we?" he said, and put his heels to his mount's flanks.

They rushed forward to the gates. Arrows struck the stone wall, clattering off harmlessly. One whistled past Samuel's ear and he ducked, concentrating on following the flanks of Tahash's mule through the gate. They entered in a cacophony of clopping hooves, and the waiting guardsmen swung the gates closed as the last Israelites slipped through. Arrows pincushioned the oak planks as they shut, and several shafts slipped through the narrowing opening until the copper-plated crossbar thudded into place.

Samuel let out his breath, only then realizing that he had been holding it. He turned to thank Avdon, and saw that the big man was staring at him in unexplained bewilderment.

JUDGE OF ISRAEL

Avdon's left hand was against his stomach; he removed it and stared a moment at the bright blood that covered it.

Then the Judge of Israel tumbled from his mule to the ground, landing on one shoulder and rolling limply onto his face.

14

Baghadh told his servants and commanders to begin packing for a journey. He was more shaken by Liora's visit than he liked to admit, and he did not know why. It wasn't as if the woman or her meddling husband had the means to interfere with any of his plans, or the plans of the Philistine Lord he served. But if she told the Elders what she had seen, or convinced Elkanah to...

So, to ease his own mind and escape the provincial people of Rama-thaim's prying eyes, he had decided to travel to Philistia himself. It was high time that he met his benefactors. A face-to-face meeting would strengthen their commitment to each other. And as quickly as events seemed to be moving, Baghadh wanted to make sure that they knew where his loyalty lay.

He eased back onto his couch, stretching slowly and cringing at the pain of his inflamed skin. The Philistines had, in the past, paid generously for information about the movements of Israelite troops, or even about the feelings and attitudes of the people. Repairing and furnishing the house in

Ramathaim had been more expensive than Reuel had planned. He glanced around the room at the gold and carnelian beads, the pins of electrum, the carved ivory bottles of unguent and perfume, the silver lamps and the intricately engraved makeup boxes of polished adamant. These were the trappings he purchased to decorate his women, and they did not come cheaply. He needed gold to complete his remodeling work and maintain the lifestyle to which he had become accustomed.

Besides, he was suddenly uncomfortable in Ramathaim. Every time he left his home, he felt as though people were watching him from the roofs of their houses or from behind courtyard walls. Who knew what rumors Liora had been spreading about him in the community? Yes, it was best that he leave town for a while.

He was also suffering even more than usual from his cursed affliction, and it was in Philistine territory that he received the best treatment. His knees ached, his pelvis ached, his vision was blurry, it hurt to move his eyes, and defecating felt as though he was being roasted from the inside out. The lesions continued to spread across his head and body, and even he was sickened at times by his own putrid smell.

No one understood the burden of his malady like the Philistines he served. He had needs, as a man, and before Lord Sarnam's lieutenant had first come to him, Baghadh had despaired of ever feeling the subtle warmth of girls' hands again. But in exchange for his cooperation, Glaucus had promised him an endless supply of willing women for his bed. Well—more or less willing, Baghadh admitted to himself, smiling. And Glaucus had been true to his word ever since, bringing him beautiful women who were blind, so that they would not run from Baghadh at the first sight of him.

Baghadh knew that not all of these concubines were born blind— burn scars around some of their eyes told a different story. But how they became blind was not his concern. No doubt the will of one god or another was at work, and they had met their fate according to some deity's sense of justice. It wasn't as if being sent to his bed was a punishment, really. He was considerate of them. He was careful to let them touch only certain parts of his body, lest they discover his affliction with their soft, slender fingers. He went through enormous quantities of perfume and incense to disguise his smell, but the cost was definitely worth it. Satisfying his lust was one of the few pleasures left to him.

Of course, eventually the concubines contracted the disease as well. When the first clusters of clear blisters appeared on their skin, Glaucus' men came, brought him new women, and took the old ones away.

It was not an unreasonable arrangement, he told himself. He allowed them to eat his rich food and drink his wine. He allowed them to practice whatever religious observances they wanted, and even provided them with incense, sacrificial crops and animals, or whatever other paraphernalia they needed for their rituals. He had learned the secrets of how to gain the favor of several important Canaanite gods in this way, and he was grateful to the women for that.

But now he needed the help of the Canaanite *Ishipu* priest that Glaucus kept among his household staff. The wizened old man knew healing rituals and complex sacrifices that summoned the demoness *Shataqat* to Baghadh while he slept, and she drove away the lesser spirits that haunted his body and caused the disease. The wrinkled priest concocted potions and unguents smelling of caper and mandrake, made Baghadh drink them or rub them on his lesions, and the following day he always felt better. The priest had kept him alive far longer than anyone expected him to live—far longer than any concubine of his who had caught the disease.

If it was not for the short-sighted, narrow-minded, naïveté of Samuel and the *Beneh*, he told himself bitterly, everyone in Israel could benefit from the wisdom, power, and experience of such healers. Baghadh could not comprehend how anyone could fail to take advantage of traditions and rituals that had been used successfully to appease the gods of Canaan for centuries before the Israelites had conquered the land. Baghadh's father, and his father before him, had recognized that such worship was not only practical—it was vital to their continued survival in the land. When children like Samuel came in pronouncing arbitrary condemnation against any form of worship other than their own narrow prescription, they put the entire population of Canaan at risk. Baghadh knew that the Philistine army was coming—and not because of some child's vision. And when they came, the worship of the ancient gods of Canaan would be the only religion tolerated from Dan to Be'ersheba. Whenever that time came—and it would be soon—Baghadh wanted to have gained the favor and approval of those gods.

"My lord," a eunuch whispered from the doorway.

Baghadh turned to face him, shaking off his angry thoughts.

"My lord, your baggage is ready," the eunuch said.

Baghadh nodded and took his cloak from the peg on the wall where it hung. "Good. Load it onto my wagon, and have the soldiers harness the horses. I want to leave as soon as possible."

The eunuch bowed low. "Yes, my lord. And if anyone asks for you, where shall I tell them you have gone?"

"Tell them that Baghadh comes and goes as he pleases!" Baghadh sneered. Then he realized that some of the visitors could be messengers sent from Philistia, and thought better of his response.

"Tell them...tell them that I have journeyed west. Tell them that I have business in Sharon.

"Tell them that I have gone to seek how I might best serve the interests of my people."

15

S amuel and his companions followed six soldiers bearing Avdon, cradled in his cloak, into the inner chamber of the Judge's palatial home in the center of Pirathon. Reuel walked alongside the Judge, deft hands never leaving the area of the wound, brow furrowed in anxious concentration.

Avdon slipped in and out of consciousness, coughing blood and breathing in thick, bubbling rasps. When they finally set him gently atop his wide divan he woke, blinking his eyes and grimacing through his wiry beard.

"Oh, stop fussing!" he grumbled, weakly attempting to push Gavriel's hands away. "It's just a flesh wound!"

"Be still, father!" Tahash said.

"Send for a healer!" said Dathan, the eldest of Avdon's sons.

"Please!" Samuel said. "Reuel is a healer—I have met no better from Dan to Be'ersheba. Let him care for your father."

Reuel ignored all of them, his entire attention focused on the huge man supine before him. After a moment, however, he looked over his shoulder at Samuel, wrinkles between his eyes and tight lips revealing his annoyance. "I need room to breathe!" he said.

Samuel nodded and began to usher everyone out of the room. "I am firstborn," said Dathan. "I should stay."

"What the healer says to you, you should do," Samuel said, and continued pushing him backwards out the door.

Reuel had taken small jars and pouches from his red chest and was mixing things from them into a fist-sized mortar: honey, blue-green verdigris, chalky white alum mixed with olive oil and red vinegar.

Samuel took a step toward him, but Reuel shook his head without even looking his direction. "You, too, my lord. Go and rest. I will work better here alone."

Samuel reluctantly allowed Tahash to lead him, Manoah, and Samson toward guest rooms in the back of the house. They had gone only a few steps when a roar of pain from Judge Avdon's room stopped them for a moment.

"Let us do as Reuel has asked," said Samuel, and they followed their guides to their quarters.

Servants brought water scented with algum oil, washed their feet, and dressed Manoah and Samson's wounds. When they left Samuel leaned back in his chair and prayed for Avdon's recovery, thinking even as he made the petition that he had brought this harm to his friend, drawing the sons of Philistia to Pirathon's gates.

For the first time since they had left Naioth he allowed himself to think about Liora and his sons, and his longing for them became a hollow ache.

He did not realize he had fallen asleep until Reuel woke him with a gentle touch to his shoulder. He sat up abruptly, embarrassed as he blinked the sleep from his eyes and wiped drool from the corner of his mouth with the back of one hand. "How is he?" he asked, standing and stretching.

"The wound will heal," said Reuel.

Samuel reached toward the ceiling, trying to ease the tightness from his back. "But?"

"But he is not well, my lord—was not well even before his injury. I have seen these symptoms before among very heavy men: pallor, shortness of breath, veins in the legs visible beneath the skin, feet bruised and swollen."

"What does it mean?" Samuel asked.

Reuel shrugged. "It means he is not as healthy as I would like. He has a strong will though, my lord. That is worth a great deal. He is asking to see you."

Samuel followed Reuel to the Judge's room and found Avdon sitting up in his bed, drinking from a steaming bowl that filled the room with the smell of spices and mutton. His normally ruddy face was pale beneath his beard; the pallor made the thread-like veins on his round cheeks seem even brighter by contrast. "Prophet!" he growled.

Samuel took the man's big hand in his own. "Here I am, my lord. It is good to see you awake."

Avdon waved away his concern. "It is nothing but a flesh wound. I will be back on my feet before sunset."

"You should take your time, my lord," Samuel said. "The wound may be more serious than you think."

"Bah!" said Avdon. "Although if you have been talking to this healer of yours, I can understand your worry. Did you ever see so somber a face?"

Samuel smiled, glancing over at Reuel. "Somber or not, when it comes to medicine, I trust him over all others."

"Oh, very well." Avdon shifted on his bed and took another long, slow drink of the broth, then wiped drops of it from his mustache and beard. "Now—to business. What brings the Prophet of Israel to Pirathon?"

Samuel hesitated. "Perhaps my news should wait…"

"Nonsense!" Avdon turned to Reuel. "Or do you think me so weak that a voice in my ears is a threat to my health?"

Reuel nodded to Samuel, smiling gently. "You may speak for a few moments. But then, the Judge should get some rest."

Samuel sat on the edge of the wide divan and briefly related Glaucus' threats, the discovery of Zimri's body, the prophecy of Gavriel, Samuel's meeting with the Elders of Ramathaim and his concerns about Baghadh, the reports Manoah had brought from the borderlands and their unexpected pursuit by the Philistines on their way to Pirathon.

Avdon listened quietly, sipping occasionally at his broth. When Samuel was finished, he set the bowl down on a table at his bedside. "Well. It seems to me that the meaning of these events is all too clear. Israel must prepare for war."

Samuel felt as though a weight had been lifted from his shoulders. "That is my belief also, my lord. The Elders of Ramathaim, though…"

"The Elders of Ramathaim are mistaking what they *wish* to be true for what *is* true," Avdon said. "I am as disappointed as anyone to see that our years of peace are at an end, but no one looking at these events objectively can come to any other conclusion than that the Philistines are planning something—and I can promise you it is no peace agreement."

"I wish I had more details to give you," Samuel said.

"The details will come, my son," Avdon said, patting Samuel's hand. "If we waited until we knew every detail before we prepared for battle, we would still be hunched over maps and registries when our enemies marched through our gates."

"What will you do?"

Avdon took a sip of broth. "I will send messengers to every corner of the land, from Dan to Be'ersheba and from the Sea to the desert." He smiled crookedly. "Some will ignore the summons, I know. But many will come. Under the banner of the School of the Prophets and the House of Avdon, my sons and grandsons will lead Israel to victory."

The big man leaned forward, trying to look out his open door. "El-da'ah!"

A young man appeared from the hallway outside. "My lord?"

"Bring my secretary, parchments, and pen and ink. And tell Dathan to get a dozen messengers ready to ride!"

"At once, my lord." The young man disappeared down the hall.

Avdon lay back against the divan's headboard and coughed weakly, wincing. "Wipe away those wrinkles, Prophet. It is for a day such as this that I was appointed Judge in Israel. By tomorrow evening, the twelve tribes will be summoned to war, and we will march forth with the might of the True God in our arms and His name upon our lips."

Samuel permitted himself a smile. "Even so, my lord."

Avdon coughed again, and Samuel felt Reuel's hand on his shoulder. "My lord—he should get his rest."

Samuel nodded, bade the Judge farewell and returned to his room, feeling hope warming his heart for the first time in weeks.

Reuel arrived a few moments later and began carefully wrapping and repacking the contents of his medicine kit.

"Thank you, Reuel," Samuel said.

The young healer glanced over his shoulder. "Do not thank me yet."

"He is recovering," said Samuel. "Even I can see that."

Reuel paused in his packing. "I will pray that it is so. In truth, he seems to be healing more quickly than I would have expected—and his strength is returning extraordinarily fast for a man so injured."

"He is not yet ready to hand over his Judgeship, I think."

"He is a natural leader, and his men love him. I am glad that it was him that you appointed, my lord, to lead us in this hour."

"It was not I. You yourself well know that it was Jehovah who chose him, and it is His wisdom alone that is responsible for Avdon's selection."

Reuel nodded absently. "Our people feel safer just knowing that such a mighty and charismatic man is ready to guide and direct them in times of trial."

"May Jehovah grant us both the privilege of seeing Avdon come into his own. It is with times like these that the scrolls of history are filled."

16

When the sun had fallen below the hills, servants escorted Samuel, Reuel, Manoah, and Samson to the great courtyard of Avdon's house for the evening meal. Entering from the south, they reclined on woven palm-leaf mats behind a long, low table of polished cedar. In front of them was the courtyard, carefully fitted stone pavers polished by the passing of countless feet. Lamps and torches hung in sconces all the way around the wall and on posts distributed like pillars throughout the open space. Their flickering, yellow light threw long, endlessly moving shadows from the dozens of people gathered for the meal. The oil in the lamps must have been sprinkled with calamus; Samuel could smell its heady scent in the air.

Along one wall, a group of musicians played the music of the circle-dance; young men and women whirled amongst the pillars to the sounds of *metsilloth* bells and copper cymbals, exultant *halil* reed-pipes, carved ivory *kinnor* lyres with strings of stretched sheep gut, gourd-shaped *nebels* strummed with plectrums of stag horn, solemn bone flutes, rattling timbrels and massive *tof* drums, each beaten by two musicians simultaneously.

Along the perimeter of the courtyard, out of the way of the spinning dancers, men and boys played with marbles or clicked stone game pieces across Chaldean *lugal* boards or intricately inlaid Egyptian *sennet* boards.

As soon as Samuel and his companions were seated, young women came forward with bowls of myrrh-scented water and gently washed their feet, rubbed spikenard oil on them and massaged some of it into their scalps.

While the dancing continued, servants brought out the evening meal: wine spiced with cinnamon, chopped cucumbers with herbs and salt, red lentils and leeks cooked in goat's milk, pickled carp, calf roasted with garlic, hot bread and *leben* yoghurt drizzled with honey.

Samuel had barely begun to eat when a commotion on the other side of the courtyard caught his attention. People began clapping and cheering, parting to allow the passage of a litter borne on the shoulders of six strong men.

It was Judge Avdon, nodding and smiling at the warm welcome. Samuel and his companions rose to their feet until the Judge was set gingerly in his place at the table with them. His face was pale, but his smile was as bright as ever.

"My lord! This is a pleasant surprise!" said Samuel.

"You should not have gotten out of bed, my lord," chided Reuel. "Your wound could easily re-open."

"Nonsense!" rumbled Avdon. "You've done a wonderful job on me, young man! A miracle worthy of a prophet!"

"Still…" Samuel put his hand gently on the man's thick forearm. "We would not count it amiss if you—."

"Bah! Speak no more of it!" said Avdon, waving away their concern. He gestured out at the crowd: his sons and daughters, grandsons and granddaughters and their families. "I have survived raising this brood, haven't I?"

He clapped his hands twice and nodded to one of the men who had been bearing his litter. The man raised a *shofar* and blew a long, hollow note. The room went quiet as all eyes turned toward Avdon.

"My friends and my family!" he said. "Today Pirathon and its people enjoy a rare honor." He extended one arm toward Samuel. "Tonight, we host Samuel ben Elkanah, the Prophet of Israel!"

People clapped and cheered until Avdon waved them into quiet once again. "It was this man that Jehovah sent to tell me of my appointment as Judge over the sons and daughters of Israel. It was he who poured the anointing oil upon my head, and who stood before the Elders of the twelve tribes to tell them of Jehovah's choice."

He paused, looking over at Samuel with a gentle smile. "All of us here tonight owe a great deal to this young man."

The crowd cheered again, and Samuel had to grip the edge of the table tightly to keep himself from bolting from the room. He forced a smile, but his stomach roiled and his mind screamed at him: *One day these people will see who you truly are, and before their eyes you will be brought low.*

"So enjoy this evening! Play, and dance, and feast!" said Avdon, clearly straining with the effort to make himself heard.

The crowd erupted in cheers again and the dancers whirled around the courtyard floor as the musicians began to play once more.

Avdon watched them with a broad, contented smile. "Sons are the true wealth of a man."

"And just how much of that particular coin have you collected now?" Samuel asked.

Avdon's grin widened. "Forty sons and thirty grandsons!"

Samson, seated a few places down the table, gave a low whistle of surprise. "How many wives do you have?"

Manoah turned toward him, scowling, but Avdon spoke before the Danite could chide his son. "Too many, my young man," he answered, laughing. "Too, too many!"

They began to eat again as beautiful female dancers spun in front of them, bare midriffs encircled with jeweled chains of gold attached to gems in their navels, hands and feet dyed with floral designs in henna; their eyes highlighted with black Egyptian kohl and green malachite.

Behind the dancers, Samuel saw that the courtyard had been cleared and men were setting up wooden pins, about the length of a man's forearm, in small holes that had been bored in the flagstones.

"What is this, my lord?" Samuel asked Avdon, pointing.

"It is called '*Malchia*'," Avdon said. "A game that is said to have come to us from Mycenae, but who knows if that is so."

"*Malchia*? King?" asked Samuel.

Avdon nodded. "Look at the way these pins are set up. Each player takes a turn rolling a pair of dice. Each roll allows him to move forward that many flagstones from the starting point. When he reaches the first pin, he is robed; at the second pin, he is crowned, and the first player to reach the final pin is given a scepter and receives the prize."

A group of men, some of whose beards were already sprinkled with grey, were lining up at the starting point, all of them dressed richly in linen garments embroidered with blue and purple and wearing rings and necklaces of gold.

"Your sons?" Samuel asked.

"My ten eldest," Avdon confirmed.

Dathan lifted a cup that rattled with the sound of dice.

"Is there some rule that the eldest must go first?" one of the other sons asked.

"Of course the eldest rolls first," said Dathan.

"How do years earn you the advantage of the first roll?" said another of the sons.

"Enough!" said Avdon, and then coughed with the effort. "Dathan rolls first."

Dathan, then each of the other sons in turn, rattled the cup and tossed the dice across the floor tiles. After each roll, a young crier chased after them and called out the number for all to hear. The players each moved forward, one at a time, arguing and grumbling about how the others were playing.

The third eldest son, whom Avdon identified as Heber, reached the first stake with his second roll. A servant carried out a deep purple robe and draped it over his shoulders. Heber looked back at his brothers. "Apparently in this game, as in life, I am destined to be first among you."

"Apparently," said Dathan, "in this game, as in life, you achieve your goals by cheating."

"How dare you!" yelled Heber.

"Enough!" growled Avdon. "Let the game continue."

The next two rounds both favored Heber again, and although two other brothers reached the robing pole, Heber reached the second pole and had a crown placed on his head.

"This goes beyond the reach of chance!" said another of the brothers. "You—crier! Heber has put silver into your hand, has he not?"

"I have done nothing of the sort!" said Heber, and the brothers erupted into a roar of argument.

"Quiet!" yelled Avdon, and the noise gradually subsided. "I do not believe Heber would do such a thing, but to prevent further complaint, let us have a new crier."

He turned to Samson. "Young man—you are neutral in this. Will you read the dice for us?"

Samson stood and bowed to the Judge. "I think it only fair to tell you that if Heber offers me money, I fully intend to accept it."

Avdon guffawed, ignoring Manoah's scowl, and broke into another round of coughing. As Samson made his way across the courtyard to the game's participants, Dathan seemed to notice for the first time that Tahash was sitting next to their father and Samuel.

"Tahash! What exactly are you whispering to the Prophet while we play?"

Tahash smiled. *Eyes flat and hard. Corners of his mouth hard.* "Nothing, my brother."

"Nothing?" said Heber. "Then why do you not join us on the floor?"

"The game has no appeal for me, I am afraid."

"Indeed?" sneered Dathan. "It does, however, provide you with an opportunity to drip suggestions from your tongue into the Prophet's ear without interference from any of us."

"Not so, my brother," said Tahash. "I have no reason to do so. I recognize that I have no chance of succeeding my father as Judge, as you hope to do."

"If only you would pass on that lesson to our brothers," said Dathan, looking at the faces around him.

The next brother rolled the dice, and as Samson chased after them, Samuel could not keep himself from muttering, "Not one of them has a chance of succeeding their father."

Tahash looked over at him with one raised eyebrow, but said nothing.

As the game continued, Avdon leaned toward Samuel conspiratorially. "Riders were dispatched this afternoon to every corner of the land, summoning the men of Israel to war. We will gather at the fortress of Mizpah—centrally located, well fortified, and with plenty of room to organize a muster. The sons of Philistia will not find us unready when they come."

"Thank you, my lord," Samuel said. "I cannot tell you how that sets my heart at ease."

Avdon patted Samuel's knee. "And when you made me Judge of Is-rael, did you not believe that I was ready for a challenge just such as this?"

"I have always trusted you, Judge Avdon," Samuel said. "But I did so because it was Jehovah who chose you, and not I."

Avdon sighed and leaned back against the pillows on his litter. "I am not blind and deaf to what is said about me among the Elders, Samuel. I myself well know that people question my appointment, and question the way I have used my position."

"Do not concern yourself with—."

"I do not," Avdon interrupted. "I do not care what is said about me, behind my back or to my face. I am not responsible for what people say—only for who I am. My heart well knows that I am doing my best to set an example for the children of Israel—and I will do my best to deal with this threat, as well."

Samuel smiled. "I have no doubt of it."

Avdon nodded and coughed again, and turned back toward the game.

In the final throws, as Samson scrambled after the rattling dice, Da-than, Heber, and another son, Zabbad all gained their crowns and robes and inched their way toward the final pole, and the scepter that awaited the win-ner. Samuel saw them surreptitiously casting glances his way as they drew closer: *eyes darting and unsteady, eyebrows raised when they caught his attention, know-ing looks and confident nods.*

So, he thought, *they think I am their route to the Judgeship.*

Dathan cast the winning throw, and Samson handed the scepter to him with a flourish. Dathan turned and nodded beneficently to the rest of his brothers.

Heber's scowl was black. "Do not think for a minute that this tells you anything about the future, brother—eh, Prophet? Tell him you will not choose the next Judge of Israel based upon the results of a game."

Samuel tried to wither the arrogant man with his eyes.

The sons and grandsons immediately regathered, this time nearly all seventy of them, lining up in two equal rows facing each other a pace or so apart. Servants brought out wooden swords, their "blades" dipped in tar, and handed one to every man.

Samuel had seen this competition before. Its origins were lost in the distant past, but it had survived in Israel for many centuries. When the swords were distributed, each man reached across the space between the rows and with their left hand grabbed the beard of the man opposite him. Thus bound to each other, they would attempt to land blows on specific areas of their opponents' bodies, thus scoring points based on the relative difficulty of the target struck. The same technique was sometimes used in serious duels between feuding parties, but then it ended in death.

Avdon shouted, "Begin!" With a series of grunts and shuffling feet, the men did their best to simultaneously strike and avoid the blows of their opponents.

"Separate!" Avdon yelled after only a few moments, and the men drew apart to take stock of their scores. Those with the lower scores retired to the sides of the courtyard to watch, and those with the highest reassembled in two much shorter lines.

The competition repeated itself twice more before a winner was proclaimed: a bear of a man named Kenath. A huge wineskin, made from an entire sheep, filled with the finest harvest of the year before was awarded him from Avdon's hand.

Kenath lofted the bloated skin above his head. "A prize fit for a lord among men!" he bellowed, and while the crowd applauded, his brothers and nephews grumbled and scowled.

The music began again and, as hemispheres of pomegranate and bowls of figs, dates, and almonds were brought to the table, Samuel covered his mouth to stifle a yawn, realizing how little his nap in the afternoon had done to alleviate his exhaustion.

Avdon saw it. "Go to your rest, my young friend. My grandsons will be up half the night—or at least until the wine runs out."

Samuel shook his head. "I beg your pardon, my lord..."

"Bah! No need, no need! Your bed has been prepared, and it would do you good to take your rest while you can get it."

He smiled broadly, and in the gleam of Avdon's bright eyes and the great muscles of his shoulders and arms, Samuel saw the courage and indomitable will that would bring men swarming to his banner, and willingly put their souls in their palms to please the Judge of Israel.

"When you wake," Avdon continued, "you will bear witness to a muster such as has not been seen in Israel since the days of your childhood!"

— —

Samuel dreamt that night that he stood in a broad, green field, the wind painting its tall grass in transient swaths of contrasting color. The ground shook, the earth before him bulged, and then it opened like the bursting of a boil, throwing black soil violently into the air. A pillar of smooth, grey stone emerged, sliding slowly upward from among the grasses. Branches and twigs split away and the pillar became a tree, its leaves dry and crumbling, its trunk colorless. Samuel wanted to step closer but he was suddenly standing above the tree, and it was barely longer than his hand, its delicate trunk grasped in his palm. He realized with a shock that it was growing out of his own stomach.

"Just pull!" an urgent voice whispered in his ear, and he gripped the tiny trunk more tightly, overwhelmed by the need to obey even though he knew the agony that awaited him, even though he did not understand the reasons behind the command. He pulled in a single, violent motion, yelling in agony…

"My lord!"

He started awake. A stranger was looming over his bed, nothing but a darker silhouette against the dark of the room.

He pushed himself to a seated position, sticky with sweat beneath his clothes. "Who is there?"

"Follow me! Quickly!"

Samuel's eyes slowly adjusted; the man was a servant he had seen at dinner. "What has happened?"

The messenger shook his head. "Reuel said you must come at once."

Samuel slid from the bed, still trying to shake the anguish of the dream from his thoughts. He padded after the servant; from the hallway outside his room, he could see orange lamplight glimmering from somewhere just ahead and hear the murmur of anxious voices. He quickened his pace.

Outside the door of Avdon's bedchamber dozens of men and women clustered, lamps clutched in their hands, some of them weeping. Samuel pushed through them.

In the room, Reuel was on his knees, hunched over Avdon's huge form where it lay sprawled on the flagstones.

His hands, his clothes, and the bedding were covered in bright blood.

Samuel rushed to his side, almost tripping over Heber's body lying motionless in a pool of foot-printed blood. In one corner of the room Avdon's son Zabbad stood, the sword in his hand dripping ichor onto the floor at his feet.

Reuel was trying to staunch the flow from the re-opened wound in the Judge's stomach. A deep red stain spread across Avdon's tunic.

Men and women prayed in whispers from the doorway, a thin breath of sound blended with the muffled weeping from the hall. Lamplight cast eerie shadows over all of their faces, painting them into creatures of nightmare.

"Reuel?" Samuel asked.

Reuel ignored him, pressing his cloth-wrapped fingers into the opening in Avdon's abdomen.

Samuel found Zabbad's eyes; the man's face was white. "He was going to kill him!" he whispered, his voice catching in his throat. "I had to…"

Samuel glanced at Heber's body again; a bronze dagger, still shiny, lay on the floor a cubit from the man's open hand.

"I tried to stop him. We struggled and…and father…father fell…" Zabbad said, pleading to be believed. "He would have killed him!"

Reuel sighed heavily and raised his head. "Not would have."

The room went silent—even the weeping from outside the door ceased.

Reuel slid his open hand down Avdon's pallid face, closing his eyes one final time. "The Judge of Israel is dead," he said.

17

Two days later, they laid Judge Avdon to rest in the burial cave of his fathers. To the northeast of the city of Pirathon, Mount Lanak loomed over the hill upon which the city was built, one steeply-sloping face of it running down to the base of the walls, breaking into rocky cliffs and nearly vertical scarps as it descended. Into this slope, tombs had been carved since long before Israel had inhabited the land, and shadowed, black openings pock-marked the pale limestone.

Liora, Joel, Abijah, and Gavriel arrived with a group of the *Beneh* from Naioth the evening before the funeral. When Samuel took her in his arms, for the first time since Avdon's death he broke down in unabashed weeping and they held each other while the children stared up at them with teary concern in their wide eyes.

That evening, Liora told him about Baghadh's actions and her fears regarding the Philistine threat. Samuel was not surprised, but he did feel rage rising within him like the coals of a fire waking to life. They prayed together for Jehovah's guidance and wisdom.

JUDGE OF ISRAEL

Samuel was called by the sons of Avdon and joined them to wrap their father's body for burial. The solemn ritual was done in silence, punctuated by lion's roars of thunder echoing among the hills and accompanied by the thrumming of rain on the roof.

In the morning, the city was packed to overflowing. Within hours of Avdon's death, a second set of messengers had been scattered to the corners of the land to summon all who would come to the funeral. By morning, people had begun streaming into the city from the countryside, a constant flow that had not stopped for two full days.

Avdon's sons seemed as intent to outdo each other in commemorating their father's death as they had been during his life. Around his palatial home and at intervals along the road leading out of Pirathon, they had built fires the size of shepherds' huts, each of them crowned with a giant bronze censer piled with incense. Cassia- and cinnamon-scented smoke drifted over the city like a dirty, white shroud.

They had asked Samuel to lead the funeral procession. As the sun rose over the shoulder of Mount Lanak, its light filtered by a layer of drooping clouds, he found himself walking solemnly down the main road of the city, flanked by a blur of ash-dusted and tear-streaked faces, his footfalls keeping step with the beating of drums from somewhere behind him. He kept his mouth closed to avoid breathing in the ash and dust the mourners tossed over their heads by the handfuls, and his own breathing in his nose was as deafening as the silence emanating from Avdon's corpse.

Over the wailing and the keening of the sackcloth-robed mourners, the haunting music of flutes and pipes drifted with the aimless smoke. Immediately behind Samuel the eldest sons of Avdon bore the Judge's huge body, shrouded in linen wrappings soaked with embalming fluids, on a wicker bier that rested on their shoulders. With each labored step, the bier creaked complainingly

It seemed to Samuel that only moments had passed before they were outside the city walls, across the plain, and had begun ascending the rocky slopes of Lanak. Footing grew less sure on the narrow path, and the sons of Avdon sweated and grunted as they struggled upward toward the cave of their father's fathers. Sparrows, swallows and fork-tailed swifts chirped brightly, diving among the fig and pomegranate trees, a discordant contrast to the droning flutes and measured drumbeats. With water still dripping from the bushes and trees from the rain the night before, everything felt fresh, as if the storm had given birth to a new world during the black of night.

Samuel felt as if a part of him had died.

When they reached their destination the music stopped, and in the ensuing silence mourners filed into the circular hollow, green with new grass. Samuel did not look at them. He could not, or would not—he himself was not sure which—tear his eyes from the massive wheel of granite that covered the cave's entrance.

Censers of copper on poles as high as a man stood on either side of the tomb, smoke snaking upward in thin, white spirals. Four of Avdon's grandsons stepped forward and rolled the stone away with a hollow, grating reminder of the tomb's insatiable emptiness. In its shadowed interior, Samuel glimpsed the desiccated remnants of bouquets of flowers laid there sometime in the distant past, the only adornment for the rotund ossuaries lining its walls.

Samuel stood next to the opening as the sons of Avdon carried their father's bier into the dank interior of the cave and placed his linen-wrapped body in the shallow grave excavated the day before. Samuel watched with cool detachment as they lowered the body into the hole, the smell of freshly turned earth mingled with the pungency of embalming liquids filling his nostrils. When the body touched the ground the dark soil clung eagerly to the white wrappings.

The scions of the house of Avdon exited the tomb and were greeted by the wives of the city Elders, proffering the cup of consolation to each of them in turn. Refilled again and again, it was passed among his forty sons. Samuel watched them drink: *Red eyes shining with tears. Nostrils flaring, as though the wine was bitter.*

Faces turned toward Samuel then, and his heart beat in his throat as he forced himself to clamber atop a platform of rock a little above the height of the crowd, trying to look as dignified as possible. He was keenly aware of the vermilion staff in his hands, and wondered if anyone believed that he was truly ready to bear its burden.

He reached the narrow platform and looked out at the expectant faces, the staff clutched in sweaty palms. A breeze blew tendrils of hair across his face and he brushed them away. He found Liora and looked into her eyes, drawing on her unshakeable calmness. He saw her belief in him, her trust that he could do what needed done. It helped him find the strength to speak.

JUDGE OF ISRAEL

"This is a dark day for Israel, a dark day among dark times. In such times, men need leaders who will guide their people in Jehovah's ways, in the ancient traditions of our forefathers.

"Judge Avdon was such a man. I counted him a friend, but he was also a friend to all the children of Israel, a man who put the welfare of his people ahead of his own, and who knew true leadership was a function of reliance on the might of our God."

He paused, noting the reactions in the audience: *nods of agreement; brows furrowed with anticipation; tilted heads and narrowed eyes of suspicion and cynicism.*

"But Avdon is dead," he continued. "He has been gathered to his fathers, and he will no more walk before us. He was a great man, and Israel will feel his loss in the days to come.

"But there is no need to despair. We are the people of Jehovah, the True God! If we seek Him with all our hearts, no enemy can defeat us! With the might of God in our arms, we will drive them before us like chaff before the summer winds."

"Who will now be our Judge?" someone from the crowd called out.

"Appoint us a Judge, Samuel!" someone else yelled.

Samuel shook his head. "We cannot appoint a Judge just because we want one. It is Jehovah who chooses—."

"Let us make one of Avdon's sons our leader!" someone interrupted.

"Give the Judgeship to the eldest son!"

Another of Avdon's sons scoffed loudly. "Has my brother already put gold into your palms?"

"How dare you!" said Dathan, and his sickle-sword hissed from its sheath.

Two dozen more swords were drawn in response, and the sons and grandsons separated into groups, each calling out the virtues of the leader he endorsed and yelling insults at all others.

"Stop!" Samuel yelled, trying to make himself heard above the tumult. "Stop!"

They took no note. He glanced down and saw one of the musicians standing a little below him. He tapped the man with his staff and gestured to him to toss Samuel his trumpet. When he complied, Samuel put the instrument to his lips and blew until stars whirled before his eyes.

When he lowered the trumpet, he crowd had gone quiet again, staring at him. "Return your swords to their sheaths," he said. "Nothing will be decided this way."

"Indeed," said one of the Elders of Pirathon, nodding sagely. "This decision must be made by the Elders of all the tribes of Israel."

"The Prophet anointed our father," said another of Avdon's sons. "And the Prophet is before us. Let him decide!"

"The Elders cannot choose a Judge, and neither can I," said Samuel. "It is not a decision...I am a spokesman for the True God, not a Judge-maker!"

"Then speak!" said Dathan. "What does Jehovah say? Who is to be the next Judge of Israel?"

"I do not know!" Samuel shouted. "As I have already told you—I do not know!"

"Are we to go into battle leaderless?" someone called out. "You yourself have said that the Philistines are threatening—."

Samuel held up his hands. "Wait! Wait! Have you not been giving ear to my words?"

He paused to gather his thoughts, afraid to wipe the sweat from his palms lest the crowd see it and know how nervous he was.

"These past years have been peaceful and prosperous ones for Israel," he began. "Already you have begun to experience the benefits of trusting in Jehovah, and in opening your ears to His commandments.

"But it is not enough to desire His help now that the threat of war hangs over us again. It is not enough to wish for a Gideon, or a Jephthah, or an Avdon to rise up and save us. If you would guarantee your safety, and that of your wives and children, you must be willing to do all that Jehovah instructs us! You must willingly cast aside all remnants of false worship, no matter how subtle or harmless you think they are. By your pure worship, in accordance with the strict dictates of the Torah, you must supplicate Jehovah with all your hearts and turn to Him when your heart becomes faint within you.

"If you will do this, you will gain the victory you cannot hope to achieve by might of arms."

"Bold words, Prophet!" said Dathan. "But three days ago you would have said to look to my father to lead us to victory. Your foresight seems to have failed you just when we needed it most."

"The hearts of men may make many plans," said Samuel, "but it is Jehovah whose purposes are carried out. I do not speak to you of the words of any Priest or Prophet. I speak of the words given to us by God himself— words every one of you has known since childhood! It is He who has promised these things! Is it not written in the Torah? And I pledge to you—if you will but awaken your ears to His words, and do these things I have told you...I, myself, I will be security to you for the fulfillment of His promises."

"Comforting!" said another of Avdon's sons snidely. "The Seer of Naioth will be our security."

"I am Samuel ben Elkanah, Prophet of the True God!" Samuel roared down at him, his anger unleashed by the man's disrespect for Jehovah's arrangement. "He is the God of Abraham, Isaac, and Jacob! He is the God who delivered our forefathers out of Egypt with a strong hand, and who brought us into this land He had promised to Abraham! Do you not know Him? He is a God who fills the hands of His chosen ones with power: Ehud, Gideon, Barak, Jephthah!"

A few cheered at the mention of Jephthah's name—there were men in the crowd who had fought at his side in Gilead during the war against the Ammonites. Encouraged, Samuel continued: "He is the God whose power swept out from the Ark of the Covenant and struck the Philistines with plague and infestation, fear and famine. He is the Almighty, the Creator, and before Him all other gods are as nothing! Is He the God you serve?"

The cheer was louder now, a chorus of "Yes!" that echoed from the mountainside.

Samuel raised his staff above his head. "He is the God who brought low all the deities of Egypt, and drowned their army in the Red Sea! He is the God who shatters Dagon, who humiliates Ba'al, who mocks Ashtoreth, who shuts the mouths of Mot and Anath! He is Jehovah of Armies and before him nothing—nothing can stand! Is He the God you serve?"

"Jehovah! Jehovah is our God!" they screamed back at him, and the scream became a chant and an anthem.

Samuel raised his arms and quieted them. "Your ears have been opened to the rumors from the west. The Philistines believe that their threats will take the strength from our arms. They wish us to exchange the glory of God for the chains of slavery! They want to bury their demon-worshiping leaders beside men like Avdon, in the tombs of our ancestors!"

The crowd grumbled, pushing in closer to where Samuel stood above them on the rock. "Let them try!" someone shouted.

Samuel moved from the highest rock platform to a lower one, a single step that took him closer to the crowd below. "The army of Philistia may be at our door."

The crowd quieted again then, the fear of reality coming back to them, hanging on his words. He planted the vermilion staff in front of himself and clasped it in both hands. "But this army is no match for our God."

They nodded. *Eyes wide and bright. Heads and shoulders pushed forward. Muscles tensed.* They wanted to believe, and he continued: "Some of you may be trusting in the protection of the walls of Pirathon, or the cities from which you have traveled," Samuel said. "But I tell you that walls alone are not enough to save us from this enemy. The swords and spears of our men are not enough to save us. Only Jehovah can give us the victory we seek.

"I, Samuel, Prophet of God, call you to meet me in one week's time at the fortress city of Mizpah. Come there with hearts and hands cleansed, and by the God that we serve, I swear you will live to see the armies of Philistia driven before us like cattle! Thence I will bring the one man whose leadership and guidance will guarantee the blessing of Jehovah."

He paused, letting the questions build in their minds. "To Mizpah I will bring Ahitub, High Priest of Israel.

"Remember the days of our glory!" Samuel continued. "When the waters of the Jordan were stopped up and our people crossed on dry land, it was after the High Priest's feet touched those waters. When the walls of Jericho fell, it was after the High Priest had led our people in a march around the city seven times. When the sun stood motionless in the sky over Aijalon, it was while the High Priest stood next to General Joshua on the plain!

"Have you not read in the Torah? 'When you go to battle against your enemies, the Priest must draw near to the people and say, "Hear, O Israel! Do not let your hearts melt within you. Do not run in panic or shudder because of them, for Jehovah your God is marching with you to fight for you against your enemies so as to save you."'"

"From the Tabernacle at Nob, High Priest Ahitub shall offer sacrifices upon the great Altar, and the smoke of his offering will rise to our God, and He will look down upon His servant, the one placing burnt offerings upon His Altar, with favor. And Ahitub, the High Priest of Israel, will march before us into the battle, if it is battle that is waiting for us at the end of these things."

"And Samuel!" one of the Elders shouted. "High Priest Ahitub and Samuel, the Prophet of Israel!"

Samuel felt the blood hot in his face. "All that I am...All that I have to offer is yours. While the smoke of the offering ascends, I will pray in your behalf to Jehovah, the God of Armies."

He looked down and saw Dathan, Judge Avdon's eldest, staring up at him. *Head cocked to one side. Corners of lips curled slightly.* "I will go to Mizpah, O Prophet." He raised his voice. "As hereditary leader of the house of Avdon, I summon all of you to the fortress of Mizpah!"

"To Mizpah!" someone shouted in response, and soon the crowd echoed with cries: "To Mizpah! All Israel goes to Mizpah!"

Samuel nodded his thanks toward Dathan. "Send messengers once again to all whose representatives are not here today. Summon Israel to sanctification."

Samuel clambered down from the rocks as the crowd began to disperse, hope again lighting their eyes. He was met at the tomb's entrance by Manoah and Samson. "Well," said Manoah. "A very pretty speech."

"Pretty enough to march the tens of thousands of Israel to Mizpah?" Samuel asked.

Manoah smiled, his beard bristling with the movement. "Whether or not—you have done it now, I am afraid: summoned all Israel against the advice of the Elders of Ramathaim."

Samuel shrugged, pretending that the realization did not terrify him. "It is unthinkable that I should stand by and wait until the Philistines are knocking on our doors."

"Indeed." Manoah nodded, and glanced over at Samson. "Perhaps this situation is just what my boy needs to bring him into his own. And my blade hungers for Philistine blood!"

Samson tried to pretend he had not heard the comment. "Why Mizpah, my lord?" he asked Samuel. "Why not gather them here?"

Samuel shook his head. "Not with Avdon's sons and grandsons at each other's throats. I need them on neutral ground, surrounded by men they must treat as equals, at the least. And Mizpah was where Avdon disclosed to my ear he was going to summon the people, before he died."

In the valley below, a group of men had begun singing, and the drums beaten in mourning just moments before began to pound out the driving rhythm of the march.

Samuel found Liora and his sons and she again took him in her arms. "I am proud of you," she whispered, her breath warm and soft in his ear.

He squeezed her more tightly, then let go to kneel and gather his sons to him.

"Are you leaving again, Papa?" Joel asked, his voice tremulous.

"I must go to Nob, to the Tabernacle," Samuel said.

"Can we go?" Joel asked.

Samuel shook his head and kissed each of his sons on the cheek. "You must return with your mother to Naioth. You must help her gather the *Beneh* and come to meet me at Mizpah."

"I don't want to go home!" Joel said. Abijah's face was growing more anxious by the moment—he did not understand what was happening, but understood his brother was upset.

"I wish you could come with me," Samuel said. "I wish it with all my heart. But I must make a hard journey, and we will meet again soon."

A young man rode up the hill to the tomb on a mule and reined it in right before the entrance. "I am looking for Manoah of Dan."

Manoah stepped forward. "I am he."

The young man slid from his mount and handed a scrap of pottery to the big Danite. "From your uncle."

Manoah scanned the ostraca and looked up, his face grim.

"What is it?" Samuel asked.

Manoah handed him the message. Scrawled on it in hasty runes were six words: *The armies of Philistia are moving.*

"So," said Manoah. "It has begun."

JUDGE OF ISRAEL

18

The moon scattered silver light across the still surface of the Great Sea, and in the windless air the rhythmic pumping of oars in their oarlocks and the creaking of rigging were the only sound that the men aboard the goose-prowed ship could hear. Lamps burned fore and aft, suspended from the stays, rocking back and forth as the boat shifted with every movement of her rowers.

She was one of dozens of similar craft making their way north toward Joppa, filled with Philistine soldiers and the equipment of war. Paralleling their path onshore was the main body of the army, tens of thousands strong, encamped now near the mouth of the river Sorek. There, all the ships save one had been dragged over the black coral onto the narrow strand for the night. From that ship, the cooking fires of the army were visible as hundreds of pinpricks of light, some reflected in the water as wavering, ethereal shimmers of amber.

Sarnam turned his gaze away from the encampment and looked again at his fellow passengers: Phicol, three other Gedhudhra and the arcane priest Sihphil, bent now over an intricately carved wooden bowl, muttering and mixing items from various pouches hidden within his voluminous black robe.

Phicol caught Sarnam's eye and smiled—not a pleasant expression on the scarred man's face, Sarnam thought to himself. But he understood the look. It was at Phicol's urging that they were on the sea in the middle of the night rather than comfortably ensconced in their tents.

Phicol had finally convinced him to undergo *threquet*, an ancient ceremony by which warriors pledged their loyalty to the savage goddess, Anat. Phicol had endured the ceremony while still a child, and Sarnam knew that it was part of what made him the warrior he was today. Some of those who survived the spell were made nearly immune to the effects of mortal weapons. They were granted greater strength in battle and dauntless courage to match it. They could endure wounds that would kill other men and continue to fight, feeling no pain.

Those who survived, Sarnam reminded himself. He had not undergone the ceremony before in part because so few did survive—and up to this point in his life he had not felt that he needed it. But as much as he hated to admit it, he was feeling the effects of age. His body did not heal as it once had. Sihphil had come up with a way to strengthen him before the ritual so that he would have a better chance of living through it than most.

His father expected him to take the risk, he knew. His father, even in death, wanted him to do everything in his power to fulfill their destiny and conquer the land of Canaan for their own. Canaan, and then Egypt.

Sihphil looked up from his muttering and stretched out his clawed hands toward Sarnam. Dangling from his gnarled fingers was a necklace of humming shells. "Wear it," the priest hissed.

Sarnam placed the chain over his head. Sihphil nodded and lifted a round, covered basket from the bilge. Its contents hissed and rasped against the woven reeds. Placing the basket in his lap, Sihphil lit a cone of incense on a small, clay bowl on the bench beside him.

"O mother of the sstallion," he droned, looking up in the direction in which the smoke was disappearing into the constellations. "O daughter of the sspring, daughter of the sstone, daughter of the heaven and the ocean, ssummoner of Shaphash!"

Somewhere nearby, a fish jumped, its gentle splash startling in the stillness of the night.

The withered priest drew the lid from the basket. The blunt, triangular head of a viper slowly emerged from within it, between Sihphil and Sarnam, tongue flicking into the salty air. Sarnam saw the light of the lamps reflected like sparks in its cold, black eyes.

"Oh Dagon, king among the godss!" Sihphil continued. "In the realm of sspiritss, at the confluence of the endless riverss, at the gathering of the two oceanss it iss to be found, it can be gathered!"

The viper raised itself higher, its cold gaze fixed now on Sarnam, easily within striking distance. Sarnam sat very still, as Sihphil had instructed him. From somewhere nearby he heard Phicol giggling.

"O Dagon," said Sihphil. "Ssend to us your power, from the water of the endlesss rivers, the incantation for the bite of the sserpent, for the ssting of the sscaled one. From him, eradicate hiss power!"

Sihphil lifted a humming shell to his lips and blew on it gently. The viper seemed to respond to the droning sound, lifting higher and weaving slowly back and forth. Sihphil played for a moment and then, the humming shell still between his lips, spread his arms and brought them sharply together directly behind the snake's head.

Sarnam did not realize what had happened until he looked down and saw the viper's head clamped down on his hand. He saw the pattern of black and grey diamonds down its long length, and the intricate perfection of its interlocking scales. Dizziness washed over him, as though he was suddenly seasick. Every movement of the boat seemed magnified dramatically. He reeled with dizziness and nausea.

Then the pain exploded within him, a burst of fire that shot from his hand up his arm and into his neck. He straightened sharply, and felt the tendons in his hand shift, rubbing against the fangs of the viper.

"That you, too, may shed your sskin and be reborn!" hissed the little priest.

Sarnam felt a heaviness in his lungs and he fought to draw breath. Sihphil bent over his bowls again and began to mix ingredients from his bags: tamarisk, date shoots, ground yellow and red powders. He crumbled a dry snakeskin into the mixture, and then wetted it with a cup of black blood. His movements thumped and echoed hollowly against the hull of the boat.

The priest shoved the bowl onto the seat between Sarnam's legs. "Bow over it, three times!" he ordered.

Sarnam found that his muscles did not want to obey him. Fear began to set in as a metallic chill in the back of his mouth, and he fought back panic. *Bow!* he ordered himself, and managed to bend his neck three times.

"Hssss," responded Sihphil, nodding. He reached over the gunwale and dipped a cup of seawater, pouring it into the bowl with the other ingredients. From one of his pouches he drew forth a serpent's skin, sewn into a long tube, sealed at one end. Tipping the carved bowl, he poured its contents into the snakeskin. It filled, taking shape as though its owner inhabited it once again.

"Now—drink!" he commanded, and proffered it toward Sarnam.

A breath of wind wafted over them, stirring the furled sails, setting the rigging to creaking, and dimpling the water all around their boat. It fingered Sarnam's thin hair, and that gentle movement felt as though someone were attempting to rip it out by the roots.

Sarnam looked down at his left hand. The viper's mouth was still clamped over it, and suddenly he could not remember if the strange shape was a new addition to his body or an appendage he had had all his life.

Sihphil looked at Phicol. "Help him."

The big warrior stepped forward, smiling, setting the boat to rocking again; Sihphil and the Gedhudhra gripped the gunwales. Phicol grasped Sarnam's chin in his calloused hand, lifted the snakeskin to the general's lips and poured the mixture down his throat.

Sarnam felt fire burn its way down to his gut. His body went rigid again, and the pain in his stomach was so intense he imagined for a moment that Phicol had stabbed him again. He wanted to retch, to writhe, to beat Phicol with his fists—but his muscles did not seem to belong to him anymore.

Sihphil stood, clutching a shroud for balance. Spreading his arms toward the starred sky, he chanted:

"To Anath we incline our facess
And take from her sstrength.
We uproot among the treess a tamarissk
We uproot among the bushess a tree of death.
The tamarissk shook off the evil
The date palm shoot desstroyed it

The bulb of the fragrant reed exiled it
The yblt plant bore it away.
Anath returnss to her housse
Anath enterss the court of godss
And our mightinesss becomes sstrong like a torrent
Sstreaming like a river."

Sarnam would have fallen then if Phicol had not caught him and lowered him slowly to the bilge. The scarred warrior's face filled Sarnam's frame of vision, but it was a visage transformed—even more distorted than normal, with eyes that glowed fire and a mouth that opened wider than should have been possible.

"You are now under the protection of Anath," Phicol said, pointed teeth emerging from behind his lips with every word.

Sarnam heard chanting from somewhere far, far away—was it from under the sea? Or was he under the sea and the singing from somewhere above him?

"Anath dances, naked and beautiful,
Her belt strung with the heads of her enemies,
Her necklace strung with their hands,
Her feet splashing in their blood."

Sarnam wanted to tell Sihphil that he did not think he was strong enough for…what was it he was doing? He was scared, and wanted to be taken out of his grave and brought back to life. He tried to ask Phicol to help him, but the boy's mouth just opened wider, until the endless black cavern hid his face, and an inky cloud emerged from it and began to swallow Sarnam. His vision dimmed, then failed altogether and he was blind, floating in an endless blackness.

"Welcome to my world," he heard someone whisper, and he slipped into unconsciousness.

19

Samuel and his companions left Pirathon the next morning, just as the orange light of the dawn began filtering down through the lingering mist and glowing across the tops of the mountains east of the Jordan. A somber quiet lay over the city, still packed to bursting with visitors from around Israel. A few of Avdon's sons and grandsons came to see them off—but not many.

Tahash, though, insisted on accompanying them. Samuel tried to dissuade him, warning him that they did not know what awaited them either on the road or at their final destination, but Tahash would have none of it. At the city gate on the morning of departure, he appeared with his traveling bag packed—a single, large goatskin pouch slung across his back.

"I still feel you should stay—for your family's sake," said Samuel.

"I am no use here," Tahash said with characteristic candor. "There are too many chieftains in this tribe even without me."

"Your place is with your brothers," Samuel said.

Tahash wrinkled his forehead and looked at Samuel dubiously from beneath one raised brow. "I think my brothers will be just as well off without me. I will never truly find my place if I do not distance myself from the shining glory of my family."

Samuel heard the sarcasm and a little bitterness in his voice. "To be a son of Avdon is an honor, though you are one among many."

Tahash smiled stiffly. "Permit me to follow you, my lord. Permit me to see if I can find a place where the honor you speak of may throw some light into a place of shadow, rather than vanishing in the brightness that surrounded the Judge of Israel."

Samuel examined the young man. *Shoulders squared. Hardness at the corners of his eyes and mouth. Eyes steady.* "Very well," said Samuel, seeing that he would not win the argument. "I have no doubt High Priest Ahitub will appreciate your support."

Tahash slung a provision pouch over one shoulder and checked the cinch on his baldric. "And a High Priest can, if he chooses, fill my hands with power," he said.

"If Jehovah wills it," Samuel said, unsure what the young man meant. "But it is not a choice for us to make."

Tahash smiled at him. "Indeed. I did not choose to be seen as the most insignificant of Judge Avdon's sons—but that is what I am, and I must accept it. You did not choose to be the Prophet of Israel—but that is what you are..."

Samuel would have responded, but at that moment Manoah, Samson, and Reuel emerged from the gate. Samson was yawning, but on closer observation, Samuel realized it was not because of exhaustion, but because of nervousness.

Neither one of us are the heroes people want us to be, he thought wryly. *All Israel waits, and watches us with hungry eyes.*

Samuel held Liora and kissed her; he felt her hot tears on his own cheek. "May Jehovah be with you," he whispered.

"He will," she whispered back.

He pulled away, feeling the separation as physical pain. "Travel always in a group," he said. "Joel—Abijah—listen to your mother."

"We will," Joel said.

"We wiw," Abijah parroted.

"And I will see you soon, at Mizpah," Samuel said.

Liora smiled. "Go."

He nodded and, taking a deep breath, turned from them as they walked slowly back through the city gates.

Samuel and his companions descended the hill upon which the city was built, following a ridge eastward until they reached a well-traveled road that circled slowly around the shoulder of a rise, following the route of a long, narrow valley below them that snaked steadily eastward. The track led them through scattered scrub and rock, still glistening with the morning's dew.

At the far end of the valley, they passed a small, unwalled settlement, a cluster of white, stone houses around an ancient well. Fathers and sons were wending their way to their fields and flocks as dawn brightened the landscape.

The road dipped into the valley then, crossing its narrow floor and ascending steeply up the other side. Turning southeast, it guided the travelers through field after field of ripe barley; gulls and swallows hopped among the furrows, snatching up worms and insects uncovered by the mattocks.

Before mid-morning they had reached the main north-south highway that transversed the land from Dan to Be'ersheba, wandering through the low hills that bordered the west bank of the Jordan. They stopped for a few moments to eat a little bread and drink from a skin of milk Tahash carried. The day was bright and clear, the sun's warmth tempered by a cool wind blowing from the northwest; Samuel imagined that in it he could smell the freshness of Mount Hermon's snows mingled with the scents of the sea.

They continued south, following the broad, flat highway through fields of well-tended farmland, populated now by fathers and their sons working side by side, their rhythmic songs echoing among the hills. Along the edges of the fields workers harvested peas, lentils, and vetch. Here and there apricot and almond trees were losing the last of their blossoms and beginning to show small, green fruit.

It was late afternoon by the time the village of Lebonah came into view ahead of them, a jumble of boxy, beige houses stacked almost atop one another and sprawled around the heel of a green hill. The road gently ascended through olive groves terraced with low walls of stacked, white stone, the shadows beneath the deep green branches dotted with the white and brown of sheep grazing on the sparse grass.

Every cubit of the nearby hills and valleys was familiar to Samuel— he and his companions were only an easy afternoon's walk from the charred husk of what had once been the city of Shiloh. The rocks and ridges around him were rich with memories from his childhood: wandering the country-side, alone with his thoughts, on the rare occasion that Ahitub gave him a break from his duties; gathering deadwood for the Altar with the Gibeonites; finding some tumbled shepherd's watchtower or some sheltered grotto in which to hide on the days that Hophni or Phinehas were more than usually cruel…

Just outside Lebonah's walls a smith had set up his forge, nestled amongst a crescent-shaped gouge in a wall of granite that jutted from a low hillside. Black smoke spiraled above the ringing of the anvil, sparks leaping angrily in its midst. It was surrounded by a wide circle of hewn oak stumps, the remains of the fuel harvested to feed the insatiable flames.

Lebonah's village gate bustled with activity. Traders and traveling merchants who had slept in the courtyard the night before now spread their wares on woven mats on the hard-packed earth: beautiful glass bottles from Minoa, carvings made from Aramaic elephant ivory, precious rolls of paper from Byblos, exotic perfumes from the lands beyond the great desert. They hawked their merchandise alongside locals set up in booths under striped, wool awnings, offering produce, flour, honey, dates, wine, golden olive oil, lamps and vessels of clay.

The village Elders had already heard of the summons from messengers sent out before Avdon's death. They met Samuel and his companions at the gate, drawing them water from the city's well and distributing barley bread and date cakes.

"Welcome to Lebonah, my lords," Guni, one of the Elders said, and they bowed.

Samuel immediately liked the man: *confident, upright posture; a quiet strength; steady grey eyes.* He wore the striped robe of a chieftain, but it was not new, and he wore no jewelry but his signet ring. His hair and beard had gone almost entirely grey, and stood in stark contrast to his thick, taupe eyebrows.

"May the peace of Jehovah be upon your households," Samuel answered.

"May your children and their children's children be blessed," Guni said.

"And may He bless the works of your hands," Samuel said.

"We are honored by the presence of the Prophet of God," Guni continued, his voice remarkably gentle. "We have not forgotten the guidance you have given us through the years, or the insight provided by the *Beneh* from the School. Your wisdom has more than once helped us find solutions to thorny problems."

"Jehovah's wisdom," Samuel corrected, embarrassed.

"Indeed," Guni said, his smile further wrinkling the skin of his face, weathered like aged leather. "Truly you do speak for the True God. But you have become more than a Prophet to us now."

Samuel struggled to think of an appropriate response, and then let the comment pass. "These are my traveling companions: Reuel, a teacher at the School; Manoah of Dan and his son, Samson."

"The prophesied deliverer!" another of the Elders said, and a murmur of awe swept through the gathered crowd.

"And this is Tahash," Samuel continued, "son of the late Judge Avdon."

"Indeed!" Guni said glancing from Samson to Tahash. "Is this the successor, then? Is Tahash to be the next Judge of Israel?"

"Even the Prophet does not know that answer yet," Tahash said. "For now, I am just his traveling companion."

"Nevertheless, welcome!" Guni said again. "This is a rare honor, indeed!"

"Will the people of Lebonah answer the summons?" Samuel asked.

"We will be at Mizpah," Guni answered. "Preparations are already underway."

"And you will spread the word throughout the villages hereby?" Samuel asked.

Guni nodded. "It is done."

Samuel breathed a sigh of relief. "May Jehovah bless you for your wisdom, Guni."

Guni raised his eyebrows. "Not at all—it is your wisdom that guides us in this time of crisis. Pray for us, Samuel. Petition Jehovah for His blessing, and He will uncover His ear to you in our behalf."

"You do not have to settle for my prayers," Samuel said. "High Priest Ahitub will be at Mizpah, there to offer prayers and sacrifices."

Guni nodded. "But men will come, not at the High Priest's bidding, for I have heard no word from Ahitub. We come at the request of Samuel ben Elkanah, the Prophet of Israel."

The fellowship bade the elders of Lebonah farewell and continued southward, plodding up a series of switchbacks that took them over a steep ridge before descending into another broad valley. Atop the ridge, a hot, dry wind whipped over the hills from the east, stirring up spirals of dust along the road. The wind was blocked as they began their descent into the valley, a broad, smooth vale green and gold with ripening wheat and ripe barley. Towering, white clouds drifted over them, and the travelers relished the cool of their shade for the few moments that it lasted.

Samuel's thoughts kept returning to Tahash's answer to Guni of Lebonah's question about the successor to the Judgeship: *Even the Prophet does not know that yet.* The answer was true, of course, but its wording had surprised Samuel. He wondered if Tahash was secretly harboring some hope that his time with Samuel would lead to his appointment as the Judge of Israel. The young man had said nothing openly about it—in fact, he appeared quite humble in his aspirations. But there was something in the way he had answered Guni...*Corners of mouth curled. Chin raised. Eyes slightly narrowed.* Samuel was not sure what these things meant, but they gnawed at the back of his mind.

Crossing one more low, rounded hill, they stared down into a winding valley with a village sprawled over a knoll in its center: Gilgal.

Manoah paused and leaned on his staff. "Gilgal will be a good place to find ourselves beds."

Samuel glanced back at him. Beyond the tall Danite, he could see the peaks of Mount Gerizim and Mount Ebal, their eastern sides ensconced now in shadow. "It will be dark soon and, much as I would like to, I suppose we cannot continue all night."

Not far from the base of the hill, the road passed a stone monument, already ancient when Joshua had conquered the land. Massive, pitted blocks of basalt, grown over now with weeds and lichen, had been arranged into two concentric circles on the plain. Legend said that the Rephaim had built it in the days of Isaac ben Abraham. The circle filled Samuel with an odd sense of comfort as they walked past, as though its permanence, and its abandonment, reinforced God's promise that the land belonged to Israel, and would do so to times indefinite.

The Elders of Gilgal were waiting at the gate when they arrived. "Welcome," one of them said. "May the peace of Jehovah be upon you."

"And may His blessings overtake you and your families," Samuel replied, a little breathless from the climb.

"Your family is well?" the Elder asked.

Samuel nodded. "When I left them. Jehovah's sheltering Hand is over them."

"News of your coming precedes you. The first of our people march to Mizpah in the morning."

"May Jehovah bless you," said Samuel.

"There is other news, my lord," the Elder said, and Samuel almost felt angry at having the respected old man refer to him by the title.

"What is it?" he asked.

"Traders arriving today from the coast have said that a Canaanite uprising of some sort is happening among many of the forced laborers in the cities of Israel. Apparently, slaves are running into the forest and forming armed bands. People are saying that they plan to attack our cities."

"Sons of Belial!" Manoah snapped. "When we will hear some good news?"

"Not for many days still, I think," said Tahash, and they followed the Elders of Gilgal into the city.

20

Lord Sarnam Ashkelon woke slowly, as though clawing his way up through dark water. When he opened his eyes, the light sliced into his brain like daggers, so painful his stomach turned and for a moment he tasted bile in his throat. He closed his eyes again.

"Drink," said a nasally voice he recognized as Phicol's.

Sarnam pushed himself up in bed, eyes still closed. His blood was tar, flowing sluggishly and reluctantly through his veins. He held out one hand and felt the cool smoothness of an earthenware cup pressed against his palm.

He took a long drink and the comforting tingle of beer swirled in his mouth. After three long drinks he tried opening his eyes again, slowly.

He was in a tent on the beach—he could hear the wash of the surf nearby, and the air was sharp with the reek of seaweed decaying in the sun. Bright sunlight outlined the tent flap beyond his feet, beyond the foot of the bed, and he avoided looking in that direction. The rest of the room was mercifully dark.

"The sorcerer said to eat this when you woke," Phicol rasped, handing him a finger-sized bundle—a grape leaf rolled around a thick, green paste and tied with a strip of seaweed.

Sarnam popped it into his mouth and swallowed it with two gulps of the beer. It was so bitter his neck muscles bunched. Phicol refilled his cup from a strainer-spouted pitcher.

"The army?" Sarnam asked.

"Ready, my lord," Phicol said. "Eager to see blood."

"And the sentries?"

Phicol smiled his twisted, gruesome smile. Sarnam found himself thinking that the young man had probably been handsome once, before he lost his nose. "The Hebrews have gone into hiding, keeping off the roads," Phicol said. "Our perimeter is very large, and the sentries have reported nothing unusual. A few travelers have come too close, but their bodies have been carefully hidden."

Sarnam nodded and took another drink. The beer was beginning to make his headache recede into the background a bit. His vision was a little blurry around the edges, and he had the distinct sensation that he was temporarily visiting his own body, looking out of his own eyes. He felt as though every sensation he experienced was happening to someone else, and that he was a spectator from inside of his own life. It was an odd feeling, but not unpleasant. It made him feel as though he could do anything.

"You have a visitor," Phicol said, unexpectedly.

Sarnam cleared his throat and spat on the floor; his sputum was olive green from Sihphil's potion. "A visitor? No. Whoever it is, he can wait."

"He has been waiting—almost a full day now."

Sarnam spun to look at him, and instantly regretted it. Waves of nausea washed over him. "A day? How long have I been asleep?"

"Two full days and a night."

"Sons and daughters of Ba'al!" he spat. "Help me up!"

Phicol assisted him to his feet and he grabbed the tent pole as the room spun around him. The movement made his left hand ache and he only then realized that it was tightly bound in white linen, and that he could barely move his fingers. Phicol saw his glance. "The snakebite will heal." He held up his own hand, back toward Sarnam. Two dark red spots within a circular scar showed where the snake's fangs had penetrated Phicols' skin.

Phicol continued. "The man says he has information for us—one Baghadh, a Hebrew. He traveled here with half a century of Phoenician mercenaries."

The room was settling into place finally, and Sarnam gingerly felt his hand under the bandage. "Baghadh? I do not remember the name."

"He says he reports to Glaucus, our garrison commander at Aphek."

"Ahh," Sarnam said, nodding. "Glaucus' spy!" He took a deep breath and steadied himself. "Very well, bring him in."

Phicol ducked out the tent door and Sarnam sat down in a carved oak chair near the tent pole. He would have preferred to stand, but was willing to sacrifice the impact of his intimidating stature to prevent falling over in front of the Hebrew.

Phicol re-entered, trailed by a squat man swathed in heavy robes, trimmed in furs and scarlet filigree. The man's smell preceded him into the tent: the rank of rotting meat poorly masked by sweet perfumes.

"My lord," said Baghadh, going to his knees and bowing until his forehead touched the ground.

"Rise," Sarnam commanded. He didn't bother to hide the disgust he knew must be showing on his features. The man was loathsome. Translucent lesions nearly covered one side of his face and neck, and the hands that were pressed against the ground were a mass of broken, weeping boils.

Baghadh clambered awkwardly to his feet. "My gracious lord, may the gods bring you all success—."

"What are you doing here?" Sarnam interrupted.

Baghadh was taken aback a moment. "I...I rode all the way to Philistia, but my contact there was gone, and...and I was told that you were the one to..."

"Come to the point, man!" Sarnam said.

Baghadh's head began to bob up and down, but the man seemed unaware of it. "I have been traveling for days to bring you news, my lord, chasing your army up the coast. I have valuable information, and I have been promised payment."

Sarnam hid his smile. He could see the man's hands shaking with fear. "I know who you are. If your information truly is valuable, you will be rewarded."

Baghadh bowed. "I rely on your generosity—."

"I'll reward you by not skewering you where you stand for wasting my time! I may even let you keep your tongue!" Sarnam shouted, though the effort made his head throb.

Baghadh took a step backward, eyes wide. He glanced over at Phicol, licking his lips and visibly shaking. "It is about Samuel the Seer, my lord."

Sarnam sat back and took another drink. "I know all too well who the mystic Samuel is."

"He is on the move, my lord! He has gone to Pirathon to tell one of our nation's leaders to rouse the armies of Israel against you."

"Has he indeed?" Sarnam said, feigning indifference. "And this is important to me how?"

Baghadh's head bobbed more quickly. "My lord...I was told to report to you any news of troop movement...any action that might be taken against Philistia."

"We will deal with Samuel," Sarnam said.

"Do not underestimate him, my lord," Baghadh said. "The people adore him as a prophet and a leader. He is the closest thing our nation has had to a king since the days of Moses and Joshua. He is the heart of Israel."

"Hearts may be torn out," Sarnam said flexing the fingers of his left hand gingerly, eyes narrowing with the pain. "And so in a single move do all plans end."

Baghadh looked from Sarnam to Phicol nervously. "And what of me, my lord? What would you have me do?"

"You will come with us," Sarnam said. "Phicol—find him a place among the baggage—where he can be closely watched."

"But my lord," Baghadh protested, "I travel with many men. If people notice that we are away from home for too long—."

"Then they may suspect you for the traitor you are. Do not make betrayal your business and then ask to be trusted!" said Sarnam.

Phicol grabbed the chubby man's arm and began guiding him out of the tent. "Phicol!" Sarnam called, and the warrior turned.

"Send for the Hunter," Sarnam said.

Phicol smiled. "Even so."

He disappeared out through the tent flap and Sarnam took another long swill of beer. The heart of Israel—that was what the spy had called Samuel. "Well, I will tear it from the nation's chest," he whispered to himself. "I will destroy him and all he cares about, just as Phicol destroyed the heart of Israel twenty years ago."

The next day, as the army prepared to move again, Phicol ducked into Sarnam's tent. "He is here," he said.

"Bring him," Sarnam said.

Phicol opened the tent flap and a man entered, bending low to pass through the entrance. He wore only a loincloth of oiled leather and a sash of leopard skin draped over his left shoulder. A curved knife with a handle of yellow ivory was tucked into the loincloth, and one end of a blowgun jutted up from behind his left shoulder. Inside, he was unable to stand erect without pushing up the tent cloths with his head. His skin was as black as charcoal and his long limbs lithe and corded with muscle. From his shaved head, down his face, chest, and arms his skin was etched with tattoos, strings of dots arranged into circles, spirals, and less identifiable shapes. Around his neck was a string of long, wickedly curved claws, and a slender finger of bone pierced his septum.

"Hunter." Sarnam greeted him.

"I come," the man said. When he spoke, Sarnam could glimpse his teeth, each filed into a sharp cone. "I pay debt. You pay totem."

"You will get your totem back, Hunter, if you do as I tell you."

The Hunter's broad nostrils flared, and his grip tightened on the spear he carried in his left hand. He would succeed, Sarnam knew. The Hunter was a being from another world, and even Phicol did not dare to cross him. He had never failed Sarnam since the day Sarnam had found him in the deserts of Egypt, as close to walking in the realms of death as a man can be. Sarnam had nursed him back to health, and the Hunter had given him his personal totem, a small, painted carving of a giraffe that was a symbol of the debt he owed the man who had saved his life.

But the Hunter could not return home without regaining the totem—to do so was a taboo that would stain his name with a disgrace he and his descendants could never outlive. Since that day, the Hunter followed Sarnam, never close enough to be seen, but always within distance of his signal: a sequence of flaming arrows fired into the night sky. He waited for the opportunity to risk his own life in Sarnam's service, and to earn back the symbol of his honor by this sacrifice.

"There is a man," said Sarnam. "A witch doctor and leader of the people who live in the lands to the east. His name is Samuel, of Ramathaim. He was last seen in a city called Pirathon."

Sarnam paused, waiting for some sign of recognition or acknowledgement in the Hunter's dark eyes. There was none. The huge black figure stared down at him with all the animation of a stone statue.

"I want you to find this man," Sarnam continued after a moment. "Find him and kill him."

"I kill him. You give totem." It was not a question.

Sarnam smiled. "Yes. Kill him and I will release you and let you return home. But I want proof! Bring me evidence he is dead!"

The Hunter blinked once. "Dead already."

"Good," said Sarnam. "Do not come back until he is."

21

Samuel and his companions left Gilgal before the sun was fully up, following the road east over a low rise and then descending into the valley below the city, its broad base broken by a dozen hills dotted with settlements and villages. Sunrise cast impenetrable shadows beneath the boughs of the olive groves that ringed the settlements, growing in neat rows between the terraces of stacked, sun-bleached stone.

The road turned south again then, neatly splitting a broad, green valley of farmland, the wheat and barley fields on either side filled with the songs of workers and the flash of moving sickles. The valley narrowed at its southern end, and the companions' route passed from the farmland and into the rocky bottom of a dry wadi filled only with a flood of pink oleanders. On either side of the road, strange red rock formations rose like mangled pillars, looking as if a giant had grabbed monstrous cylinders of clay and kneaded them with his hands. In some places, it appeared that tubes had been cut through the rock and Samuel wondered what force could have produced such tormented shapes.

The road continued meandering through the hills until they reached the foot of the Mountain of Abraham. They circled away from the mountain's steep northern face until they could look up a narrow path of switchbacks leading up the southeastern side.

"I cannot pass without seeing the top of the mountain and standing in the footsteps of Abraham," Samuel said. "I can meet you in Bethel if you wish. It is but a short distance from here to the city gates."

"I would like to see the view as well," said Samson. To Samuel's surprise, the others agreed and they turned from the road and made their way slowly up the steep path, weaving back and forth through scattered sheep and goats grazing on bright spring grass among the pale rock that littered the ground. Shepherds carrying lambs or singing to their flocks waved and called out greetings to them as they passed.

For a short distance they walked in the shadow of a grove of ancient, untended fig trees, slender suckers jutting skyward from their gnarled branches. Near the hill's top, their path punched through a chest-high patch of baca bushes and scrub, scraping at their legs as they climbed.

On the other side, the last stretch of track carried them to the mountain's level top, green with new grass emerging from the red earth and speckled with white lilies, red and purple anemones, asphodels in white and pink, and elegant white cyclamen with delicate scarlet stripes. They stopped there, breathless and overcome with awe at the view before them.

They were poised atop one peak of a ridge of mountains stretching like a backbone north and south, nearly on the border between the territories of the tribes of Ephraim and Benjamin. To the west, at the foot of the hill, the ancient city of Bethel huddled within its walls on a stony plateau, a jumble of multi-storied buildings seemingly built right atop one another, a mass of hard angles and sun-bleached, mud-brick walls. On its northern side, a weed-shrouded tumble of rock marked the only remains of the ancient Canaanite city of Luz, burned by Joshua during his conquest; his descendants had built Bethel on its ruins. From their vantage point they could see how the trade roads seemed to flow like spokes from the hub of Bethel, reaching out to all four corners of the land: north toward Shechem, south toward Be'ersheba, west toward Joppa. On the western route, a caravan of camels and a single wagon were wending their way toward the mighty oak forests of Sharon and, beyond them, the sea, two day's travel distant.

Farther south, sunlight gleamed from the white buildings of the Jebusite city of Jerusalem, crowning Mount Zion. To the east, they could just glimpse the ruins of Ai, a mound of tumbled white stone that seemed to be receding into the green hilltop.

Only paces from where they stood a weathered, pitted pillar of basalt jutted up from the grass; at its base was another stone the size of a yearling lamb. A circle of bare earth was worn around them both, evidence of the passing of countless feet.

"Here were we first called Israel," whispered Tahash.

Samuel let the wonder of the place flow through him, goosepimpling his skin. On this hilltop, Abraham had once camped. Here he had spoken to Jehovah, and been given the promise that had centuries later brought their people to this land: "*Lift up your eyes from where you are and look north and south, east and west. All the land that you see I will give to you and your offspring to times indefinite.*"

Two generations later, Abraham's grandson Jacob had returned to this same spot. During the night, his head resting on the smaller of the two stones, in his dreams he had been granted a vision of a ladder ascending to heaven, and Jehovah had changed his name to Israel and repeated to him the promise He had given to Abraham.

Jacob had later raised the standing stone to mark the site and named it Bethel, the House of God. The stone stood there still after the passing of nearly nine centuries. It remained one of the most sacred places in the Promised Land.

Samuel walked slowly across the grass to the ancient menhir. Its top was stained dark with repeated anointings of oil, and its surface worn smooth by weather and countless adoring touches. He brushed it, feeling the tiny pits and dimples passing under his fingertips. *This stone was raised by Jacob's hands.* It was a piece of history people could touch. It was a bone of the Promised Land, lifted from its flesh as a reminder of the promise all Israel relied on for their very existence: their divine right to inhabit Canaan. Abraham, Isaac, Jacob—all of them had died without seeing the fulfillment of that promise.

But their faith had been strong. The stone stood here in symbol of it, defying wind and rain and the ravages of time, as if to tell Samuel, *All that Jehovah promises will come to be. Strengthen your hands, and let your heart not become faint.*

But his heart was faint—at times it melted within him. He looked southwest, to the gleaming of the sun on the far-off dunes of Philistia. He feared the dark power that even now might be marching from those shores.

He did not like to admit it, even to himself, but he feared what it could do to his reputation almost as much as what it could do to his flesh. *Will I be yet another in a long line of servants of Jehovah who are remembered as much for their failings as for their successes? Will I be remembered at all?*

He let his eyes travel farther inland, to the hilly country in which the villages of Ramathaim and Naioth rested, hidden by rolling hills and forests. There, between the threatening armies of Philistia and himself, were Liora and his sons. He could only pray for them, and trust in God to watch out for them while he was gone.

Thinking about his family made their separation more immediate. Samuel placed both of his palms on the stone and looked at the blue sky overhead. *Please, Jehovah. Tell me what to do. Watch over Your people for the sake of Your great name. Let it not be said that the God of Israel could not protect His people against the false gods of Canaan. Use me in whatever way You can. If it be Your will that I be martyred for this cause, I willingly go to my death. But save this, Your people, I implore you.*

Samson, standing behind him, unknowingly interrupted his prayer. "I cannot imagine doing this."

Samuel let go of the stone and turned to face him. "Doing what?"

Samson gestured at the monolith. "This. Placing a landmark that people would visit and honor centuries after my death. Growing up, we all hear the names: Abraham, Isaac, Jacob, Joseph, Moses, Joshua. But in the stories they are more like legends than earthling men."

He reached out and ran his fingertips across the stone. "And then you come here," he continued softly, "and you see the work of the patriarchs' hands. And suddenly, they are legends no longer, but men like you and I, who sweated and toiled and laughed and wept under the sun."

Samuel nodded, still staring out toward the endless blue of the sea. "Do you suppose that their faith waxed and waned like the tide, as ours does?"

Samson looked at him sideways, the skin between his eyes wrinkling. When Samuel did not explain his question, Samson just shrugged and slowly circled the stone, his eyes embracing every detail of its surface. "People just do not do things like this anymore…When was the last standing stone erected?"

Samuel thought a moment. "You know—I cannot remember. Is it the Witness Stone that Joshua set at Shechem? I think so…"

Samson whistled. "Three centuries ago. Why so long, do you think?"

Samuel shrugged. "Because since those days there have been no more Joshuas. Such men no longer walk the earth. As you said—they are more legend than men. And legends are not born in a day."

They descended the mountain path and followed the valley a little farther until they reached the foot of the plateau on which Bethel was built. There, the road passed a massive, gnarled oak tree, its shadow a pool of cool darkness across their path.

"Allon-bacuth—the Great Tree of Weeping," Samuel said.

Isaac's wife, Rebekah, had named the tree six centuries before, when they had buried her childhood nurse, Deborah, under the shadow of its boughs. Afterward, the Canaanites had adopted the site as a place of false worship until the conquest by Joshua. The grave marker was now long gone, and the tree itself had become the remembrancer of that ancient chapter of Israel's history. Its roots, Samuel thought, stretched both down into the earth and back into the past.

A delegation of Elders greeted them at the city gate. One of them stepped forward, bowing. "May you have peace, Prophet of Israel. I am Elishama, grandson of Judge Tola, chief of the Elders of Bethel."

He was a dignified looking man, Samuel thought. He had not yet seen sixty years, and his frame was tall and powerful, but Samuel saw that his hands were not callused. His hair was white and fell to his shoulders in thick curls, though his beard, stark over his bronzed skin, was neatly trimmed around his cheeks and ears.

Samuel and his companions bowed. "And may peace return to your household, and your city," Samuel answered.

"I pray that it will be so," Elishama replied. "How are your wives, and your children?"

"My two sons are at home with their mother," Samuel said. "They are in God's hands."

Elishama nodded. "May He continue to watch over them."

"You have been told to why we are here?" Samuel asked.

"A messenger from Judge Avdon's household rode through the city two days ago," Elishama answered. "He said that Samuel is leading Israel into war."

Samuel was taken aback. "Did he? It would have been more accurate to have said Samuel was summoning Israel to Mizpah to be sanctified by Ahitub, the High Priest. We may still hope to avoid war."

Elishama raised his eyebrows. "I am glad to hear you say so. But rumors of a Philistine army moving up the coast are whispered by travelers from Sharon. Is that not the reason for the summons?"

"The reason for the summons is to strengthen the nation's determination to serve Jehovah with their whole heart, mind, soul and strength," said Samuel. "How that will play into the plans of the Philistines we will have to wait and see."

Elishama looked puzzled, but let whatever questions he was pondering pass. "Well. Let us refresh you from your journey and take you to see the congregation of Elders."

Samuel, Manoah, Samson, Reuel, and Tahash followed Elishama through the gate and into the town square. It was huge and cacophonous, bustling with activity. Women surrounded an ancient well at its center, coming and going with water jars on their heads or hips. Camels laden with clay vessels and wrapped bundles scowled or spit at passers-by, their soft, long-lashed eyes belying their temperaments. At their feet turbaned Ishamaelites with gold rings in their sharp noses sat cross-legged on woven mats, hawking goods laid out on the street before them. Beggars in tattered clothing, blind, deaf, or lame, stood or leaned on sticks near the gate, calling for gifts of mercy. Shops surrounded the square, tents or awnings fronted by low tables or rugs rolled out upon the dusty ground; herbs, pottery, copper cooking vessels, leather tack, and jewelry hung from pegs and tent poles. The smells overwhelmed Samuel's nostrils, reminding him of his childhood in Shiloh: flatbread baking in pit ovens, roasting meat, the mingled sweat of men and animals, all blended with dust kicked up from the ceaseless passing of sandaled feet. The enthusiastic cries of merchants hawking their goods cut through the clamor: grain, wine, olive oil, tent cloth, garments, metal ware—all were available for a price.

As they left the square a group of swarthy Edomites stepped in front of Samson. One of them, a sharp-featured man with a black, oiled beard that came to a point a handbreadth below his chin, bowed to the young Danite with a flourish.

"Welcome, my lord! I can see that you are a man of wealth and exquisite taste!" he said. "There are so few in this crowd who can truly appreciate what I have to offer—I beg you—pause just long enough to swallow your saliva, and sample my wares."

Samson, frowned, irritated, but courtesy required a polite response. "My friends and I are here on urgent business—."

"Ah! Just so! What I offer can make your hurried meals into feasts of delight. Behold!" The man proffered a wooden box, and then opened it dramatically. Inside, the box was divided into six rectangular compartments, and each was filled with powdered spices. "Galbanum! Pure frankincense! The finest myrrh, straight from the secret lands beyond Egypt! My suppliers brave rivers of crocodiles and behemoths to bring this across the desert! They purchase it from a tribe so savage they use dried pieces of their own flesh as money!" He leaned toward Samson conspiratorially. "They say that every gerah of frankincense represents a lost life, so dangerous are the lands from which it comes!"

"Indeed?" said Samson. "Then I would be remiss to pass up such an opportunity."

The man's eyes lit up, but Samson licked his index finger and stuck it unceremoniously into the receptacle of frankincense, then into his mouth. "Fair," he said a moment later, nodding. "But not the best I have tasted."

He walked away as the Edomite, mouth open, looked from his open box to Samson's back. "But...but my lord..."

Samson flashed a smile at Samuel as they passed from the square onto the street, and Samuel shook his head and rolled his eyes.

Elishama led them to a beautiful home near the center of Bethel, a sprawling two-story structure built around a spacious courtyard and surrounded by a strong wall and gate. On the two-level rooftop, a handful of women spoke in low tones, their rhythmic movements accompanied by the rasping of a flour mill being turned. In the courtyard, about two dozen men sat in a circle on a patchwork of rugs laid on the flagstones, dipping thick-crusted bread into wide dishes of golden olive oil and black vinegar.

They rose as Samuel and his companions entered. "The Prophet of Israel!" Elishama announced, and they bowed.

"Please—be seated." Samuel set the example, taking his place in the circle, and the men shifted to allow Manoah, Samson, Reuel, and Tahash to join him. Two young women carried in bowls of milk and plates of dates and set them before the men.

"Eat!" said Elishama, and Samuel gratefully took a drink of the milk, only then realizing how hungry he was.

They ate in silence for a few moments and Samuel took the opportunity to observe the Elders of Bethel. Some of their faces he knew, although he remembered few of their names. He was surprised and saddened to see that almost half of them wore amulets on slender chains around their necks: crescent moons, cats, monkeys, or heart-shapes in red and blue. They were charms, probably from Egypt, and the Torah forbade them. They had, nonetheless, become popular in the past few years.

"Well then," said Elishama, burping and setting down his bowl of olive oil. "Now there is salt between us."

Samuel smiled. The phrase referred to the inviolable bond between two people who had shared a meal. "Then let us speak frankly to one another," he answered.

"Even so," said Elishama. "I suspect you have come to ask us to lead the men of Bethel to Mizpah."

Samuel nodded. "I have. We must——."

"You do not have the authority to ask us to go anywhere, Samuel ben Elkanah," Elishama interrupted.

The courtyard went quiet, all eyes turning toward Samuel. Men froze with their hands halfway to their mouths.

"Indeed," continued Elishama, "nowhere in the Torah does it put into a prophet's hands the authority to do anything—other than to speak the messages he is given."

Samuel felt his face reddening. "I am not trying to overstep my responsibilities."

"Perhaps not. But that does not mean you are *not* overstepping. You are the Prophet of Israel. Surely you know what is written in the book of *Devarim* regarding the role of a prophet."

Samuel knew it was pride that motivated his words, but he spoke them anyway, reciting the memorized words just as they were written, just as Ahitub had drilled them into his head: "'I will raise up for them a prophet like you from among their brothers; I will put my words in his mouth, and he will disclose to their ears everything I command him.'"

"And have you received a command from Jehovah to summon all the people to Mizpah? Why not to Nob? Or Shechem?"

"Is not your real question 'Why not to Bethel?'?" Samuel asked.

Elishama looked at Samuel as though he were a child speaking out of turn before his Elders. "Is it Jehovah's words that you bring us, or Samuel's?"

"Do you not remember the rest of what Jehovah said to Moses on that day in front of Mount Horeb?" Samuel asked. "'If anyone does not give ear to My words that the prophet speaks in My name, I Myself will call him to account?'"

Elishama raised his white eyebrows. "And Jehovah continued, 'But a prophet who presumes to speak in my name anything I have not commanded him to say...'" He trailed off, looking absently toward the sky, feigning forgetfulness. "What was it Jehovah said next?"

Samuel did not answer, although he knew the words: *That prophet must die.*

"So I ask again," Elishama said, "Is your summons to Mizpah the word of Jehovah, or of Samuel?"

"It is the word of Avdon, divinely appointed Judge of Israel, his last command to the nation before his death," said Samuel.

Elishama shook his head. "I think that it was only Avdon's repetition of Samuel's command. And Avdon, as you say, is dead."

"Is it only by the word of Jehovah that our people should be gathered together for sacrifice and repentance?" Samuel asked. "Must we wait for a divine invitation to praise God, or to renew our vows to Him?"

"If you feel the need to renew your vows, then by all means go to Mizpah and do so," said Elishama. "But it is quite a different matter to ask us to."

"I would think that a grandson of Judge Tola might see the Egyptian charms hanging around the necks of his chiefs and recognize that a need for repentance could exist—even in the holy city of Bethel!" Samuel said.

The Elders around the circle scowled and grumbled, but Elishama smiled. "Believe me when I tell you I mean no disrespect. But do not try to instruct me in the worship of God. Not every righteous man subscribes to your antiquated interpretation of the Torah, Samuel."

"You are making a mistake, Elishama," Samuel said.

"I acknowledge that you think so. But I am afraid that your opinion is not the shaper of my views. Unless I hear the summons from the High Priest in Nob, or you can tell me that Jehovah gave you the words you carry now to the cities of Israel, I think that I will stay behind the walls of Bethel."

Samuel glanced as surreptitiously as he could at his companions. Reuel was staring daggers at Elishama; to Samuel's surprise, Manoah looked angry as well.

But it was Tahash who spoke. "Do you put so little trust in one whom Jehovah himself has declared trustworthy?"

"Judge Gideon was entrusted by Jehovah with great responsibility, but he made an ephod in Ophrah, and all Israel drew away from the Tabernacle and began worshiping it," Elishama said. "Not all that loyal men do—though it is motivated by the best of intentions—fulfills the will of God."

"What if I told you I am very confident that High Priest Ahitub will join his hand with mine in summoning Israel to Mizpah?" asked Samuel.

"Because of your influence over him, or because Jehovah commands it?" Elishama asked. "I would tell you that your confidence is, itself, presumptuousness."

Reuel, Manoah, and Samson all came to their feet together, and Samuel saw the Danites hands close over the hilts of their swords. "Do not dare to accuse the Prophet of Israel before my eyes!" said Manoah through clenched teeth.

Elishama raised one hand dismissively. "Sit! Sit! I have accused no one of anything!"

Elishama's men who had been standing near the courtyard gate made their way toward the gathering of Elders, their hands drifting to their swords as well.

"Sit, please!" Elishama said again. "We are all brothers here!"

"Father," Samson asked, not taking his eyes from Elishama's face, "am I allowed to be a brother to one who says he would defy the word of the High Priest?"

Elishama's expression was so smug Samuel wanted to erase it with his fists. "Do not put words in my mouth, boy," the Elder said. "If the High Priest commands it, I will go to Mizpah, or to Be'ersheba, or across the sea. Does not the Torah also say, 'Go to the priests, and to the Judge. Inquire of them. And you must act according to the decisions they give you. Be careful to do everything they direct you to do. Act according to the law they teach you and the decisions they give you. Do not turn aside from what they speak in your ears, to the right or to the left. The man who shows contempt for the Judge or for the Priest who ministers in the Holy Place must be put to death.'"

Samuel stood. "Then I have wasted enough of your time here. We will continue on our journey to Nob, and I will send back to you the word of High Priest Ahitub—in writing, of course."

Elishama chuckled. "No written command is needed. If you tell me Ahitub's words, I will trust that you speak the truth."

"Very generous," Manoah growled.

"I do not plan to return here," Samuel said. "A messenger will have to do."

Elishama stood then, and the rest of the Elders followed his example. He called to one of the guardsmen standing nearby. "Bring these men provisions for the rest of their journey, and a donkey to carry them." He paused and turned back to Samuel. "Unless you wish to stay the night in Bethel, and continue on in the morning?"

"No, my lord," said Samuel, not bothering to hide his sarcasm. "Your hospitality is overwhelming, but we must reach Nob as quickly as possible, and on the way we must speak to the Elders of Ramah, Mizpah, and Gibeah."

"Very well." Elishama bowed. "Then we wish you a speedy and a safe journey."

Samuel looked slowly at each of the faces of the Elders of Bethel standing across the rug from him. "In a few days' time, men and women from Dan to Be'ersheba, from Sharon to the Jordan—and beyond, from Gilead across the Jordan—will be assembling at Mizpah by the word of High Priest Ahitub and the word of Samuel, Prophet of Israel. Each of you should think very carefully if you truly wish to stand alone against the rest of the sons of Israel in this."

Elishama looked as though he was going to respond, but Samuel turned on his heel and strode out of the courtyard, Manoah, Samson, Tahash, and Reuel at his heels.

22

"After three days, Abraham raised his eyes and saw the place in the distance."—The Scroll of Bereshith

Samuel, Manoah, Samson, Reuel, and Tahash continued south from Bethel later that same day. The road was now a broad highway and they regularly passed the wagons and camel trains of traders from north and south. Huge, puffy clouds towered above them, darkening as they gathered over the hills of Samaria. They were now only a long day's walk from the banks of the Jordan to the east, and perhaps two days from the shores of the Great Sea in the opposite direction.

By early evening, they were approaching the hill upon which the city of Ramah was built. They stopped briefly at the city gates, just long enough to take some water and a bit of bread from the Elders who were waiting there to meet them.

Samuel asked them to respond to the summons they had received earlier by messenger, to join Israel's forces at Mizpah.

"All that you have spoken to us has come true, Prophet," one of the Elders said. "You advice has been as the advice of the True God. If you ask us to gather at Mizpah, then at Mizpah you will find us."

The afternoon's light was fading into dusk, and so Samuel left the gates of Ramah as quickly as possible. The road turned sharply west, and they rejoined the main highway south for a short time before leaving it to follow another well-worn track across the low hills. Thunder rumbled over the mountains to the west, and a few moments later, it began to rain.

In moments the rain became a deluge. The road dropped into a deep wadi then, meandering along its rocky bottom under the shadow of the hills upon which Mizpah was built.

"We need to move more quickly," Manoah said over the noise of the downpour. "We do not want to be in this riverbed in the rain!"

They struggled onward. Samuel's clothing was cold and stuck to his skin uncomfortably, saturated and growing heavier with each step. It was becoming more difficult to see, and they slipped and stumbled over the wet, tumbled rocks that lined each edge of the road. Samuel's frustration and exhaustion became anger at Elishama for acting in a way that had prevented them from stopping in Bethel for the night. He knew that the choice had been up to him, but he refused to carry all of the blame for the miserable circumstances they now found themselves in, unreasonable as he knew his thinking might be.

The rain stopped, as abruptly as it had begun, as the little fellowship entered a narrow defile that wound between massive boulders half-buried in the hillsides. Sycamores, cedars, oaks, and other trees spread their branches over the yellow flowers of newly-blossomed acacias.

As they reached the opening of the defile Tahash, walking in front of Samuel, stopped abruptly, his right hand drifting to the hilt of his sword.

The others stopped, too. "What is it?" asked Samuel.

Tahash was silent a moment, scanning the shadows under the trees. "I am not sure…"

The trees and rocks around them were quiet except for the sound of water dripping from the branches. Manoah and Samson drew their swords as well. Manoah glanced at Samuel over his shoulder. "Wait here."

Reuel stayed with Samuel as the three warriors moved forward, their hair dark and plastered over faces gone pale in the waning light of evening.

After a few cautious steps, Tahash knelt on the road, extending his hand slowly toward something in the wet grass that Samuel could not see. "It is some kind of snare," he said.

"On the road?" Samson asked. "Set for what?"

"Or for whom?" Manoah said.

Samuel never knew if it was some inner sense or a whisper of sound that warned him, but at that instant he flinched away just as a spear hurtled across the road from the shadows of the rocks. The weapon's shaft glanced off of the staff in his hand and its tip buried itself in the flank of their donkey. The animal squealed and sprang forward, plowing into Samuel and Reuel and knocking them to the ground.

Samuel rolled back to his feet just as the donkey collapsed onto the road, thrashing and screaming. Manoah, Samson, and Tahash were yelling and running towards him, swords flashing dully in the half-light. Samuel instinctively looked in the direction from which the spear had come just in time to see a strange spinning circle flying from the rocks...

A weighted net dropped neatly over the three warriors and they tumbled to the ground, tangled in the cords and in each other. Samuel had a glimpse of Manoah, his face red with fury, the flat of his sword blade smashed against his chest and left cheek as he struggled to free himself.

Movement from the rocks caught Samuel's eye and he turned. A figure scrabbled over the boulders, hunched and moving like a huge insect. The figure's long, thin legs were bare: he wore only a loincloth, revealing stick-thin limbs and skin as black as midnight shadows. Poised like a spider about to pounce on its prey, his features were indiscernible in the dusky light.

Reuel stepped between Samuel and the strange figure, bronze knife in hand. Without hesitation the black man leapt toward them and for the briefest instant, Samuel caught a glimpse of triangular white teeth and intricate tattoos across an ebon, cadaverous face.

Acting purely on instinct, Samuel raised his staff and struck the man as hard as possible with its butt end.

Their attacker shrugged off the blow as he landed almost atop them and wrenched the staff from Samuel's hands with a grip like iron. He tossed it behind him contemptuously, and it clattered among the rocks.

In a single smooth movement the black figure drew a knife from his leopard-skin sash and tackled Samuel. The prophet clawed at the rocky ground of the road, trying to get out from beneath the powerful, wiry limbs on top of him. It would have likely been his final act, but at that moment Reuel hurtled into the figure, screaming and slashing with his knife.

"Let him go!" Reuel screamed.

The two men tumbled to the ground and rolled over once. Samuel got to his knees and began instinctively crab-crawling away from the unknown attacker.

"No! Aaaah!" he heard Reuel scream, and spun around.

The black man was now on top of the young prophet, his long fingers clamped around the *Beneh's* neck. Samuel pushed himself to his feet, still shaky from the attack, looking for an opening.

Then a rock collided with their attacker's shoulder, striking a glancing blow that sent him tumbling to the ground. Reuel scrambled away on all fours, gasping for breath.

Samuel turned to see Manoah, free of the net now, loading another stone into his sling as he rushed toward them.

"Son of Belial!" the big Danite screamed as he ran.

Samson and Tahash were right behind him, swords drawn, their battle cries echoing in the narrow defile.

The black man bared his pointed teeth and drew the strange, curved knife from his sash. In the same movement he bent his long legs, leapt over Samuel's head and landed atop the nearest rock. He dodged one more rock from Manoah's sling, looking down at them with teeth bared as though he was about to attack, a trickle of blood running from his shoulder where Manoah's stone had struck him.

He must have thought better of it. He turned silently and vanished, disappearing into the rocks. Manoah and Samson raced after him but returned a moment later, empty handed.

"Not a trace," said Manoah, panting and red-faced. "Not even a footprint."

"What was that?" said Reuel, finally catching his breath.

"I have heard stories of these men," said Manoah. "A tribe, tall and thin, with hair and skin as black as night. They are said to come from somewhere far to the south of Egypt—so far south that the stars are strange. They are lion hunters, it is said. I have heard that they drink blood before a hunt. Pharaoh Ramses kept some at his court as slaves, or for entertainment."

"Whomever he was, he targeted Samuel first," said Samson.

"Maybe because the rest of us were armed," Manoah said.

"He threw a spear!" Samson said. "It would have made no difference if his target was armed or not!"

"Were you trying to escape the net?" Manoah asked. "Or just trying to entangle us further with your thrashing?"

"Thrashing?" Samson asked, scowling.

"First Glaucus and now this!" Samuel said, changing the subject. "Can we not even travel the highways of our own country anymore in safety?"

"Enough talk! We need to get out of this wadi!" said Tahash.

They moved quickly then, fresh energy flowing through their veins, although they jumped at every hint of movement in the shadows. Reuel retrieved Samuel's staff from among the rocks. Clambering out from the wadi, for the rest of their route they put up with rough, trackless country in order to gain better visibility of their surroundings.

Ahead of them, Mizpah perched atop a low plateau of grey and white limestone stretching south and west. Its top was broad and level, green and gold with grain fields. To the east and the north, the hills were neatly terraced and strung with roping grapevines running between groves of gnarled olive trees. They stayed atop a ridgeline as it crossed a shallow saddle, looking down at the road below them. In the distance, they could make out a small group of travelers, but the fading light gave the fellowship no indication of who they were.

As they neared the gates, the walled city became a silhouette against the sky, now beginning to show stars peeking out from between banks of clouds. Above Mizpah's walls its central keep towered, a massive bastion whose foundations had been laid in General Joshua's day. From his previous visits Samuel knew that the tower was surrounded by its own thick wall, and from three hundred years of history he knew that these defenses had never been breached.

Samuel's musings were interrupted by Manoah's asking a sentry at the gate to summon the Elders of Mizpah to meet them.

"Who shall I say asks it?" said the sentry, holding up his lamp to try and illuminate their faces.

"Tell them that Samuel the Prophet is waiting in the dark outside their gate," Manoah said.

The man's eyes widened and looked at the traveler's faces for just an instant, obviously unsure which was Samuel. "As you have said, so it shall be done!" he said, and scurried off into the city.

The other sentries posted offered the travelers water and bread and they took it in gulps. Samuel hadn't realized how hungry he was—fear had pushed all other thoughts from his mind, it seemed.

A cluster of lamps appeared out of the darkness in the city, nearing until Samuel could make out the faces of four Elders, shadowed into sinister masks by the flickering light. They bowed, and then one stepped forward and kissed Samuel on each cheek.

"Samuel ben Elkanah!" he greeted.

"Here I am, my lord," Samuel responded.

"I am Ahlai, chief among the Elders of Mizpah. We welcome you to our city—we did not expect you until tomorrow, or we would have been more prepared."

"Give it no more thought, I beg you," Samuel said. "Right now we are looking for nothing more than a warm bed."

"And so you shall have it!" said Ahlai. "Please—follow me, and be guests in my home for the night."

They bid goodnight to the other Elders and followed Ahlai down one of the narrow roads leading from the gate. Warm lamplight glimmered from windows on either side of them, splashing pools of wavering orange onto the streets. The domestic sounds that floated from windows as they passed made the exhaustion of the day fill Samuel in a rush, and the thought of sleep pushed all others from his mind, save one: *Liora. Where are you at this moment, my love? Are you and our sons safe, and happy?*

"We received news that you have summoned all Israel here, of course," Ahlai said, interrupting Samuel's musing. "We are deeply honored, my lord, but...but what will you do here?"

"Jehovah will show us what to do. If you can prepare for the arrival of those who answer the summons—they will need to cleanse themselves ritually, so water will be needed outside the walls in troughs or shallow pools. You will also need to prepare for a sea of tents to be set up outside the walls, and to ready accommodation for as many as possible inside the walls. Spread the word among the inhabitants to be prepared to house guests on their rooftops and in their courtyards."

"Should we expect an attack?"

"I do not know, but we would be fools not to make some preparation for one. Many of the men who answer the summons will come without weapons and armor, and we will have to do what we can to arm them if the Philistines do attack."

Ahlai nodded. "I will have the tower stocked with food and other supplies."

"And organize the Levites to be ready to sanctify the men for battle."

"As you have said, so it shall be done," said Ahlai. "But will you not be arranging these things? We assumed you might take over leadership of the city once you arrived."

"No," said Samuel. "I leave for Nob as early as may be in the morning."

"Nob? Is the Ark again at the Tabernacle?"

"No—I go to fetch the High Priest. Perhaps you can choose a place from which he can address the nation—atop the great tower, or from the wall near the gate."

Ahlai stopped in front of a plastered wall and swung open a tall, well-crafted wooden gate. Young men and women came out from the courtyard and began to lead the travelers to their beds atop the house.

Samuel hesitated. "I know I have asked a great deal of you."

Ahlai shook his head. "Give it no more thought, my lord. All that Samuel, the Prophet of Israel has said will be done."

They broke their fast early the next morning with figs and a little cheese, and left while the dawn was limning the hills in Gilead with umber. Samuel stopped just outside the gates and paused for a moment, looking at their route to the south. A valley descended into the lowlands, where the road vanished in a thick fog that lay like a sea around unbroken hills for many days' journey south. "Nob and the House of God," he whispered. "Would that I was traveling to you for some other reason."

The followed the road south and then east, funneled through forested hills by the valley in which they walked. The sun rose bright and clear, but by mid-morning massive banks of clouds began gathering over the hills, throwing all into shadow. The wind gusted from the north, hard-edged with the cold of Mount Hermon's snows.

The farther south they traveled, the more populous the hills around them grew, until from any given point on the road they could see half a dozen settlements or villages crowning hilltops or nestled in their shadows.

It was only a little after mid-morning when they came in sight of the city of Gibeah. The city and its tower, built atop the spine-like ridge of the central mountain range, stood higher than the surrounding hills and were used as a lookout point and a fire-signal post in times of war. The north-south road ran at its feet; it had become an important stopping point for traders and caravans on their way north or south.

Not far outside the city gates, just above the trade road, a bulwark of chalk cliffs loomed. Stark white against the green of the landscape above and below them, even in morning' shadow they seemed to Samuel to gleam. "The White Cliffs of Gibeah," they were called, a towering escarpment of pillar-like ridges broken by shallow caves and overhangs. In the days before Israel's conquest of the land, it was said that Canaanites had used the cliffs as an execution ground, throwing criminals from the heights to be smashed on the rocks below.

Inside the gates, amidst the craftsmen and merchants in the city square, Samuel and his companions were greeted by the Elders of the House of the Matrites. Samuel knew the men—all Israel did, as they were a pros-perous family of the tribe of Benjamin, with a reputation as fierce and pow-erful fighters. Abiel was the patriarch of the clan, a man who had seen eight decades in the city of his forefathers. His son, Ner had taken over for him as active leader of the family, and he introduced Samuel to his brothers in turn: Abdon, Zur, Ba'al, Nadab, Gedor, Ahio, Zechariah, and Mikloth. All of the men of the Matrites were huge—towering above Samuel and his compan-ions but also broad of shoulder and thick in the chest and limbs.

Ner also introduced them to his son Kish, a long-limbed, black-haired, muscular monster of a man Samuel's age whose renown in battle was already talked about from Dan to Be'ersheba. *Kish Kephir*, he was called, *Lion of the Rocks*—a name earned during a battle on the heights of a stony crag not far from Gibeon.

"I would like for my son, Saul, to meet you as well," said Kish, his voice a gravelly rumble. Samuel noticed that his mouth hardly moved in his lean face when he spoke. "But I did not know to expect you this morning. Saul is tending to the herds on the hills to the west. He will be disappointed that he was not here to greet the Seer of Ramathaim."

"It seems likely that we will meet soon enough," said Samuel.

"At Mizpah," said Ner, nodding. "We are already preparing to an-swer the summons."

Samuel clapped a hand on Ner's thick shoulder. "I confess I was relying on your ability to convince the men of Gibeah and its dependent towns to come. But I am afraid that is not likely to be the last thing I ask of you. No matter how things turn out at Mizpah, we will need men to lead a nation that is lost after Avdon's death."

"Are you continuing on to Nob, then?" Ner asked, shrugging off the compliment.

Samuel nodded. "We leave for the Tabernacle immediately. I want to be on my way back to Mizpah with High Priest Ahitub by tomorrow morning."

"The route is dangerous, I am afraid," said Ner.

"Dangerous?" Manoah looked at him askance. "On the highway? In the heart of Israel?"

"A band of Philistines has been patrolling the road. They are at least forty strong, and heavily armed. They have thus far let travelers pass unmolested, but rumor suggests they are looking for you, Seer."

Samuel closed his eyes and sighed. "Have you seen the garrison commander who leads them?"

Ner nodded. "An ugly fellow, with a strange growth on his neck…"

"Glaucus." Samuel shook his head. "I did not imagine he would follow me this far."

"There is something else as well," Kish rumbled. "I almost hesitate to speak of it, as it may be nothing more than a story."

"A story about what?" asked Manoah.

Kish shrugged. "Several patrols have come back with tales of a strange figure glimpsed in the night: a tall, black-skinned man haunting the shadows. And there have been deaths—bodies of sentries or other soldiers found, throats cut or dead without any apparent cause. As I said, it is probably only rumor—."

"It is more than rumor," said Tahash.

"Indeed?" Ner pursed his lips. "You seem to be the destination for more than one traveler, Seer."

Kish turned to his father. "Let me join my hand to theirs, Father. Let me lend what aid I can in helping them get to Nob safely."

Ner looked at his son for a moment. Samuel saw that it was not hesitation, though: *pupils widening, features softening, head cocked at the slightest angle, corners of the mouth upturned ever-so-slightly.* It was not hesitation. It was pride.

"Gather your things my son—that is, if you will have him." He directed the last at Samuel.

"We will have him," Samuel answered. "But only if you assure me that his absence will not deter you in any way from leading the men of Gibeah to Mizpah."

"I have already sent messengers to Beriah, the chief of the Elders of Benjamin," Ner answered. "He will join his forces with our own. We will be at Mizpah to welcome you when you arrive."

Samuel looked over at Reuel and smiled. "Then we will bring Ahitub to you there. May Jehovah be with us all."

23

Cheran arrived back at Joppa in the early morning hours, just as the wind began to force the palms and Aleppo pines perched along the shore to bow to its authority, and to toy with the gulls and cormorants overhead, tossing and swinging them like toys. He felt a palpable sense of relief on hearing the rhythmic surge of the surf and the screams of the gulls—they were the sounds of his second home, here with his in-laws.

Only when he was within sight of the walls did he realize the extent of his own exhaustion. He had traveled non-stop since leaving Naioth, and fears for the safety of his family had haunted every step. His one comfort on the journey had been that he no longer felt any concern about Gavriel. He knew that the Prophet Samuel would take care of him—that his son was safer and in better hands now than Cheran's own.

He climbed the ascending road toward Joppa's gate, paralleling the beach. He breathed deeply of the salt air and the smell of seaweed decaying on the low ledge of rock that formed the natural breakwater that made Joppa's harbor the most valued on the eastern shore of the Great Sea.

Foaming waves swept through the gap in the middle of the barrier, just wide enough for a ship to pass through if it were too drafty to approach through the shallow waters of the broad, northern entrance. Half a dozen ships were anchored in the harbor; on one of them, the crew was shipping the oars and pulling the anchor chain. The wind carried their shouts and the hollow rattling of the oars in their oarlocks to him even over the wash of the surf.

He reached the gate. It was open, as was typical of Joppa--the stream of traders, merchants, and travelers did not stop day or night, and a city like Joppa that relied on their good will did all it could to be accommodating to their business. There was very little activity in the square yet—Joppa was not a town of farmers who rose before dawn. Some fishermen were already on the water in their boats, but the fish along the coast were more active in the early afternoon and the evening.

He made his way down the quiet, shadowed streets to his in-laws' home. Inside, it was dark and quiet and deserted. A shard of pottery had been left on a lamp stand—the only thing out of place in the tidy house. He picked it up and turned it over. On the back marks had been inscribed: the letters G and R and an extremely rough sketch of what he thought must be a sheep. He allowed himself a smile. *GR. Gath-Rimmon.* His wife and children and their relatives had traveled together to their home in Gath-Rimmon to see if it was safe and to care for their animals.

For a moment, he wondered if he really should feel relieved—their decision had put them closer to Philistine-occupied territory, but they would know to be on their guard while there, and his father-in-law was a wise man.

There was a little food in a basket hung from the ceiling: cakes of pressed figs and raisins. He took one of each and made his way back toward the city gate, nibbling on them.

At the gate, Joppa was beginning to wake. Shop and market owners were laying out their wares on low tables or rugs spread atop the packed earth. Yawning olive oil merchants carried earthenware jugs on their shoulders to their booth near the northern gatehouse. Spice traders, their fingertips orange or yellow from handling their wares, laid out bowls of ochre, red, umber, brown, and green powders in neat rows on the ground at their feet.

Cheran felt more relaxed than he had in days, and he climbed the stone steps to the top of the gatehouse tower, rested his elbows on the battlements and munched contentedly on the date cake. Sentries leaned on their spears at the city's corner towers and in a few places along the wall. Cheran allowed himself to believe that his family was safe, waiting for him in Gath-

Rimmon. He breathed deeply of the sea air and let the warmth of the rising sun behind him seep into his bones.

One of the sentries wandered over. "North, South, or East?"

It took Cheran a moment to realize what the man was asking. "Oh—from the east, from Ramathaim."

The guard nodded. "Then no doubt you've already heard of the summons."

"Summons? No."

The guard smiled subtly, as a man who knows he has a story to tell that will please or surprise his audience. "My brother just returned from Avdon's funeral late last night."

"Judge Avdon? He is dead?"

The guard chuckled. "You have been out of touch, haven't you? Yes, Avdon is dead—killed by one of his sons, some are saying."

"Is there a Judge to replace him?"

"Not yet. But—as I was about to tell you—the Prophet Samuel has summoned the entire nation to Mizpah. Some think he will choose a new Judge there."

"Why has Samuel summoned the whole nation? He does not need the Chieftains or the Elders to choose a Judge."

The guard shrugged. "I do not know. Perhaps we are to be readied for war."

Cheran would have asked more questions, but the rattling of six wagons passing through the gate below drew both of their attention. The guard wandered down the battlements to talk to the other men on duty.

Cheran watched the wagons form a line in the square, the oxen that pulled them stretching in their yokes to try to nibble at the grain mounded on the wagons in front of them.

The drivers began talking with the few Joppans who were in the square. It was a sizable delivery even for a port city like Joppa—the wagons were piled high, and only the taut camel skin stretched over the bulging load kept the grain from spilling over the sideboards. Cheran estimated that the cargo would fill the hold of at least two Phoenician transport ships completely, perhaps with grain left over for a third.

He rubbed sleep from his eyes, yawning; he could feel the gusting wind blow into his open mouth, as though it was trying to suffocate him.

When he opened his eyes, he thought that he saw something move under one of the wagons' camel-skin coverings.

He stared at the spot, but the movement was not repeated. He tried to tell himself that it was only a rat, stowed away and stuffing himself on freshly harvested barley, but his gut warned him otherwise. Not sure what he was doing, he started back down the steps to the courtyard.

The flagstone landing of the stairway deposited him only a few paces from the nearest wagon, but Cheran was surprised to be met there by one of the drivers. The man was beardless, like an Egyptian or a Philistine, with thick, curly, brown hair and hazel eyes.

"May you have peace, my lord," the man said, his accent thick. He stood directly between Cheran and the wagon.

Something in the man's face made Cheran uncomfortable—a sneer perhaps, hidden in the corners of his eyes. "And peace be with you," he answered. Acting as though he was in a hurry to get somewhere, he tried to walk past the man. The driver put his arm around Cheran's shoulder and began gently but forcibly steering him away from the wagon. "Do you have some interest in our grain, my lord?" he asked.

At that moment, a trumpet rang out from the wall. The cries of the sentries echoed through the city: "To arms! To arms!"

Cheran broke away from the merchant, who smiled at him coldly. The man's reaction angered him, but he did not have time to think about it. He raced with other Joppans back up the stairs to the top of the wall as guards pulled the gates closed and dropped their heavy crossbar into place with a thud that echoed across the square.

Atop he wall he saw the reason for the alarm: ships were sailing into the harbor through the gap in the breakwater—a dozen had already entered, and more were coming as he watched: swan-prowed ships, every one filled with armed and armored Philistine soldiers.

24

Joppans ran from the city streets in droves, swords and spears in their hands; the battlements on the sea-facing western wall filled with men and spears. Guardsmen were handing out weapons, and a spear was shoved into Cheran's hands.

The ships began beaching, their passengers disembarking in a rush of shouts and the flash of drawn swords. Scattered among the regular soldiers, Cheran could see the black uniforms of the dreaded Gedhudhra and the lean forms of their hounds.

"They come only by ship and leave behind their horses and chariots?" a man standing beside him wondered aloud. "They will never make it over the wall!"

Cheran was not a warrior, but he knew this was no siege. There were not enough troops to surround the city effectively; it was too easy for Joppa to receive reinforcements by sea…

An instant too late, he realized his mistake. An explosion of sound and movement from the square spun him around. Dozens of Gedhudhra leapt from under the skin coverings on the wagons, bursting from their hiding places within the piles of grain. They were on the gate guards in seconds, slaughtering them and removing the gate's crossbar before any of the Joppans could react.

The gates swung open as the attackers outside the walls reached it and Philistine warriors flooded, unhindered, into the city square.

The soldiers around Cheran all pushed for the stairways at once; those who were unable to get down hurled their spears or fired their arrows into the enemies below them. Cheran raised his own spear, but by the time he did so Philistines were tangled with Joppans and he dared not throw it.

Men were pushing him from behind, and he was swept onto the stairs and down them. The flashing of swords, the ear-splitting ringing of iron weapons, a red mist of blood and the screams of the dying surrounded him. For an instant, through the crowds he glimpsed a handful of Joppa's Elders leading dozens of men in a charge from one flank.

Then a sword blade whipped past a handbreadth from his nose and he threw himself backward instinctively, smashing against the bronze edging of a shield behind him. The bearer—Israelite or Philistine, he did not know—pushed him away violently, and he stumbled forward, leaning on his spear shaft to catch himself. The same Philistine who had leveled the first blow at him was swinging again, but the iron sword bit into the oak shaft in Cheran's hands. He twisted the spear and nearly succeeded in pulling the blade from the man's hands, then jabbed the spearhead in his direction.

Something heavy slammed into him from behind and he pitched forward, forearms scraping on the rocky ground. In a maze of moving legs and fallen bodies he crawled away as quickly as he could, then scrambled to his feet and, ducking and dodging, ran from the melee.

He broke free of the crowd near a booth where a potter's wares had been smashed and trampled into the rug on which they had been displayed. Backing up against the wall he paused to get his breath.

Movement atop the houses nearby caught his eye. Philistines were running there, carrying large, clay vessels with lit torches attached to their wooden lids. One of them paused twenty-five paces from where Cheran stood and tossed the vessel into the street below him.

It hit the ground and exploded in a great *whoosh* of flame. Cheran was aware for an instant of searing heat and a feeling like a massive fist slamming into his chest. The next thing he knew he was laying on his back on the ground, his face painfully hot, his ears ringing, struggling to get air back into his burning lungs.

Everything around him—dry earth, stone steps, plastered walls—was on fire. He crawled to his feet, coughing, and stumbled away. He managed to find his way down another street and fell against the outer wall of a house's courtyard, coughing uncontrollably. He heard another explosion somewhere nearby, followed by the sound of people screaming.

He forced himself to keep moving. Arrows hissed overhead, their tips streaming flames as they carried destruction to other parts of the city. He was almost trampled by a donkey galloping madly past, its fur singed and still smoking. The whole city was going up in flame, as though the attackers did not care what spoil remained for them to carry away.

He turned down an alley, trying now to make his way to the wall, hoping to find some postern gate through which he could escape. He emerged onto a broader avenue, choked with battling soldiers and screaming, fleeing Joppans. A knot of Gedhudhra was moving in formation down the street, their swords ablaze. Whenever they made contact with a person, weapon, or shield, fire splashed like liquid from their blades onto whatever was nearby, leaving a path of fear and flame in their wake.

Cheran ducked into another alley before he was caught up in the fighting again. Ahead of him two women were herding and carrying their children away from the conflagration. He paused, trying to get his bearings. The air around him was thick with smoke, and he realized he had only a guess as to which direction he was facing.

Shouts of command and battle cries burst out behind him and he turned, startled. Back on the avenue, the Joppans had organized themselves into a battle line at last and managed an orderly charge against the Philistines. Cheran saw the two forces meet in the choking air. The Gedhudhra and armored Philistine troops cut through the defenders' ranks almost effortlessly, spilling bodies onto either side of the road. He turned again and fled down the alley.

He emerged on another street and caught a glimpse of what he thought to be the southern wall some distance ahead of him before the smoke shrouded his view again. Then he looked down and realized that he was standing amidst dozens of dead bodies—men, women, and even children lying in pools of blood and offal in the dusty street.

He felt himself unraveling and knew only that he must escape—all other desires were driven from his mind by the incomprehensible carnage and the melting of his heart. His legs were moving him forward, toward the wall he had seen, but he could not seem to collect his thoughts.

The swirling smoke parted again, affording him another glimpse of the city wall. Not far from where he walked, a home had been built against the fortifications and its inhabitants had set up a ladder leading from its roof to the top of the battlements. Cheran did not think about what he would do once he reached the top of the wall. He only knew that the ladder could take him out of the choking air, away from the screams and the death that threatened to swallow him up.

He heard someone approaching and ducked through a gate and into a courtyard. The door to the home inside was open, and the interior of the house yawned dark and still. He pushed his back against the inside of the courtyard wall and waited, trying to slow his labored breathing.

He heard a whimpering cry from somewhere to his left and turned his head slowly toward the sound. From where he stood, he could see the bare calf and foot of a young leg poking out from behind a small, upturned cart. He shuffled toward it, unconsciously trying to be quiet even though any sound he made would have been easily masked by the cacophony all around him.

He crouched when he reached the cart and the person hiding must have seen him at last, because he or she cried out in terror and began crawling backwards away from him. An instant later he saw that it was a son of fourteen or fifteen years, his face streaked with dirt, tears, and blood.

"Sshh!" Cheran held out his hands imploringly. "Sshh!"

The boy curled into a fetal ball and began to cry. Cheran glanced over his shoulder to make sure no one was coming through the gate, and then eased closer. "I am a son of Israel. I am a friend," he whispered.

The boy's reaction was unchanged. He rocked back and forth a little, whimpering. Cheran wanted to take him in his arms, but he sensed that any touch would be too much for the boy at the moment.

Instead, he kept talking in a low voice. "I can help you get out. I can help you escape."

The boy glanced over at him with wide eyes and the rocking slowed.

"Do you want to escape? I can help you to get free."

The boy stopped moving and stared at him, his chin quivering.

"We need to move quickly," Cheran said. "I need you to get up now, and follow me."

To his surprise, the boy did as he was asked, standing with his shoulders pulled together and his head sunk into them as though he were expecting a blow.

Cheran nodded encouragingly. "Come quickly."

He moved to the courtyard gate and the boy followed, a silent shadow so close behind him that Cheran was afraid he would tread on his heels as they walked.

He glanced at the avenue outside. Nothing moved except the smoke hanging like a shroud over the haphazardly scattered bodies. He took a deep breath and felt his heart pounding against his ribs. "Now!" he whispered.

They dashed into the avenue. Cheran led his shadow south towards the wall he had seen earlier. They skirted burning debris and corpses, some of them hacked and scorched beyond all recognition.

Something moved in the smoke ahead and Cheran leapt for the concealment of a nearby wall. He reached for the boy to pull him to cover as well but the child instinctively recoiled, his eyes widening and his teeth bared.

A knot of Philistine soldiers stepped from the smoke. Cheran was hidden from their view, but the boy still stood in the open roadway. They saw him immediately. The boy screamed and began fleeing. Cheran looked back and forth from the soldiers to the boy's back, trying to figure out what he could do.

Then one of the Philistines raised his bow and shot. The boy's arms spread wide and he fell on his face on the dust of the roadway. The arrow clattered against a fence or gate farther down the road.

Cheran squeezed his eyes shut, gritting his teeth. He wiped his running nose with the back of his hand, and it came away wet with tears and muddy mucus.

He glanced around in a panic and immediately saw across the road a courtyard with a wooden ladder ascending to the roof of a white-plastered house. *Go! Go now! Do not think!* he urged himself, and scrambled to his feet. Eyes locked on his goal, he dashed across the road and through the gate, not stopping or even looking at anything until his fingers were wrapped around the ladder's smooth stringers.

He took a deep breath, coughing on inhaling some of the smoke, and climbed. As he cleared the height of the walls, he felt a vast emptiness at his back, as though he were exposed to the view of the entire world. Stepping from the last rungs over the parapet and onto the roof, he dropped to a crouch and risked a glance back toward the street.

Three Philistine soldiers were standing there, staring at him.

He turned and ran across the roof, their shouts and the sounds of their footfalls like a wind at his back. He reached the edge of the roof and leapt from the parapet to the next roof, a distance equal to his own height. He fell to one knee when he landed but pulled himself back up and continued running.

At the edge of the next roof he paused and looked over his shoulder. The soldiers had climbed the ladder and were following him across the housetops. He stepped onto the parapet in front of him and leapt again over the gap between houses, planting one sandal on the parapet of the next roof, rolling his weight forward to land awkwardly on his knee and shoulder atop layers of drying strands of flax.

The soldiers were shouting behind him again, and an arrow whispered past his head and bounced off the rooftop ahead of him. Cheran ran in a crouch across the housetop to the opposite parapet. A ladder poked up from the other side of it.

Sure that an arrow was about to pierce his back he steeled himself, then swung over the parapet and half-climbed, half-slid down the ladder to the alleyway between the houses. Without looking back he ran as fast as he could down the alley toward the city wall.

When he emerged from between the houses, he could see a postern gate in the wall ahead of him. He stumbled toward it, eyes stinging in the swirling smoke. He reached the wall as the smoke thickened and he felt his way along the stones, coughing and squeezing his eyes shut. More shouts sounded from across the street and an arrow struck the wall next to his head. He ducked and ran as quickly as his near-blindness would allow.

His searching hands found the wood of the postern. He fumbled with the latch as another arrow *thunked* into the oak planks. Then a searing pain burned across his left arm and he flinched away, yelping, even as a third arrow bounced off of the gate. His tunic sleeve was torn and blood flowed down his bicep to his elbow.

He put his shoulder to the postern and it ground open. Clutching his wounded arm in his right hand, he stumbled out of the city of Joppa toward the cover of the trees.

26

The big Benjaminite Kish joined Samuel, Reuel, Tahash, Manoah, and Samson as they left Gibeah, retracing their steps for a short distance to the north. The son of Ner appeared in a leather kilt and sandals laced up to his knees. He wore nothing else but a pair of wide, leather belts crossing each other over his broad, hairy chest and passing over the slopes of muscle that descended from his thick neck to his burly shoulders. A wide-bladed, bronze battle axe hung from the straps on his back; a sling was tucked into his belt next to a stone pouch.

On re-connecting with the main road, they headed south again, passing through the settlements that dotted the hills on either side of them, growing denser the farther they traveled.

The road paralleled a chain of rounded, limestone hills that reached all the way to Jerusalem and beyond: Mount Scopus, upon which Nob was built; the Mount of Olives, covered in clusters of palm, myrtle, oil, and its namesake trees; and the Mount of Ruination, only an short distance from the base of the peaks of Zion and Moriah, on which Jerusalem was built.

JUDGE OF ISRAEL

Clouds rolled in from the west and settled into a grey-blue mass overhead, darkening the morning's light, heavy with the scent of rain. Thunder rumbled ominously from the mountains of Samaria.

They were within sight of the road that led east to Nob when Kish stopped and pointed at the softer earth at the edge of the road.

"Sons of Philistia," he said.

The dirt was churned by the hoofs of shod horses and the narrow tracks of iron-bound chariot wheels.

The sight of the markings brought memories back to Samuel in a rush, images of the last time he had seen Philistines near the Tabernacle, of fell Gedhudhra pouring into Shiloh like a black scourge, limned by the fire of the city burning...

Manoah scowled. "The dogs think they can foray through Israel with impunity." He spat on the tracks.

Almost simultaneously, it began to rain, a torrential downpour that soaked everything in moments.

"I guess you should not have spat," said Samson wryly.

They plodded forward as the road beneath their feet melted into slime. Water poured in broadening rivulets from the high ground to their left, spilled across the road in swirling masses of muck, then rushed down the shallow, rocky ditch on their right.

Samuel hunched his shoulders, the cowl of his traveling cloak pulled tight around his head. Rain dripped from its edge onto his nose and cheeks and some of it seemed to have somehow found its way to the back of his neck. Through the dim light ahead, he saw the road disappear into darkness beneath a grove of cedars. The companions hurried forward toward the broad, sheltering branches.

Under the cedars it was even darker, but the rain slowed to larger drops falling from the ceiling of branches, the broad boughs deflecting most of the downpour. Shaking the drops from his cowl, Samuel saw that there were still patches of completely dry ground around the bases of some of the trees.

"Do we wait here for the rain to ease, or try to make it to Nob as quickly as possible?" Samson asked, half-shouting to make himself heard over the rain.

Kish squinted up through the branches at the dark sky. "Let us put off that decision until we get to the far side of the grove. Perhaps the rain will have lightened by then."

Cold and uncomfortable, they started forward again. They had not taken a dozen steps when a spear hurtled silently from the darkness to their left. Samuel saw it only as a hint of movement in the corner of his eye, and then Tahash was shoving him out of the way, shouting. As though the entire world had slowed, Samuel watched the whirling spearhead slide along Tahash's ribs, parting the fabric of his tunic, before vanishing into the trees on the other side of the road.

Four swords were drawn almost in unison and the group formed a rough circle, peering into the shadows below the trees. Nothing moved. No birds called; no rodents scurried in the underbrush or among the dripping tree branches. Kish slowly hung his axe over his shoulder and unwound his sling from his belt, drew a stone half the size of his fist from a pouch at his side, and placed it in the sling's hollow.

All remained silent. "Keep moving!" ordered Manoah. "Let us be the ones to decide where we next meet this shadow."

They crept forward. Samuel saw a slender line of red, like a random seam across Tahash's tunic. Their eyes searched the forest to their left, every muscle tensed in expectation.

Samuel did not even hear the next attack. Pain pricked his shoulder, as from the bite of a fly, and he slapped at it. His hands encountered, not a fly, but a slender dart, the length of a finger, no thicker than a stalk of wheat, a bundle of downy, yellow feathers at its tail.

He pulled it free—it had barely penetrated his skin. Its tip was coated in some black substance.

"Sons of Belial!" said Manoah, and then another dart appeared in Reuel's neck, buried almost to the feathers. The young prophet yanked it free.

"Run!" said Tahash.

They raced down the road, Manoah and Samson swinging into a rearguard position. Samson clutched his shield now on his left arm, peering beyond it at the shadows beneath the trees as they ran.

Samuel saw the road emerge from the grove ahead. The rain had not eased, but the sheltering branches of the cedars had turned from a welcome protection to a lurking place for unnamed fears.

They were just about to break clear of the trees when a shape, as black as tar, swung from the branches above them. Long, bare legs smashed into Tahash's chest, hurling him backward into Kish, and both of them went down in a heap of flailing limbs. The black figure swung back onto a thick limb, clutching it like a monkey, then leapt again and landed in a silent crouch in front of Samuel.

Manoah and Samson launched themselves at it, howling. The figure spun, one leg raised to shoulder height, and kicked Manoah in the chin, sending the big Danite spinning off the road and into the brush. He kicked again toward Samson but the young man ducked and lunged with his sword. The black figure danced clear of the blow, drawing his strange, curved knife in the same movement. Before Samson could recover from his lunge, the Hunter's long fingers clamped down on the Danite's wrist, squeezing and shaking, ropelike muscles taught beneath his ebon skin. Samson roared with pain, and smashed his shield against the man's shoulder, but their attacker held on until the sword fell from Samson's nerveless fingers. The Hunter, still gripping Samson's wrist, leapt from the ground, spinning his body horizontally to land a solid kick against the side of Samson's face. Samson tumbled from the road as well.

The black figure turned to face Samuel. The Prophet clutched his staff, unable to breathe. Only seconds had passed since the man had swung down from the trees and all four of Samuel's protectors were on the ground or trying to clamber back to their feet.

The Hunter smiled at him, revealing pointed, white teeth. "Nimehatari. Nimekifo, matokeo ya utafutaji kwa-ungo."

Samuel had only the briefest of instants to hold out his staff in front of him in an attempt at defense when the Hunter dove for him. The strange, curved knife flashed, and the vermilion staff fell in two pieces, severed as though it were a dried reed. The Hunter smiled at Samuel again. "Kifo."

Samuel dropped one half of the staff, holding the other in both hands as if it was a sword.

At that moment something happened that no one could have predicted. Lightning flashed directly above them, striking a treetop and raining sparks down on all of their heads. The thunder did not rumble—it erupted, shaking the ground and knocking the breath from Samuel's lungs. A dead branch, as thick as a man's thigh, crashed through brittle boughs above them and landed with stunning force on the Hunter's shoulder. The big man all but collapsed under the impact, shrieking like a cat and stumbling clear, his shoulder torn and bleeding.

Samuel glanced behind him; Manoah and Samson were on their feet again, blades in hand, moving forward; Tahash and Kish, still looking unsure on his feet, were not far behind. Reuel was standing unnaturally still in the road, white-faced, his eyes distant and glassy.

The Hunter crouched and then leapt straight up, his long legs launching him high enough to grab an overhanging tree limb. Pulling himself up with the agility of a monkey, he leapt to another tree, swung from one branch to the next, and slung himself to the ground among the underbrush. He glanced back once, eyes narrowed with hatred, and vanished without a sound into the forest.

The company stood in silence for several moments. Samson moved first, running into the woods—although not in the direction the Hunter had disappeared.

"Samson!" Manoah yelled. "What are you doing?"

Kish moved unsteadily to follow him. "That thing could still be out there!"

Samson was scanning the forest floor. "It's gone!"

"Of course it's gone!" said Manoah.

"No! The spear! The spear he threw is gone."

"Nonsense," said Manoah. "It's just hidden..."

Samson shook his head. "I watched it land—it stuck into this tree." He pointed at the trunk of a sycamore. "Look—here is the mark it left."

"Dog! Son of Belial!" Manoah growled, slashing through a tree limb as thick as his arm. "Who sent this devil to haunt our steps?"

They were quiet for a moment, searching the shadows under the trees.

"Could he have had someone else with him?" asked Kish.

"If he did, why didn't they come to his aid?" asked Tahash.

Samson walked back toward them. "And if he didn't...then how did he retrieve the spear?"

Thunder boomed again nearby and the rain seemed to intensify. "We have no time for these questions now," said Manoah. "We need to get moving."

Samuel grasped Reuel's shoulders. "Are you alright?"

Reuel stared at him, pallid forehead wrinkled, eyes still glassy. "I do not know..."

The rest of the company was already moving. Samuel draped Reuel's arm across his own shoulders and supported him. "Come along—we will be at Nob soon enough."

Reuel nodded weakly and allowed himself to be led forward.

They left the cover of the trees. The road was cut into the side of a steep hill and a distance ahead of them it transversed a narrow ravine, filled now with rushing, muddy water. To their right, the water fell in a widening waterfall into the depths of a valley below. Samuel could just hear Manoah's voice over the cataract, yelling at Samson. "Did you even wound him?"

Reuel was getting heavier. "Manoah!" Samuel strained to be heard over the sound of the raging water. "Something is wrong with Reuel! I think the dart was poisoned!"

Samson ran back and draped Reuel's other arm over his own shoulders. Together, he and Samuel helped the near-unconscious man to stumble forward.

"You were also hit—is it alright with you?" Manoah asked.

"It barely punctured my skin," Samuel said.

They reached the ravine and paused, looking for the best way to cross the churning cascade to reach the road on the other side.

"The underlying roadbed is sound!" shouted Kish. "Hold onto each other, and trust in your staves if you have them!"

They stepped into the flow. The current sucked at their legs, but the water was no deeper than their knees. At one point Samuel looked down the valley where the flood disappeared into a distant canyon, growing stronger as the flow was fed by dozens of other streams and rivulets.

The volume of water swelled. Rocks and branches washed against Samuel's legs, threatening to knock him over. He stumbled forward.

"Run!" Kish suddenly roared.

Instinctively, Samuel looked up. A torrent of dark water crashed toward them, a flash flood of mud and debris. He leapt forward, pulling Reuel with him; to his right, Samson was doing the same, fear etched on his young face.

The water hit them like a wall of rock, slamming Samuel down on his face against the roadbed. He held his breath and tried desperately to claw his way free of the flood. At one point he grabbed someone's leg, and then felt them pulled away by the force of the current.

Then arms were under his armpits, hauling him out of the mud, dragging him backward on his heels to the road beyond the flood. Coughing and wiping muck from his face and eyes he turned to see that it was Samson that had pulled him clear. Kish was dragging Tahash out in much the same way, and Manoah was thrashing around in knee-deep water, trying to keep his footing.

Then Samuel saw Reuel. Beyond Manoah, the young man's head pushed clear of the brown water for a moment, panic in his mud-smeared eyes.

"Reuel!" Samuel yelled, scrambling to his feet.

Kish was beside him, and they splashed back into the flood together. Reuel's head vanished again, then came up a little farther away, his arms flailing as he tried to grab anything solid. The flood was sweeping him toward the far edge of the roadbed.

"Reuel!" Samuel yelled again, his voice drowned out by the cacophony. Then something heavy under the flowing water slammed against his ankles and he went down in the mud, thrashing. When he stood again, Kish was still splashing toward Reuel; Manoah a few paces ahead of him.

"Samuel!" he heard Reuel yell, his voice thin over the tumult. Then the shoulder of the roadbed under the flood collapsed, washing into the valley below with a roar. Reuel went with it, vanishing in a maelstrom of debris and brown foam.

Samuel pushed forward as fast as the rising water would allow, but then more of the road began to collapse, its edge disappearing as though an invisible mouth was eating it away, vanishing in the newly born river flowing far down into the valley below.

Samuel scrambled clear of the collapse. With a roar, the entire road sloughed off, leaving only a gaping gouge in the side of the hill, filled instantly by the rushing waterfall.

"Reuel!" Samuel yelled again, his voice hoarse and completely swallowed up by the sound of the storm.

But Reuel was gone.

27

They searched for nearly half of the day for Reuel, clambering down mud-slick slopes into the sodden valley to comb both sides of the river. The rain eased, then stopped, but the clouds remained—a dark, glowering presence looming over their search, as though threatening to renew its onslaught at any moment.

"He could be halfway to the Dead Sea by now," Manoah said when they finally re-assembled in the late afternoon, exhausted and covered in filth.

"Or buried in the mud beneath our feet," said Tahash.

Samuel glared at him, even though he knew that the young Ephraimite was right.

"We cannot give up while any hope remains," said Samuel, his voice hoarse from calling his friend's name.

Manoah shook his head in agreement. "No. But neither can we delay any longer our quest to bring Ahitub to Mizpah."

There was a long pause as the members of the fellowship faced each other, no one wanting to say what they all knew must be said.

"Then here we must part ways," said Kish at last.

Manoah nodded. "Here is what I suggest: Samuel—you must continue to Nob. It is you who must bring the High Priest to Mizpah. Searching for Reuel will be a bitter and hopeless task, so I volunteer myself and Samson to do it. Tahash, Kish—you can escort the Prophet to Nob. If Jehovah is willing, we will meet again at Mizpah."

Samuel sighed, hesitant to make a decision that could someday end up haunting him. "I am willing to accept your advice…"

"It was not advice," said Manoah. "Only ideas. This decision is yours."

"For myself," interjected Tahash, "I am staying with Samuel, whatever you others may do. His and my destinies lie together."

"Perhaps," interjected Samson, "after we find Reuel, my father and I can travel back to Naioth for you and make sure that your family and the *Beneh* have made it safely to Mizpah."

"That would, indeed, ease my heart," said Samuel.

"It is settled, then?" Kish was anxious to leave. None of them had forgotten the tall, black warrior who was hunting them.

Samuel nodded. They shouldered their provisions. Kish and Tahash led Samuel up the steep slope toward the road to Nob.

"May Jehovah be with you," Samuel said, bowing to Manoah and Samson. "May He grant success to your hands."

They parted as the afternoon was beginning to wane, the change almost imperceptible beneath the heavy clouds. Samuel found a stick in the debris to replace his staff. He deliberately chose one that was crooked and knotted and more than a little uncomfortable to his hand; somehow the discomfort seemed like a fitting punishment for allowing his vermilion staff to be destroyed, and for allowing its giver to be lost.

He clambered up the hill behind Kish and Tahash, slogging through the still-sodden ground. They reached the road at last and, as the water drained and the soil became dry again, they began shedding the mud that caked their legs and feet. Each step became lighter, but it did not feel that way to Samuel.

They followed the road as it circled the base of Mount Scopus, moving through ancient forests and ascending toward the hilltop on which the city of Nob was built.

The walk was surreal to Samuel. His friend, his loyal companion, was gone. He was overwhelmed, but not with sorrow or even a sense of loss. He was overwhelmed by his lack of emotion, his inability to latch onto any feeling and truly make it his own. Reuel was almost like a son to him, and yet he could summon nothing more than a sense of emptiness and unease. Samuel wondered what was wrong within himself that he would react to his friend's loss with such ambiguity. Why was he not weeping uncontrollably? Why was he not completely incapacitated, as he knew Reuel would have been had their positions been reversed?

Instead of anguish, he felt as if it were not only wrong, but somehow impossible for him to carry on with his life after Reuel's disappearance. How could he put one foot in front of the other, continuing in his quest, acting as if it had not happened? He knew that, as Manoah had said, they could not stop: events had been put in motion that involved the entire nation. The children of Israel were assembling at Mizpah and Samuel had to bring the High Priest to them.

But to carry on felt like some sort of betrayal of Samuel's friendship with Reuel. Reuel deserved more than a few moments' reflection before carrying on with life as it had been before his death. It did Samuel no good to tell himself that it was what Reuel would have wanted. What his friend wanted and what he deserved were two different things, as they were with all people.

How ironic it was that people almost never got either one.

He was still caught in his own thoughts when Tahash appeared next to him and laid a hand briefly on his shoulder.

"I have prayed that Jehovah watch over Reuel," he said.

"Thank you," said Samuel. "I will continue to hope that prayer is answered."

Tahash glanced forward to where Kish led them, eight or ten paces ahead. "I hoped to talk to you alone for a few moments."

"Speak," said Samuel. "My ears are uncovered."

"On the day that you were called as a Prophet..." Tahash hesitated, licking his lips. "You heard Jehovah's voice, I know, but...but was there anything else that made you feel certain you were Jehovah's choice for this assignment?"

Samuel frowned, confused. "Anything else?"

"A feeling—a sense of knowing, deep inside, that this was now your purpose in life?"

Samuel shrugged. The rawness of his sense of loss brought a rare candor to his lips. "To be honest, Tahash, I have always had my doubts about my choosing—I still do, to this day. It seems unbelievable that I could possibly be the one Jehovah has chosen for His Prophet. But He has spoken to me, and asked me to repeat His words to His people—and that makes me, by definition, a Prophet."

"Exactly!" Tahash's eyes widened, and he nodded enthusiastically. "You *knew* that you were a Prophet, beyond all doubt, whatever anyone else said or believed!"

"There were many who doubted at first—there are still those who doubt," he said, thinking of his brothers.

"Woe to the doubters," Tahash said. "They cannot undo what God has done. You yourself well know that you are the Prophet—that He has called you to this lofty purpose. There is no point in fighting it."

Samuel suddenly wondered what it was that Tahash was talking about. Obviously there was more going on in the young man's head than idle curiosity about Samuel's appointment.

"What is this about?" he asked.

Tahash looked around as though to make sure they were not being overheard. "I, too, have received an appointment at Jehovah's Hands," he whispered.

Samuel stopped walking. "What? When?"

Tahash grasped his elbow and urged him forward. "I do not wish everyone to know about this yet," he said. "I do not wish to become an object of adoration to others."

"Why would you become an object of adoration, Tahash? What has happened?"

Tahash's Adam's apple lurched. "I have been chosen to be the commander of Israel's armies at the upcoming battle."

Samuel was taken aback. "I was not even certain there was going to be an upcoming battle! When did you receive this appointment? Why did you not say anything?"

Tahash's brow furrowed. "It was not at a specific time...it is more of an understanding that has been growing within me ever since you came to Pirathon..." He looked up at the sky, squinting, as though trying to recapture a memory. "I feel it in my heart, as though Jehovah Himself had spoken to me."

"As though? So Jehovah has not...You believe you are appointed because you *feel* it is so?"

Tahash looked over at him sharply. "You just told me yourself that you felt you were a Prophet, beyond all doubt—that in spite of what others might think, you knew it was true."

"But Tahash—I know because...because Jehovah *does* speak to me."

Tahash nodded excitedly again. "Yes—yes! For you, the appointment comes with that assurance. For me, though, more faith is required. Being chosen as the commander of the army of God is not accompanied by any sign. It cannot be proven to those who will not believe until that day that I take up my task at the head of the warriors of Israel."

"Are you sure about this, my brother?" Samuel asked. "Are you sure of what you feel?"

Tahash clapped a hand on Samuel's shoulder. His eyes were wild. "More sure than I have been of anything in my life." He glanced forward at Kish. "Let us speak no more of it, though. I do not wish to reveal myself yet."

He nodded knowingly to Samuel and fell back behind him on the road.

Reveal myself? Samuel thought. The whole situation did not feel right, although Samuel had to admit that his own appointment must have seemed equally strange to the people around him when it had happened. Did he have the right to question what Tahash said—to accuse him, even in his own heart, of deception? Who was he to say that Tahash could not have been chosen by God for a special task?

He wondered if his hesitancy to believe the young man's claim was actually his own arrogant belief that Jehovah would not have made such an appointment without telling him first.

He decided to let the matter rest for the time being, and hoped that in the coming days Jehovah would make his path clear.

Samuel breathed a sigh of relief when they came in sight of the walls of Nob, although seeing armored guards permanently posted outside the gate, spears at the ready, made him unspeakably sad. When he was a child the Tabernacle guardsmen had been ceremonial and few. Since the destruction of Shiloh, they were trained and well-armed, and, in Samuel's mind, their martial presence cast a pall over the sacredness of the place.

They were still several hundred paces from the wall when Samuel realized that something was happening outside the city. A crowd was gathered, still and quiet, on the western shoulder of Mount Scopus. A hundred paces from the wall, the afternoon breeze toyed with hair and garments, fluttering like flags in white, blue and earth-tones wrapped loosely around their human standards. The somber wailing of a pipe drifted on the wind.

"What is going on?" Kish asked, nodding his head toward the crowd.

"I am not sure," said Samuel.

He turned from the road and strode across the grassy hillside, Kish and Tahash following. Wet grass soaked sandals that had just begun to dry. As they drew closer to the crowd, the lowing of a cow echoed off the rounded hills around them. They wove their way through the throng, penetrating far enough to get a view of the reason for the assemblage.

In the middle of a wide open space in the center of the people were a Chief Priest, four Levites, and a young cow, striking for her umber coloring. A Levite held a rope of linen that had been tied around her neck. Not far behind them a rough pyramid of cedar, pine, and fig wood was stacked so that it provided a cave-like opening in one side.

"The Red Heifer," said Samuel quietly.

"What?" Kish leaned closer to him so that he could whisper the question. "What are they doing?"

"It is the Ceremony of the Red Heifer. They are about to make the sacred ashes used to sanctify holy water."

The Chief Priest's stark white robe of thin wool was nearly transparent in places where his skin, wet from ceremonial immersion, touched it, or where the water had dripped from his hair and beard to form "V"'s over his chest and back.

"I have never witnessed this ceremony," whispered Samson.

Samuel nodded. "Few have. It is rarely performed, and there is no fanfare surrounding it, so that only those who happen to be at the Tabernacle when it takes place are privileged to see it."

"That is Ahimelech, is it not?" Samson asked, gesturing toward the Chief Priest.

"It is. He has been kept for seven days in the House of Stoves, everyday sprinkled with the last of the ashes of the previous red heifer. This morning he was washed from head to toe and dressed in a robe that was woven expressly for this occasion."

JUDGE OF ISRAEL

The crowd quieted and Samuel turned to see that Ahimelech was addressing them. "The words of Jehovah came to Moses and Aaron in the wilderness, saying: 'Bring a red heifer which has no defects and which has never worn a yoke, and give it to the heir of the High Priest. It is to be taken outside the camp and killed in his presence. Then he is to take some of its blood and with his finger sprinkle it seven times in the direction of the Tabernacle. The whole animal is to be laid into a fire by the Levites as a burnt offering in his presence. Then he is to take some cedar wood, a sprig of hyssop, and a red cord and throw them into the fire. After that, he is to wash his clothes and pour water over himself, and then he may enter the camp; but he remains ritually unclean until the evening. The Levite who burned the cow must also wash his clothes and pour water over himself, and he also remains unclean until evening. Then a clean man is to collect the ashes of the cow and put them in a place, sanctified and holy, outside the camp, where they are to be kept for the sons and daughters of Israel to use in preparing the water for purification. The man who collected the ashes must also wash his clothes, and he remains unclean until the evening. This regulation is valid for all time to come, both for the Israelites and for the foreigners living among them.

"'And the water of purification must be made in this way: some ashes from the red heifer shall be taken and put in a pot, and clear water added. Into this should be dipped a sprig of hyssop and the water sprinkled upon the one who is unclean, his tent, and all that is in it. This must be done on the third and on the seventh day. After that, the man must wash his clothes and pour water over himself, and on the setting of the sun, he will be clean.' So it is written in the Torah of Moses."

Ahimelech approached the heap of wood and beckoned to the Levites holding the red heifer. They led it in a circle and forced it to walk backward until its hindquarters were inside of the cave-like opening in the woodpile. Levites on either side of it pulled tightly on opposing ropes wound around its neck so that it could not move. The heifer was facing west, toward the reddening sky of sunset. Ahimelech stood beside it, also facing west. He extended his right hand, gripping an obsidian blade. Without looking he placed the blade's edge under the heifer's neck, and then placed his left hand, palm up, under the blade. Still facing west, he slashed up and toward himself.

The heifer opened her mouth as if to low again, then opened and closed it several times silently, almost as though chewing. Her neck gaped;

blood poured from the wound, filled Ahimelech's left palm, trickled in a scarlet line down his arm and pooled at the heifer's feet. Then the animal's front legs buckled and she lay down, ensconced in the stacked wood.

Ahimelech dropped the knife and dipped his forefinger into the blood in his palm. Turning at last, he sprinkled it seven times in the direction of the Tabernacle. Then one of the Levites approached, a burning torch in his hands, and Ahimelech took it from him and tossed it into the wood.

The flame leapt from branch to branch, roaring to vociferous and insatiable life. Ahimelech held up a handful of branches, twigs and needles still attached. "Is this cedar wood?" he asked the crowd.

"It is cedar wood," they intoned.

Ahimelech nodded; in his other hand he held up three stalks of hyssop, each with three buds. "Is this hyssop?"

"It is hyssop."

The priest nodded again and bundling the cedar with the hyssop in his left hand, he held up a red ribbon. "Is this scarlet?"

"It is scarlet," the crowd responded.

He tied the scarlet around the bundled branches and threw the bundle into the fire, atop the burning, hissing corpse of the red heifer.

Ahimelech faced the crowd and spread his arms above his head. "May Jehovah bless you and keep you. May Jehovah make His face shine toward you, and may He favor you. May Jehovah lift up His face toward you, and assign peace to you."

"Jehovah our God is One!" the crowd responded.

Ahimelech lowered his arms and began pacing toward the city gates. He drew close enough for Samuel's companions to get a good look at him: a thick, stolid man a little shorter than Samuel with thinning brown hair and dark, deep-set eyes.

"It has been a long time, Samuel," Ahimelech said. "I have been praying you might come."

"We saw Philistine tracks just outside the city," said Samuel.

"A marauding band has been wandering through the countryside, trading in iron," said Ahimelech. "They know that we are not organized to act against them."

"But chariots at the foot of Mount Scopus?" Samuel asked.

Ahimelech nodded. "They have become very bold."

"You know why I am here?

Ahimelech smiled. "Do you mean your summoning the entire nation to Mizpah? Yes, I think I heard something about it."

Samuel rolled his eyes. "I need to speak with your father."

The smile disappeared. "I will take you to him. But I must warn you—he is not well, Samuel. His years have not been easy ones."

"No indeed!" Samuel said. "He had to raise you!"

But Ahimelech did not smile in return. "I must go into seclusion for a time, and ritually bathe—I can take you to him after sunset."

Samuel nodded. "After sunset it is, then. At your father's house."

Sadness passed over Ahimelech's face, like the shadow of a cloud before a storm breaks. "At my father's house," he repeated, almost in a whisper, then turned and walked toward the city gate.

28

*"Then Abraham loaded the wood onto Isaac, and took
in his own hands the fire and the slaughtering knife, and
they continued on together."—The Scroll of Bereshith*

S amuel and his companions strode solemnly across the grass a few paces behind the rough circle of priests who encircled Ahimelech with
linked hands, shielding him from anyone who might accidentally come
in contact with him and thus become ceremonially unclean. The land rose
gently to the gates of Nob, framed on either side by the alert figures of the
Tabernacle Guard, spears pointed skyward, swords hanging from their hips.

They passed through the gates. Inside, the first thing Samuel saw
was Tirzah racing across the square toward him, her *tsa'iph* threatening to
come loose. She threw her arms around him. "Samuel! Oh, Samuel—it is so
good to see you."

She held him by his shoulders at arm's length. "Let me look at you!" Her eyes drank in his face. "The same uncertain mouth—the same sad eyes. As if only your skin has aged."

Not only my skin," Samuel said, patting the top of his forehead where his hair was beginning to thin.

She laughed, the uninhibited laugh that he remembered so well from their years together. "How are Liora, and your sons?"

"They were well when I left them. So much has happened since then, though—I wish I knew what they were doing right now."

She nodded, her smile undimmed. Samuel felt more comfortable in her presence than he had since he left home. She was the same Tirzah who had been his anchor, his comfort and the closest thing he had to family while he was growing up in Shiloh. Behind her tanned skin, wrinkled now around the eyes and mouth, beneath her long hair, now streaked with grey, was the young woman that had stood by his side when the evil of Hophni and Phinehas threatened to destroy him.

She bowed and greeted Tahash and Kish. "I know the name of the house of the Matrites," she said to Kish. "It is an honor to have you here."

"Are we not the least of the sons of Benjamin?" Kish said, bowing in return.

Nervous movement caught Samuel's eye a few paces behind Tirzah. A young man stood there, head bowed, mouth closed tightly but lips in constant motion, as though he were chewing on every surface of the inside of his mouth.

Tirzah saw Samuel looking his way. "Come closer, Ichabod," she said. "You remember Samuel."

"Samuel the Prophet," Ichabod said softly.

"May you have peace, Ichabod," Samuel said, taking a step toward the young man.

Ichabod took a step backward, head sinking lower into his shoulders.

"It is alright, Ichabod," Tirzah said, going to him and wrapping her left arm around his shoulders.

Samuel smiled as brightly as he could, wondering if the young man could tell that the smile hid an embarrassed discomfort. Something was wrong with Ichabod, probably due to his premature birth on the day of his father's, his uncle's, his grandfather's and his mother's death. His mind was not whole and as his body aged it became apparent that his mind would probably never catch up to it.

"Let me take you to the Tabernacle," Tirzah said, and they fell into step behind her as she made her way through the streets of Nob. Ichabod trailed behind them, muttering to himself.

Everywhere, the city had adapted over the past twenty years to accommodate the needs of the Tabernacle and the crowds it drew. The streets were thick with sacrificial animals being led to the Altar or to storage pens southeast of the Tabernacle Courtyard. Penitents, coming or going, choked the streets as well, and Samuel and his companions struggled through them like fish fighting their way upstream.

They passed a hall to the right of the road, its stacked-stone walls plastered from waist height up.. Through tall windows with smoothed oak sills, Samuel caught a glimpse of rows of boys seated, cross-legged, on a grey wool rug. On their laps rested rectangular plates of fired clay, each covered on one side by a layer of translucent, ochre beeswax. As the voice of an unseen Levite instructor drifted through the open windows to the street, the boys—eyes narrowed, tongues poking from the corners of their mouths—inscribed their lesson into the wax with styli of split reeds.

Samuel remembered his own lessons, many years before, when Ahitub had brushed honey over the beeswax, knowing it would keep Samuel writing for the reward of repeatedly licking the sweetness from the nib. It was only years later that Samuel had realized the unconscious lesson Ahitub had been giving him: that the words he wrote must be taken from the page to become a part of him; that they were, indeed, sweet and nourishing to the one who took them in.

The Tabernacle's Curtain Wall rose up before them, taller and thicker than the one in Shiloh had been, and the open gates were made of oak planks as thick as Samuel's forearms. Music drifted from inside, the Levite Chorus singing one of the Psalms of Moses to the accompaniment of the orchestra:

> Jehovah will become for me
> A bastion of security
> And my God the Rock that safeguards me
> He will turn back
> My enemies attacks
> And will bring them to silence by their own plans

JUDGE OF ISRAEL

Jehovah our God will bring them to silence.

Once through the gate, Samuel was welcomed by a familiar face at
every turn: old men who had served with him when he was young; young
men to whom he had become a mentor and guide; women who had grown
alongside Tirzah in the Chorus.

Beyond them, gray smoke spiraled from the gleaming bronze of the
Altar, breathed skyward by the endlessly licking tongues of the Eternal
Flame. Samuel stopped to look at it, remembering sitting in the mud, the
ashes of the Flame scattered over himself and the sodden ground, the feeling
of incomprehensible loss and displacement that swept through him in the
moment when he thought the Flame had died...

"Samuel?" Tirzah's voice broke his reverie and he turned to see the
group was several paces ahead, standing and waiting for him.

Kish and Tahash's foreheads were wrinkled, their eyes narrowed.
But Tirzah's wide, laughing mouth was curved into the subtlest of smiles,
and her eyes were soft and wet with sympathetic memory.

Samuel shook off the ghosts of the past and moved forward once
again across the flagstones, past the taut, cloth walls of the Tabernacle itself.
Within it was the most sacred place in Israel—the Holy of Holies, a perfect
cube of fabric and acacia that had once housed the Ark of the Covenant. In
some ways, the whole purpose of the Tabernacle was as a resting place for
the Ark. Now, the Ark resided within another cubic compartment in the city
of Kiriath-jearim, at the home of Abinadab, under the watchful care of his
sons, Eleazar, Uzzah, and Ahio. There it had stayed since Jehovah had recovered it from the Philistines after the battle of Aphek. Somehow, the Tabernacle without the Ark inside seemed strangely hollow to Samuel.

Attached to the east wall of the Tabernacle, behind the room that
had once been Samuel's and the Room of Scrolls, were the simple quarters
of Ahitub, the High Priest of Israel.

Leaving Tahash and Kish outside, Samuel followed Tirzah through
the door posts under a lintel mottled with the stains of Passover blood.
Light spilled from the doorway in a semi-circle on the floor; the rest of the
room was dark, the windows shrouded with heavy curtains. Samuel squinted
to let his eyes adjust. Slowly shapes emerged from the darkness, limned in
the light of a pair of oil lamps.

A long couch was centered against one wall, and the lamps flickered
petulantly on lamp stands on either side of it. Upon the couch, propped up

by pale linen bolsters sat a wrinkled, old man. His bony chin, adorned with the sparse white remains of a beard, drooped to his sunken chest, and not even the lamplight penetrated into the black caverns around his eyes. A woolen shawl swathed his shoulders and the rest of his body was only a series of undefined lumps and ridges beneath layers of wool blankets. Samuel would have thought he was asleep except that the bony fingers of his right hand gripped a beautifully carved vermilion staff, its surface an inscribed maze of whorls and lines. The swollen knuckles were white with the intensity of that grip.

"My lord Ahitub!" Samuel strode to the old man's side, cradling his head against his chest, kissing the stringy white hair. He smelled of musty incense, sweat and lye, masking the unmistakable odor of old urine.

The Priest spoke, but so softly Samuel could not make out the words. He knelt to see his mentor's face. "What did you say, my lord?"

"My child," Ahitub said in a quavering whisper. "Prophet of the true God, Jehovah."

Samuel felt tears in his eyes. It was not the deep lines that seamed the old man's face, nor the age spots upon his temples, nor even the shadowy remains of a voice that woke a bitter anger in Samuel's heart. It was the dullness he saw in the High Priest's watery eyes. The light of care that had once shone there had many times kept Samuel from giving in to despair, stars that had illumined an otherwise black existence.

"I am sorry for coming unannounced and unexpectedly, my lord," Samuel said, raising his voice and wondering if the old man thought he was shouting.

The merest hint of a smile played at the corners of Ahitub's mouth and eyes. "At least you are not waking me in the middle of the night to tell me that God is talking to you."

Samuel unconsciously examined the High Priest for the expressions and body language of his true feelings. He saw nothing. Ahitub's body, frail and skeletal, did not move. It was, he thought with hollow fear, like trying to read a corpse.

The High Priest coughed, his mouth closed, shutting his eyes afterward exhaling through his nose as though exhausted. "We should let my father rest," Ahimelech said.

Samuel nodded. "May Jehovah be with you, my lord," he said, leaning close to Ahitub. "I will return when you have rested."

Ahitub smiled weakly, and Samuel allowed himself to be led out the door into the Tabernacle Courtyard. Kish and Tahash waited there, concern in their narrowed eyes.

"I am sorry, Ahimelech," Samuel said. "I did not know, or I would have come sooner."

"What could you have done?" Ahimelech said bitterly.

"I could have been here for *you*, my brother."

Ahimelech turned toward him, anger wrinkling his nose. "Why? He is dying, and I am not ready. There is nothing any of us can do to change that."

"Do not give in to despair," Samuel said. "He will not die yet. He will lead us, just as he always has."

"Lead us? He can barely get out of his bed!"

"He is stronger than you think!" Samuel felt himself getting angry, and wondered why.

Ahimelech shook his head. "Thirty years under Grandfather's thumb left its mark, even if it is not visible. For my father there were no easy years. He went from the corruption of Grandfather and Great-Uncle Hophni to being High Priest of a nation in ruins—a task he never wanted. Then mother died..."

"I have known your father longer than you have," Samuel said. "He has quiet reserves of strength that will amaze all of us."

Ahimelech tried to smile. *Mouth moving, but not his eyes.* "I'm sure you are right. In any case, let us speak of something else."

Samuel put his arms around the young man's soldiers. "Let us break bread together, and you can disclose to my ears all that has happened here since I visited for Passover."

Ahimelech nodded and they moved toward the dining booths on the northern end of the Courtyard. But Samuel could not stop himself from looking back over his shoulder, to the shadowed entry of the High Priest's room, where the open door's black revelation looked more than anything like the entrance to a tomb.

29

Lord Sarnam Ashkelon followed his troops into Joppa, surveying the destruction all around him with grim satisfaction. Bodies were every-where—few of them, he was glad to see, were Philistine corpses. He had, of course, prayed to Ba'al and to Dagon for success before the battle, as he always did. But this time, he had offered a prayer and a sacrifice to Anath as well, and he had felt, as he spoke the words and watched the smoke ascend, her cruel smile of approval. Something had happened as a result of that prayer, just as Phicol and Sihphil had assured him that it would. As he drew near the battle, he felt his heart racing as it had not since his youth, when he had been initiated in blood on the battlefields of Caphtor.

Sihphil did not accompany him—the priest remained aboard one of the boats, guarded by a half-dozen of the Gedhudhra, although he claimed that he needed no bodyguard. He did not have the physical strength to ride into battle anymore, his body broken down by the torture he had endured in Egyptian captivity.

JUDGE OF ISRAEL

As soon as Sarnam passed through the city gates, a knot of Hebrew men rushed from behind a burning storefront, spears flying. One of the missiles grazed Sarnam's left side as he drew his sword. His Gedhudhra bodyguard made short work of the men, but when they saw a weapon in Sarnam's hand they allowed him to face one of their attackers himself. When his blade bit into the man's flesh, a thrill swept down his spine and he felt light-headed and expansive, as though he were abruptly connected to everything in the universe around him, as though he could feel the pulsing heat of its life coursing through his own veins. He was filled with a ravenous longing to control that life, to feel it as it died under his blade.

Every stroke renewed and strengthened the feeling, and before he even realized it, he had hacked the man to pieces, laughing with ecstasy. There was strength in his arms, strength! It was as though youth had returned to his muscles, and a forgotten joy to his heart. He stopped only because there was no more life in the gobbets of flesh on the ground before him, and he immediately cast about for another enemy to destroy, his chest heaving with anxious eagerness for another kill.

He realized that he was experiencing what Phicol must feel every time he spilled blood, and in an instant his understanding of the brutal, scarred warrior increased tenfold.

The Gedhudhra were looking at him strangely, but he didn't care. "Burn it!" he commanded.

One of them pointed at him. "My lord—your arm!"

He glanced down. His left forearm had been deeply slashed—almost to the bone. The wound opened and closed like a macabre, lipless mouth when Sarnam moved, and he laughed again. He hadn't felt the blow at all—and even now, it only stung mildly.

"Bind it!" said another of the Gedhudhra to an infantryman standing nearby.

"Do not bother," Sarnam said, silently blessing Anat. "It does not bleed."

The Gedhudhra stared in awe, realizing it was true. Only a thin trickle of blood ran across his forearm from the wound, and already it was congealing into a thick brown paste.

Sarnam raised his eyes. "I thought I ordered you men to burn this place!"

Infantrymen were summoned, bearing urns of his latest weapon: a potion that Sihphil had told him was invented centuries before by their ancestors. Sarnam did not know all the details of its manufacture, but he knew it contained refined bitumen mixed with sulfur, lyme, and olive oil, thinned and blended in the costly oil pressed from terebinth berries. It burned with incredible heat, and it stuck to whatever it came in contact with. Water only spread it and made it burn more hotly, and it could not be removed from the body unless the skin itself was peeled away.

The soldiers began to disperse through the city, packing the urns to the rooftops of houses to cast them onto the streets below where they exploded into gouts of spreading flames. In moments, the entire city of Joppa was burning.

Sarnam made his way through the smoke-choked streets looking for a fight. He found that he didn't want to think about his plan for attack, the movement of his troops, or the details of his campaign. They all seemed like unwelcome distractions taking him away from what truly mattered now, in the moment: finding enemies whose blood he could spill.

Another cluster of Hebrews, arranged in loose formation, assembled in the street ahead of him, and the Gedhudhra quickly moved into protective positions, surrounding him with a hedge of swords and spears. Sarnam pushed his way through them to the forefront, his heart pounding, his thoughts purifying into one overwhelming desire.

The Gedhudhra were nervous at the sight of him so directly exposed to danger. "Today, you are not my bodyguard," he called, never taking his eyes away from the assembled Hebrews. "Today, we are brothers. In this moment, I share in your danger, and in your glory."

Raising his sword, he led the charge: "For Dagon and Anath, and the glory of Philistia!"

They hurled themselves at the Hebrews. The battle was short but fierce; the Joppans fought with the fearlessness of men who are defending their homes and their families. Sarnam respected that, and his admiration for them grew even as he cut them down. There were brave men among the Hebrews. It was too bad they had set their faces so resolutely against Dagon.

Then a burly warrior with a tangle of curly auburn hair raced toward him, bronze khopesh raised, and teeth bared in fury. One of the Gedhudhra leapt between them, but the Hebrew barreled into him like an angry bull, sending the black-clad guardsman flying.

Sarnam raised his own sword and they smashed into each other like two stags in rut, bouncing off and stumbling away with the force of their collision. Sarnam spun and saw the Hebrew lunging toward him again, kho-

khopesh sweeping down toward his left side. Sarnam was not carrying a shield. Instinctively, he raised his left arm to ward off the blow and felt his enemy's blade hit his forearm with a force that jarred Sarnam's teeth in his jaw.

He spun away, swinging his own sword in a wide arc that found its mark in the big Hebrew's thigh. The blade bit deep and his enemy collapsed to the road, face white with pain and the loss of the blood that poured onto the ground around him. Sarnam raised his blade again; the Hebrew raised his own sword limply, eyelids fluttering. Sarnam swung downward with all his strength, battering the feeble defense aside and delivering the killing blow to the base of the man's neck.

The rest of the Hebrew soldiers had been dispatched by the Gedhudhra, and Sarnam looked around with a giddy joy at the sprawled corpses. He saw that, once again, his men were staring at him with awe in their cold eyes.

"What?" he snapped.

"Your arm, my lord," one of them said, pointing.

It was only then that Sarnam remembered the sword stroke he had blocked with his forearm, and glanced down to assess the wound.

There was none. He could feel an ache where the sword had made contact, but no mark.

"Truly, you are favored of Anath," another of the Gedhudhra said, and Sarnam heard them whispering among themselves: "He cannot be injured..."

"His flesh has been charmed against weapons..."

"...invincible in battle..."

Sarnam ignored them. "Do we have reports in yet?"

One of his captains nodded. "The city was contained, my lord."

"No escapees?"

"One, my lord. A single Hebrew managed to find his way out a postern. One of our men pursued him while another came back to get assistance. By the time he returned, the man who had been pursuing the escapee had been killed."

Sarnam turned to one of his bodyguards. "Find me that simpering cretin, Baghadh."

The guardsman nodded and loped off. Sarnam made his way back to the city gates, climbing the stone steps to the top of the wall. He watched as the survivors from Joppa were led, bound in a long chain, toward the beached ships. Some would be taken to Philistia to serve as slaves in the Pentapolis, but most would be sold to the Tyrians who would ship them to whatever land was paying the highest price for human flesh.

"My lord?"

Sarnam recognized the sycophantic voice immediately, and he did not turn to face Baghadh. "I have a task for you."

"Anything, my lord, to prove my loyalty to—."

"A Hebrew escaped from the city. I need you to find him and kill him."

"Kill him?"

Sarnam finally turned to face Baghadh. Even in the fresh sea air, he could smell the odor of rotting flesh. "I cannot afford to have him carrying news of our whereabouts, our strength, or of this victory to the rest of your people."

Baghadh nodded. "I will send one of my warriors immediately..."

"Not one of your warriors. I want you to do it, Baghadh. Alone."

"My lord, you honor me," Baghadh said, bowing. "But perhaps a soldier would be a better choice. I am not a warrior, nor do I have the strength to travel swiftly..."

"No?" Sarnam drew his sword, still sticky with blood. "Isn't there any way we might...motivate you to find hidden reserves of strength and resourcefulness?"

Baghadh bowed lower. "Of course, my lord."

"Yes, you will. And then you will find out what the Sorcerer Samuel is planning. My army will be in the heart of Canaan in a matter of days. If you fail to do as I ask, it had better be because you are dead. Because if this task is not done and you are breathing when I next see you—and I will see you again, Baghadh—then I will have Sihphil devise a way to keep you alive long, long after life has become an unendurable agony."

"As you say, my lord," Baghadh mumbled.

"Then why are you still here?"

Baghadh scrambled to his feet and fled down the stairs.

Sarnam leaned back on the battlements and looked out across the forest that lay between Joppa and the heartland of Canaan. "At long last, Father," he whispered his eyes going unfocused. "At long last I will fulfill our destiny. I will name our new capital city for you, and I will fill this land with your glory and the glory of our gods."

30

Cheran stumbled through the forest, following game trails or wandering across trackless land—any route that took him up the hillsides and into the mountains of Samaria. He wept as he went, clutching his bleeding arm and trying to catch his breath.

His only thoughts were for his family, praying silently and aloud that they were safe. But the pages of his prayer were illustrated in his mind with images from Joppa: the slack faces of slain friends, the greasy blackness of smoke rising from burning corpses, and his last glimpse of the city before he had entered the cover of the trees—men, women, and children being led in slave-lines towards the waiting Philistine ships.

His relief at not finding his family at Joppa was so intense it brought tears to his eyes. In the midst of his weeping, though, he felt sick inside, disgusted that he could feel anything positive in the face of what he had just seen. He wanted to thank Jehovah for delivering his family from the destruction, but how could he do so when God had allowed so many other families to die or be captured? What had he or his wife done to deserve greater protection than any of their neighbors or relatives? Were his children more righteous than the sons and daughters who lay now, forever silenced, in their scorched houses and courtyards?

He was exhausted to the point of delirium, and his legs moved woodenly through the undergrowth, tripping and stumbling every few steps. He did not know where he was going—just that he must put distance between himself and the horrors that he had witnessed. Sometime in the future, he knew, he would have to find his family and make certain that they were safe. But a part of him feared traveling that path, both for the danger of being caught by the savages who had sacked Joppa, and in dread of what he might find when he did catch up with those he loved. He could not face that possibility and stay sane. It was best, for now, not to think about them and to focus on finding Samuel, and then on getting somewhere that he could hide and rest.

The land cleared for a distance, and he wandered, exposed, over broad grasslands, splashing his way across the dozens of small tributaries of the Yarkon River that snaked over the plains, fighting his way through dense clusters of reeds and groves of broom trees and thorn bushes. Where the streams broadened in babbling stretches of clear, pebble-bottomed water, he pushed through the brakes of cane and white-blossomed oleander and knelt to drink the sun-warmed water. He did not stay long—flies and mosquitoes were thick in the damp heat, and sullen yellow lizards watched him from the muddy banks. He paused just long enough to make a poultice of wild herbs and clay and pack it on his still-bleeding wound.

The fields and moorlands were awash in flowers: anemones, mallows, narcissus and iris quivered in the sea breeze. They seemed pale somehow, drained of their ability to impart joy, even as the bright sun overhead did nothing to lighten his mood. He found himself listening without really hearing the twittering of the army of birds harvesting seeds from the spring grasses. When they fell silent as the shadow of a hawk passed silently over the swampy land, Cheran fell to a crouch and scanned the horizon in every direction, nerves on edge, haunted by the specter of Joppa.

When he stumbled from the cover of a forest of oaks onto the great north-south trade road, he paused for only a moment before crossing it and following a narrower track that led east.

He had walked fewer than a hundred paces before he heard the sound of horse's hooves approaching from behind.

Not far ahead a hillock brooded over the road, crowned by an acacia dripping with long, yellow blossoms. He clambered up the hill. The bush was neither dense nor thickly covered in leaves, and Cheran lay on his stomach on the red earth behind it in order to avoid being seen. The pose limited his own vision to the road directly in front of him, so he quieted his breathing and allowed the *clip-clop* of the horse to tell him where his pursuer was.

The sounds drew nearer. Mosquitoes buzzed annoyingly His fear faded in the face of a mindless anger that welled up unexpectedly in his chest and throat. He did not know who was coming; he feared he had been followed. But he silently vowed that if it was a son of Philistia, he would choke the life from him in vengeance for even one of the corpses that today fed the gulls in the ruins of Joppa.

The horse's footfalls slowed. Had he been seen? Had he left obvious tracks when he left the road to clamber up the hillock? He cursed himself for failing to hide his prints and wished for some kind of weapon, in spite of the fact that he really did not know how to use one.

The hoof beats came to a halt. He could just make out the horse's auburn-maned head through the acacia branches, but the rider was still hidden. The horse whinnied, and Cheran saw a hand reach forward to pat it on the neck.

For some reason, seeing the skin of the rider extend from his voluminous sleeves fanned Cheran's rage into an inferno. Screaming so loudly it hurt his throat, in a single movement he rose to his feet and leapt from the hillock, tackling his pursuer and toppling him from his horse.

They landed in the grass on the other side of the road. The rider was tangled in his cloak and thrashed wildly as Cheran rained blows on him with his fists.

"Stop! Stop!" the figure shouted, his voice muffled by his cowl that had become partially wrapped around his head. Cheran ignored him.

The man thrashed even more. "Stop! I am a Manassite! I am a Manassite!"

Liar! Thought Cheran, but he stopped punching for a moment.

The man pulled his cowl away from his face. It was the bearded face of an Israelite, although scarred and deformed by some loathsome disease. "Why are you following me?" Cheran asked breathlessly.

The man licked his cracked lips. "Get off of me, and I will tell you!"

Cheran hesitated a moment, then let the man go and rose to his feet. His pursuer did so as well, brushing leaves and twigs off of his traveling cloak.

"By the bones of my fathers, man—what did you think you were doing?"

Cheran remained suspicious. "Who are you? Why are you following me?"

"I am Baghadh, an Elder of Manasseh and advisor to the Prophet Samuel," the man said. Cheran saw that his blows had torn some of the pustules on the man's face and blood and clear fluid mingled on his pocked cheeks.

"I escaped from Joppa even as you did," Baghadh continued. "I saw you leave, then saw you traveling a short while later—from a distance, across the swamps of Sharon. I have been trying to catch up with you ever since."

"I have never seen you in Joppa before."

"I was only there on business, for the day." Baghadh shook his head disgustedly. "Of all days for me to come through those gates."

Cheran allowed himself to relax a little. The man's speech was definitely that of an Israelite. "Where are you going?" Cheran asked.

"I was going to ask you the same thing. I need to warn my family, of course, but when that was done I was going to respond to the Prophet Samuel's summons."

"Summons?" Baghadh asked.

Cheran nodded. "Samuel has called all Israel to gather at Mizpah."

"Mizpah?" Baghadh wrinkled his brow. "Why Mizpah?"

Cheran shrugged. "I just found out about it myself. The rumor is that he may choose the new Judge of Israel and prepare our people for war. Jehovah may have already disclosed the attack on Joppa to his ears, but I want to bring him the news just in case."

Baghadh clapped a hand on his shoulder. Cheran could not help but flinch at the sight of the lesions that ran down the back of his wrist and disappeared under his sleeve. "Our paths may lie together for a while, then. I, too, was going to alert the Elders—perhaps in Shamir. The signal fires must be lit; Israel must be summoned to war. You look like you could benefit from a little time on horseback. I will walk for a while and give you the opportunity to rest."

"May Jehovah bless you," Cheran said and stepped toward the mount.

But he had not even completed the step before pain like a terrible flame exploded in his back, below his shoulder blade. He felt something happen inside of his chest and he suddenly struggled to get enough air.

As though time itself had slowed, he turned and saw Baghadh standing behind him, pupils widened, mouth open as though in ecstasy, a bloody dagger clutched in one hand, red ichor covering the hand and sleeve.

Cheran collapsed onto his chest on the road, struggling to breathe. He coughed and spattered the stones with flecks of crimson.

"We should probably get you off of the road," Baghadh said from somewhere beyond Cheran's vision. "We wouldn't want you to get stepped on by some passing mule."

The Manassite laughed and grabbed Cheran's ankles, dragging him to the edge of the road and through the dry grass a short distance. Every jolt and tug sent waves of agony and nausea through Cheran's body, and as he continued to fail to get a breath, his vision seemed to be fading into a red mist.

Baghadh dumped him behind a sandstone boulder and knelt down to look him in the eyes. He tapped Cheran on the forehead with one finger. "I have come up with a better idea. How about if I leave you here to feed the ravens and the wolves, while I ride to tell the Elders of Samaria that I have just returned from Sharon, and that the rumors about the Philistine attack are untrue?"

He laughed, a cruel, mirthless sound. Cheran tried to speak but could not get his breath. "Then maybe I can send Glaucus to finish the job he was supposed to do in the first place—find your family and send them to join you in Sheol."

Cheran knew he should have been afraid, or angry, but all emotions seemed to have left him. There was only a great weariness, and he fought to keep his eyes open, even as he wondered how this man knew Glaucus or Cheran's family.

Baghadh chuckled again. "You people are so sure that you can just ignore thousands of years of religious tradition and blatantly reject the gods that have inhabited this land since long before Joshua walked its hills. And now, look! Pidray, the Daughter of Lightning has shone on me. Tallay, the Daughter of Dew has refreshed me; Arsay, the Daughter of the Soil has supported me, and Ugar, the Daughter of Fields has guided me. Ba'al has heard my cries for help, and sent his daughters to bring me success."

He spat on Cheran's face. "Tell me, Cheran—what has Jehovah done for you?"

Cheran felt distant, and knew with cool detachment that he was about to lapse into unconsciousness, a sleep from which he would likely never wake. Baghadh moved away from him, and then suddenly loomed over him again, his eyes squinted and his yellow teeth bared in his flushed, lesioned face. He kicked Cheran savagely in the ribs. "Fool!" he snarled, then scurried to the road. "Stupid fool!"

Cheran's vision faded, then returned, and he heard the hollow clopping of a horse's hooves galloping back in the direction of Joppa. He lay there in perfect stillness until the sound faded into silence.

Cheran's whole body ached, but he had not felt Baghadh's final blow as pain. When the Manassite's sandal had connected with his ribs, Cheran had heard—and felt—it *snap* something in his chest. But even as it did, he inhaled sharply and reflexively. This time, his lungs—or at least one of them—filled with air. The spots and the redness vanished from in front of his eyes, and waves of agony washed over him as he came fully awake once again.

He rolled onto his chest, the twisting movement sending nausea washing through him. His own weight on his chest made it even more difficult to breathe than it had been. But he needed to be face-down. He needed to see the leaf-littered ground in front of him.

Gavriel. I am coming.

Reaching out with one bloody hand, he began inching toward the road.

JUDGE OF ISRAEL

31

Two days after the sack of Joppa, Lord Sarnam Ashkelon led his men from its smoldering ruins eastward, deeper into the land of Canaan. From the hill on which Joppa was partially built the army traveled east-northeast across broad, flat lands of cultivated fields occasionally pierced by the ragged edges of the great oak forests of Sharon.

By mid-morning, they had reached the banks of the Yarkon River, and they turned onto the road that followed it toward its source at the base of the highlands of Samaria. A layer of grey-blue cloud, whisping toward the earth in long tendrils as it reached the mountains ahead of them, dimmed the morning dramatically and turned the air cool and damp. The road, dry but rutted by the passing of many chariot and wagon wheels and countless pounding hooves, wove alongside the shallow river, sometimes right on its banks, other times distant enough that neither the water nor the thick vegetation around it were visible through the scattered oaks.

Where the Yarkon itself was visible, its brown water hid the wary bodies of behemoths and water buffalo, their black snouts and nostrils just protruding above its dark depths. From time to time a sudden splash and concentric rings on the surface of the water told of a snake or another small creature vanishing into the protection of the river.

The armies of Philistia reached Aphek in the early evening and were welcomed to the city by the garrison that had been posted there by Sarnam two decades earlier, after his victory at the first and second battles of Aphek. The rest of the Axis Lords and their additional troops that had marched north from Philistia joined them there as well, swelling the army to tens of thousands. From Gath, the Rephaim had come; dozens of the giants were now encamped outside Aphek's walls, huddled around glowering cooking fires. There were no tents on the field—the Rephaim slept in the open, sometimes still encased in their heavy armor and with no covering but their brown cloaks made from stiff cow pelts.

The garrison commanders at Aphek (except for Glaucus, who was somewhere in the east still, hunting the sorcerer Samuel) had prepared well for the arrival of the troops: wine and beer had been brought into the city by the wagon load, and now the vats were opened and the people feasted and drank by firelight until the moon had passed its zenith in the dark sky above them.

The following morning trumpets burnished by the orange light of dawn blared from Aphek's watchtowers. Like a serpent waking from a cold night, the Philistine forces eased into motion. In the vanguard a pack of lithe war hounds strained at their leashes, held by the Master of Dogs and his men. Behind him marched rank on rank of infantrymen bearing a forest of spears that waved above them as though blown by a confused wind. Dust quickly coated their sweating skin; many faces were shrouded in black cloth wrapped to cover nose and mouth. A moving wall loomed behind them: the armored Rephaim, their footfalls heavy, craggy faces impassive. At their heels Phicol rode at the forefront of the cavalry: scores of armored chariots and high-stepping stallions, each bearing a driver, an archer, and a lancer.

The air was still and oppressively hot. Dust enveloped them, filling noses and mouths with metallic dryness, then soared into the sky above them to be whipped inland by the high breeze from the Sea. The road crossed broad wheat fields held by the troops at Aphek, and cut through intermittent fingers of oak groves that extended down from the great forests of Sharon to the north. The flatlands began to rise and buckle, the road winding now around steep hills, cliff-edged with whitish-yellow stone, capped with spring's bright green grass.

The road turned south and the hills began to soften. By late afternoon they had reached a forest of pines, oaks and sycamores that stretched into the distance to the north and east. There the army encamped in the shadow of the trees, setting up tents in the rolling fields.

Sarnam gathered Phicol and the Gedhudhra as the sun fell below the treetops. Leaving the army in the hands of the other Axis Lords, he led his hand-picked force quietly through the trees toward Naioth.

They had the advantage of surprise, although Sarnam knew they did not need it. The troops he had chosen could have destroyed the School and the city even if the entire population had been waiting to oppose them.

They were not. When the Philistines charged into the dark hamlet they were met by silence.

Naioth was empty.

Sarnam sent three of the Gedhudhra to scout the city itself. They returned a short time later: the city was vacated as well.

Sarnam drew his sword and split one of the scouts from shoulder to navel. He was pleased to discover that even that bloodshed brought him a measure of enjoyment, in spite of his rage at the escape of Samuel and his acolytes.

"Burn it!" he ordered. "Burn it all."

Torches were lit and barrels of his fire-oil were dumped in homes and meeting halls. Flames were already licking skyward when Sarnam called Phicol to him again. "Have them drag as much wet fuel as they can in from the fields and forest. I want to make sure this sorcerer sees the smoke of his home being put to the torch, no matter where he may be hiding. And send a message back to the troops. I want the hounds ready to hunt these people down!"

He returned to the encampment irritated and dissatisfied. Sihphil was waiting for him in his tent, but the wizened priest had fallen asleep on a divan in the corner, and Sarnam did not wake him. Whatever element of surprise they had enjoyed had now been lost for certain. It would not be long now before the Hebrews knew the details of his troop strength and movements, if they didn't already. His experience with them as an enemy told him what to expect next: they would mount a fierce resistance, no matter how sure they were to fail.

They would fail this time—he knew that the gods of Canaan were backing him, and he did not doubt their power in the land. But he remembered all too well the might of the Hebrew's mountain god as well.

Sarnam's evening was brightened, though, a short time later. His bodyguards announced that Baghadh had returned, and the little man was guided into Sarnam's command tent. Sihphil awoke and rose to his feet.

"My lord." Baghadh got on his knees and bowed. Sarnam could see how much it pained him to do so.

"Get up. Did you find the man?"

Baghadh slowly got to his feet, looking equally pained. "More than that, my lord. He is even now feeding the crows and the wolves."

Sarnam sank into his chair. "Good. You have obviously benefited from the favor which the gods bestow upon me."

"No doubt, my lord. Perhaps even more than we were expecting."

"What do you mean?"

Baghadh smiled slyly. "He revealed something to me before he died."

"Well?" Sarnam scowled at him.

"Samuel has summoned all Israel to the city of Mizpah, my lord. Within a few days most of the nation—men, women, children, old people—will be gathered there."

"It isss a ssign," said Sihphil quietly.

"If you can kill Samuel and other key Elders in front of the rest of the people," Baghadh continued, "you will be able to conquer the entire nation without losing valuable Israelite slaves in a war."

"Ba'al, Dagon, and Anath will bring you a great victory at Mizpah," said Sihphil.

"I will pray that it is so. But we will not plot our course by relying on a single wind," said Sarnam.

"You have another plan?" Baghadh asked.

"Indeed. I am sending you to Mizpah. When the time comes, you will open the gates of the city for us."

Baghadh's eyes went wide. "But...but my lord...I will not be permitted near the gates!"

Sarnam shrugged. "Then you had better figure out a way to get to them without being given permission."

"Please, my lord!" There was real fear in Baghadh's eyes. "I have been running nonstop for days now! I am not a well man, as you yourself know—."

"You will be a dead man if you wait any longer to obey my orders!" Sarnam snapped. "I am trusting you with this last task, if you want to prove your worth to me and your loyalty to the Axis Lords of Philistia. But if you fail to do as I have asked, there will be no cave deep enough to hide you from my wrath."

Baghadh swallowed loudly. "So be it, my lord." He bowed again, and scurried out of the room.

Sarnam waited a few moments after he had gone, then turned to Sihphil. "That is one plan I cannot rely on."

"Perhapsss. He iss frightened enough, I think, that he will do hiss besst to obey."

Something in the priest's tone made Sarnam worry. "But...there is something else that concerns you?"

Sihphil sighed, as though fighting exhaustion. "The omenss were clear, but they did not predict that the acolytes of Sssamuel would have fled, or that the city would be emptied."

Sarnam frowned. "The omens were wrong?"

"I am not sssure. I fear that sssomthing in the sspirit world iss working againsst uss."

"One of the godss?"

Sihphil shook his head slowly and looked at Sarnam from under heavy lids. "No. Your father."

32

"Wake up! Wake up!"

It was not the words, but the stinging slap on his left cheek that startled Reuel into wakefulness. He was damp and cold. His eyes opened. A face was staring down at him, a round face with beady, dark eyes too close together over a freckled, button nose and a thick-lipped mouth. The lips were opened in a sneer, but the expression's intended effect was softened by the bearer's marked lack of teeth: only three still clung to the man's top gums, all on his right side.

"Haa Haa! Awake now, eh? Yes, now you're awake!" The man grabbed a handful of Reuel's hair and pulled him into a sitting position.

As soon as the man let go, Reuel scooted away from him and glanced around. His head was pounding and his body ached everywhere, as if he had been beaten from head to toe. He did not remember being beaten, or even being attacked...

The memories returned in a rush. The flood on the road to Nob. The churning water. Tumbling from the roadbed. Being pummeled by unseen objects in the water until he slipped into unconsciousness...

Samuel.

The man in front of him slapped him again. "Awake? Are ya awake? Did the river wash the sense right out of ya? Haa Haa!"

Reuel started to rise to face his attacker, only then discovering that his wrists were bound tightly behind his back, and his legs had been hobbled with a short length of rope.

It was also at that moment that he realized that he was surrounded by people: men and women, children and grey-headed—all of them roped together and sitting or lying on the rocky soil. Some of them appeared to be Israelites, others Canaanites, one clearly an Egyptian from his features, skin color, and the stubble on what was once a shaved head. All of them were covered in dirt and their eyes were flat and dull, focused on nothing.

They were the eyes of people who had given up hope.

"Haa haa!" The man said again, folding his arms over his striped, woolen robe. "Glad ya are awake! Glad ya can walk, so we do not have to drag ya! Haa haa!"

Reuel noticed the man was wearing a necklace of amulets: animal charms, figurines of Ba'al, Ashtoreth, and deities Reuel didn't recognize.

"Who are you?" Reuel said, surprised to hear his voice come out as a thin rasp.

The man reached behind Reuel and grabbed the rope that bound his hands, yanking it upward so that it pulled Reuel's wrists almost to the height of his neck. Reuel yelled as he felt the tendons in his shoulders popping and agonizing pain lanced through his neck and upper arms.

"Who am I? I am the man who holds your rope, boy! That is all ya need to know. I am the man who holds your rope, until someone pays me so that they can hold your rope! Those are the last words I expect to hear out of your mouth!"

He let go of the rope and Reuel fell forward onto his shoulder and face. Jarring pain erupted in his forehead to accompany the agony in his shoulders. He tasted blood and dirt in his mouth.

"Haa haa!" Reuel heard the man laughing over his shoulder.

He rolled onto his side and sat up again, blinking away tears of pain, trying to blow the dirt from his right eye. His captor walked to a chain of three wagons, and Reuel noticed that the ropes that bound the prisoners were attached to a pole that spanned the rear of one of the wagons. They appeared to be full of cheap pottery, metal ware, and weapons, a few dust-covered garments and skins, and miscellaneous lidded containers and cloth bags. At the back, near their captor's head, a heavy clay pot swung pendulously from a rod that jutted up and back like a flagpole. Smoke spiraled lazily from the pot's mouth, and several implements poked from its top.

Below the smoldering pot was a man on his knees. His head lolled onto his chest; his arms were stretched unnaturally over his head, and his hands were bound and tied to the highest point on the wagon's sideboards.

Their captor drew a bronze knife from his belt and cut the suspending rope: the captive pitched forward onto his face in the dirt. For a moment, Reuel thought he was dead, but then he rolled slowly onto one shoulder.

"Haa haa! Ready to walk again, my lord?" their captor mocked, bowing exaggeratedly. He gestured back toward the train of prisoners. "Your entourage awaits! Haa haa!"

The prisoner did not move. Smiling, their captor withdrew one of the implements from the smoldering pot. It was a copper rod, one half as thick as a thumb and wrapped in leather as a handle, the other half filed or forged down to needle thinness. Their captor, as unemotionally as if he was handing a friend a piece of bread, sank the implement into the thigh of the man lying on the ground.

Reuel flinched and felt his stomach turn as the prisoner twitched uncontrollably with agony. He did not cry out, though—he did not make a sound.

"There! Haa haa! That put some life back into those limbs!" said their captor, withdrawing the implement. "Now perhaps you have the strength to get back in line!"

He did not wait for an answer. Instead, he grabbed the man by his thick, black hair and dragged him across the rocky ground to where Reuel was tied. Swiftly and efficiently he tied the captive's hands behind his back and fastened them to the rope like the rest of the prisoners. Striding toward the front of the line, their Captor called out to six other men who rode on or stood near the wagons, and the train lurched forward.

Still in a daze, Reuel took several moments to realize what was happening. When he saw the roped prisoners scrambling to their feet, some of them being dragged forward kicking wildly to try to get their feet under them, he jumped up and tried to help the ones nearest him in whatever way he could with his own hands bound behind his back. One was the man the Slaver had burned. Reuel saw that he was about his own age, stripped to his undergarments and beaten so severely that his chest, stomach, arms, and legs were a mass of purple, red, and sulfur-yellow bruises.

The chain of human wares got to their feet and trudged along behind the wagons. Reuel looked around to try and get some sense of where they were, but he did not recognize the stretch of road they were on—it was not a main trade route, he knew. His best guess was that they were somewhere to the west of Jerusalem, heading south.

Their captor walked beside the last wagon in the train with a bowlegged gate that made his shoulders and head rock back and forth rhythmically.

"Halt!" he called after a short time, and the chain ground to a stop. The beady-eyed man scrambled up a low bank to the west of the road where a small cluster of ancient oaks was growing, their massive trunks wrinkled and scarred with age. He circled the trees a few times, pawing at the bark and muttering to himself. When he finally climbed back down to the road, he clutched something in his dirty fists.

"Haa Haa! It is those bugs!" he called out to his six companions. "The bugs that the Phoenicians make the purple dye out of."

"Two handfuls?" one of his men responded. "You stopped for two handfuls of bugs?"

"They are valuable! Do not ever pass up something of value—isn't that what I always tell you?"

"That's what you always tell us," the man confirmed, glancing at the wagons piled high with miscellany and shaking his head.

Their captor ignored him. He dumped his treasure into a cloth bag on the back of the nearest wagon. "Move on!" he shouted, and they slowly eased forward again.

Then Reuel saw the distant gleaming of a flame atop one of the highest peaks visible, and another farther north.

The signal fires of Israel, lit to alert the nation to a threat.

The Philistines were coming. That had to be what the lighting of the flames meant. The nation was being summoned to war.

The man beside him stumbled, nearly pulling Reuel down with him. Reuel tried to help him back to his feet as they were dragged forward, forced to continue moving by the prisoners ahead of and behind them.

"Thank you," the man whispered.

Reuel was about to answer when a voice from behind him interrupted. "Do not talk to that one. Do not touch him if you can avoid it."

Reuel craned his neck to see the speaker. It was another prisoner—his accent and short-cropped beard identified him as a Canaanite. "Why not?" Reuel asked.

"He is been singled out for particular attention," the Canaanite said, thrusting his chin in the direction of their Captor. "Do not give them any reason to think you are connected with him, or you will find there are worse things than being chained like an animal to a Slaver's cart."

"Slaver?" Reuel felt a fool as he began to realize the full scope of his predicament.

The Canaanite looked at Reuel as though he were out of his mind. "Where did you think we were going? To a harvest celebration?"

Somewhere ahead of Reuel someone in the chain stumbled and he was jerked forward. When he regained his balance he looked over at the man tied next to him. His lips were chapped and bleeding, his eyes dark and hollow, but somehow his face was still both handsome and proud. Not only was he hobbled and his hands bound behind his back, but additional loops of rope had been tied around his neck and waist. The flesh of his arms and his legs was pocked with inflamed, red wounds—the marks of the heated, copper implement the Slaver used for torture.

"I am Reuel," he whispered to the man.

The prisoner did not look at Reuel when he spoke. "I am Jiram. But he is right. Do not let them see you talking to me. I do not wish to be the cause of any further suffering."

They walked forward in silence for a while then. Reuel tried not to think about the pain that wracked his body. His muscles were stiff and bruised, and wounds he could not see on his head and hip throbbed and burned with each step. He was worried that if the wounds went untended they could become infected. He already felt nauseas and he hoped it was due to fear and hunger rather than some sickness raging through his body.

The Slaver and his six companions led them along lesser-used roads, at times leaving the road entirely where the landscape permitted the donkeys to pull the wagons across the open ground. The farther south they traveled, the drier and more barren the landscape became. They stopped once mid-morning and Reuel watched in horror as the Slaver trudged to the back of the string of prisoners to cut free an elderly man who had fallen to the ground and was no longer moving. The Slaver kicked him several times in the stomach and chest and when the old man did not respond, he ordered the train to move on, leaving the body in the dirt in the middle of the roadway. A woman's muffled weeping haunted the dry wind.

As they eased forward, the Slaver walked along the line with a worn skin of water, splashing a mouthful on each of his prisoner's faces. They waited for him with mouths wide, necks outstretched—like baby birds in a nest, Reuel thought.

When the Slaver reached Jiram, Reuel saw that the young man was staring at his own feet.

"Haa! Very good!" the Slaver said. "You accept your fate at last. Let the gods provide you with water if they want to. I will not."

Jiram neither moved nor spoke.

"Did you hear me, boy?" the Slaver said, grabbing Jiram's hair and pulling his head up so that he was staring into the boy's eyes.

Jiram still did not speak. The Slaver raised one hand as if to strike him, and then brought it down gently, palm patting Jiram's cheek.

"We will spare your pretty face," he said. "Pretty faces bring higher prices in the markets of Be'ersheba—there are men there who would pay a fortune to own a pretty face like yours."

He let go of Jiram and splashed Reuel's face with water. Reuel was ready and caught a mouthful.

Fighting his desperate urge to swallow, he held the tepid, gritty liquid in his mouth until the Slaver had moved down the line farther and had his back turned. Then he bent down to Jiram and placed his lips on the young man's as if in a kiss. Jiram understood what he was doing and opened his mouth. Reuel spat the water into it, and Jiram swallowed, then coughed horribly into his own bare shoulder for several minutes.

"I should not have accepted that," Jiram said when he had stopped coughing. "Now you have had no water."

"Do you know where I was before I was captured?" Reuel asked. "Drowning. I have had water enough to last me for days."

The Slaver started yelling and his companions whipped the wagons forward and the captives to their feet. When they were underway again, two of the men who traveled with the Slaver walked back alongside the chain of prisoners. Reuel saw one of the captives, a son of fourteen or fifteen years, glance their way.

"Eyes forward!" the guard snapped.

The boy flinched away and his father (whose wrists were not tied) wrapped his arms around his son's shoulders protectively.

"Let go of him!" the guard snarled. "He needs to learn to take his stripes like a man. Soon enough, you will not be around to watch over him anymore."

"Just think of it!" the other guard said. "Once we reach the markets of Be'ersheba, the two of you could find yourselves headed toward opposite ends of the world!"

The father released his son and the nearest guard punched the young man in the face, then laughed uproariously as the dazed boy stumbled, trying to keep his footing, and blood poured from his nose.

By early evening they were marching along the salt-encrusted shore of the Dead Sea. On the hills to the west, they passed clustered black-and-brown tents of nomadic shepherds that faded like mirages against the dun-colored walls of the wadis. Once two shepherdesses appeared atop a nearby hill as though by magic, their black robes fluttering in the hot wind, their veils aglitter with silver dowry coins. Reuel knew they would do nothing to help the captives. They were a solitary people who lived by an ancient code that was centered on a single precept: the survival of their culture in a hostile land.

Jiram stumbled every few steps, and his face had gone white. Reuel moved closer to him. "Try to lean on me as we walk," he said.

"I dare not!" Jiram said. "If the guards see you—."

"I will take my chances with the guards," Reuel said. He locked his bent elbow against Jiram's elbow. "Try to let me carry some of your weight."

Reuel was not sure if he was actually helping or just providing a measure of emotional support, but Jiram continued to stumble forward until they reached their destination: a desolate spot on the shore of the Dead Sea where the Slaver decided they were going to camp for the night. The wagons stopped and the prisoners collapsed where they stood.

Jiram was asleep instantly, his breathing raspy and shallow. Reuel lay down next to him. He tested their ropes briefly, but it was obvious the slavers knew what they were doing. He was not going to get loose on his own. He was on his way to Be'ersheba, and no one even knew he was alive.

33

Mid-morning of the day after Samuel and his companions had arrived at the Tabernacle, Ahimelech sent a messenger to tell him that Ahitub was again awake and ready to see him.

Samuel entered the High Priest's room to find him still in bed, propped up in a sitting position by bolsters on either side of him. His vermilion staff was vertical in his right hand as though it, too, supported some of his weight. There was no one else in the room.

"My lord!" Samuel got on his knees next to the bed and took the High Priest's left hand between his own palms. "How is it with you?"

"Everything is changing, Samuel," Ahitub said, his voice stronger than the day before, but still thin and phlegmy. "What the High Priest once was, he is no longer."

Samuel smiled. "The years catch up with all of us, but our minds and hearts become mightier each day."

"No," Ahitub said. "It is the role itself that is changing. Priest, Prophet, Judge, General—what are any of them now, and what will they be tomorrow?"

"You speak in riddles, my lord," Samuel said.

"Perhaps. But only because it is a riddle to me as well."

Samuel was quiet a moment, wondering what thoughts passed through his mentor's mind after a lifetime of sacred service.

"Ahimelech has disclosed to my ears that you wish me to come with you to Mizpah," Ahitub said at last.

Samuel nodded. "After the death of Avdon, and the revelation of a new Philistine threat, the people are ready to return to Jehovah with all their hearts. They only lack a High Priest to tell them what to do."

Ahitub shifted under his bedclothes. "We have already told them, Samuel. Now it is time to show them."

"My lord?"

"Aaron and his son Phinehas—they were men born for days of war. Their Priesthood was one of action. Other High Priests were born for days of peace, of teaching and guiding our people through planting and harvest." He sighed deeply. "I was not born to lead men into battle."

Samuel grasped his mentor's hand more tightly, feeling the slender bones under the dry, paper-thin skin. "You could, if it was needed. Men would follow you to their deaths and count it a privilege. But today, our nation needs their Priest as a sanctifier, not a general."

"And what do they need from their Prophet?" Ahitub asked. "And are you ready to give it to them?"

"I do not understand."

"We have already told them what to do, my son. Now it is time for you to show them."

"Show them what, my lord?"

Ahitub sighed. "Seeing one's own death drawing close leads the mind on unusual paths, Samuel. I cannot expect the young to be able to follow those paths with ease."

"Do not speak of death, my lord. You are needed in Israel for many years more before you are gathered to your fathers."

Ahitub smiled at Samuel, a look of such compassion that it made Samuel's heart ache. "The length of our lives is not determined by the wishes of our friends, my son. If it was, you would live to times indefinite."

"As would you, my old friend."

"But our people's history is built on stories of those whose deaths have meant as much as their lives."

Samuel frowned. "Manoah said something similar to me, just days ago. He said, 'It is our willingness even to martyr ourselves in the service of our God that is our greatest power.'"

"How is Manoah, and how is Samson?" Ahitub asked.

"Samson bows under the weight of his destiny. Manoah, I'm afraid, has become consumed by thoughts of vengeance."

Ahitub nodded and sighed. "But he is a man who will not hesitate to give his life doing what he believes to be God's will." He turned toward Samuel. "What about you, my son?"

"Me?"

"Are you prepared to give all in the service of our God?"

The High Priest's look was so intense that Samuel's throat went dry and his skin suddenly felt cold, as though an icy draft had entered the room. "My lord? Are you saying...are you telling me...?"

"That you must be prepared to give up everything, Samuel. Everything. Jehovah uses those who have truly learned to rely on him. He strips them of everything sometimes, so that they may trust in His strength, and not their own. They must, for at times He asks them to give the ultimate sacrifice."

Samuel rose to his feet and squared his shoulders. "I am prepared to die in the service of our God."

Ahitub raised one eyebrow. "Why do you assume that the ultimate sacrifice is your life? For some men, yes. But for you? There are worse things to you than dying a martyr's death."

Samuel's mind was spinning. The conversation was not going at all like he had imagined it would. Why were they talking about him at all?

"In any case," said Ahitub, leaning hard on his staff to push himself up a little in bed, "I will do as you have asked. I will prepare to go to Mizpah, to sanctify the children of Abraham."

"I hope that I have not asked too much of you, my lord."

"I will pray that Jehovah gives me the strength. If he does not, then I will die, and another man will march at your side to Mizpah."

"Is it in your power to leave today?"

Ahitub took a deep breath and let it out slowly. "We shall see. Find Ahimelech and send him to me."

"Just as you say, my lord." Samuel kissed Ahitub's wrinkled forehead and strode toward the door.

"Samuel! Wait!"

Samuel returned to the bedside. He saw that Ahitub's eyes were pale and watery, but behind them was the shadow of his old intensity. Ahitub pushed his vermilion staff into Samuel's hand. "Take this, my son."

Samuel looked down in confusion. "It is unthinkable, my lord."

"You can, and you will. This is the staff my grandfather Eli carved for me from the branch of an almond tree when I was a son of thirteen years. It is called *Mish'eneth*."

Samuel ran his hands over the polished, vermilion-stained wood. The grip had been carved with a pattern of interlacing almond leaves, the rest of the staff with a maze of whorls and lines. "I remember. That is the name Aaron gave to his staff that Jehovah caused to produce buds and blossoms and ripe almonds in the days of Korah's rebellion."

Ahitub nodded. "Aaron's staff still rests inside the Ark of the Covenant, in Kiriath-jearim. It was, perhaps, presumptuous of me to adopt the name, but I was young."

"This is the staff of a High Priest," Samuel said, examining the intricate carvings around the grip. "It is a matter of debate if I am even an Elder of my tribe."

"You yourself well known that you are more than an Elder, Samuel. Why do you insist on pretending you do not matter, when you know you do? Are you that desperate to hear people say it to you over and over again?"

Samuel looked at the floor. "Perhaps I am."

"Why? Does repetition make it truer? Or do you value the judgment of your fellow man more than you value the approval of God?"

"Whether or not I have God's approval is a question that He does not give us a clear answer to," replied Samuel. "How we are treated by the people of God is our best indicator of how He sees us."

"Indeed? So is Jehovah controlling the words and actions of men, then?"

"You know that is not what I mean. But whatever opinion…I am not a man who can accept the possible signs of God's favor as certainties! I cannot afford to! I am my reputation, and my reputation lies in the hands of men!"

"The hand of Jehovah is cut short, is it?" Ahitub asked.

Samuel did not answer, but tried to hand the staff back. "Keep this, my lord."

"I will not!" said Ahitub. "Accept it, and may it serve you as well as it has served me as you walk before the people of Israel."

"You will come to Mizpah, then?" Samuel asked.

"If Jehovah permits it. Perhaps I will consult the Urim and Thummim. But I do not think we will leave today, my son."

Samuel felt fear and urgency gnawing at his stomach, but he hid it from the High Priest. "As you say, my lord."

Samuel made his way toward the Altar of Burnt Offering, crowded with supplicants and animal corpses-to-be. He smiled to see that someone had planted an herb garden near one side of the curtain wall, removing a few of the flagstones to make way for neatly trimmed clusters of coriander, horseradish, cumin, garlic, mint, and rue. Their determined smell fought its way through the pervasive odor of smoke, incense, and burning flesh.

He found Ahimelech at the Altar. "The Elders of Nob want us to leave for Mizpah now, without my father, and carry the Ark with us into battle," Ahimelech said as soon as Samuel was close enough to hear him.

"Did we not already learn that lesson at Aphek?" Samuel said.

"How was my father when you left him?"

"Much better than yesterday. We had a lively conversation. It reminded me of my youth."

"What do you mean by 'much better'?" Ahimelech asked.

Samuel hesitated. "He does not feel that he can travel today. Tomorrow, he told me."

Ahimelech nodded. "Speak to me honestly, Samuel. Can we wait that long?"

Samuel was taken aback. "We will wait as long as it takes! There is no replacement for having the High Priest bless the nation."

They paused as a half-dozen Levites passed carrying two-handled, woven baskets filled with powdery stacte drops, yellowish-white onycha taken from the muscles of mollusks, and galbanum from fennel—all ingredients in the sacred incense.

"A group of merchants arrived today," Ahimelech said, nodding toward the baskets.

"Did they bring any news?"

"Indeed. They said that there has been some sort of Amorite uprising in Kiriath-jearim, and in other places. There are no details yet, but something major is happening."

"Summer and winter have arrived in one day," said Samuel.

Ahimelech nodded. "May Jehovah preserve us."

34

Manoah and Samson's route from the flood that had taken Reuel was to follow the churning, brown water slowly downstream, one on either side of the flow. The leaves of the underbrush and the stalks of grass were dripping from the rain and within a short time both father and son were soaked from the hips down. They moved slowly, scanning the earth for any sign of the young prophet or his body. Samson tried to look for the color of a prophet's robe, but the taupe wool would have been very similar to the silt in color. His eyes began to ache with the effort of scanning as much ground as possible.

By the time evening was drawing close the water had vanished into the thirsty ground, leaving behind murky puddles and a trail of dark silt and debris coating the tumbled stones in the bed of the wadi.

The first meaningful sign they discovered was a fresh set of wagon ruts and a jumble of footprints where the silt paralleled a road for a short distance. They paused, crouching to peer at the tracks.

"Three wagons?" Samson asked, fingertips brushing the tracks lightly.

Manoah nodded. "And dozens of unshod feet."

Samson glanced up in the direction the wagons had gone. "Slavers."

"Could be. But that's no reason to believe that Reuel is with them, or that he was ever here."

Then why did you bring it up? wondered Samson, but he kept his thoughts to himself.

Manoah stood, pushing his shoulders back to stretch aching muscles. "It will be dark soon. I'm not sure how much farther we should continue."

"There are hundreds of places we passed already that Reuel could have wandered from the path of the flood and left no track or sign," said Samson.

"Or we could have simply missed whatever tracks were left," said Manoah. "In either case, we dare delay no longer in returning to Naioth to check on the Prophet's family. Reuel, if he has survived, will have to look out for himself."

"Jehovah will watch out for him," Samson said.

"If it is His will. But whether or not, there are people in Ramathaim who may need our help—and we must be at Mizpah in a handful of days."

They turned northwest then, following the trade road through the hills in the direction of Samaria and Ramathaim. That night they slept in Gibeon again, arriving there well after dark. They were up before dawn the next morning, retracing for a time the steps of their journey of a few days before, then turning onto the road that cut through the forested mountains to the northwest, angling toward Timnath-serah and Ramathaim.

They did not talk, content to leave each other to their own thoughts. For Samson, those thoughts wandered uncomfortable paths, second guessing their decision to abandon Reuel to his fate. He understood why his father had chosen to do so, and he could not fault his logic. What bothered him was the seeming callousness with which he had made the decision. How could they so lightly abandon an innocent child of Abraham whose life was almost certainly in danger?

He did not say anything to his father. There was no need. He knew exactly how he would respond: he would reason with Samson on the logic behind his decision, defying him to come up with a better solution. And Samson knew he could not—the lives of the people in Ramathaim who were threatened, the urgency of their arrival to the summons at Mizpah out-weighed the slim possibility that they might find Reuel and rescue him.

He admitted to himself that, eventually, he would likely have made the same decision as his father. It was the speed at which Manoah had made it and the exercise of cold logic in the absence of any expression of concern or regret for Reuel's welfare that bothered him.

By late afternoon they had reached the forest that bordered Naioth to the southeast. They were just entering its borders when Samson grabbed his father's arm and pointed to the sky ahead of them. "Look!"

Greasy smoke wafted toward the scattered clouds, and the inky shapes of carrion birds soared and circled through it.

They rushed forward, leaping through the forest underbrush until they burst clear of the trees in sight of the School.

There they froze, staring. The smell of ash and the sharp, sweet odor of burning flesh filled Samson's nostrils as he scanned the scene: charred skeletons of homes and outbuildings, blackened and crumbling. The beams and joists of stacked-stone houses had failed and the roofs had col-lapsed atop furniture and personal belongings. Gardens, orchards, vine-yards—all were razed to the ground. The charred carcasses of cattle, sheep, and goats lay haphazardly between the houses and on the paths, some of them still seeping greasy smoke.

"Search for survivors!" Manoah said, whispering in the morbid si-lence.

They separated and began combing through the wreckage of the buildings. By the third house he had searched, Samson was convinced that they were, thankfully, not going to find anyone. The homes were empty of people, though some of them held the blackened corpses of animals, charred so extensively that he could sometimes not even identify what creature they had once been.

He met up again with his father on the narrow road that passed through the hamlet. "Anything?" Manoah asked.

Samson shook his head. "They must all have escaped."

"Or been taken prisoner," Manoah growled.

"And left not one body? Someone would have fought!"

"The Philistines could have taken the bodies!"

"To what purpose?" asked Samson.

"I do not know!" Manoah snapped. "They are animals, and do not act with the logic of men."

Samson let the matter drop. "We have not yet checked the Prophet Samuel's house."

Manoah sniffed and spat on the ash-dusted ground. "Well, let us get to it."

They strode up the low hill on which Samuel's dwelling had been built. His courtyard gate was not burned, but it had been torn from its hinges. When they could see inside the courtyard itself, both of them stopped abruptly.

Crimson smears on the flagstones of the courtyard told of something being dragged very recently over the stones—something that was losing an enormous amount of blood.

Both men drew their swords in unison, and Samson swung his shield from his back onto his left arm. They crept, knees bent, through the gateway and eased across the flagstones. Samson tried to still his breathing as the Zebulunite weapons masters had taught him, straining to hear any sound coming from inside the house itself. He felt the inner stillness that old Bocheru had taught him creep through his muscles; his training began to take over his body.

When it came, he did not need to strain to hear it. Something fell with a crash, followed by a cracking thud. The two men leapt toward the open door, one of them taking up position on either side of the dark entryway, swords at the ready. Samson took the right side, silently slipping his shield onto his right arm and his sword to his left hand. He was suddenly appreciative of, if not grateful for, his father's decision to bind his right hand for days at a time when he was young, in the manner of the tribe of Benjamin, forcing him to become ambidextrous.

Both jambs were smeared with blood and black ichor, and a gobbet of unidentifiable raw flesh lay across the threshold.

Father and son looked at each other, nodded once almost in unison, and burst through the doorway, howling.

The howl was choked off—what they saw took the breath from their lungs.

Two lions, huge thick-maned males, seemed to fill the room, looming side by side over the carcass of a donkey. Their victim's skin was nearly gone; they had torn open its rib cage and were feeding on the organs. Their muzzles and claws were smeared with blood, and in the moment that the two Danites appeared, their mouths were open just enough to reveal their dagger-like, crimson-streaked teeth.

Men and beasts stared at each other for a moment that seemed to stretch into eternity.

Then both lions roared, a sound so loud it shook plaster from the walls and rained debris on the heads of the two men who dropped instinctively into protective crouches next to the door. Samson felt his insides quaver with the strength of that roar, and though he gritted his teeth and kept facing forward, his heart seemed to stop in his chest.

Both men dove for the doorway. Manoah was closer—he made it out just ahead of Samson, who landed with his shoulder pressed against the inside of his shield, rolled once, and came to his feet with his sword at the ready.

Manoah was already spinning, his iron blade raised above his head. The first of the lions slipped out the door almost slowly, head down as if to show he was unafraid. Without hesitation, Manoah brought his sword down right onto the lion's muzzle, just in front of his eyes, and in a single stroke sheared away the beast's entire nose and jaw.

The lion leapt away, its roar turned to a gurgling rasp. Rolling and thrashing at the empty air, it tried to attack but was unable to see or smell its prey. Samson raced after it, waited just long enough for the beast to roll to its feet once again, and then plunged his sword through the animal's neck behind his ears. The lion convulsed once, so violently it nearly threw Samson to the ground and ripped his hilt from his hand, then collapsed onto the bloodied flagstones.

Samson yanked his sword free and spun just in time to see the second lion burst through the doorway in a flying leap, sending plaster and wood splinters flying in every direction as his muscular shoulders tore the top half of the opening two hand-spans wider than it had been. Manoah leapt clear, but the huge cat hit the ground and turned in a single, fluid motion, launching himself at the big Danite.

Samson was already running. He saw Manoah swing with all his strength at the giant form descending on him, but the lion batted the sword away mid-leap and landed on the Danite with crushing force.

Samson heard Manoah bellow in pain and rage. He did not go for the kill; in that moment he wanted only to get the beast off of his father. He slashed downward with his blade at the lion's tawny hindquarters and the sword jarred his arm as its edge struck bone somewhere in the beast's hip.

The lion turned so quickly that for an instant Samson was staring at its bloodied tail and its open mouth at the same time. A huge paw flashed past his view, its claws shredding the leather of his shield and effortlessly hurling him across the courtyard.

He bounced off the plastered wall and landed on his face and chest on the flagstones. Struggling to get air back into his lungs, he pulled himself to his knees. His left arm throbbed and he withdrew it from the shredded shield's straps, letting the broken wood and leather clatter to the ground.

Across the courtyard, Manoah stood defiantly with his sword held before him in both hands. Only a few steps away the lion paced, eyes locked on Manoah's tall form, tail dragging and leaving a smeared line of blood on the flagstones behind it.

Samson struggled to his feet, leaning against the wall for support. His head spun and he tried to focus on what was happening in front of him.

The lion charged Manoah again; this time, the big Danite dodged to one side and slashed downwards as the cat slipped past. It was only a grazing blow, and the lion landed, spun, and jumped again before Manoah could even finish turning around. Both tumbled to the ground in a flurry of fur and blood.

Instinct and training sent Samson stumbling across the courtyard. He heard a strange sound behind him and looked back before he realized it was the sound of the tip of his sword, clasped loosely in his right hand, dragging over the stones as he walked.

He shook his head to clear it and drew his dagger from his belt. He held it loosely; clenching his left fist sent stabbing pains up his arm. "Hey!" he shouted, trying to get the lion's attention.

The big cat snarled and rolled off of Manoah; Samson heard pain and anger in the sound. Manoah was crab-crawling backwards, his left shoulder a mass of blood and shredded cloth, a third of his sword blade coated in bright blood. The lion tucked its back legs under it and prepared to pounce.

Samson hurled the knife at its head.

The dagger spun through the air and the blade vanished in the flesh behind the lion's ear. It turned to face Samson, roaring again: Abruptly, Samson's entire world seemed to be consumed in gleaming, white teeth and a bellowing fury that was far more hatred than hunger.

Samson roared back at it and leapt forward, sword raised. Out of the corner of his eye, he saw his father get to his feet and move forward as well. The lion turned from one to the other, snarling.

Come for me! Samson silently called.

The lion obeyed. Fluid and silent, it uncurled its long body, forelegs stretched out before it, hind legs nearly horizontal.

Time congealed. The beast grew until it filled Samson's vision, open mouth roaring with the stench of carrion, the odor of sweat and dust thickening the air. Samson did not think, but let his muscles respond with pure instinct. When the lion was an arm's length from his own body, he plunged his sword through its ribs and into its beating heart with all his might.

In the same instant, the lion's bulk hit him and he was crushed onto the flagstones. The back of his head cracked against the rock and pain exploded through him, reddening his vision.

All went still. Fading in and out of consciousness, Samson realized the lion was lying atop him, but it was not moving. He tried to pull his way free of the cumbrous corpse, but could only wiggle a little to one side. It was enough, though, to see the tip of his sword's blade protruding from between the lion's bony shoulders.

Manoah stumbled over to him a moment later, his face beneath his beard white with blood loss. Together they heaved until they had rolled the corpse away and Samson could pull himself to his knees, still struggling to get his breath.

"Sons of Belial!" he heard Manoah whisper, and he nodded his agreement.

"Samson!" Manoah hissed urgently.

Samson looked up and followed his father's eyes to the top of Samuel's roof chamber.

Another lion stood there, the biggest lion Samson had ever seen, massive and muscled, with a huge, tar-black mane and a black-tipped tail. A fierce, white scar curved from the corner of his left eye down his tawny cheek. His neck was arched proudly as he stared down at the two men below him. Still as an idol, he stood for several moments, watching.

Then he turned with cool deliberation and leapt from the rooftop to the yard behind it, landing silently and vanishing in two bounds into the scrub and rocks.

Samson heard his father exhale slowly and turned to face him. "He did not leave because he feared us," Samson said.

Manoah shook his head. "No. Jehovah was watching over us today."

Samson struggled to his feet, still dizzy and a little nauseous. Stumbling, he ducked back into Samuel's house and gathered some scraps of cloth from a shredded blanket. His father sat gingerly on a bench in the courtyard while Samson bound his shoulder. The wound was long and gaping, but miraculously no tendons had been cut and the bleeding was already slowing.

"What do we do now?" Samson asked as he worked.

Manoah shifted on the bench and winced. "Ahh! We return to Samuel at Mizpah. Hopefully we do so before the Philistine dogs who have done this reach him."

Samson tied two knots in the cloth, securing the bandage. "And the Prophet's family?"

Manoah bent his left arm and gingerly raised his elbow a hand span, gritting his teeth. "They are likely somewhere between here and there. Let us hope we can find them."

"Let us hope, indeed," said Samson. "Before war catches up to them."

"War is already upon us," Manoah said, glancing around at the destroyed School. "What has been started here can only end on the field of battle."

35

Reuel woke in the cold, blue hours before dawn, when the light of sunrise was just easing over the hills of Ammon and Moab. He remained where he was for several moments, lying on his back in a field of dew-dampened herbs and grasses, staring up at the fading stars. The musky smell of wet earth filled his nostrils. His body ached all over, but he knew the real pain would begin when he moved.

Abruptly he remembered Jiram and turned his head to check on him; pain like a burning heat stabbed through his neck as he did so. Jiram lay next to him, also on his back. His eyes were open.

"Did you sleep?" Reuel whispered.

"A little."

Reuel gingerly raised himself to his elbows and looked around. Spring's grasses sprouted knee-high all around them. Reuel crawl as far as he could without pulling on the tethering rope. Within his arm's reach, hidden under half flattened weeds, was a dwarf mallow, its saw-edged leaves young and soft, its flower stalks already weighted with clusters of disc-shaped fruits.

He took a deep breath and lay down again on his back, pulling his knees tightly against his chest. Gritting his teeth against the pain in his shoulders, he worked his tied hands down the back of his thighs, then over his feet. In a few moments, they were in front of him.

He paused to catch his breath, then got to his knees and gathered the leaves and the fruits, caught two grasshoppers half-frozen under the grass, and collected a handful of wild vetch.

"Eat." Reuel poured the double handful of wild food on the ground next to Jiram's head.

The young man rolled onto his left side and looked at Reuel with knitted brows. "Why are you doing this for me?"

"Because you need to eat!"

"You have no obligation to help me. You know that you could yourself suffer for doing so." Jiram gestured toward the pile of food with his chin. "And you have not eaten."

"I am a healer," said Reuel. "I cannot treat your wounds, but I can do my best to make you strong."

"I am not a Hebrew."

Reuel smiled. "Yes, I had figured that out."

Jiram swallowed once, looking now at the food.

Reuel reached out and began feeding it to him: first the mallow cheeses, then the bitter vetch leaves, and lastly the grasshoppers, biting off and spitting out the heads. Jiram ate slowly, chewing each bit for a long time and swallowing with difficulty due to the dryness of his throat.

When he had finished he lay back down on his back again. "I am in your debt, Reuel."

"Nonsense. I have a better chance of escaping if the man I am tied to is not half-dead."

Reuel felt, rather than saw, Jiram's smile. "Where do you come from?"

"I am a servant of Samuel ben Elkanah, the Prophet of Israel," Reuel said. "I live at the School of the Prophets in Naioth."

"I have heard of Samuel," said Jiram. "It is said that he wields great power, and can strike his enemies with plague and famine."

"He is beloved of our God, Jehovah," Reuel said. "I do not believe anything is beyond the reach of the power God will give him. Even now, he prepares our people for war against the Philistines."

Jiram exhaled disgustedly through his nose. "Lord Ashkelon will not stop until he possesses all of Canaan. It is not only you Hebrews who call the Philistines 'enemy'."

The crash of something being thrown against one of the wagons and a series of curses alerted them that their captors were waking. Reuel lay back down and closed his eyes, determined to get a few more moments rest before they started moving again.

"Thank you, Reuel the servant of Samuel," he heard Jiram whisper.

Only moments later cries of pain and the sounds of bodies being dragged over the grass alerted them that the wagons had begun rolling again. Reuel could move more freely now that his hands were in front of him, and he helped Jiram to his feet. Grateful for the cool morning air and the dew that kept the dust down, they continued trudging south.

The day was very still. From the road they could look down on the pale cobalt waters of the Dead Sea, rimmed by a wide shore of white salt. Visibility was limited by the haze of evaporating moisture, but the still water reflected the tawny limestone cliffs of Moab, broken by outcrops of basalt and charcoal-grey limestone. The heat grew more oppressive with each footstep until the prisoners felt as though they were walking through an oven.

The Slaver, apparently blessed with boundless energy, cursed and yelled at them to hurry, but even the donkeys pulling the wagons were lethargic and the line would move no faster.

The sun was a circle of angry flame in the sky above them when they reached an oasis alongside the road. Clusters of date palms curved gracefully skyward, casting welcome shadows on an oval of tamarisks and rushes. At their center a small, shallow pool huddled under the shadow of a pale grey boulder seamed with streaks of bright green moss.

The Slaver yelled something that Reuel could not understand, and the wagons ground to a halt.

To Reuel's surprise, the Slaver untied their rope from the rear wagon and walked back toward the center of the human chain, grasping its loosed end in his hands.

"Haa haa!" he said, smiling broadly. He slowly made his way down the line, untying the prisoner's hands, but leaving tied the rope looped around their waists. "We have a long way to travel tomorrow—a long, dry way. Haa! So today, you get all the water you can drink!"

When he reached Reuel he looked down at the young man's hands, in front of him rather than behind his back as were the hands of the others.

The Slaver smiled. "Haa! You are not the first to do this, boy. I came up with an answer to this kind of cleverness years ago. I just run hooks through the flesh of your forearms, and tie the rope to the hooks. Haa! That discourages cleverness, eh? Haa haa!"

When the Slaver had untied all of their hands the captives looked at each other nervously, rubbing their wrists as they were loosed, not trusting any generosity from their oppressors.

"Follow me!" The Slaver, pulling the rope, led them through the hip-high reeds to the clear pool. His six partners followed; two of them held stocky, recurved bows, their bellies reinforced with long, narrow plates of aurochs horn. The guards took up positions around the pool, kneeling to drink but glancing up frequently to keep an eye on the string of captives. The two archers stood side by side, arrows nocked.

The Slaver tossed the rope to the ground. "You all look like I'm trying to poison you! Haa! I need you alive when I reach Be'ersheba—alive and awake, or you're worthless to me on the slave block. Here is free water, and if I can convince you fools to drink it, you're more likely to survive the journey!"

His assurances were enough for several of the parched captives. They lunged forward, pulling the rest of the line with them as they fell to their knees on the muddy banks and lowered their faces to the now-dirty water. A moment later, the rest of the captives had joined them, including Reuel and Jiram. Reuel could feel the silt against his teeth as he drank, but nevertheless the water seemed the most refreshing beverage he had ever had.

After several long draughts, he raised his head and looked around. The six guards were standing again now, a few of them holding full skins of water, some leaning on the shaggy palm trunks looking almost as exhausted and hot as Reuel felt.

Movement in the reeds across the pool caught his eye, and he turned to see a man push free of the dense grasses to reach the now-muddied water. He was dressed like a Benjaminite shepherd: a simple wool tunic belted at the waist with a wide, leather belt. A mantle of white wool lay over his shoulders, surprising in the heat, and his belt was draped with a wide stone-pouch, half a dozen slings, and a bola with smooth stone weights.

He stopped and looked across at the string of prisoners and their captors. His eyes narrowed, and he drew his turban off of his thick, curly hair and used it to wipe his face and close-trimmed beard. Only a few paces from where Reuel knelt, the Slaver tensed, staring at the new arrival, his right hand going to his sword hilt. His eyes shifted to his two archers, as if to reassure himself that he was well protected.

The Benjaminite squatted at the pool's edge and began to scoop water into his mouth with one cupped hand. He rinsed his turban and wrung it out, then placed it back on his head and adjusted its band. Reuel watched him carefully. Benjaminites moved differently than anyone else. The men of the tribe were all ambidextrous, made so by their fathers who alternately bound one of their hands throughout their childhood. The change was subtle, but watching someone doing even simple tasks and not favoring one hand lent a strangeness to their movements, instantly recognized but not easily defined.

The Slaver must have decided the man posed no threat, and he went back to rinsing his head from the skin of water he had collected. Reuel stayed still, squatting on his haunches, watching the Benjaminite. For a moment, he had seen something in the man's eyes...

The Benjaminite stood again. "That is quite the cargo you are transporting," he said across the still water.

The Slaver scowled. "Move on, stranger. This is none of your business."

The Benjaminite shrugged. "Maybe not."

He looked up at the blazing sun, squinting, then turned back to face the Slaver. "Of course, if any of those people are my countrymen, then maybe it is my business."

"I'm warning you," snapped the Slaver. "Unless you have an army with you, you had better walk away. Now."

A hint of a smile played across the shepherd's face. "No, no army. Just me."

He looked down at his feet, and when he raised his eyes, a loaded sling was in his hand. "Just me and a handful of stones."

The Slaver spat in the pool and turned to the archers. "Kill him!"

Before the men could even raise their bows, the sling whirled once around the Benjaminite's head and a stone shot across the pool. Faster than the eye could follow, it clipped the top of the first archer's head and sent him tumbling to the ground, hand clutching the wound; it continued and hit the other archer in the temple, felling him like a timberman fells a tree.

Howling, the other four guards and the Slaver drew their weapons and rushed toward the Benjaminite. His sling whirled again, and this time the stone shot past his attackers and smashed into the pot of coals suspended from the third wagon. It shattered, scattering smoking embers into the mass of random goods the Slaver had collected. A garden of flame blossomed.

The Slaver turned, wide-eyed. "My treasures!" He raced toward his burning loot.

The mule yoked to the third wagon bolted forward, trying to escape the flame and startling the other mules who likewise began to trot away from the oasis. They quickly picked up speed, the wagons careened in three different directions while the Slaver waved his arms, yelling madly.

Reuel looked back just as the first soldiers were reaching the Benjaminite. He felled the nearest with another sling stone shot from a dozen paces. The three remaining closed on him, swords raised. As soon as they were within reach he whipped the loose end of his sling across the nearest ones eyes; it snapped like a whip and the man tumbled backward and fell in the water, clutching at his face and howling.

Another soldier swung his sword at the shepherd's head and he lunged backward to avoid the blow. The grasses and reeds caught at his heels and he fell on his backside among the growth. The guard loomed over him, sword raised for the killing stroke.

The Benjaminite's fall, though, was a feint. From his position on the ground he whipped his sling so that it wrapped around his attacker's legs, then he somersaulted forward toward the man. The guard, legs bound together, crashed onto his back in the reeds.

The last soldier was on top of the shepherd then, khopesh slashing. The Benjaminite rolled clear of the blow and onto his feet. One of the bolas was in his hand and he swung it in a whirling criss-cross pattern in the man's direction. The guard retreated a step, just long enough for the Benjaminite to adjust the bolas' whirling direction so that its weighted end cracked against the head of the man on the ground, struggling to untie his legs. He crumpled.

The final guard lunged forward, khopesh held out before him. The bolas was still swinging, and the Benjaminite let a few more inches of its cord slip through his grasp. The next spin brought the stone down on the guard's head, and he fell silently to the ground.

Without taking a breath the Benjaminite sprinted around the pool toward the Slaver, who was still trying to calm the mule yoked to his burning wagon. The Slaver was oblivious to his presence until the shepherd's sling wrapped around the his neck like a garrote. The Slaver clawed at the cord, his legs flailing as the Benjaminite dragged him backwards to the edge of the pool. While the man thrashed and kicked futilely, the Benjaminite tied the garrote around a palm trunk so that the Slaver's back was pulled tightly against it. In moments, he had yanked the Slaver's hands backward and tied them behind the tree with slender, leather lacing.

The Slaver choked and struggled. Ignoring him and the captives, the Benjaminite loped from fallen guard to fallen guard, resting one ear over each of their mouths to see if they still breathed. Two did—he dragged them to the palm trees next to their leader and bound their hands tightly, leaving them lying face down in the sandy soil.

The prisoners were disentangling themselves; Reuel helped Jiram to get free of his bonds. It took several minutes--the knots were tight and the cords wrapped around his neck were thin.

When Reuel looked up again it was just in time to see the Benjaminite returning with a dead bird in his hand. Drawing an obsidian knife from a pouch at this belt, the shepherd slashed open its breast and pulled out the breast and internal organs. With deliberate slowness, he draped the offal from the garrote encircling the Slaver's neck.

Blood dripped down the man's chest and shoulders. "You are mad!" he said, choking with the effort. "What are you doing?"

The Benjaminite did not answer, just stared at the Slaver, his bloodied obsidian blade still in his left hand.

"Please!" the Slaver pleaded. "I am a wealthy man."

"You need a lesson in the value of human life," the Benjaminite replied.

"A lesson? Thank you, my lord!"

"Do not. I am leaving you for the jackals that will come to this pool as soon as dusk arrives." He reached forward almost tenderly and touched the bleeding organs. "The tracks around the pool tell me that a pack of them comes here every night. But just in case they planned to go elsewhere this evening, the smell of this carrion will draw them."

"Please—no! No! You can't!" the Slaver pleaded.

Reuel finished untying Jiram and strode to the wagons. The one that was burning had overturned and its contents were scattered across the sandy soil, some of them still on fire. Reuel moved among them, searching. A moment later he found an oilcloth bag of date cakes, a skin of wine, and an earthenware jar of honey.

He was about to turn away when from the corner of his eye he spotted the corner of a red box. Pulling it clear of some plant debris, he stared at his medical kit. Inside, its contents had clearly been soaked during his time in the river, but many of them were still salvageable.

He returned to Jiram and fed him the dates. "Slowly."

Jiram nodded and consumed the cakes in tiny bites. "Again, I thank you."

Reuel stepped over to the Slaver and tore his outer garment off of his body; it came away in wide strips. The Benjaminite watched with a bemused expression on his face. "What are you doing?" the Slaver begged pitifully.

Reuel ignored him and tore the cloth further into bandages. He used them to wrap Jiram's wounds with honey, wine, and a selection of healing herbs from his kit. "It is less than ideal," he said. "But it will ease the pain and help you to heal."

The rest of the captives had begun to scatter, helping themselves to whatever supplies they could gather before they fled.

A shadow fell over the sand where Reuel and Jiram knelt, and Reuel looked up to see the Benjaminite looming over them. He was staring with narrowed eyes at Jiram. "I came to rescue Israelites. You and the others...you just happened to be in the right place at the right time."

"Nonetheless," said Jiram, "I am grateful."

The Benjaminite scowled and gestured toward Reuel. "If you hadn't somehow earned the compassion of this one, I would probably have killed you myself."

Reuel saw his expression as he spoke the words: there was no kindness in the shepherd's eyes, but neither was there any rage. He would not have killed the unarmed man, no matter what he claimed, even if he wanted them to think so.

"You are welcome to join me as I travel north," the Benjaminite said to Reuel. "You, though..." He gestured to Jiram. "You will have to find your own way."

Jiram nodded. "So be it." He turned to Reuel and placed one of his scarred hands on each of the young prophet's cheeks. "We have broken bread together. Now there is salt between us."

Bowing, Reuel gave the formal response: "I accept the burden of this salt."

"I will not forget you, Reuel," said Jiram. "May the gods one day grant to me the opportunity to repay the kindness you have shown."

Jiram bowed, then strode to the wagons and released one of the mules from its traces. Mounting it, he waved once, then wheeled and rode off toward the west.

Reuel watched him for a moment before his thoughts were interrupted by the Benjaminite. "And you? Where are you going?"

"I need to find my master at Mizpah."

"Mizpah? Is your master there in answer to the Prophet's summons, then?"

Reuel turned to face him, pride making his heart pump a little faster. "My master is the Prophet."

"Indeed?" The Benjaminite's eyebrows arched. "Then we are well met." He bowed. "I am Jedaiel, of the tribe of Benjamin. Our paths, it appears, lie in the same direction."

"You travel to Mizpah?" Reuel asked.

"Yes," Jedaiel said. "To Mizpah, and to war."

Reuel picked up his box of healing supplies and tucked it under one arm. "Lead on."

The Benjaminite Jedaiel nodded and, ignoring the pleas of Slaver and his waking guards, the two men marched swiftly to the north.

36

Samuel woke with a hand gently shaking his shoulder. "Samuel! Samuel!"

He opened his eyes and saw Tirzah's long face, hollowed by the shadow of the oil lamp she held in one hand. "Samuel—come quickly."

He sat up and slid out of bed, still groggy and unsteady on his feet as he wrapped his *me'il* around himself and followed her through his door.

Outside, the moon was a thin sliver of silver and the Great Altar glowered with deep, red coals. They padded across the dew-dampened flagstones. By the time the cool night air had fully wakened him, Samuel knew where they were going, and a knot in the pit of his stomach warned him that what he found when they got to their destination was not going to be good.

Two Levite guards stood outside High Priest Ahitub's door. There also were gathered Ichabod and a group of Under Priests and Levites.

Tirzah and Samuel slipped through the open door of the High Priest's room. Inside, Ahimelech knelt next to the old man's bed, tears making flashing lines down his cheeks in the yellow light of the oil lamps.

Samuel knelt next to him. He felt like he was expected to speak, but he did not know if he should address Ahitub or his son, and he could think of no words to say. He looked from Ahimelech's anguished face to the pale, wrinkled mask that now hid the man who had been like a father to Samuel for the first dozen years of his life.

"Samuel." The High Priest's voice was the shadow of a whisper.

"Here I am, my lord," Samuel whispered back.

"The Judge of Israel..." Ahitub said.

"No, my lord. Avdon had been gathered to his fathers. It is I, Samuel."

"Show them, Samuel. Show them!"

Samuel glanced at Ahimelech, then back to Ahitub. "Show them what, my lord?"

The High Priest coughed and his breath rasped in his throat. Tirzah held a rag to his lips and dripped water onto his tongue. After a moment he turned his head on his bolster so that he could look in Samuel's eyes. "Jehovah has taken everything now."

Samuel reached out and caressed the old man's wrinkled cheek; his skin felt like papyrus. "No, my lord! Jehovah has given you friends, and a hope—."

Ahitub cut him off. "Not me! Jehovah has taken everything...from you!"

The room went silent except for Ahitub's rasping breath and Ahimelech's quiet weeping.

Samuel felt as though he needed to fill the silence, although he wondered if that was because he was uncomfortable or that he felt others were. "You are safe for eternity, my friend. Safe in the memory of our great God."

Ahitub's eyes closed and he smiled. "I am safe. I have given my all for you, O Jehovah! I have given my all!"

"Yes, my lord," Samuel said.

Ahitub's eyes opened and he looked over at Samuel once again. "What are you willing to give?" he asked.

Then the High Priest's breath rattled in his throat and he slumped into stillness.

The room was as quiet as the death that suddenly filled it. Then Ahimelech and Tirzah began weeping more loudly as Samuel reached up and gently closed his mentor's eyes. "Goodbye, old friend," he whispered. "May

Jehovah bless you and keep you. May Jehovah make His face shine toward you, and may He favor you. May Jehovah lift up His face toward you, and assign peace to you."

Ahimelech was on his knees, still clutching his father's hand. Samuel turned to him and gathered the Priest into his arms. "May Jehovah be with us all," he whispered into Ahimelech's ear. "But especially with you, my friend. You are now the High Priest of Israel."

37

Her mother had named her Yiddishah. She was a daughter of thirteen years when she was driven from her family and her town on the plains south of Mount Tabor, near the River Kishon. But for her, that was not an ending. It was the beginning, her second birth.

It happened in this way: One of the slaves that served in her household had told her and her sister about a Canaanite ritual that was being held on a nearby hilltop, a ritual to beg the gods for fertility for the land of their parents, and for themselves. The slave had told them that if they attended it when they were young (her sister was only a daughter of eleven years at the time), it would guarantee that they would have many children.

Yiddishah did not remember very much of what had happened that night after they snuck away to the hilltop. She remembered a drink, bitter and thick, being poured down her throat by a woman with kohl smeared around her eyes. She remembered fear, whirling, naked bodies all around her and chanting voices, the eyes of the looming idol of Ba'al seeming to watch her wherever she went. She remembered the crushing weight of men's bodies on top of her, along with a frightening pain in her loins and a sadness so deep it did not have a name.

Then she slipped from the world and found herself running, terrified, in a land of darkness and shadows, pursued by the dead—ghostly figures who chased her endlessly, begging her to carry messages to their loved ones in the land of the living...

When she woke the next morning, she was alone in a grove of oaks on a small hill. Revelers from the celebration were unconscious on the ground all around her, but the priests and priestesses were gone. She got to her feet, her head pounding, her inner thighs and hips so sore she could barely walk.

She found her sister just a few paces away, lying on her face in the matted grass. When she shook her, her sister did not wake. When she rolled her over and saw what had been done to her, Yiddishah knew that her sister would never wake again.

That night she did not return home. After burying her sister's body in the sandy soil with no tools but her own hands, she traveled to the temple of Ba'al on the plain of Jezre'el. She did not know what she intended to do, but when she arrived the priests welcomed her. One of them, an old man she remembered vaguely from the night before, told her that the god Mot had taken her sister, and that for a price, he could let Yiddishah speak to her once again. She told him that she did not have any money. He told her that Ba'al was pleased to accept the tender coin of flesh in lieu of gold and silver.

After he took her on a wool blanket on the floor of his tent while two of his fellow priests watched, he led her to a tent of goat's hair, so black inside that she could not see her hand in front of her face. There, he lit a single lamp that burned with the scent of spikenard. He performed an ancient ritual that he told her only those beloved of Mot could ever master.

She paid close attention to everything he did: every chant recited, every arcane gesture, every ingredient sprinkled into his potions.

When it was done, dancing wisps of light, like glowing smoke, appeared before her, and as she watched they took the shape of her sister. She saw her, and heard her voice like an icy breeze in her ear. The priest told Yiddishah that she should not have been able to see the ghost—that only the one performing the ritual could see it, although others might hear its whispered words. But Yiddishah saw her—an evanescent form as though made from smoke and steam, a roiling cloud of light and darkness that had her sister's face.

Yiddishah begged her forgiveness, hot tears burning her cheeks. When she heard her sister's voice telling her it was alright, that she was safe and happy, Yiddishah wept as she had never wept in her life, a storm of tears that washed her clean inside.

The moment that her sister's ghost faded into the darkness again, Yiddishah turned and plunged a knife through the old priest's throat. While he bled out on the floor of the black tent, she gathered his amulets and charms, his magical ingredients and, cutting an opening in the back of the tent, fled back to her home.

When she returned to town, breathless and covered in blood, she told her father and his family what had happened. She had known they would be devastated to learn that her sister was dead, but she had expected that sadness to be tempered by the knowledge that she was safe and happy in the underworld, and that her death had been avenged. Yiddishah assured them that she could bring her sister's ghost back for them, so that they could see her and speak with her for themselves.

They drove her from the town. They called her an abomination. Years later, she found out why she was not stoned as the Torah prescribed—some of the Elders, in spite of their protestations, secretly desired her services.

She fled to the sacred grove where her sister had died. There, with her own hands, she built a makeshift house from deadwood stacked and bound together with withes. Inside it she began to experiment with the magic she had learned and found that she was able to summon the spirits of others who were dead—in some cases, people who had died decades before. She found that they could tell her things, secrets no one else knew, secrets about lost treasures, unreported crimes, and hidden lusts fulfilled in the darkness. They warned her when she was in danger. Sometimes they would do her bidding, especially when that meant executing her curses on those who had forced her to live the life of banishment she now endured.

Other times—more often than not—she could summon nothing. But she learned to watch the people who came to her for help. She learned how to speak to them, what questions to ask, what assertions to make and how to phrase them. She learned that most of the time she did not require the help of any spirits to give them the answers they sought.

The people of her town feared her. But they also knew the value of her power. Soon, they began to come to her for help. First it was locals. Then, as her reputation spread, it was people from all over Samaria. Like the priest who had taught her, she took her payment in gold or, from the men who appealed to her, in pleasure. She made a name for herself, a name the dead promised her would be remembered to times indefinite.

They called her the Ghost-Wife, the Witch of Endor.

❖ ❖ ❖ ❖ ❖ ❖ ❖ ❖ ❖ ❖ ❖

Sarnam crested the rounded hill with Sihphil and a hand-picked guard of Gedhudhra. Nestled among the ancient oaks was a hovel built of sticks and branches. Its door was a flap of leather, as stiff as wood and with its cracked edges curled from weathering and improper tanning. Smoke swirled around the top of the dome-shaped home as though hesitant to leave.

He heard Sihphil hiss beside him: "She isss here."

Through the sharp odor of smoke Sarnam detected other smells: the pungency of spices, the sickly sweetness of rotting flesh. "Yes, but is she alive?" he wondered aloud.

Sihphil glanced at him briefly from under his heavy lids, and then led the way forward to the Ghost-Wife's door.

"Witch!" Sarnam called out. "I come for your services."

"You come for your needs."

The voice came from behind them and Sarnam, Sihphil, and the guards all spun to find the speaker. A few paces behind them a young woman stood among the oaks, her chin lowered almost to her chest. None of them had heard her approach; it was as if she had just appeared.

She stood as still as an idol, her brown, stringy hair falling about her dirty face and hanging in front of the torn, stained woolen sack she wore as a dress. Thin limbs jutted out from it like twigs, but the shift did little to conceal her voluptuous curves. Her feet were bare, blackened with dirt and with thick, yellow nails. A necklace draped around her slender neck was heavy with golden amulets to the gods of Canaan.

Through the veil of her hair, Sarnam could see her eyes. They were pale green, so pale they would have seemed almost colorless had her skin not been so darkened by sun and dirt. He was pleased at the way those eyes sent chills down his spine.

"You wish to speak to the dead," the Ghost-Wife said. It was not a question.

Sarnam nodded.

She took a few steps closer, walking toward him sideways like a crab. She craned her neck toward him, sniffing. "You wish to speak to...your father?"

He nodded again, impressed.

She glanced at the guards. "These are not needed."

"Wait for us at the foot of the hill," Sarnam told them.

After they had left, the Ghost-Wife led Sarnam and Sihphil into her hovel, muttering to herself as she went. Sarnam had to bend almost in half to fit through the tiny, arched door. Inside, a meager cooking fire smoldered in the middle of the room, filling the top third of the domicile with smoke before it could escape through cracks in the ceiling. Bunches of dried herbs, bones, and the desiccated bodies of small animals hung everywhere, and idols and charms peeked from dozens of nooks and crannies.

"Did you bring payment?" she asked.

"I did," Sarnam said. "What will your services cost me?"

"You are old, and the sorcerer is even older," she said. "I am not interested in your wrinkled flesh. I want five gold shekels."

Sihphil counted out five freshly minted shekels into his clawed hand and handed them to her. "Five gold sshekelsss," he said, and reached into a pouch hidden in the folds of his robe. He proffered another item: "And a scarab from the tomb of the Apostate, Pharaoh Akenathen."

Her eyes widened and she snatched the scarab from his hand, examining its malachite surface inlaid with pearls, emeralds, and silver. "For this price, I will call forth Mot himself."

"I have no desire to commune with the god of death at this time," said Sarnam. "As you have said—I must speak with my father."

She nodded and reluctantly set the scarab aside. From a woolen bundle she unwrapped a large bowl formed of smoky glass, one of the most beautiful Sarnam had ever seen. Doubtless of Minoan origin, it was worth a small fortune. Humming and chanting to herself, she mixed olive oil and honey in the bowl, stirring it with one long fingernail. "Sit!" she commanded, pointing to the floor against the wall of her hovel.

They obeyed as her chant rose to a higher pitch. She placed the bowl between them and waved a wand of myrtle over it. Sarnam felt the unsettling hollowness in his stomach that always accompanied communing with the gods. The Ghost-Wife added powders and thin strips of something to the mixture in the bowl and began to speak aloud.

"By the names of the spirits of the fifth camp of the first firmament I conjure thee! *Neninah!* Thou who resteth in the grave upon the bones of the dead, I ask that thou accept this offering from my hand and do my bidding!"

Something moved, like colorless smoke, above the mouth of the bowl.

"Bring me the father, the son of the grandfather who is dead, and make him stand erect and speak with me without fear, and have him disclose unto my ears the truth without fear, and I shall not be afraid of him. Let him answer the questions I shall put to him."

A chill crawled down Sarnam's spine and he *felt*, rather than saw, a presence in the room with them.

"He comes," she whispered.

The room went cold, as though the sun had vanished from the sky and, in its absence, the chill of night had set in. Sarnam saw the air moving over the glass bowl like waves of heat that distorted what was behind it.

"He rises," the Ghost-Wife said. "He rises feet first from the land of the dead."

"What do you see?" Sarnam asked.

"An old man with a strong, beardless face," she said, staring into the nothingness between them. "He wears the armor of the sons of Philistia."

"Father..." Sarnam whispered.

The Ghost-Wife stiffened. "He turns toward you. He sees you now."

"And his face?" Sarnam asked, feeling suddenly like a boy again, longing for his father's approval.

She paused. "His face is full of sorrow, or anxiety."

"Father," Sarnam whispered again. "Father, what have I done? Why have the spirits and the gods turned away from me?"

The Ghost-Wife was silent a moment, nodding. "He believes you have not yet fulfilled your destiny."

"Egypt..."Sarnam breathed.

The Ghost-Wife nodded. "He knows...he understands that you are trying."

"What should I do?" Sarnam asked.

"I am sensing that he has a purpose in mind for you," the Ghost-Wife said. "Some important step to accomplishing your goal...something he perhaps wants you to do now...on opportunity you have only recently learned about..."

"Mizpah." Sarnam nodded.

"Mizpah," the Ghost-Wife agreed. "The city of the Israelites."

"Curse them!" Sarnam said.

Suddenly the Ghost-Wife's voice changed, becoming deep and gravelly, harsh with authority and anger. "Destroy them! Wipe them and their god off the surface of the ground! Do not fail me, my son! Do not curse me to an eternity of suffering in this place, watching all the work of my life undone!"

"I will not fail you, Father," Sarnam said.

"The gods will be with you—I have sacrificed much in this place to assure you their aid. Ride into battle with confidence."

"I, too, will sacrifice to them," Sarnam said.

"I long to see you again, my son," the Ghost-Wife growled. "I long to feel your warmth in my arms in this cold place."

"Father..."

The Ghost-Wife quivered as if overtaken by palsy. Coming back to herself, she looked over at Sarnam with wide eyes. "He is fading. I am losing him."

"No! Father!" Sarnam cast about with his eyes, trying desperately to catch sight of the vision. "Hold him, witch!"

"He fades..." the Ghost-Wife repeated. "He says that your time is coming...that you will achieve...destiny..."

"When?" Sarnam reached for her but Sihphil grabbed his arm, holding him back. "When?"

"When the sky and the ground open before you, and a heart is offered up on an altar of stone...know that the day of...your destiny has arrived," the Ghost-Wife said.

"Father! Father!"

A stiff breeze blew through the hovel, scattered the smoke of the little fire. The Ghost-Wife sighed, then opened her pale eyes and fixed them on Sarnam. A thin sheen of sweat covered her face. She smiled slightly.

"Go, prince of Philistia," she said. "Go to your destiny."

— —•— — —•— — — —•— — —•— — — —•— — —•— — — —•— — —•— — — —•— — —•— —

When Sarnam had gone, Yiddishah doused the mixture in the bowl to stop the heat and smoke that helped convince her customers that a spirit hovered above it. She smiled to herself, knowing that the Philistine Axis Lord had left satisfied and impressed by her abilities. That was good. His endorsement would surely draw more customers to her.

The fact that she had not raised a spirit, that she had done nothing more than tell him what he wanted to hear, made the experience that much more gratifying.

38

The inhabitants of Nob fled, rather than departed. They fled as though pursued by an enemy they knew they could not escape. If the Elders of Nob tried to stop them, Samuel did not hear about it. But it would have been to no avail. Ahimelech—refusing to wear the clothing of the High Priest or to be formally installed—claimed his newfound authority for one reason only: to escape the city where his father had died.

Samuel had tried to convince him to take up the priestly garments, or to use the sacred lots, the Urim and Thummim kept in the ceremonial breastplate, to determine Jehovah's will for them.

"I am not worthy to touch them," Ahimelech responded, and would brook no more discussion of the subject.

Samuel understood what he was feeling. He tried to help, to tell him to believe in himself, and in Jehovah's choice of him as High Priest.

"Jehovah's choice?" Ahimelech snapped. "Was it Jehovah's choice that my father died here tonight?"

Samuel gave up easily. His words sounded hollow in his own ears: *Trust Jehovah. Trust in His choice of you. Believe that you must be worthy and able to fulfill the purpose He has set you to.*

They were the words he had heard from others all the days of his life. He did not believe them himself; how could he now ask someone else to?

So they fled Nob, in the direction of Mizpah, for there was nowhere else to go. "You must offer the sacrifices and sanctify the people there," Samuel told his friend.

"I will not," Ahimelech said. "I go to Mizpah because my father agreed to go, and I would have followed him there."

"Your father would also have offered the sacrifices when he arrived. He would have been the High Priest that our people need him to be."

"I am not my father," said Ahimelech, and strode with heavy steps down the road ahead of Samuel.

They were hundreds of people, strung out along the road for farther than Samuel could see: men, women, children, young and old, sound and lame. Samuel stayed close to Ahimelech, worried about him. They were surrounded by Priests and Levites, Tirzah, and Ichabod; Kish and Tahash flanked Samuel on either side. Ahimelech moved woodenly, his red eyes fixed on the road in front of him.

Samuel swung Ahitub's staff, *Mish'eneth*, alongside him as he walked. The High Priest's hand had been larger than Samuel's, and the staff did not fit his palm well. Within the first few minutes of travel it began to chafe, then to blister, but he did not stop to wrap it or do anything else to alleviate the pain. The pain felt appropriate somehow, as if it was a reminder that he, an unworthy sinner, still lived while a righteous man lay embalmed in a temporary sepulchre beneath the Tabernacle.

He thought he caught some of the people who walked with them casting dark stares in his direction, and he assumed it was because they recognized the staff. He did not blame them—he knew it was not right that he should carry it, but he could not defy Ahitub even after his mentor had died. Especially, he realized, after he had died.

It struck him that a staff was a strange symbol of power, though every cultue seemed to use it as one. It was a crutch, a sign of weakness, an admission of one's inability to stand on one's own. And yet the most powerful men on earth carried one in front of all their subjects, and were not ashamed.

Their first glimpse of Gibeah was just before mid-day. A black haze hung ominously over the city. Kish did not say a word, but rushed forward, followed by Tahash, Samuel, and the few other Gibeahites that had been at Nob.

They rushed through the gates—left wide open and scorched—and were greeted by a scene of horror.

The city square was choked with dead bodies sprawled across the flagstones, and Samuel gagged from the smell of rotting meat swarming with flies. The ravens and crows hopping among the carrion were barely disturbed by their arrival; they croaked in protest and went on tearing ribbons of flesh from the corpses. Furtive movement in a nearby building caught Samuel's eye, and he turned to see a jackal loping away, dragging a human arm.

Kish was running from body to body, turning them to look at their faces, silently mouthing names as he identified people he had known. Tahash ran off through the streets, returning a few moments later with his sword drawn. Samuel noticed its blade was still clean.

"The dead seem confined to the square," Tahash said. "It appears that the rest of the inhabitants escaped."

"Or were taken captive," growled Kish.

Tahash put a hand on the big Benjaminite's shoulder. "There are no signs of that, my friend. The dead who lie before us are warriors of your city, and surely more than just warriors would have died if they were defending their women and children from capture."

Kish did not look comforted.

"The Elders had already agreed to answer the summons to Mizpah," Samuel added. "Your people had already left when the Philistines arrived."

"I must go to my home," said Kish. "I must see if my family left word or sign for me."

"Go," said Samuel, and the tall Benjaminite loped off into the smoldering wreckage.

Samuel turned and began walking down another street, among the burnt buildings, seeking air that was free of the stench of decaying flesh. He was haunted by the sight of the corpses at the gate—not just because of the horrific sight, but because he felt inextricably connected to every death caused by Philistine hands. Had he in some way brought this down on his people?

It was as though the scorched, smoking bodies on the flagstones had become offerings on an invisible altar, unwilling martyrs to someone else's cause. He wondered if they had felt they had a choice in the matter, or if they had died not understanding the purpose for which they had been forced to give their lives.

He let his feet take him, without thinking, deeper into the city. On either side of the road were homes whose roofs had collapsed into the rooms beneath them and then burned until all that was left was a misshapen skeleton of stacked stones and blackened poles. Through burnt-out window openings, Samuel could see remnants of people's everyday lives, reminders that these were once homes, filled with people and belongings that had been handled by many generations of the same family—filled with the past's memories and the future's hopes.

He stopped in front of one of the houses, staring through the blackened door. "What am I doing?" he whispered to himself. He was no national leader. He had never wanted to be. He had only wanted to get Judge Avdon to lead, and High Priest Ahitub to guide the nation. And now both of them were gone, and the nation was gathering to Mizpah, awaiting leadership. Awaiting him. What was he going to tell them? What was he going to do?

He was just turning to walk back toward the gate when a rustling noise from somewhere behind him alerted him to movement.

It was all the warning he got. Something crashed into his back and sent him flying headfirst into the shell of a house. His body broke through a scorched timber, knocking the wind from his lungs, and then crashed against a wall. As he scrabbled to his feet, gasping for air, he sucked charcoal dust into his lungs and began to cough.

When the tears cleared from his eyes and he got to his feet again, the light from the doorway outlined a figure standing there: a tall, skeletal figure with skin as black as charcoal.

The tattooed face of the Hunter was so dark the whites of his eyes seemed as though they belonged to another creature, and he had stolen them to gain its powers of vision.

"Prophet." The Hunter's accent was thick, but it did not conceal the hatred with which he said the word.

Samuel did not have time to think about what he could have done to earn such intense ire—he turned and fled through the debris of the house, ducking beams and squeezing through a half-collapsed doorway in search of a rear exit.

He found one and pushed clear into a narrow alleyway.

The Hunter appeared as though he had swooped down from the sky, landing in a crouch in front of him, his strange, curved knife clutched in his right hand.

Samuel felt his heartbeat in his throat and ears. He slowly crouched until one hand rested against the roadbed. The Hunter smiled, revealing his white, pointed teeth.

Without warning, he sprang at Samuel like a lion. Samuel grasped a handful of dirt from the road and tossed it into his attacker's eyes and open mouth, then threw himself to one side with as much speed as he could muster.

The Hunter snarled as he missed Samuel by a hairsbreadth, tumbling to the roadbed with his eyes tightly closed. Samuel raced from the alley onto the nearby street, then turned and began running back toward the gate as fast as his legs would carry him.

An instant later movement to his left caught his eye, and he glanced up to see the Hunter paralleling him atop the burnt houses, leaping from wall to wall and roof to roof like a huge, black cricket. Samuel tried to run faster, and barely noticed the shadow that suddenly slipped across his path.

He turned and leapt in the same movement, hurling his body clear of the Hunter descending on him like a diving hawk. Samuel stumbled and fell hard against a wall, bounced off of it and tumbled to the gravel road.

Just as he pushed himself to his feet, something slammed into him; he cringed, and then hands were grabbing at him, pulling him away. He stopped flailing and looked over his shoulder to see one of the Levite guards pulling him backward.

Samuel jerked free as Kish, Tahash and three other Levite soldiers charged at the Hunter, now standing in a crouch in the middle of the road, arms spread wide as though he were about to embrace someone, one hand clutching his long spear.

Tahash swung at the Hunter's head but the black man ducked, then twisted to one side to avoid a sweeping blow from Kish's axe. The spear swung in a wide arc, catching one of the Levite guards in the cheek and sending him tumbling away in a flash of blood. The Hunter leapt toward a nearby wall and sprang from it toward Tahash, arms outstretched, spear still clutched in his right hand.

Tahash swung savagely toward his attacker and Samuel heard the *crack* of Avdon's son's blade connecting with the thick spear shaft. The Hunter's thrust nevertheless missed by only a few fingers' width, and Tahash spun away, nearly falling in his efforts to get clear.

A Levite tried to take advantage of the opportunity to leap toward the Hunter's back with his own spear in his hand. The black warrior did not even turn, but simply shoved the butt end of his spear backwards with such force that it transfixed the Levite through the stomach. For a moment everything seemed to freeze as the Levite hung grotesquely from the shaft. Then the Hunter jerked it free and spun around once again, hurling the spear so hard it went completely through the third Levite guard and buried its tip in a nearby wall.

Kish and Tahash charged toward the Hunter again, but the black assassin bounded onto a wall, then a rooftop and raced away, leaping from housetop to housetop until he vanished from sight.

Neither Kish nor Tahash pursued him.

"Someday," growled Kish, letting the haft of his axe rest on the ground in front of him, "I am going to kill that man."

Samuel abruptly remembered where Kish had been. "Did your family...did they leave you any sign...?"

Kish nodded. "It appears that most of our people fled under the guidance of my father and some of the Elders before the Philistines arrived. They should have reached Mizpah—or somewhere near it—by now."

Samuel checked the bodies of the fallen Levites—all of them were dead. He was about to say something to the warriors who had saved his life when the sound of a turmoil at the gates caught his attention. He strode toward the sound, Kish and Tahash following.

At the gate, he was met by Manoah and Samson, looking much more travel-worn than they had the last time he had seen them. Samuel looked around them at the crowd anxiously. "Reuel?"

Manoah shook his head. "We did not find him. But I think he is still alive."

"You *think*?" Samuel snapped.

Manoah took his shoulders. "Samuel—we had to come back. We have more important news."

"More important than the fate of my friend?" Samuel asked, anger and fear overwhelming his other emotions.

Manoah nodded. "As you can see all around you, the Philistines are already here, in Israel. They are going to reach Mizpah before us."

"Yes?"

Manoah looked grim. "They have been to Ramathaim, Samuel."

Samuel felt the ground fall out from under his feet. It felt as though he had just learned he had done something unfathomably terrible, and its consequences were about to be visited on those he loved. And there was nothing he could do to stop it, only stand and watch as what he loved was punished for his wrongs.

"Ramathaim is destroyed," said Manoah. "Ramathaim and Naioth."

"And the people?" Samuel whispered.

Manoah shook his head. "We found no one—and no bodies."

Samuel glanced around him and found Kish's craggy face, spattered with the blood of one of the Levites. He felt a cold anger seep through him. A passage from the Torah came into his mind and, although he did not know why, he recited it like a litany: "Blood pollutes the land, and no expiation can be made for the land for the blood that is shed in it, except by the blood of him that shed it."

Kish nodded. "So says the Torah." The big Benjaminite sheathed his axe and turned back to Samuel. "Let us go and expiate the sins of the Philistines, and give to the Land of Promise the blood that it is due."

39

U nder the cover of the treed hills of Samaria, dozens of families made their slow, boisterous way southwest. The route they had chosen was not the most direct one to their destination, but it was the least likely to encounter marauding bands of Philistines. Some of the tracks they followed were little more than trails wending through stones and cedar forests, not wide enough for a chariot to travel.

At the head of the somber group Samuel's father Elkanah strode in the place of the leader, but Liora knew he would have strongly argued with that characterization. When she had convinced the *Beneh* to leave Naioth against the desires of the Elders of Ramathaim, Elkanah had not hesitated to tell her that he disagreed with her decision and her way of handling it. Hannah had not spoken to her since they left, choosing instead to communicate her feelings by her uncharacteristic silence.

Liora tried to reason with Elkanah—and with some of the other Elders—arguing that they would have left for Mizpah in answer to Samuel's summons anyway; she was only asking that they leave sooner rather than later. But Elkanah was worried about having to answer for his headstrong son's actions—and now the actions of his son's wife—to the other Elders of Ramathaim.

But the hesitancy of all of the Elders had crumbled before the urging of the people when they learned that little Gavriel, the youngest prophet at the School, had been granted another vision. Several of the older *Beneh* interpreted it as referring to an imminent attack on the town and the fear engendered by this prediction was enough to move many of the townsfolk to insist on evacuating immediately.

Liora looked around her. The *Beneh* showed none of that fear. They marched with confidence in Samuel as their spiritual guide, and in Jehovah as the God who was as real to them as their own brothers and sisters. It was how Samuel had taught them.

Or, she reflected, they were putting on a very brave face. She wondered if any of them knew that the true lesson Samuel was teaching them by his example: to try to behave bravely, to act as though your heart was not melting in order to give comfort to those around you.

Not far ahead of them the trail rejoined a wider road again. A scout loped back toward them. "Elkanah! Elkanah!" he called.

The line came to a halt for a moment until the breathless scout reached them. "Here I am," said Elkanah.

"We have found a Danite alongside the road—he is badly injured...I think...we think he may not recover."

Elkanah glanced back at Samuel's brothers behind him. "Keep the line here for a moment."

Elkanah followed the scout up out of the trees to the road, and Liora quietly kept a few paces behind them. When they emerged, half a dozen scouts were propping up a dirty, bloodied figure in the tall grass on the roadside. Liora was only two or three paces away from him before she recognized the man.

"Cheran!" she said.

Cheran's eyes fluttered open. "Betrayed..." he rasped.

Elkanah glanced around them worriedly. "By whom?"

"Baghadh...," said Cheran.

Liora turned to one of the scouts. "Find a healer—quickly! And bring Gavriel!"

The scout ran off to do as she asked, and Liora got on her knees next to the injured man. His tunic, front and back, was brown and stiff with dried blood, and he grimaced with each labored breath. "We're going to need a litter," she said to no one in particular.

Elkanah knelt down beside her. "Betrayed by Baghadh? Why? How?"

Cheran reached out one hand and grabbed Elkanah's forearm with a grip like a vice. "Mizpah...the Philistines know...the Philistines are coming to Mizpah..."

The group fell silent for a moment, the full import of the words slowly sinking into their consciousness. Then the healer rushed up to them, pushing Liora and Elkanah aside and kneeling next to the injured man, pulling off Cheran's shirt and treating the half-closed wound on his back.

Liora glanced up and saw that Elkanah was staring at her. "We are walking into a trap," he said.

She shook her head.

"Liora! An unarmed, unprepared nation is gathering as if we wanted to make it easier for the Philistines to slaughter us. Obviously, I'm not saying that this is what Samuel intended, but nevertheless—we are walking into a trap!"

"Do not underestimate your son," she said, quietly and confidently.

"Samuel is no war leader! Judge Avdon is dead! We have not won a battle against the Philistines since the days of our fathers grandfathers—and since then their arms have only grown stronger, while we, militarily, have grown weaker!"

She reached out and took one of his large, calloused hands in her own. "The Prophet of Israel called the entire nation together at Mizpah. The Prophet of the True God summons the children of Israel, and the children respond. When we get to Mizpah, all of our people and our prophets and priests, do you think that Jehovah will abandon us?"

The intensity of his glower did not diminish, and he shook his head slightly. "Were we not the children of Israel when the Philistines slaughtered forty thousand of us at Aphek?"

Four men arrived with a litter and set it next to Cheran; the healer continued his work.

"Your husband's prophecy is not a guarantee of deliverance from all harm," Elkanah continued a moment later. "This is a snare whose trigger is about to be tripped!"

Liora nodded. "Yes, it is."

He looked at her askance. "Now you agree with me?"

"I never disagreed that this was a trap, Elkanah. It is a snare most deadly that will crush its prey into destruction."

His brow remained furrowed.

"But it is God who has set it," she said. "He has used his Prophet to set a trap for the Philistines that they will not escape from. And just as He purposed, they rush to their destruction."

Elkanah stared at her a moment longer before she finally saw a hint of a smile creep into the corner of his eyes. "May Jehovah grant us all your faith, girl."

She only smiled in response.

"There is just one thing, though, Liora," he added, standing as the healer and scouts helped Cheran into the litter.

She looked at him, waiting.

"If this is a trap, as you say...then we are the bait."

40

"And Isaac said to Abraham his: "Father?" Abra-
ham answered: "Here I am, my son!" So Isaac
continued: "Here we have fire and wood, but where is the
sheep we are going to sacrice?"–The Scroll of
Bereshith

The congregation from Nob left the city of Gibeah behind them, but the horror of what they had seen there traveled with them, as did the foreboding that it had planted in their hearts. They moved toward Mizpah with an increased sense of urgency, knowing that at least part of the Philistine army was somewhere ahead of them, wondering what other horrors it had unleashed on their people.

JUDGE OF ISRAEL

Samuel felt the crushing weight of responsibility on his shoulders. *How did this happen?* he kept asking himself. Somehow, in his efforts to prepare his people for a potential attack, in his desire to protect and safeguard them, he had managed to put the entire nation in terrible danger. As though he were working on behalf of their enemies, he had gathered all of them to one location. He had done so without asking them to arm themselves or ready themselves for battle.

He had prepared his entire people as a sacrifice on an altar of his own design.

He had, albeit unknowingly, chosen them all to be martyrs to his own cause.

It sickened him to realize that alongside his fear that he had led his people to death and imprisonment was an equally great concern that he had destroyed whatever reputation he might have gained during his years as the nation's prophet. He thought back to men of fame in the annals of Israel's history: Korah, who lived a long life with a reputation as a wise man and an able leader—until his rebellion against Moses and Aaron. In that single moment, all the good he had done was lost to history. In that single moment, his name had become forever synonymous with rebellion and divine judgment. Or Abimelech, the son of Judge Gideon—he had once been renowned for his charisma and his loyalty to Jehovah and the Torah. Now history remembered him only for ill-conceived plot to become Israel's first king, for his ignominious death when an old woman dropped a millstone on his head from atop the tower in Thebez, and a crippled Abimelech committed suicide by means of his squire's sword.

Both of them—in fact, all of the examples he could think of had ended the same way: in the death of one who had lived long enough to see his own name become a curse. It was a just punishment, of course. But it was also an act of mercy for the one judged. Freedom from life also freed him from living with an eternal shame.

There were things that were worse than dying.

Samuel wondered if he was about to discover one.

Jehovah will save his people. Jehovah will not leave his loyal ones. Ahitub and Tirzah had drilled those words into his mind during his years at the Tabernacle in Shiloh. And he believed them. Seeing how Jehovah had managed to preserve the holy tent with all its ancient accoutrements—and even more so, how Jehovah had cleaned wickedness from the midst of his people and left the nation and their faith intact, had convinced Samuel beyond ever doubting again that Jehovah could, and would, act to save his people from annihilation—physical or spiritual. He had seen with his own eyes how Jehovah had resurrected the Eternal Flame from its scattered ashes, and had preserved the links between the modern nation and their ancient history and traditions.

But there was a price to be paid for such deliverances. In his youth, that price had been paid by Eli, Hophni, Phinehas, Mara, the Rephaim Saphold, and tens of thousands of Israelite men who had died on the battlefields of Aphek. But it was no coincidence that three of the men whose death had purchased Israel's ultimate victory were the men who had failed to properly lead the nation in Jehovah's way: the High Priest and his two sons.

Sacrifices on the stone altar of the land of Israel.

Who would be sacrificed this time? he wondered. And, although he knew the answer, he could not help but ask: who has misled the nation now? Whose foolishness would, this time, cost the lives of righteous men?

He saw his father's stern face in his mind, heard his voice: *Do not mistake your fears and thoughts for the truth...We are all of us just men.*

How was it, Samuel wondered, that his father always spoke so simply, but so truthfully? Thinking on his words now, they seemed undeniable. But at the time they had sounded like cowardice, or at least excuses for inaction.

Now they sounded like a very justified condemnation.

"May I speak with you, Prophet?"

The voice startled him from his thoughts and he turned to see Manoah approaching from where he had been walking alongside Kish and Tahash. "Do you need my permission?" he asked.

Manoah came alongside him and smiled crookedly. "No. But in case someone was inclining their ear, I thought I should show a little more formality."

Samuel guffawed. "Anyone who saw you showing formality would know it was an act."

Manoah smiled, but the expression faded quickly. "You realize the situation we find ourselves in, do not you?"

Samuel blushed, wondering how Manoah could have known what he was thinking. "I...I suppose..."

"We are on the brink of a war with the sons of Philistia," Manoah continued. "For the first time since Samson was born, we are about to face the full might of the Philistine army."

"I am afraid I cannot share your enthusiasm," said Samuel.

Manoah turned to face him, his eyes shining. "Do you not see? This is what Samson was born for—this moment! This battle! He has been trained. He is of age. And now he has been swept onto a battlefield that could determine the survival of our nation! Can there be any doubt that his time has arrived—that Samson will, at last, take up the task for which he was born?"

Samuel let himself entertain the possibility. It was certainly appealing—if for no other reason than that it took the weight of the nation's salvation off of Samuel's shoulders.

But it did not *feel* right. Samuel didn't know why he should give any credence to his feelings after all that had happened, but it seemed too easy. It did not...did not *cost* the nation enough.

"What is it?" Manoah asked, scowling at Samuel's hesitation.

Samuel shrugged. "Once again, Manoah—you know as much as I do. I wish I could give you some assurance, but...I do not know."

"It is your job to know, Samuel," Manoah growled. "The people are looking to you for guidance—or do you not see that, either?"

Samuel felt anger rise like heat to his neck and face. "I am not the leader of this nation! I have never been, nor do I ever wish to be, the leader of this nation! Have you asked Ahimelech about this? He carries the Urim and Thummim! If you really want an answer, go to him!"

Manoah rolled his eyes. "You yourself well know that right now Ahimelech does not know his own hands! He is barely holding himself together, Samuel—and it is rumored that he refuses to accept the High Priesthood or use the sacred lots."

Samuel said nothing, overwhelmed. After a moment, Manoah laid a hand on the Prophet's shoulder. "Samuel—at least let me send Samson ahead with some scouts to bring us back news of our enemy. At least let me give my son this opportunity."

Samuel nodded. "I trust your advice in these matters above anyone else here, Manoah. Send out whatever scouts you wish."

Manoah vanished back into the line of people behind them on the road, and Samuel plodded forward, trying not to think of anything.

Samuel did not see the scouts leave. He kept the crowd moving steadily down the roadway. The hills on either side of them were bright with new grass and sprinkled with white and pink cyclamen, bright red poppies, anemone, and asphodel. A few clusters of trees broke up the smoothness of the hills: oaks, almond trees white with blossoms, pomegranate and wild apricot jutting up from the galaxy of flowers like fountains of bright color. They had stopped in the midst of a herd of several hundred cattle, and the wide-horned beasts grazed contentedly on either side of the road. Calves suckled greedily under their mothers' legs even as the cows tried to walk, while others bounded across the grass in mad dashes that led nowhere. Samuel did not see the herdsmen, but that was not unusual—these cows, from Bashan, were powerful and wary, fully able to protect their young from whatever predators might be prowling the hills at night.

It was not very long afterward that he saw the scouts returning, moving slowly down the road toward him and others in the vanguard of the travelers from Nob. At first he was puzzled by their lackadaisical pace, but then he realized that two of them were supporting the third between them.

Samuel called a halt when the sentries reached them, and Manoah, Kish, and Tahash appeared at the same moment as though they had been summoned. When the big Danite saw who had returned, his face turned so red with anger that for a moment Samuel was afraid he was going to have to call on the Levite guards to hold the man back.

Samson had his arms draped over the shoulders of the men on either side of him. He was hopping on one foot, holding the other off of the ground completely. Samuel rushed forward to him. "Are you alright?"

Samson's crooked smile made an attempt at appearing, but pain and embarrassment prevented it.

"He appears to have sprained an ankle," said one of the scouts supporting him.

"Fell in an accursed hare hole—twisted his foot badly," added the other.

Samson and Manoah just stared at each other, red-faced, both jaws knotted, both sets of nostrils flared.

Samuel took the place of one of the scouts. "Go and find a healer," he told him.

Samuel and the other scout helped Samson hobble to a rock alongside the road where he could sit down. Manoah, Kish, and Tahash followed. "What did you find?" Samuel asked, deliberately directing the question to Samson.

Samson lowered his eyes and half-shrugged. "He can tell you," he murmured, gesturing toward the other scout with his head.

Samuel would have pushed the point, but the scout responded immediately. "The advance force of the Philistines is encamped at Mizpah. The Philistines have surrounded the city and blocked off every approach."

"And the city itself? Have they attacked the city?" asked Samuel.

The scout shook his head. "They appear to be waiting for the rest of their army. We met a trader who said the main force is not far away, approaching rapidly from the west."

"Did you see any damage to the walls of Mizpah, or any...any signs that a battle had been fought?" asked Samuel.

"No," said the scout. "No destruction, no bodies. But the city is filled to bursting. A second city of tents surrounds the walls—tens of thousands of our people who cannot fit inside. Israel has responded to your summons, my lord."

"Are the men outside the city...are they protected?" asked Samuel.

The scout nodded. "It appears that what armed men and soldiers there are among our people have set up a perimeter around the tent city, and the Philistines have not yet tried to breach it."

Manoah finally tore his scowling gaze from his son. "The Philistine army—infantry or cavalry?"

"Both," said the scout. "But primarily infantry. One cavalry unit—maybe two. Chariots with scythed wheels."

"Rephaim?" asked Kish.

"Not that I saw, my lord." The scout hesitated a moment, as if unsure of his next words. "My lord—they were feasting on the flocks and herds from the countryside. I did not know..."

"Did not know what?" Samuel asked.

The scout looked up, his brow knotted. "They butcher animals without slaughtering them, my lord. Did you know? They cut off the part they wish to eat, bandage the wound, and keep the animal alive. They...they eat them in pieces, my lord."

"Practical," said Tahash grimly. "That way the rest of the meat does not spoil."

Manoah nodded. "Practical—if you have the heart and mind of a dog!"

Samuel sighed and glanced down the line of travelers. "We need to gather all of these people together and meet with the Elders of Nob and the High Priest—and any other experienced military men among us. We need to figure out how we are going to get into that city."

"I'm not sure how much room will be left inside the walls," said the scout.

"Room or not," said Kish, "we cannot stay here." He turned and looked to the west. "The main forces of Philistia are on their way, and we do not want to be caught between the hammer and the anvil."

"Can we fight our way through their advance force?" Samuel asked.

Manoah shook his head. "Unlikely—not with our numbers comprised primarily of townsfolk: women, children, and our elderly. Even if we made it through, we would lose hundreds in the attempt."

At last, Samson raised his head. He was not smiling, but Samuel saw the familiar, rascally gleam in his dark eyes. "I have an idea," he said. "But I'm going to need Kish, Tahash, and three fast horses."

41

Reuel and the Benjaminite Jedaiel traveled north as swiftly as they could, trying to moderate their pace to make sure they did not give out from exhaustion before they arrived. They followed the trade road—broad, straight, and relatively flat as it sliced its way through the land from south to north. There was little traffic, and all that they encountered were trade caravans from Egypt and Edom or from Lebanon, Aram and the distant north, camels plodding forward with their bobbing gait.

Jedaiel told Reuel that they were only a short distance south and east of Tekoa, making it possible for them to reach Mizpah in a day if they really pushed themselves. Reuel was exhausted from his ordeal in the hands of the slavers, but he forced himself to keep up with the Benjaminite's hurried pace. They did not speak much as they traveled, saving their breath for climbing the hills in the road.

By mid-afternoon, they were within sight of the dust cloud that hung over the Philistine columns marching ahead of them. "There are tens of thousands beneath that cloud," Jedaiel said.

"And Mizpah is on the other side of them," Reuel added.

"We will have to leave the road for a while," said Jedaiel. "If we go much farther forward, we will run into their rearguard and scouts."

Reuel scanned the rough hills around them. "Traveling cross-country will be slow here."

Jedaiel shrugged. "Better a live dog than a dead lion. We will just have to go as fast as we can."

Reuel nodded, thinking to himself that he didn't know if he could keep going at a faster pace—especially across trackless country.

"Then we had better get started," said Reuel quietly.

Jedaiel smiled and nodded. "Keep your eyes and ears open, Reuel."

They scrambled up a low hill to the west of the road and hiked northward through the scrub. A short distance later they crested a hill and Jedaiel stopped and pointed toward the Philistine army. "Look—Mizpah."

Beyond the cloud of dust a rounded hill, like an inverted bowl, rose from the surrounding valleys. It appeared to be crowned with a tall, white wall and at its peak a single, thick spire jutted skyward, gleaming in the light of the afternoon sun. Reuel could just make out masses of men and tents that covered the base of the hill, outside the walls, as well as the valley plain around it. "O Jehovah," he prayed aloud, "Please bring my master safely within those walls."

Jedaiel clapped a hand on his shoulder. "Let us go and see how your prayer has been answered."

They moved forward again, slipping through hillsides of scattered oaks, sycamores, and almond trees awash in white blossoms and the pale green leaves of spring. Birds flitted around them, chirping brightly as they gathered nesting materials and ate the buds from the pomegranates and olives; clearings were filled with the humming of bees collecting nectar from chrysanthemums, red and black poppies, and white cyclamen. The incongruity of the scene almost angered Reuel—how could such peaceful beauty exist alongside the evil and wholesale destruction that was about to be unleashed on the land?

They crossed a ridge that was more densely treed. The new grasses and herbs of spring softened their footsteps as they slipped through the trunks like shadows. Twice, Jedaiel stopped them, pulling Reuel down to crouch behind some weathered stone or dense cluster of broom trees. The first time Reuel saw nothing. The second time, though, while they waited in silence a Philistine sentry in pleated kilt and feather-crested helmet crossed their path only a few dozen paces ahead of them, scanning the trees warily.

The next time they broke clear of the trees, they stood on a craggy knoll that jutted out from the side of a cliff, bare of anything but a few weeds clinging to shallow patches of soil that had collected in divots in the rock. A boulder was poised on the edge of the knoll as though waiting to be trundled down the hillside below. Crouching behind it, they scanned the view before them.

A series of descending hills stepped down to the level of the trade road, the higher ones covered in a multi-textured layer of evergreen and deciduous trees covering the full spectrum of greens, the lower dotted with brush and scrub and patches of blue-grey rock. At the bottom of the steps the great road wound through the hills like a giant, camel-colored snake. There, the army of Philistia sprawled out before them, a dark flood that oozed down the road toward Mizpah, spilling over both of its banks onto the land on either side.

"How many are there?" Reuel stared in awe.

"I would guess fifteen thousand." Jedaiel shaded his eyes with one hand. "Maybe twenty."

Reuel felt his throat go dry. "So many…"

Jedaiel glanced back toward him. "This is just the main force." He pointed at the city of Mizpah in the distance. "The advance is already at Mizpah, and is likely several thousand strong."

"How do we get past them now?" Reuel wondered aloud.

Jedaiel nodded. "Good question. Now there are two forces—well, one and a half—between us and the city."

"I must get back to my master," said Reuel, as much to himself as to Jedaiel.

But the Benjaminite wasn't listening. Shading his eyes again, he squinted toward the city. "What is that?"

"What?"

Jedaiel leaned closer to Reuel so the prophet could follow the line of his extended arm. "There—between the Philistine army and the advance's camp. Another crowd is hurrying forward…"

"Yes! I see it!" Reuel strained to make out the details of the group, but they were just a dark smudge on the otherwise empty section of road leading up to Mizpah.

"There are a few hundred people there, as well as wagons and a handful of mounts." Jedaiel was frowning now, his cheeks pulled up as he squinted against the light of the sky. "They are not moving in an orderly…I do not think they are soldiers."

Reuel stiffened. "Then…they are Israelites."

"I think so. But from where, and what are they doing between the two armies?"

"Whatever they are doing there, they are our best chance for getting into the city!" Reuel felt hope lighten his breathing. "They will have to somehow penetrate the advance force, just as we have to!"

"That does not mean they have a better plan to do so than we do."

"No—but several hundred may succeed where two may fail."

Jedaiel cocked his head doubtfully. "In my experience, it usually works the other way around."

"Nevertheless," continued Reuel, "we may be able to help each other. If they are, as you suspect, not an army, then they may need all the able bodies they can get to penetrate the Philistine defenses."

Jedaiel was silent for a moment. "Well. It does not feel right to abandon them without determining what their situation is. We should at least try to contact them, and that means joining them at least temporarily." He turned to face Reuel, his face grim. "It is time to infiltrate the enemy forces."

Without any further explanation, the Benjaminite returned to the trees and began quickly making his way downhill toward the road. Reuel followed him, his thighs aching as they descended the steep slopes. Reuel felt as though he was making enough noise to be heard all the way across the valley in comparison to Jedaiel's silent footsteps. He tried to watch the way that the Benjaminite walked: knees constantly bent, each step carefully placed to avoid brittle sticks, feet rolling heel to toe.

It seemed only moments had passed when they reached the first valley crossing their route. Again Jedaiel stopped them, holding up one hand, palm forward. Reuel crouched behind some brush but Jedaiel remained standing, taking one of his slings from his belt and loading a rough, fist-sized stone from the forest floor.

Jedaiel had the sling whirling around his head before Reuel even spotted his target: another Philistine sentry, four dozen paces below them. The sling stone collided with his left temple with such force that it knocked him from his feet. He did not make a sound, and he did not rise.

"We have crossed their sentry line," Jedaiel whispered to Reuel. "It will be harder from here." He proffered one of the slings from his belt. "Do you know how to use a sling?"

Reuel shook his head.

Jedaiel nodded and tucked the weapon away again. "Very well. Stay close."

They crept forward. The forest had transformed for Reuel. Every shadow now concealed furtive movements; every gulley was a potential hiding place for the enemy. They had not gone far when Jedaiel stooped and loaded another stone into his sling. Reuel ducked behind a tree, scanning the forest until he saw what had caught the Benjaminite's attention: a pair of sentries, paralleling their course two dozen paces down the hill. Both carried spears, casually held horizontally at their sides.

Jedaiel stood perfectly still, sling tails in his right hand, cradling the loaded stone in the other. He watched the two men walking forward until both were lined up where he wanted them. The sling whirled once and the stone hurtled between the trunks almost silently.

The stone hit the farther soldier squarely in the temple and he dropped silently and instantly. His partner had time only to turn toward his fallen companion in confusion when a second rock struck him in the back of the head. He toppled onto the body of the other soldier

"Quickly!" hissed Jedaiel, and bounded down the hill toward the two men. Reuel followed; when they reached the bodies—both men were already dead—Jedaiel began to strip them. After a moment, Reuel realized what he was doing and bent to help him.

In a short time they were clothed in the uniforms of Philistine warriors: tunics, pleated kilts, cross-laced sandals, and feather-crested helmets. "Leave the weapons," Jedaiel ordered, and when Reuel looked at him quizzically: "Do you know how to use a sword?"

"How complicated can it be?" Reuel asked.

Jedaiel's face was expressionless. "Yes…as I said: leave the weapons. Any advantage they might give someone untrained like you would be eliminated by the way they will hinder our movements."

They continued downward and Reuel quickly recognized the wisdom in Jedaiel's advice—if traveling quickly and quietly had been difficult before, it was all but impossible with the additional weight and awkwardness of the bronze helmet and the ill-fitting clothing. Reuel could just imagine what it would have been like with a sword twisting at his hip or a heavy shield slung across his back.

The next time they saw Philistine scouts it was two groups at the same time. "Keep walking," Jedaiel said. "Wave if they wave to you but otherwise act as if you have not seen them."

Now they could glimpse the edge of the main force in the valley below them, hear the rumble of their movement and taste their dust in the air. Jedaiel had plotted their route perfectly: they were on course to reach the road just ahead of the Philistine vanguard. Reuel's heart pounded so loudly in his ears that he was sure their enemies could hear it even over the sounds of the army. "Even in this clothing, I do not think I look like a Philistine," he said.

"You do not," said Jedaiel without turning.

"I was hoping for a little encouragement!"

"Be encouraged if we survive."

Jedaiel changed course and began to parallel the road while still descending toward it. Reuel was breathless and his muscles ached, he stumbled frequently over the underbrush. They were within a few dozen paces from the road when Reuel realized that their current course would put them in plain view of the Philistines in moments.

"Jedaiel!" he hissed.

"Keep walking," said the Benjaminite.

"But we're going to be—."

"Keep walking!" Jedaiel repeated.

Reuel followed him as they closed the gap and stepped onto the dusty road. A few dozen paces ahead of them four Philistines in a scythe-wheeled chariot, flanked on either side by half a dozen other men, walked slowly down the road. Reuel was relieved to see none of the black uniforms of the Gedhudhra among them, but he was not sure why—Gedhudhra or not, the soldiers were more than a match for the two of them. He felt completely exposed, as though he had already been discovered as an imposter.

Behind them, seventy paces or so back, a string of half a dozen chariots led the vanguard. No one seemed concerned about Reuel and Jedaiel's presence—at least not that Reuel could detect. Jedaiel stooped and filled one filled one of the wide pouches on his belt with stones from the roadside, then began loping toward the chariot ahead of them. Reuel followed him, a few paces behind.

"Faster," Jedaiel hissed. "We need to catch up to that chariot."

"Faster?" Reuel panted. "Shouldn't we have stayed hidden as long as we could?"

Jedaiel glanced back at him, but did not slow. "You could not walk quickly enough through the forest and hills to overtake them."

Reuel fell silent, only then realizing what a burden he must be to the hardened warrior and how kind Jedaiel had been not to say anything about it.

They drew up behind the chariot. Jedaiel wrapped a strip of cloth around his nose and mouth to keep out the dust that roiled from the vehicle's wheels, and Reuel tried to cover his mouth with his sleeve, squinting to keep the dirt from his eyes.

"Message from the Gedhudhra!" Jedaiel shouted, his voice slightly muffled.

The men in the chariot turned and the vehicle slowed.

A bola was in Jedaiel's left hand and a loaded sling in his right, although Reuel had not seen him remove either from his belt. Jedaiel kept them concealed behind his back.

"Well?" said the spearman on the chariot. "What message?"

"You've been relieved of your duties," Jedaiel said, still approaching the rear of the vehicle.

Confusion wrinkled the soldier's forehead and nose. "Relieved?"

Jedaiel nodded. "Permanently."

In the space of a heartbeat the bola struck the chariot's driver at the base of his skull, just below his helmet; he tumbled over the front of the chariot into the harness. A sling stone followed the bola, hitting the archer, his bow already half-raised toward them, directly between the eyes.

"Now!" Jedaiel yelled and sprinted forward.

Now what? Reuel wondered, dashing after him.

As the warriors on either side of them drew their weapons and charged toward the chariot, Jedaiel leapt onto the vehicle, a short sword in his left hand and a bola whirling in his right. The shield bearer caught the bola stone below the chin and flew out of the chariot as though he had been tossed by a Rephaim. The spearman whirled toward them, lunging at Jedaiel with his weapon. The Benjaminite parried the blow with the Philistine sword that seemd to have appeared in his hand, then swung the bola downward; it wrapped the spear shaft three times and Jedaiel jerked, yanking it from the Philistine's hands and pulling the warrior forward onto Jedaiel's extended sword. The blade disappeared in the spearman's stomach and before he had even hit the ground Jedaiel was clambering over the front of the chariot and onto the harness.

The horses had slowed and were weaving in confusion. The Philistine soldiers closed from either side, howling.

"Reuel!" Jedaiel yelled, raising his sword and hacking at the traces. In three swift blows he cut the chariot away. Its tongue dropped and dug into the roadway and the vehicle swung dramatically sideways, and then rolled over twice in the middle of the road.

Jedaiel clambered atop one of the horses and grabbed what remained of the traces of the second horse. "Mount up!" he yelled at Reuel, who dashed forward to obey.

But the Philistines were at his heels. Jedaiel had to let go of Reuel's mount to throw two more bolas into his enemies, felling the first two soldiers with blows that struck them squarely in the forehead. The loosed horse was a war stallion and whirling slings and shouts did not frighten him, but he lunged forward to get clear of the action. Reuel dashed after him, his vision filled by dust and flicking hooves.

"Yaaah!" yelled Jedaiel, urging his mount forward.

A spear hissed past Reuel's head from behind, just missed the horse ahead of him and clattered onto the dusty road. He glanced over his left shoulder as a Philistine, only a pace behind, raised his black blade above his head.

Reuel tore his helmet off and swung it with both hands to parry the blow. The force of the sword-stroke smashed the helmet from his grasp; it hit Reuel in the forehead before falling to the road at his feet and rolling away.

He reeled from the blow, stumbling backward, struggling to focus. A thunder of movement to his left sent him lunging away, but not fast enough—someone grabbed his collar in a grip of iron. He twisted, thrashing at his captor.

"Stop struggling!" he heard Jedaiel's voice yell and he looked up to see the mounted Benjaminite half-dragging him along the road.

The horse ahead had slowed and Jedaiel galloped alongside it, pulling on Reuel's collar as the prophet grabbed the mount's mane and clambered onto its back.

Arrows whispered past their head and Reuel turned to see the entire vanguard of the army thundering toward them.

"Ride!" Jedaiel yelled, digging his heels into the horse.

Crouching low over his mount's neck, Reuel galloped after him down the dusty road.

42

S amuel turned when he heard the thundering of hooves and cries of "Make way! Make way!" from behind him. Two Philistine soldiers galloped toward him, driving their mounts hard. The crowd parted and the riders reined to a dusty halt in front of him.

"Reuel!" he yelled, his heart leaping in his chest.

Manoah grabbed the bridles of the high-spirited mounts as they pranced in place, foaming. "Easy! Easy!"

Samuel's friend smiled down at him, his hair wild and wind-blown, looking somehow younger than when last Samuel had seen him. "My lord! The Philistines are at our heels!"

Screams of fear from the rear of the line of travelers punctuated Reuel's warning. The entire mass of people on the road surged forward. The elderly were lifted into wagons, and whips cracked behind the mules pulling them. Fathers swung children onto their shoulders or pulled them urgently forward by the hand, and mothers clutched swaddled babies in their arms, hurrying down the road with fear stark and bright in their eyes.

"Wait!" Samuel shouted. "We cannot get through! The advance guard!"

He was completely ignored as the crowd pushed toward Mizpah with a single thought in their minds: to put more distance between themselves and the army that bore down on them beneath a forebodeing column of roiling dust.

Manoah, still clutching the horses' bridles, craned his neck toward the hills to the west. "Where is Samson?"

Now Samuel could hear the Philistines, even through the tromping of sandals and hooves and the shouts and weeping of the people around him. The ominous sound of galloping chariot horses and the fierce urgings of their drivers rumbled like distant thunder..

The dust column approached over a hill just behind them.

Samuel spun in circles, surrounded by a maelstrom of movement, as though he were a lodged stone in a flowing stream. The echoes from the hills played tricks on his ears, reverberating as though another army was galloping toward them from the green valleys to the west...

And then over a rise in those hills, like a black wave of arcing horns, flailing hooves, and hurtling flesh, hundreds upon hundreds of cattle surged downhill toward the road. Behind them Samson, Kish, and Tahash galloped, howling and pushing their horses like madmen. Each of them whirled a torch tied to a rope over their heads, scattering sparks in a circle around them and driving the stampede forward with panic in the whites of their bovine eyes.

The Benjaminite Jedaiel was the first to react. "Get clear!" he shouted at the fleeing Israelites all around him, kicking his heels into his mount and galloping toward the descending herd. Reuel turned his own horse toward the crowd, urging them to the eastern side of the road, trying to create some type of barrier between them and the stampede.

Now the crowd saw what was happening, and those on foot rushed from the dirt roadway onto the grass and scrub to the east or took shelter on the eastern side of the wagons. The stampeding cattle thundered onto the vacated road, turning to follow the path of least resistance.

In a flash of understanding, Samuel grasped Samson's plan.

"Run!" he yelled at the top of his lungs. "Follow them! Hurry! Follow them!"

The herd raced past and people near Samuel obeyed his urging, confusion on their faces but trusting in the guidance of the Prophet of Israel.

They fell into place in the dust-choked road behind Tahash, Samson, and Kish, running in blind obedience, urged forward by hope.

The few mounted men among the fleeing Israelites whirled their mounts to the south and followed Reuel and Jedaiel. They were joined by the able-bodied men who carried any kind of weapon—mostly staves, sickles, pruning hooks, bows, and slings—who fell back to form a makeshift rearguard under Manoah's shouted directions.

Samuel, torn between fleeing and supporting the rearguard, looked up and down the road. The Philistine army pursuing them was clearly visible now, a dark stain that swallowed up the road and land on either side of it. At its forefront ranks of chariots hurtled forward, spewing clouds of dust that hung over the loping infantry behind them like a shadow of the death they bore.

Samuel flinched as arrows began falling among the Israelite rearguard. Manoah rallied the determined farmers, Levite guards, and townsfolk and they made an orderly retreat, moving as swiftly as they could toward Mizpah while maintaining a defensive line.

Jedaiel thundered past Samuel so suddenly that the Prophet leapt to one side of the road, raising his hands to shield himself. The Benjaminite didn't seem to notice him; he galloped into the rearguard and, sling whirling overhead, faster than the eye could follow, hurtled stones into the approaching chariots.

Drivers and horses began to fall; chariots careened sideways into one another, or tipped onto their sides in the road where the vehicles following them collided with them in spectacular explosions of dust, wood, and leather. The road was too narrow to allow the Philistines to move forward in large numbers. The chariots were pressed together where their scythed wheels threatened one another.

Slingers from Manoah's rearguard joined the Benjaminite's efforts and sent a hail of stones into the Philistine van even as the Israelites continued to flee headlong toward the city in the wake of the stampeding herd. The slingers targeted the galloping chariot horses; sling stones *thunked* into the mounts' bronze head armor, and some went down in a tangle of flailing legs and traces. Every felled stallion left another scythe-wheeled chariot in the roadway, hindering the charge of the Philistines behind it.

The Israelites crossed another low rise in the road and suddenly the Philistine advance was before them, a sprawling camp of makeshift tents and smoldering fires. Feather-crested soldiers scurried toward the road, tightening armor straps and collecting weapons, hastily assembling in a defensive line.

The terrified herd of cattle thundered toward them. As soon as they appeared, to a man the hardened warriors scattered clear of the tossing horns and flailing hooves, parting like the waters of the Red Sea beneath the staff of Moses. The stampede burst through the advance guard, and the Israelites were close on their heels.

But as soon as the cattle were past, the Philistines returned to their positions, closing on the Israelites like the jaws of a trap.

Manoah was ready for them. His most well-armed soldiers flanked the Israelite rearguard. They never stopped moving, fleeing toward Mizpah even as they maintained the best defense they could muster against the Philistine advance. Kish, Tahash, Samson, and Jedaiel stood together at the center of the rearguard, and wherever they went, they left a swath of death in their wake.

Now the cattle were stampeding through the Israelites camped outside the walls of the city, but Gadite cattlemen from Gilead leapt onto horses and mules or ran with long sticks in their hands, herding the cacophony through the sea of tents as deftly as a weaver threads his needle through the loom.

When Samuel at last stopped running, he was in the middle of a roiling mass of people weeping and panting before the massive gates of the city of Mizpah. As the cattle were herded harmlessly into the valley plain to the north, the Philistine advance drew back from Manoah's rearguard, not yet ready to engage their enemy.

Then a dull thud and the creaking of bronze hinges announced the opening of the gates, and people poured from the gap like a flood. Samuel scanned the faces and, at the realization that he was—temporarily—out of harm's way, relief washed over him with such intensity that his knees seemed to want to fold of their own volition.

Just outside the walls Priests in white robes and turbans stood before troughs hastily dug in the dry ground. With the assistance of the Levites, they ceremoniously poured water from tall urns onto the dirt, where it splashed across their ankles and bare feet. It was called "the Offering of Tears," an ablution that acknowledged their humility by symbolizing that the offerers, like the water, would one day return to dust.

"In this way," the Priest intoned, "do we vow to part with our sins, and to retain no more of them than this vessel does of the water that is in it."

Men and women stood all around the offering, heads bowed or hands raised, faces strained in the peculiar emotional intensity of silent prayer.

The crowd parted momentarily in front of him, and for an instant he had a view of the wide opening between the stone guardhouses.

A woman was walking there. To Samuel, she seemed somehow alone, separate from the sea of faces all around her. Wind and movement had loosed long strands of her dark hair from her *tsa'iph*, and several blew across her nose and cheeks, as though they were the remnants of a shredded black veil. Three young boys clung to her unadorned linen skirts, as though clutching solidly fixed stones in an unexpected flood.

Her eyes found his—her steady, dark eyes, calm in the midst of the maelstrom of movement all around her, like still pools beneath the shadows of a forest whose treetops are tossed by a storm.

"Liora," he whispered, and rushed into her arms.

43

"To this Abraham replied: "God will provide the sheep, my son." And they continued on together." – The Scroll of Bereshith.

Liora's hair smelled sweet and nutty, like spring flowers and olive oil, and in her arms Samuel felt a completeness, as though pressed against her yielding warmth he had slipped into a place formed just for him.

Joel and Abijah were pulling at his robe, and he released his wife and knelt to gather them into his arms. "Papa," Joel whispered warmly against his cheek, and the emotion in his son's voice pierced Samuel's heart with a pain that was as welcome as water, and breath.

"Cheran is clinging to life," Liora said when he stood to face her again.

"What? Why—what happened?"

"We found him badly injured on the road. He said only that Baghadh has betrayed us."

"Did he tell you how?" Samuel asked.

She shook her head. "He said only that the Philistines knew we were gathering at Mizpah. But at Naioth, with my own eyes I witnessed Baghadh plotting with Glaucus."

A metallic taste burned in the back of Samuel's throat. "May Jehovah see it, and may his betrayal whirl back upon his own head. Is Cheran awake?"

She shook her head again. "He has not regained consciousness since shortly after we found him."

"Then Joppa…?"

"Fallen," Liora said.

"My lord Prophet?" a small voice asked, and Samuel looked beyond Liora at Gavriel, looking up at him from beneath lowered brows, his chin tucked against his chest. Samuel knelt and took the boy in his arms.

"I am so glad to find you safe," he said.

"Did you see them, my lord?" Gavriel said. "The people outside dumping water on the ground?"

The boy's vision came back to Samuel in a rush: *a city, where people were dumping water on the ground…the water they were dumping turned into a big river. It crashed into the black clouds…*

"Then it all went down," Samuel whispered.

Gavriel nodded, eyes wide.

"My lord!" An approaching voice from behind Samuel spun him around. Reuel pushed through the crowd and they embraced.

Samuel felt tears burning his eyes. "I was sure…we were afraid you were lost."

"I nearly was," said Reuel through unabashed tears. "I was captured by Canaanite slavers and dragged halfway to Beersheba. But Jehovah was with me like a terrible Mighty One. He sent a deliverer to me, a Benjaminite named Jedaiel."

"Cheran is seriously injured," said Liora to the healer. "Can you come to him?"

Reuel hefted his battered red box of herbs and salves clutched beneath one arm. "Lead on."

Samuel kissed his wife and his sons. "Return to me quickly, my love," he said.

Reuel and Samuel's family threaded their way through the crowd toward the city center. They had barely stepped away when Samuel found himself face to face with Manoah, Samson, and Manoah's wife Na'amah. A few steps behind them were Samson's two younger brothers.

Manoah had his arm around his wife's shoulders. No matter how many times he saw her, Samuel was always shocked by her incredible beauty. Even now, as a woman who had seen four and a half decades under the sun, her gently curled, tar-black hair, her large green eyes and her wide, sensuous lips turned men's heads wherever she went.

"You are all well, are you not?" Samuel asked.

Manoah nodded. "We had to fight our way through at the last, but we are uninjured."

"Does that mean you have become the hero of Israel finally, big brother?" one of Samson's siblings asked him, and Samuel could not miss the mocking tone in the young man's voice.

Manoah turned on him, scowling. "Samson fought with an honor and skill that the two of you could learn from." He turned back to Samuel. "Ahlai has called an assembly of Elders at the entrance to the keep. We were just on our way there."

Samuel and Ahimelech followed the men through the choked streets of the city. On either side of their route, homes and shops were crowded with people, from their entries to their rooftops. Here and there spears or farmer's bills jutted up from the crowd, but they were few and far between. Samuel did not see a single armored man among them, and he hoped that they were all posted at the walls.

Samuel kept his head down and tried to avoid eye contact with anyone, afraid that if he was recognized he would be swarmed with people asking him what they should do. To his relief, the people that milled and flowed all around him were too overcome by their own anxieties to notice much of anything beyond the welfare of their loved ones.

Several blocks into the city they passed a smithy spouting black smoke, its coals roaring under the breathing of the bellows. Heat rolled from it in an invisible wave. Half a dozen smiths in leather aprons worked side by side, hammering bronze plowshares and pruning hooks into daggers and swords, and sickles into curved khopesh.

At the pinnacle of the city, a stout gatehouse of weathered stone hunkered at the base of the towering keep. Several dozen men were gathered inside the gatehouse, whose entrance was encircled by armed guards who held back the pressing crowds. Many of them were Phoenicians; Samuel took this to mean that Baghadh was somewhere within. Manoah introduced himself and his companions to the guards and told them that Ahlai had sent for them, and they parted to allow the group to join the Elders.

Samuel was surrounded by familiar faces. Ahlai, chief of the Elders of Mizpah stood near Dathan and the sons of Judge Avdon—including Tahash, who had rejoined his brothers. Guni of Lebonah; proud Elishama of Bethel, the Benjaminites Kish and Jedaiel, there in the absence of Ner; Manoah and his sons; Ahimelech; and Baghadh, looking—shockingly—even worse than he had the last time Samuel had seen him. Samuel was surprised that he would dare to show his face among the Elders, but the fact that he did so made Samuel wonder about what Liora had told him. Would Baghadh have come if he had truly betrayed them to the Philistines? Or was he simply unaware that anyone knew? In any case, Samuel realized that most of the guards posted around them were Baghahd's men. He had, as always, brought an entourage.

"Brothers!" Ahlai called them to order. "Thank you for responding to the Prophet's summons." He glanced around the faces suddenly, confusion wrinkling his forehead. "Where is Ahitub? Where is the High Priest?"

All eyes turned toward Samuel and Ahimelech, standing beside him. Samuel waited for Ahimelech to speak, but the man only stood silently, staring at the ground a few paces in front of him.

Samuel cleared his throat. "High Priest Ahitub has lain down with his forefathers."

Silence swallowed the gathering in a single moment. "May Jehovah preserve us!" Elishama whispered.

"Where is Ner?" Samuel asked Kish.

"He has led the Benjaminites of Gibeah into the hills," Kish growled. "Apparently my grandfather was not confident in the strength of Mizpah's walls."

"He must return!" Samuel said, confused by the certainty he felt that his words were true. "Can you convince them of our need?"

Kish was silent a moment. "I can try. But they will incline their ears to the voice of our patriarch, and he has ever been resistant to putting our people in danger if he feels that victory is unlikely. Even if I go, they may not return with me."

"So be it," said Samuel. "Go, nevertheless."

"Tell him that Tahash, son of Avdon, summons him," Tahash said, and the entire group turned to look at him.

Kish shook his head in confusion. "I will tell him that the Prophet of Israel summons him. If anything moves him, that will."

The big Benjaminite stepped from the gathering of Elders, disappearing in long strides through the crowd beyond the circle of guards.

After a protracted pause, Ahlai spoke again, but his voice was heavy. "We have done as you instructed, Prophet. All those summoned have fasted since arriving. Outside the walls, the Priests and Levites have organized ablution offerings in symbol of our repentance of past sins."

"And so now we have water, and Priests, and Prophets," said Elishama, "When what we need is an army."

"We have an army," said Baghadh. "I have brought thousands of Manassites with me, and each chieftain here represents thousands more fighting men. But does anyone really think war will be our salvation?"

"Are you suggesting we take no action?" asked Dathan.

"Your father is no longer here," said Baghadh. His voice expressed regret and sorrow. Samuel saw otherwise: *eyes flat and cold. Jawline hard.*

"But if he was, my father would have led an army against this enemy," Dathan responded. "He said as much, before his death."

"And perhaps, under the leadership of Jehovah's Judge, that army might have stood a chance against this enemy," said Baghadh. "But Avdon has lain down with his forefathers."

"I have heard people saying that you think you are Avdon's successor," said Dathan, his eyes narrowed.

"I have never said so!" Baghadh held up his lesioned hands in protest. "Though I have heard others suggest it."

Samuel looked at the men around him, trying to see if their faces reflected his own anger and disgust at Baghadh's words. "How many of these 'others' have received gifts from your hands?" he asked.

Baghadh scowled, wrinkling the crusty pustules around his mouth. "I need not stand here and be subjected to the criticism of this man who bears the vermilion staff under his own authority."

"Under my authority!" growled Manoah. "As an Elder and prince of the tribe of Dan."

"Ahh," Baghadh purred. "A Danite is now appointing the Elders of Levi? This is beyond the scope of even your great influence, O Manoah."

Manoah looked as though he were about to rip Baghadh limb from limb, but Ahimelech intervened. "Look more closely at the Prophet's staff, Baghadh. Do you not recognize it?"

Baghadh glanced at the staff. Although he doubted if anyone else noticed, Samuel *saw* Baghadh's reaction: *pupils dilating; eyes widening slightly; sudden tightness in jaw and neck; his body stiffening in an abrupt stillness.*

But Baghadh just shrugged. "Should I?"

"It is *Mish'eneth*, named for the staff of Aaron that sprouted almond blossoms and was placed forever in the Ark of the Covenant. It was given to the Prophet of Israel by my father, High Priest of Israel."

Baghadh's sneer did not diminish, and he looked around at the group in unabashed disgust. "I can see that you are determined to oppose me, and the will of your own people. Very well. I know when I am no longer welcome. But I warn you—the Prophet Samuel does not lead this nation. There is another leader who has already been appointed by God."

"Who?" Ahlai asked.

Baghadh turned toward Samuel. "Ask Samuel the so-called Prophet. And then ask yourselves why he has not disclosed this to your ears!"

Ahlai looked at Samuel, forehead wrinkled. "Samuel?"

Samuel glanced over at Tahash, suddenly unsure of what to say. "I…Someone did speak to me about this…"

"But you decided that no one could possibly be appointed by Jehovah without your approval," sneered Baghadh.

Samuel shook his head. "No. That is not it at all. I simply have had no time to…to determine…"

"You have said enough, Samuel," said Baghadh. "My brothers—think carefully about what you are doing. If you choose to follow Samuel, or the one whom he appoints, you will be answerable for the consequences."

He turned on his heel and strode from the group, flanked by his contingent of guards. Tahash followed him, glancing back at Samuel with narrowed eyes.

When he had gone, Ahlai turned to Samuel. "People are saying that you secretly appointed him as Avdon's successor, and are going to make the appointment public here, today. They say that is why you did not appoint any of Avdon's sons—because you already knew Baghadh was the one to replace him."

Samuel was about to reply when he was interrupted by cheering and shouting from the crowd outside the gatehouse. The Elders turned and saw, above the heads of the people, Baghadh standing behind a parapet on a high rooftop, arms spread wide as though to embrace the adoration of the crowd.

Tahash stood next to him, nose in the air, and behind them were three or four dozen richly armed and armored Manassites.

"What is this?" Samuel heard Ahlai say.

"People of Israel!" Baghadh called out, and the crowd quieted. "I have had my ears opened to your fears! I have seen the power in the arms of the enemy that even now sets up camp outside these walls! In spite of this great gathering of the children of Israel, the Philistines have many times the number of our armed men. Let us be realistic. Do we have the might of arms to defeat this enemy? The House of the Matrites has fled into the hills; our brothers of other tribes have failed to respond to the summons or are scattered. Some of our men are busy guarding cities in the south, where the Amorites are even now staging an uprising against us.

"And here we wait—most of us unarmed, burdened with our wives, and our children, and our old men and women. We cannot fight! We cannot! We would be forced to watch our wives and children slaughtered before our eyes! And who would lead us in such a fight? Avdon is dead. And I have just learned that High Priest Ahitub has also fallen asleep in death."

The announcement came as a shock to many in the crowd, and for several long moments all other sounds were swallowed in the wailing and keening that erupted.

"We must acknowledge the reality of our position!" Baghadh shouted over the uproar. "If we had a Judge to take Avdon's place, then we could march behind him into battle without fear, confident that Jehovah would bring us the victory." He looked meaningfully in Ahimelech and Samuel's direction. "But our Priest and Prophet have failed to provide anyone to fill that role."

Baghadh paused long enough for the real meaning behind his words to sink in. Then his voice took on a note of desperation. "I say there is only one course open to us now, no matter how distasteful it may seem: we must approve a leader who will represent us in a full surrender, and throw ourselves on the mercy of the Philistine Axis Lords."

"Mercy?" Manoah shouted up at him. "We would better entrust ourselves to the mercy of wild dogs!"

Baghadh shook his head and waved his hands, palms outward, in front of his chest. "No—no...I have been among them, worked with them in business and trade. They are reasonable men, and they do not want to see all of us dead! If we submit to them, they will at least spare our wives and children—and they may allow all of us to live!"

"At what price?" Samuel shouted up to him. "As slaves beneath the whips of their taskmasters? At the cost of our freedom to live and to worship as we choose?"

Baghadh glanced at him briefly—eyes narrowed and jaw clenched—but then turned back to his audience. "How long will you keep uncovering your ears to Samuel? He who has put you in this situation, who has drawn all of you here and made you an easy target for your enemies?" He pointed an accusing finger in Samuel's direction. "If Samuel wanted the nation destroyed, he could hardly have conceived of a better plan to accomplish his goal!"

People in the crowd began grumbling and shouting, but Samuel knew only some of it was anger directed at Baghadh. There was too much truth in the man's words for Samuel—or anyone else--to dismiss them out of hand. There was too much truth for Samuel to challenge them here, in front of people who would all be witnesses to his humiliation if Baghadh were to appear to get the better of him.

"But I do not believe Samuel intended for this to happen," Baghadh continued, his voice softened by his pretence of magnanimity. "He is a Prophet who has served his nation well. But he is not a man of the shield, or a leader to men of the shield. His mistake was in ordering all of us here, to Mizpah, when doing so was beyond the range of his authority and wisdom. Examine the Book of the Wars of Jehovah—is there any precedent for preparing for war by gathering an unarmed people, along with women and children, in response to the threat of attack?"

"And you feel you are qualified to lead us?" Manoah yelled.

"Me? I would never suggest that I am...I did not come here today to promote myself. But we have remained safe these past years by lying still lest we cause the Philistines to see us again as a threat. Has anyone here forgotten the lessons of Aphek, and how our armies fared against the iron blades and chariots of Philistia?

"And yet," he continued, "here we find ourselves yet again. Once more under Samuel's guidance we are arrayed against the might of the Philistines. Only this time, we are unarmed and unprepared for battle.

"It is not the first time Samuel ben Elkanah has led us astray. We have gathered here today in repentance, as evidenced by the offerings of abnegation we have witnessed and participated in outside these walls. But repentance for what? Because we have sinned against Jehovah by listening to the voice of Samuel and separating the Ark of the Covenant from the Tabernacle! We stand here pleading for the help of our God even while we allow His Holy Ark to remain in Abinadab's store room! Jehovah has brought this punishment down upon us, and our only hope is to beg the mighty Philistines for their mercy."

"They stand, armed and armored, before our walls!" shouted Manoah. "Do you think they will simply walk away now because we ask them to?"

"The Danite makes a good point!" Baghadh responded, before anyone else could. "But we may be able to pacify them by offering them some prize."

The crowd was quiet for a moment, and then a rumble grew to a roar as people discussed what Baghadh meant by the comment.

"What prize?" someone from the crowd nearby shouted. "You know them—what prize would they accept?"

Baghadh looked down from his place atop the house, and his cold eyes found Samuel. "Who has been their enemy since his youth? Whom do they hold responsible for the plague that swept their nation two decades ago, and cost them their spoils of war: the Ark of the Covenant? Whom do they blame now for gathering the nation in hostile opposition to them? Who has sent his minions throughout the countryside preaching hatred of our neighbors in Canaan, and proclaiming all their ways an abomination?"

He extended one finger toward Samuel, as though he wished to skewer the Prophet upon it.

"Give them Samuel ben Elkanah," he said.

44

The crowd had fallen nearly silent again at Baghadh's words.

"Do you dare suggest such a thing?" Ahlai said, anger roughening his voice.

"Do we dare fail to at least consider the idea?" Baghadh shot back. "Samuel has repeatedly sworn that he would give his life for his people. Does anyone here doubt the sincerity of that claim?"

Samuel felt, rather than saw, the sidelong looks of the crowd.

"This day does not have to end in a destruction of our people!" Baghadh continued. "But if we fail to placate the Philistines, they will march on us and destroy us all! You will watch your wives and daughters raped, your children slaughtered around you until the streets of Mizpah run red with blood!"

He turned and gestured toward Tahash. "Or, we can accept the leader Jehovah has chosen for us, and give him the authority to negotiate our surrender with the Philistines."

Elishama took a step nearer to Ahlai. "We have to at least consider surrender," he said, almost in a whisper.

"Do we?" Ahlai said, but Samuel could hear in his voice that he knew Elishama's words were correct.

Reuel abruptly pushed through the crowd until he spotted Samuel.

"Cheran?" Samuel asked as the young prophet rushed to him.

Reuel shook his head. "I'm sorry, my lord."

Samuel sighed, feeling as though his world were unraveling. "We were too late."

Reuel shook his head again. "No, my lord. His injuries had already begun to heal, and although they were serious, I do not think they were any longer deadly."

Samuel looked at him in puzzlement. "Then...?"

"He was poisoned," Reuel said.

"Poisoned?" Samuel felt abruptly light-headed. "But how? And why...?"

He abruptly remembered. Liora had told him. Cheran, when he was still conscious, had claimed that Baghadh had betrayed them. No one knew what he had meant. And now that knowledge, and Baghadh's only accuser, had been brought to silence.

He looked up at Baghadh, who was speaking again, but Samuel could not hear what he was saying. A roaring in his ears mingled with the pounding of his heart and the grinding of his teeth.

But the crowd was shifting toward Baghadh now; more faces were turned his direction than toward the Elders still clustered within the gate-house. Those who had turned away from him were now looking at Samuel, their eyes wells that were drained of courage and confidence.

"My lord Samuel," someone said, and Samuel looked over to see one of the *Beneh* peering at him from between the guards. *Arms held tight against body. Shoulders drawn in. Head lowered.* "What do we do?"

The volume of the crowd was rising; Ahlai's hands were above his head as he shouted for calm. "Jehovah has abandoned us!" someone shouted.

Then the blat of a *shofar*, a ram's horn, cut through the cacophony. Stillness descended, except for the rustling of sandaled feet and puzzled whispers.

Ahimelech appeared beside Baghadh, lowering the horn he had blown, his lips reddened in a bright circle from the mouthpiece. There was something in Ahimelech's look that Samuel could not read, as though the High Priest had at last found the confidence he had lost in the wake of his father's death. But Samuel knew that was not quite what he was seeing in Ahimelech's eyes, and in the stolid set of his hips and shoulders. It was a newfound confidence, but not in himself…

Ahimelech raised his arms, spread wide over his head. "People of Israel! Hear me! I am Ahimelech ben Ahitub, heir to the High Priesthood of Israel."

Silence spread, like ripples on a pond, from the cluster of Elders. The sounds they could hear now were those of the soldiers and people near the wall and outside the gate: a few shouts and calls, the distant bleating and lowing of animals.

"Today," Ahimelech continued, "I have uncovered my ears to the words of the children of Israel. I know what you desire from me: assurances that Jehovah will be with us, and guidance as to what we should do in the face of this enemy. I stand here to disclose to your ears that I am ready to provide such guidance, and such assurance."

A hesitant murmur rolled through the crowd. The people shifted, and Samuel found himself across the circle from Ahlai, Dathan, Guni, El-ishama, Jedaiel, Manoah and Elkanah.

Ahimelech slowly rotated as he spoke, arms still extended, casting a net with his words and his eyes. "But you would be fools to believe that I, barely free of the short-sightedness of youth, could take up leadership of this great people. You would be fools to trust to the words of a young, untried, unconfirmed—and oftimes unwilling—High Priest."

Ahimelech paused, his dark eyes scanning the crowd. Samuel felt a chill creep down his spine. There was an energy that seemed to emanate from his friend, as though Jehovah was pouring His spirit out through Ahi-melech's words.

"But I do not ask you to do so," Ahimelech continued. "Do not give ear to my words, for were it not for my father's guidance, I would be the most thoroughly lost of any man here.

"Do not give ear to my words," he repeated. "Listen to my father's. Ahitub ben Phinehas was one of the greatest High Priests our people have known. For twenty years he has guided, taught, and provided for our people with a kind and gentle heart. Were it not for his faith, we would have noth-ing to fear losing."

"Ahitub has been brought to silence!" someone shouted; Samuel thought he recognized Baghadh's voice, but he could not be sure.

Ahimelech did not flinch at the harsh words. "Ahitub has lain down with his forefathers," he confirmed. "But he foresaw this day. And in his wisdom, and his love, he knew what we would need to do to survive it. He knew, and on the night that he died, he passed on that knowledge to me."

Samuel reeled in shock. Ahitub had told Ahimelech what they should do? All this time that they were wallowing in fear and anxiety, all this time that Samuel had struggled to maintain his own confidence while trying desperately to plot the nation's course...and Ahimelech had said nothing?

"In truth," Ahimelech continued, "we all know what it is that we need: a leader, chosen by Jehovah, who can guide us to victory, or escape, or both."

He paused again. "We need a new Judge of Israel."

The murmur in the crowd grew in volume and intensity. Still struggling with his anger of Ahimelech's secrecy, it was several moments before Samuel realized that his childhood friend was walking slowly toward him.

Ahimelech stopped a single long pace from Samuel, staring him in the face. His eyes were the steadiest Samuel had ever seen.

Ahimelech slowly raised one arm and extended his index finger toward Samuel. "Behold! In this way did High Priest Ahitub instruct me before his death: look to the bearer of the High Priest's staff *Mish'eneth*, Prophet of our nation and faithful servant of our God.

"Behold: Samuel ben Elkanah, the Judge of Israel."

45

"Finally they arrived at the place that the true God had shown Abraham, and he built an altar there, placed the wood upon it, bound Isaac hand and foot, and put him on the altar atop the wood." – The Scroll of Bereshith.

S amuel passed slowly through the shadow of the gatehouses, thrown like pillars of darkness onto the city square by the afternoon sun. Each step was a deliberate decision, a mechanical act of will. As though he were watching himself in a dream, the sound of his breathing, the thump of *Mish'eneth* on the ground, the murmuring of the crowd on every side—each became preternaturally clear and distinct.

He was outside the gate then, following the broad, dusty road as it descended into the valley below, the crowds parting before him as though he were Moses on the lip of the Red Sea. His right hand burned where he clutched *Mish'eneth*; the blisters that had formed were beginning to break open, but he felt as though the stinging gave him something to cling to, some familiar reality in a world that had suddenly been turned on its head.

His goodbye to Liora and his sons had not been one of spoken words. Joel and Abijah knew only that he was leaving, and from the tears that Samuel tried to hide they knew that this parting was something more than they understood.

He had stood and faced his wife and she had held out her soft, slender hands; he had grasped them and remained still, as though some invisible barrier lay in the distance between them. There were tears in her eyes also—but they were the dew of a dawning hope and joy. In that moment, whatever she might have been feeling, she gave him only her strength.

He had dropped her hands when Reuel had appeared beside him, draping a yearling lamb across his shoulders, whispering unheard words into his ear.

Now we must show them what to do. They were Ahitub's words, some of the last he had spoken to Samuel. Samuel wanted to believe that he didn't know what they meant, that he didn't understand how they applied to the crisis Israel now faced.

But it wasn't true. He understood perfectly.

A new Isaac.

Now we must show them what to do.

And what was Jehovah asking them to do? To put faith in Him, and to march, without fear of death, into certain annihilation.

But Israel would survive. Jehovah would preserve them through whatever trials time threw at them. But individuals—individuals would be required to make a final sacrifice on an altar that no man had seen, but that cast its shadow into every corner of the land.

Baghadh had gotten exactly what he wanted, though Ahimelech's announcement had stolen from him any joy he might have taken in the victory. Samuel was, indeed, offering himself to the Philistines. But it was Jehovah alone who would determine if the sacrifice was accepted.

Samuel realized that his feet had carried him clear of the crowds amassed around the walls of the city and into the broad field that still lay empty inside the ring of the Philistine army. He marched forward, having no destination in mind until he saw a mound of stacked boulders, stark against the green verdure. Several stones supported a massive dolmen laying atop them, its smooth upper surface looking strikingly like a gargantuan, basalt tabletop. Other stones were scattered over the surface like misshapen dishes tossed aside by long-vanished giants.

Samuel adjusted his course slightly toward the mound, staff swinging at his side. He felt warmth and wetness in his hand and, without taking his eyes from the boulders, knew that blood and water flowed from the blisters that had broken open.

He could hear the roaring of the Philistine army now, building as they saw him making his way toward them: swords crashing against shields, drums pounding and trumpets blaring over the dull thunder of tens of thousands of voices raised in murderous rage. He wondered what was happening among the Israelites behind him but he did not turn. He could not let them see him appear to hesitate or fear. In this hour, they needed a Judge who marched against their enemies unflinchingly, who demonstrated to them the most primal meaning of faith.

The faith of Isaac. The faith that willingly offered, and sometimes sacrificed, even life itself to a greater cause.

He understood now.

For so many years he had wondered that Jehovah would choose him as His Prophet—him, a child without lineage, wealth, talent, or position, who had failed to distinguish himself even as a man. No matter how the people might see him, Samuel knew he was no role model, no paragon of piety or faith or obedience to the Torah. He knew, just as Jehovah knew, the true depth of his weaknesses and the shape and color of his sins. He was a man like any other, and he had dared to allow himself to be made into a leader.

Pride is before a fall, and loftiness of spirit before stumbling. So went one of his mother's favorite proverbs. And he had allowed himself to be lifted to such heights that there could be no recovering from his fall. That day had come at last, the day he had feared since Jehovah had spoken to him one night in the Tabernacle, so many years ago.

God had chosen him and brought him to this place, this time, because his death was necessary, a fitting conclusion to the life and times of a Prophet who was not worthy to be remembered as a leader to his people. He had been given this one final task before his name was wiped out of Israel's memory.

Now we must show them what to do.

He reached the mound of stones and shifted the weight of the lamb on his shoulders. On the side that faced him, a hillock ascended to a series of half-buried rocks that formed a natural stairway to the top. Leaning on *Mish'eneth* he climbed, straining at the huge steps. His head cleared the top of the tableau and he saw beyond it the dark line of the Philistine army, milling beneath a cloud of dust.

The top of the platform was half-covered by scattered chunks of limestone and basalt, chipped free by wind, rain, snow, and ice. The skeletal remains of a desiccated oak twisted up from a tangle of dead branches like a withered hand. Strands of dry, yellow grass, caught somehow in the branches, whispered like the last remnants of hair on an old woman's head.

Samuel lowered the lamb from his shoulders and it lay on the rock, tucking its black legs under its body. It looked up at Samuel as if to say: *I am staying right here.*

Samuel lay *Mish'eneth* down and began to gather stones. A thin coating of dust softened their roughness. His right hand left an imprint of blood on each one, mottling the stack he built from them.

It took shape slowly: the length of a man's height, the width of his shoulders. *Large enough for me to lay upon*, Samuel thought, and the idea was anguish and satisfaction all at once. He suddenly thought about what the Elders of Ramathaim—and even from all over Israel—would think of what he was doing. If he had seemed to them to have gone beyond his authority before, what of now? What of his decision to build an altar, like Noah had done when the waters of the Great Flood had receded, like Abraham and the patriarchs had done in the days before the Torah? Like Gideon had done to replace an altar to Ba'al, but only by the command of Jehovah? Like Manoah had done, but only at the request of an angel?

The stones stacked with a hollow clacking that seemed amplified by his elevation. Uncut stones not held together by mortar, pitch, or lead—just bone-chips of the land, stacked upon its flesh, a link between earth and heaven.

When the altar was as high as his knees and he had exhausted almost all the rock on the tableau, he stared down at his work. The weight of what he was about to do hung heavy on his shoulders and neck.

The lamb raised its head and looked up at him, eyes round and trusting. "You were born for this day," Samuel whispered, wondering if he spoke to the lamb or to himself.

A new series of horn blasts and a roar echoed from the Philistines. Samuel turned; men and horses shifted restlessly in patterns that looked like the scurrying of insects.

Soon now.

Half a dozen long steps took him to the ancient oak, and he gathered an armload of dead wood and grass. It rasped and crackled with every touch, and as he carried it toward his altar he left a trail of bark and small twigs.

After two more trips he had covered the altar with a tangled stack of fuel as high as his chest. He brushed the dirt and bark from the front of his *me'il*, although even as he did so he wondered why. He did not expect to be seen in the garment ever again.

He knelt again and unsheathed his bronze knife. *It should be an obsidian blade,* he thought, the sacred rites of the Tabernacle speaking to him as clearly as though Ahitub were whispering in his ear.

Swiftly, before further thought could stop his hand, he reached out and slit the lamb's throat. It did not move; its eyes went flat, and a stain of scarlet slowly spread across the white wool of its neck, and chest.

He lifted the corpse—it felt heavy and unwieldy, as though even the creature's bones had become disconnected. The dry wood crackled as he laid the lamb upon it. Randomly, he wondered, *Why do people lay corpses upon the altar with such care? Neither the corpse nor the protesting wood can feel what is being done to them.*

He removed his flint from the pouch at his belt and struck a spark in a clump of dry grass nestled between two of the rocks of the altar. It lit on his first attempt, and he wanted to take it as a sign that Jehovah supported what he was about to do.

The flame roared through the dry wood voraciously, and black smoke smelling of burning wool and fat swirled into the clouds above him.

He lifted his staff again and raised his arms toward the sky. "Accept this offering in behalf of Your people, O Jehovah," he shouted, so loudly his voice burned in his throat. "Accept this and look upon them with favor. Save them, Jehovah! Save them!"

He lowered his arms and walked to the edge of the stone plateau. "Take me, instead," he whispered.

I have failed my people, he thought. *They may not realize it yet, but they will, and all the nation will see, at last, the purpose for which I was chosen by Jehovah*

He looked at the limestone beneath his feet and smiled. *I, too, am an offering on an altar of stacked stone.*

He raised his eyes to the dark line of the Philistines. "Take me," he said, and at that moment the armies of Philistia surged forward like water released at the breaking of a dam, pouring toward Samuel in a flooding black stain.

46

Lord Sarnam Ashkelon stood in the largest chariot in his army, surrounded by his driver, a spearman, a shield bearer, and Sihphil. All around him, chariots steeds sawed fitfully at the reins and chariot wheels shifted forward and backward incessantly. His own black horses, though, stood almost rock-still, waiting with disciplined patience the crack of the driver's whip.

Sarnam couldn't believe the Hunter had failed him. He could not imagine how a Hebrew sorcerer like Samuel could possibly have escaped the black assassin's blade. He wondered if Samuel had a great deal more power than Sihphil thought, and had used some dark and potent magic. But magic or not, Sarnam had thought the Hunter would be more than a match for the young mage.

But the gates of Mizpah were open. Perhaps Baghadh had succeeded in his task—although Sarnam knew it was more likely that they remained open because thousands of Hebrews were still encamped outside the walls, unable to crowd into the packed city. They would not close the gates now except as a last resort, when they had given up all hope that those outside the walls would survive.

Movement among the Hebrews caught his attention, and he watched in confusion as the dense mob parted as if to make way for an attacking force. But no force came. Just a single man, staff in hand, a bundle across his shoulders.

"What is this madness?" he asked himself.

"The ssorcerer Ssamuel..." said Sihphil.

Sarnam strained to make out any details of the man who approached, all alone, across the fields. His eyes had become less keen in the last several years, and he felt an unreasoning irritation tightening the back of his neck as he failed to discern anything more than the form of a man walking, getting nearer...

The figure—no doubt Sihphil was right, and it was Samuel—climbed atop a huge stack of boulders in the middle of the field and began to stack rocks on it.

Sarnam looked over at Sihphil. "We are watching the actions of a madman."

"Sssss. Not mad. He isss a true believer."

"As am I." Sarnam gripped the familiar leather handle of his sword, still sheathed at his side.

In a short time, a crooked finger of greasy black smoke snaked skyward from the stones. Samuel clambered down from the rocks and began marching through the grass toward them again.

Sarnam turned. "Phicol..." He changed his mind abruptly. "No, not you. I do not want him dead yet. Chilian!"

The captain turned smartly. "My lord?"

"Go and see what this sorcerer wants."

Chilian nodded and barked an order at his driver; his chariot lunged forward and hurtled across the field in a cloud of dust. It ground to a halt only a few paces from Samuel, and the dust drifted over him and dissipated in the breeze.

They talked for only a moment before Chilian wheeled the chariot around and galloped back to the line.

"I bring a message, my lord" he said, trying to catch his breath.

"Well? Loose your tongue!"

"My lord—Samuel the Prophet invites the Axis Lords and their armies to surrender, and offers his assurance that if we do so, their god Jehovah will have mercy upon us and we will be spared to become servants in the homes and fields of the Hebrews. He further says that if we do not surrender then they will engage in *jihad* against us, and they will strike every soldier with the edge of the sword and bring every soul of ours to silence."

For a moment no one said anything; then Phicol laughed his wheezing, nasally laugh. Several other Gedhudhra captains joined him.

Sarnam was not amused. "He *is* mad!" he snarled, looking back across the field. Samuel was again atop the great stone, standing with his staff held in front of him, looking as though he planned to take on the army single-handedly.

"Take me out in front of the men!" he ordered his driver, and the chariot lurched forward and made a wide circle until Sarnam was once again facing the phalanxes of his army.

"Philistines!" he roared, and the army cheered and drummed their swords against their shields.

"Once again, we face the Hebrews. As they did two decades ago, they dare to oppose our right to this land. In their audacity, they seek to make us slaves."

The army grumbled; shouts of "Death to the Hebrews!" echoed from all corners.

"Will you leave your children enslaved to these hill-folk? Will you pass on to your grandchildren an inheritance of chains?"

Rage erupted through stamped feet, pounded shields, screams of men and of horses.

"I know this in my heart and soul," he continued when they had quieted. "The day will come when these Hebrew churls and the pretender they follow will be laid low. Look to the sky!"

Overhead, grey clouds had begun to amass, sullen and glowering.

"Ba'al haunts the clouds today, lightning in hand," he continued, "and when his anger is released it will scorch this brood from the surface of the land. On that day, Canaan will ring with praise to Dagon, the father of the gods. On that day, the bright faces of Ba'al and Ashtoreth will shine upon us.

"We stand at the dawn of that day. From this sunset forward, men will look back on we who fought here today and speak of us as the right hand of the gods. Today, we become immortal!"

The army's roar was deafening; the ground shook with their pent anger.

JUDGE OF ISRAEL

Sarnam drew his sword and pointed it forward, toward Samuel standing atop the rock, toward the city of Mizpah.

"Philistines! Tear that city to the ground!"

Shaking the earth with their onslaught, shrouded in a cloud of dust beneath a darkening sky, the Philistine juggernaut surged forward.

47

"Then Abraham put out his hand and, taking the slaughtering knife, prepared to kill his son."–The Scroll of Bereshith

S amuel stood with his legs apart, his staff held in both hands above his head as though pointed at the massing, charcoal clouds. Blood from his blistered hands had smeared, red over vermilion, on the polished wood.

"Please, Jehovah. Hold Your protecting hand over Your people today."

He thought of Aphek, and of the day that Beriah the Benjaminite had arrived at Shiloh with the news of Israel's second defeat. "Not again, Jehovah," he whispered, knowing that his thoughts and worries were already known to the God from whom not even the deepest secrets could be hidden.

The smoke from the makeshift altar swirled upward, vanishing into the darkening sky.

A dull rumble like thunder shook the stone beneath his feet. He lowered his eyes from the clouds and saw the Philistine army surging forward.

He gazed skyward again. "Save them, Jehovah. Accept this sacrifice in their behalf. Do not punish this people for my sins."

He was still looking upward when the clouds began to coalesce, spinning sluggishly in a circle of grey, blue, and green. Another rumble shook him, and this time there was no doubt that it came from the sky. Flashes of unseen lightning played in the depths of the clouds.

A sudden wind tossed his hair around his face and sent a chill through his body; he felt more keenly the heat of the altar fire at his back.

The Philistine army closed on him, spread now across the plain in every direction. A knot of chariots led the charge; dozens of Rephaim giants lumbered among the infantry, enormous axes cradled in their arms. Brassy Philistine horns blared; churning hooves tossed earth and dust behind them. Samuel could feel the rumbling of the charge through the rock on which he stood. Its intensity grew and even as it did so, Samuel saw a change in the Philistine charge, a sudden hesitancy…

The rock under him lurched and he realized that it was not in response to the thunder of hooves. An earthquake rolled across the valley plain; the stacked stones of his makeshift altar rattled behind him. Samuel fell to one knee, bracing against the staff to keep from losing his balance completely.

The rumble of the earthquake grew. Horses screamed reared in terror. Two chariots collided, one of them careening onto one wheel before tipping over completely and spilling its occupants.

Thunder ripped through the air once again, so loud it shook the breath from Samuel's lungs. He stumbled backward, eyes drawn by a maelstrom of flashing lights overhead.

The coalescing clouds spun into a towering, black pillar that spiraled ponderously earthward, as though it was a colossal hand reaching for the battlefield. Lightning flashed again in its grey-green depths, explosions of red, blue, and white.

When the forked tongues burst free of the cloud, they struck like cobras of terrible brightness. The thunder buffeted him, traveled through him; Samuel fell back, still clutching the staff and shielding his eyes.

Forking branches speared, crackling, into the battlefield in a dozen places with explosive force, tossing men, chariots, and dirt upward. When the dust cloud cleared, wherever the lightning had struck the charred bodies of men and horses lay still and smoking in blackened circles on the field.

The earthquake built in intensity. Charging soldiers stumbled, unable to keep their feet. Horses fled in every direction, dragging their scythe-wheeled chariots through their own ranks and leaving a bloody swath of destruction in their path. Lightning crashed again, the thunder so loud it rang like the song of iron swords in Samuel's ears.

The Philistine army had lost their momentum but continued moving forward, following the knot of chariots that still rolled in spearhead formation toward Samuel. Again and again the lightning stuck, splitting the army into smaller and smaller pieces, each time leaving a patch of charred earth and dead bodies behind it.

Samuel felt the gigantic stone on which he stood shifting on the stack beneath it. Behind him the altar began to shake apart, spilling coals across the flat stone. He watched in awe as the ground under the Philistine charge was rent in a dozen places, great chasms opening and swallowing men, horses, and chariots by the dozens. More lightning yielded a thunder so powerful it shook the breath from Samuel's lungs and for a moment he thought it would rattle *Mish'eneth* free of his grasp. Philistine soldiers dropped swords, spears, and shields, trying to keep their feet and stay clear of runaway chariots, chasms opening in the ground, and the ceaseless strikes of lightning that blinded them from every side. Hardened warriors fled in every direction.

The chariots that had led the charge kept coming, though. Ahead of the worst of the damage, they hurtled toward Samuel, stallions swerving and rearing to avoid lightning strikes and chasms in the crumbling ground. In the leading chariot Samuel saw once again the huge figure he had glimpsed earlier, a whip in his hand, driving his horses forward mercilessly.

He pulled himself to his feet again and nodded. "Take me, Jehovah."

48

*"But Jehovah's angel called to him from heavens: "Do not touch
the boy or do anything to him. I know now that truly you fear
God- you have not even withheld your only son from me." And
Abraham looked up and saw a ram trapped by its horns in a thicket.
So Abraham took the ram and offered it in place of his son." –
The Scroll of Bereshith*

L ord Sarnam Ashkelon had taken the crop from his driver and he
whipped his stallions savagely, whipped them until he felt blood from
their torn flanks spraying back against his face in a crimson mist.

This was the battle he had been born for.

He felt the hunger of Anath growing inside him, a craving for the
feel of flesh beneath the keen edge of his sword, a longing to watch the light
in the eyes of his enemies go dull. He felt childishly petulant that the He-

brews were so far away, impatient that he had to wait a little longer before the slaughter began.

Phicol was the only one visible in his peripheral. As he had not for many years, Sarnam led the charge against the enemy. "For you, father," he whispered.

The solitary figure of Samuel still stood atop the rock, but Sarnam rejoiced to see above his head a dark pillar of lightning-wreathed cloud. Ba'al had come to join the battle. The god of storms rode with the Philistines.

When the horses first slowed, tossing their thick necks against their traces, Sarnam did not realize what was happening; he did not feel the unsettling rippling of the earth. But then lightning struck around them in brilliant flashes, so bright that for several moments afterward all he could see were streaks of red and white.

When his vision cleared, he glanced over his shoulder. Already, his army was in disarray. Bolts of lightning blasted among them; he watched a contingent of Rephaim burned into a smoldering mass of corpses.

Fear gripped him. Why did Ba'al fight against them?

Then he felt the lurching of the ground beneath his slowing chariot. His horses reared and screamed, slewing the vehicle sideways so abruptly that the spearman tumbled over the side and onto the whirling scythes on the wheels. On either side of him the earth began to split apart, chasms appearing as though someone was tearing the ground like an old garment. Men, chariots, and horses all followed rocks and soil into the depthless dark, screaming and clawing as they vanished into the schisms.

Lightning flashed again, right in front of him, and the horses reared crazily. Sarnam clung to the rail as the vehicle went up on one wheel. He heard the frightened whinnies of the stallions until the thunder struck, and then he heard nothing but the sound of his brain rattling between his ears.

He hit the ground, blinded and deafened, and a stabbing pain lanced down his back from his left shoulder. Rolling to his feet he cast about wildly, still half-blinded by the flash. He could hear the horses thrashing, faint over the ringing in his ears, and the sound of men screaming, but he could not see anything clearly. Holding his sword out in front of him like a blind man's stick, he stumbled forward.

A few moments passed before his vision cleared. The chariot lay upon its side, the horses hopelessly tangled in their traces. He saw white bone jutting from one slender leg, and another stallion had a trickle of blood running from one side of its mouth. Only one of his men still moved, rasping as he tried to extract himself from beneath the crushing weight of the chariot. His face was slack and white.

The next flash of lightning brought Sarnam to his knees. The ground rolled beneath him and he felt a desperate fear, like none he had felt in his life.

"Dagon! Ba'al! Anath! Give me your strength!" he shouted at the glowering sky.

Phicol's chariot caught up to him, then another. He had not even had time to acknowledge them before the ground rolled again and tore open in jagged crevasses right under their wheels. Phicol leapt clear of his chariot just as it vanished into the darkness, its occupants screaming and clawing at the root-tangled soil. The other chariot was overturned by its horses; then one of the mounts tumbled forward into the widening chasm. Kicking and squealing, the other horse, then the chariot, followed it into the bowels of the earth.

Sarnam looked over at Phicol and raised his sword. "Forward! For the glory of Philistia!"

The noseless warrior looked at him for a moment, scarred face blank, eyes flat. Then he smiled his twisted smile. "I do not think so," he said.

Phicol turned and began loping off of the battlefield, weaving among the debris of men and animals.

"Curse you!" Sarnam screamed after him. "Curse you to the deepest pits of Mot!"

Phicol did not turn or slow.

Panting now, involuntarily cringing every few moments at the rolling of the thunder, Sarnam looked back at his army. The charge had ground to a halt as every man and beast looked for a way to escape the web of chasms with one eye on the grumbling sky.

Sarnam turned back toward Samuel. The Prophet still stood upon the rock, staff held upright above his head, outlined by the smoke swirling into the dark clouds above him. Somewhere in the back of his mind Sarnam noticed that behind Samuel, a circle of blue skies opened over the city of Mizpah, and he wondered why the city was being spared the wrath of the god of storms.

At that moment, Lord Sarnam Ashkelon remembered the words of the Ghost-Wife of Endor's prophecy: *When the sky and the ground open before you, and a heart is offered upon an altar of stone, know that the day of your destiny has arrived.*

He felt hope blaze in his heart again and he limped toward the lone figure poised atop the mass of stones. Pain lanced down his left side but he ignored it, eyes locked on his enemy.

"Today it begins, father," he whispered through clenched teeth. "Send me the power of Ba'al and Anath! Send me the blessing of Dagon!"

Lightning sizzled not more than a dozen paces away and the dry grass erupted into flame, crackling voraciously as it spread. Sarnam coughed on the bitter smoke but did not slow.

He stood almost at the base of the stones. Whatever powers Samuel wielded, it had not been enough. Though his army might be scattered, he, Lord Sarnam Ashkelon, beloved of Anath, had made it through the Prophet's every defense. The sky and the ground had opened, and now Samuel's heart was about to be offered on an altar of stone.

His father was there with him.

He had succeeded at last.

Lightning struck again nearby, but this time Sarnam did not flinch. He felt bathed in the warmth of Anath's protection, felt the heat of her anger pouring out through him, the instrument of the gods. He had always known it was so. Since his boyhood, since his earliest battles on the shores of Egypt, he had known.

He was favored by the gods.

He was destined to be remembered.

Samuel was directly in front of and above him now. Sarnam almost laughed—the renowned prophet was still little more than a boy.

"Is this your *jihad?*" Sarnam yelled up at him.

Samuel looked down from the roiling clouds, still clenching the staff, and met his eyes. Sarnam felt a chill run across his scalp and down his neck.

They were the fearless eyes of a fanatic.

They were the eyes of a man who would stop at nothing.

"Do you think this display can stop the might of Philistia, Samuel?" he yelled, gesturing skyward. "Lightning and thunder are the playthings of Ba'al! I do not fear them! I am Sarnam, Axis Lord of Ashkelon, beloved of Anat. I ride on the chariot of Ba'al. You cannot harm me!"

Samuel's expression did not change. "It is not me you need to fear."

For one instant Sarnam realized what was about to happen—an instant so brief that it barely allowed for a single, terrified thought: Ba'al did not bring this storm.

Jehovah, the God of the Hebrews, did.

"Anath! Ba'al! Father!" he pleaded.

Then he was enveloped in white heat, and vanished from the surface of the ground.

Samuel saw it happen. He shielded his eyes and went to his knees as the thunder seemed to shake ground, air, and flesh with a power that was so far beyond comprehension that it was not felt, only feared.

Then Sarnam was gone. Where he had stood was only a charred circle of black, smoldering soil.

A sound from behind him turned his eyes toward Mizpah. Israelites poured out of the city, singing and shouting, rushing down the hill from Mizpah's gates toward the shattered Philistine forces. Standards fluttered above their divisions: the lion of Judah, the grape cluster of Ephraim, a shining sun of Reuben, an open tent for Gad, a slender palm for Manasseh, a donkey for Issachar, a sycamore for Asher, a ship for Zebulun, a leaping hind for Naphtali, a coiled snake for the tribe of Dan.

The men outside the city fell in behind them, hastening past Samuel's position on the rock. He glimpsed Tahash, Manoah, and Beriah at the forefront of their tribes. Moments later, he saw his father Elkanah rush past, followed by two dozen of the *Beneh*, armed with knives, staves, and farm tools.

For just a moment their eyes met, and Samuel knew that in that moment his father no longer saw Samuel as his son, but instead as a man that he would serve, and follow.

As the Prophet and Judge of Israel.

Something changed in Samuel at that moment, something invisible but so profound that it transformed the man he was into someone that he did not even know. He felt, for the first time in his life, like a leader of men. But it did not feel the way he had imagined it. The Israelites who ran past him on all sides looked to him now. They had put their lives into their palms for him, and would do so again. But they did so because they believed he was the *mashiach*, the anointed one of God. They did so because they believed that following him would lead to victory and glory, and because it was he who had stood beneath the whirling clouds, limned in the light of God. It was he who had been named by the High Priest—and, therefore, by Jehovah—as the Judge of his people.

But Samuel saw what his appointment truly meant. For every good deed men remembered, they would recall two errors. For every man who honored him, there would be another who would despise him.

For every victory he enjoyed, he would suffer two defeats.

Judge of Israel. Savior of his people.

It was a role no man could fill.

As the vanguard reached their enemy, the ground rumbled once again and the yawning crevasses folded shut; the only sign that they had existed were scars of freshly turned dirt crisscrossing the plain. The Philistines that had not yet fled took up their weapons once again, forced to fight whether they wanted to or not. The two armies collided, the clash of battle rang out, and from Samuel's high place he watched his brothers sweep into the enemy like a storm-tossed wave.

The Philistines rallied, gathering around their surviving captains and falling in behind the few remaining groups of Rephaim. Their hearts were gone from the battle, almost all of their chariots destroyed, but they fought now instinctively for their own survival. Even after their losses, they outnumbered the Israelite soldiers by many thousands. They gathered in a defensive line; it swayed and bent as men rushed in from both sides of the conflict.

The line began to crumble in both directions. The conflict descended into a melee, the Philistines fighting with such reckless abandon that Israelites died in scores.

Blood streaked the grass below Samuel and he watched Israelites falling under their enemies' swords and spears. The remaining Gedhudhra formed a wedge and pushed deep into the Israelite line, a seemingly invincible spear point of destruction. The earlier mayhem had shattered any semblance of order among the tribes and they could not mount an organized defense. Rephaim marched alongside the Gedhudhra, unstoppable, massive axes swinging.

"Sovereign Lord Jehovah! Please!" Samuel pleaded. "Do not let it be said that the gods of Philistia and of Canaan are greater than You! Please, Jehovah! Execute Your vengeance upon them!"

Thunder, distant now, rumbled again, but its sound transformed into a resonant ringing, not like thunder at all.

Then Samuel recognized the echo of horns, horns blowing wildly in the distance. He spun and saw yet another force, thousands strong, flowing down from the hills beyond Mizpah, their banners fluttering proudly above them as they ran.

The horns increased as they neared until Samuel could see the insignia upon the banners: the wolf of Benjamin. Ner and Kish ran at the forefront, slings whirling, felling Philistines as they came. Drawing their swords with a roar the Benjaminites burst upon their enemy and instantly shattered the Gedhudhra wedge.

The army of Israel raged unchecked now across the plain, and the power of God was in their arms, and His light was upon their faces, and they sang out with the joy of battle and victory, and like a shining wave they swept their enemy from the plain.

And Samuel sank to his knees, every heartbeat a surprise, and letting his head fall upon his chest, wrapped his arms around himself and began to weep.

49

hree days later the commanders and tribal chieftains gathered at a hastily erected camp outside the city of Mizpah. Ahlai arranged for a tent to be set up for Samuel and his family some distance behind the command tent.

Samuel left Liora and his sons there along with Hannah and Reuel. Elkanah had not returned yet, but Samuel assured Hannah that was no cause for alarm.

"Thousands are still in the field, Mother. They may not be back for several days. Some of them will not return here—they will follow their Elders back to their homes. For all we know, Father is waiting for us at Naioth."

She was comforted very little by his words. Samuel could not blame her. He would not admit it to her, of course, but he was worried as well. He felt somehow that he had not earned his own survival—that he had been a spectator to the courage and selflessness of other men. He knew it was not entirely true, but the knowledge did not free him from the guilt and embarrassment that haunted the dark recesses of his mind.

Samuel took up *Mish'eneth* and strode to the command tent. When he ducked through the entrance there were already more than a dozen men inside: Ahlai of Mizpah, Manoah and Samson (still supporting himself on a crutch), Dathan ben Avdon, Guni of Lebonah, Elishama of Bethel, Kish for the House of Ner, and Ahimelech.

Samuel and Samson embraced. "How is your ankle?" Samson asked.

Samson flashed his rascally grin. "Reuel forced me to drink some soup—I think it was made from mule urine, bark, and bat quano. It was, as you can imagine, delicious. But the pain is all but gone."

"The swelling is down as well," Samuel said.

They were interrupted by Ahlai calling for their attention. "The Philistine forces are broken," said Ahlai when the group quieted. "Many thousands were brought to silence as they fled from here to Philistia—some of our warriors chased them almost as far as Aijalon, where their new commander, a monster named Phicol, attempted to muster some sort of organized defense. Apparently, he felt that the broad valley plain would allow him to deploy his chariot forces to deadly effect.

"He failed, and our men drove the dogs back to their cities on the plain. By now, as far as we know, the fighting has stopped and the Philistines are licking their wounds and weeping before their stone idols."

"Are most of our men returning here?" Dathan asked. "Or are they going to their homes?"

"Most appear to be slowly filtering back here," Ahlai said. "They return ready to do as the Prophet—that is, as the Judge of Israel asks, whatever that may be."

For a moment all eyes turned toward Samuel, but he did not reply. He had begun to formulate an idea of what he would ask of the people, but he was not yet ready to put it into words.

Manoah broke the awkward silence. "There is another concern. It appears that Tahash, son of Avdon, is calling men to his banner, claiming his divine appointment as General of Jehovah's armies. Baghadh is, of course, with him, lending weight to his words."

"And are men responding to his summons?" asked Guni.

Manoah nodded. "Certainly the tribe of Manasseh is—and others. Many believe that he is Jehovah's anointed one."

"And are we sure that he is not?" Elishama asked.

Again, faces turned toward Samuel and Ahimelech. Samuel avoided their eyes for a moment, thinking. Then: "As Baghadh indicated at Mizpah,

Tahash did speak to me about his belief that he had been chosen by Jehovah."

"His belief?" Elishama said. "Then you doubted him."

Samuel shook his head. "I can neither confirm nor deny his claims. But his appointment did not come through the mouth of Priest or Prophet. In fact, it sounded to me as though he may have been basing his belief on a feeling within himself that he was...was meant for great things."

Samuel glanced at Dathan; he was red-faced. "My lords—I, too, have reason to doubt my younger brother's claims. He is a strange man, sometimes given to wild musings and fits of melancholy or elation. More than once he has come to me or one of my brethren to express his conviction that he had discovered his true purpose in life. Each time, the 'conviction' passed, swept away by the strength of a new 'calling.' I am afraid Baghadh might be using those weaknesses to mislead Tahash, and create for himself a puppet-General through whom he can wield control over Israel's armies."

"How many follow him?" asked Guni.

"I do not know," answered Manoah. "But the number seems to be swelling by the day."

"Follow him to what?" asked Elishama. "The war is over, is it not?"

"Jehovah has given us a great victory," said Ahlai, "but I, for one, will wait a little longer before I declare this war to be finished."

"Why?" Elishama asked. "Do you know something we do not?"

"I know that this Phicol who has taken over command of the Gedhudhra and the Philistines is a savage animal," Ahlai said. "I do not think he will accept defeat and do nothing, nor be content to retreat to the Pentapolis and give up on his nation's ambition to rule all of Canaan."

"There is something else we must consider," said Ahimelech. "Reports continue to filter in about the growing uprising of the Amorites. Men who have returned from Aijalon report that escaped slaves have joined independent tribal leaders and begun to amass a sizeable army in the hills around the city. Aijalon's walls are strong, but there is genuine fear that a rebellion from within and without will turn the city over to Amorite control."

"Giving them control of the pass," said Ahlai. "That would be a blow indeed. Have there been any skirmishes?"

He glanced around the group, but all were silent or shaking their heads. "They are waiting, then," he continued. "But for what?"

"We can hardly mount an attack—or even a defense—against this uprising until they present some concrete threat," said Elishama. "So what do you want us to do, Prophet? My men are anxious to return to their homes."

"As are all of us," said Ahlai. "Your men no more than any other, Elishama. But I am sure all of us want to be sure that whatever action we take is approved by Jehovah."

He turned toward Ahimelech. "Could we not consult the Urim and the Thummim?"

Ahimelech shook his head. *Eyes narrowed. Muscles in jaw clenching and unclenching. Eyes downcast.* "I may be Ahitub's heir, but I am not High Priest."

"Surely that is but a formality," said Guni.

"The installation of the High Priest is much more than a formality," Ahimelech snapped. "And I will not cast the sacred lots until every step of the ritual has been done in exact accordance with the words of the Torah."

The group fell uncomfortably silent. "I am Judge of Israel," Samuel said. "I will choose a course of action for us. But not this moment. I need to think, and pray." He remembered vividly watching the Philistine army collapsing in front of him in the midst of lightning strikes, and the ground opening beneath their feet. "Jehovah will show us the way. Or do you think He has saved us at Mizpah just to abandon us now?"

A soldier Samuel did not know pushed his head inside the tent. "Judge Samuel?"

"Yes?"

"Reuel has sent a message saying to come to him immediately."

Samuel frowned. "Did he say why?"

The guard shook his head. "No, my lord. But he told me not to leave until I saw you on your way. He said it was a matter of extreme importance."

Samuel bowed to the Elders. "Please excuse me. I will return as soon as may be."

He ducked out of the command tent and made his way back toward his family. He did not know what he wished the Elders would do, but he felt an unshakeable confidence, like nothing he had felt before in his life. He could not argue with the events at Mizpah. Jehovah had protected him. Jehovah had used him to save His people.

He was within sight of his family's lodging when he heard a woman wailing, her piteous cries emerging from Samuel's own tent...

"No," he whispered, and broke into a run.

Reuel emerged from the door and hurried toward him. "My lord…"

He stopped when they were face to face. Inside the tent behind his friend, he could tell now that the wailing was his mother, Hannah.

"My father…" Samuel could barely whisper the words.

Reuel swallowed hard. "I am so sorry, my lord."

Samuel felt something harden inside of him, a wall behind which his explosion of emotions quickly cooled. In their place came a cold acceptance in which fear, doubt, and even grief, had no place.

"What have you learned?" he asked Reuel.

Reuel could not meet his eyes. "They found him at the end of the valley, my lord. They are bringing him back now."

"He is…"

"Yes, my lord. Your father is dead."

Judge of Israel

50

In the ancient orchards on the hillsides to the northeast of Mizpah, the apricot and the almond trees were showing off their beauty. The rich green of the grass beneath them was dusted with delicate white and pink blossoms shaken free by the hot eastern wind. As though in proud competition with the carpet of petals, myriads of wildflowers stretched elegantly skyward: white and pink asphodel and cyclamen, red and purple anemones, deep red poppies, and scattered clusters of hollyhock and chamomile. Their perfume swirled around Samuel as with every step he crushed stem, leaf, and flower beneath his sandals, scattering bees and tiny white butterflies concealed amongst the rainbow.

While he walked, the nation waited. The knowledge did not bother him. He had been given the assignment to lead Israel in this time of crisis—he, Samuel ben Elkanah. If Jehovah had entrusted the task to Samuel, then the people would have to wait until Samuel decided what to do. He had not asked for the responsibility—he had not wanted it. But now that he had it, it felt surprisingly *right*, as though his life had been building to this moment.

His mother's voice, chiding him for his pride, was not silenced, but it was only a shadow of a thought in the back of his mind, an echo from a past that was gone now beyond recovery. It was locked away behind the wall he had built to contain his father's death.

He wondered what Elkanah had thought when his son was proclaimed Judge of Israel. The question brought the inner brightness of a smile to his mind in spite of the pit of anguish that yawned deep within him, buried beneath carefully crafted walls of logic, duty, and fierce determination. He wished he could have seen the look on his father's face.

He wished that he could know that what it had shown at that moment was pride.

He climbed a small rise, leaning more heavily on *Mish'eneth* as he ascended. His palms burned; he wondered that such smooth, polished wood could produce blisters so prolifically. But that, too, felt right: a small reminder of the lofty standard his mentor had set for him, and for anyone in Israel whose hands had been filled with power. The staff reminded him that he was not the man Ahitub had been. It reminded him he had not yet grown into his assignments.

As if he needed a reminder.

But he was different. He knew now with a cold certainty that, in spite of what his family might think of him, in spite of what Baghadh might be saying, Jehovah had filled his hands with power. He did not take it lightly—the knowledge that with a word he could send thousands of men into battle and death was sobering, to say the least. But they would go, if he asked them, and willingly.

They would go, not for Samuel, but for the Judge of Israel.

And however unlikely a candidate he was for the assignment, he trusted Ahitub above any man...He had almost thought *any man alive*. Ahitub would not have made a mistake in his selection—not in something as important as this.

He, Samuel ben Elkanah, was Jehovah's choice to lead their people in battle against their enemies, and to serve as the arbiter of the Torah for the children of Israel.

Prophet of Israel.

Judge of Israel.

He knew also that if he chose to denounce Tahash's claims, the people would abandon the young man in an instant. With their divinely aided victory fresh in their memory, the people believed that their Prophet and Judge could do no wrong—that to follow him was to follow in the footsteps of God.

The thought was tempting, but he did not wish Tahash ill. He felt a measure of responsibility for what became of the young man. Samuel felt that he had missed an opportunity to help him when Tahash had first told Samuel about his feelings, and in the days of travel they had shared afterward. It was easy to tell himself that there had been no time, that the string of crises that had haunted their steps from the time they had left Pirathon had not allowed him the luxury of discussing the matter further, of helping Tahash to see the true nature of divine appointment.

But it was an excuse, he knew—an excuse to assuage his own sense of guilt. If Reuel had come to him with a similar concern, Samuel knew he would have made the time to talk to him.

He did not want to turn on Tahash now when, whether the young Ephraimite knew it or not, he needed true friends more than ever.

He paused in his walk and sat slowly on a flat stone nested in tall grass and cyclamen. Laying the staff across his knees, he scanned the landscape around him: a stippling of spring colors enshrouded the hills, broken here and there by the distant, subtle movements of grazing sheep or cattle.

Ten paces in front of him an oak jutted up from the wildflowers, only half again as tall as Samuel was. It was dead, and had been for a long time—its bark had crumbled to the ground and its skeletal trunk and limbs bleached bone-white by the sun. From one of its branches a small black bird stared at Samuel as if trying to decide if the appearance of this stick-wielding figure was sufficient reason to abandon its warm resting place.

Stark white branches. Tar-black bird.

There were no intermediate colors, no browns or greens or greys to soften the contrast. Even the light contributed, the slanting sunbeams casting a hard-edged shadow of the tree on the gently waving grass.

Stark white branches. Tar-black bird.

Sometimes there was no middle ground.

Sometimes what must be done was obvious, but the very idea was so frightening, so unthinkable that no one dared accept it.

But he was the Judge of Israel. It was his responsibility to accept for the people what they could not accept themselves.

Now we must show them what to do.

Father. I am so sorry. I failed you. I will not fail your people.

He stood and strode back toward the command tent as the evening wind, smelling of blossoming fields, tossed his hair across his face and shoulders. Men looked up as he wove through the city of tents that had sprung up outside the city and its storm of smells: cooking fires, animals, roasting grain. He did not acknowledge at his audience, but he could feel the awe in their eyes.

He reached the command tent and pushed inside without hesitation; Ahlai, Manoah, and Guni, poring over wrinkled vellum maps, looked up, startled.

"Spread the word among the Elders. Tomorrow, just after sunrise, they are to assemble to the northeast of the city."

"For what purpose?" Manoah asked.

"To uncover their ears to the words of their Judge, the Prophet of Israel," Samuel said, and ducked out of the tent before they could question him further.

Sweeping bands of white clouds, like the tails of horses blown by a strong wind, swept in from the sea during the night, and dawn broke in a brilliant display of reds and yellows. Sunrise painted the wispy clouds with its palette, fire-orange against cool blue.

The wind that had borne the clouds eastward was spent by dawn and the grassy field northeast of Mizpah waited in warmth and stillness as the Elders, commanders, and chieftains of Israel gathered there, filtering through the anguished trunks of the ancient orchard.

They found Samuel waiting, *Mish'eneth* held in front of him in both hands. Arrayed around the Prophet were Ahimelech and two dozen of the *Beneh*, as still and inscrutably silent as their leader as the dawn oranged their faces.

When the gathering men saw the reason Samuel had summoned them, as one their eyes widened and their mouths opened in stunned disbelief.

Behind the Prophet and the *Beneh* a standing stone had been erected, a massive monolith of grey-white limestone stabbing up from the dew-dampened grass, socketed in a freshly-dug hole. A broad circle of ground around it was trampled smooth with sandal prints in the packed earth that had been removed from the hole.

When all had assembled, Samuel nodded to Ahimelech. The young Priest took an alabaster jar and emptied its golden contents over the top of the pillar: olive oil speckled with myrrh, saffron, and spikenard. As the oil trickled down the sides of the stone, Samuel raised his hands, the left still holding *Mish'eneth*.

"Hear me, O Israel. I, Samuel ben Elkanah of the tribe of Levi, Prophet and Judge of Israel, do hereby dedicate this stone as a sign to times indefinite to the sons of Israel of the victory Jehovah has given us in this place. It has been raised from the flesh of the ground, a bone of the land that was promised to our forefathers Abraham, Isaac, and Jacob. It shall be called *Evenezer*, the Stone of Help, because Jehovah has proved to be our Helper from the day that our nation was born in the shadow of Mount Sinai down to this day. May it remind our people of the town of Evenezer, where Israel gathered before the great defeat we suffered at Aphek in the days of my childhood. May it remind us that the power for victory lies within Jehovah's hands, no matter what enemy may be arrayed against us."

Ahimelech stepped forward and raised his arms toward the assembly. "May Jehovah bless you and keep you. May Jehovah make His face shine toward you, and may He favor you. May Jehovah lift up His face toward you, and assign peace to you."

"Jehovah our God is One," the Elders chorused instinctively, but Samuel could see their true feelings on their faces: *eyes downcast but in constant motion; shifting nervously where they stood; lips and jaws tight.* It was fear he saw, fear, guilt and uncertainty. Not even their grandfather's grandfathers had ever seen a standing stone erected; they were a relic from another age, from the time of the Patriarchs or the days of Moses and Joshua. They wanted to trust Samuel, but this was asking a great deal.

If only you knew, Samuel thought. *The real surprises are yet to come.*

"By the power of Jehovah's Hand we have driven our enemies back into the land of Philistia," he continued. "But still they hold the trade route in their iron grip, as they have since the days of my childhood. Aphek, Lod, and Gibbethon are in their hands. And in spite of this defeat, their numbers are not going to stop growing. More Philistines will continue to arrive, refugees from other places, immigrants on their way here even now, new children born. If we allow these dogs to remain in the cities belonging to the sons of Israel, then this will just be one more battle in a war without end."

"What are you suggesting?" one of the Elders asked.

"We must retake Aphek, Lod, and Gibbethon—now, while the Philistines are still reeling from their defeat, and before one among the Axis Lords takes up Sarnam's sword."

He paused, waiting for a response, but none came. The Elders just stared in shocked silence. Finally, Elishama broke the hush. "This is madness! We risk losing all that we have gained here! The people are not ready. The Philistines may have fled, but that does not mean we can march up to a walled city defended by trained, iron-armed warriors and capture it!"

Samuel shifted slightly so that he was directly in front of the standing stone from Elishama's perspective. "Until now, Jehovah has helped us."

"Why not just let the Philistines go back to Philistia, and take on this challenge another day?" said Guni.

"I intend to let the Philistines go back," said Samuel. "I intend to make all of them go back—even those who now inhabit our cities. And then we will follow them there."

"To Philistia?" Ahlai asked, eyes wide.

"To the coastal plain they call Philistia," Samuel said. "But let no son of Abraham call it by that name. It is Israel. It was promised to Abraham, Isaac, and Jacob and to their descendants to time indefinite."

Everyone began talking at once until Samuel raised his arms for silence.

"Has Jehovah promised you victory in this?" Ahlai asked.

"He has always promised us His help, if we do His will," said Samuel. "Why should this be any different?"

"But...It is one thing to defeat the army here, on our territory, when the sky and the ground fight for us," said Guni. "It is quite another to march into their own land and face their fortified cities and their gods. After their defeat they will be better prepared. Every able-bodied man in Philistia will join the fight with them, and their armies will swell far beyond what we have yet seen. And they will be fighting for their homes and families."

"Jehovah has filled them with dread," Samuel said. "Do you think they will quickly forget their battle against earth and sky?"

"Their priests will convince them that they have regained the favor of their gods," Ahlai said. "They cannot afford to do otherwise."

"And we cannot afford to squander this opportunity to carry battle to their doors!" Samuel said. "If we do not do this, if we leave the trade route in their control, if we allow them the freedom to lick their wounds while we pretend that we have accomplished something, then more of our people will be brought to silence to hold or regain what we won today." *And those who died here will have died in vain,* he wanted to add, but did not.

"They will not readily give up their homes and fields," said one of the Elders.

"We are not asking them to give them up," Samuel said. "We will take them."

"What of the High Priest?" Elishama asked. "What have you to say, Ahimelech?"

"Do you even need to ask?" Ahimelech replied. "The Prophet and Judge of Israel speaks. Prophet *and* Judge! A man who has proved his faithfulness to you for two decades, a man who has led us to an impossible victory on the very ground on which you stand! He is the *mashiach,* the chosen one of Jehovah. I will not defy him."

There was silence for a few moments but for the sounds of grasshoppers chirruping and the dawning of a breeze moving through the wildflowers.

"If the Prophet and Judge of Israel leads us, I will follow," said Ahlai then. "To Philistia, or to the ends of the earth."

"This campaign is nothing more than what Jehovah asked of our people in the days of Joshua," added Manoah. "Let us finish the *jihad* begun centuries ago."

"Awaken your ears to the Prophet," said a voice from the back of the crowd. Faces turned, and then parted to make way for the hooded form of Baghadh, limping forward with Tahash at his heels.

"Awaken your ears to the Prophet," Baghadh repeated, gesturing toward Samuel with a dramatic sweep of his arm. "After the events of the last few days, can any of us doubt that he is the Fist of God?"

Uncomfortable silence settled over the group. *With what are your hands busy, Baghadh?* Samuel wondered, a knot forming in his stomach.

"I have spoken to the Elders of Manasseh," Baghadh continued. "They are ready to put their lives in their hands for you, Samuel. All of my warriors also await your call."

Samuel, unsure how to respond, glanced at Tahash's face. *Lips tightened. Eyes looking down and to one side. Shoulders back, spine straight. Pride and shame.*

"And you, Tahash, my brother?" Samuel asked.

"'And I shall raise up a Prophet for them from amongst their brothers,'" Tahash quoted. "'And My words shall be in his mouth, and just as I command him, so will he speak to you. And it must occur that anyone who fails to give ear to My words that the Prophet speaks in My name—it is to Me that he will have to answer.' So says the Torah."

Samuel nodded. *A very political answer. Baghadh himself could not have done better.*

"Then we are decided," he said. "Send word to any who have returned to their homes. Let the men sanctify themselves for war. As in the days of Eli, we march on the city of Aphek."

51

Over the next two days, Baghadh and Tahash put the full weight of their popularity and authority to work in organizing the men of Israel who responded to the summons. Soldiers arrived from all four directions, from a half-dozen brothers traveling together to bands of a thousand or more streaming in under the ensignia of a tribal chieftain. Mounted messengers galloped through the gates to report that their tribal leaders would meet the army of the Judge of Israel at some point along the route to Aphek.

All day and night the valley rang with the pounding of smith's hammers as weapons were repaired and sharpened, or plowshares and pruning hooks were converted into spears and swords.

On the evening before they were to march west, each Chief of a Thousand gathered their legion before them in an appointed location outside Mizpah.

"Who among you has built a house, but has not yet been able to inaugurate it?" the Chief asked. "Who has planted a vineyard and as yet received no yield from it? Who has become engaged but has not yet married?"

Any who answered in the affirmative were dismissed from the army. Lastly, the Chief of a Thousand asked, "Who fears this battle, and whose heart has become faint within him?"

The Torah required that men answer the question truthfully. When those whose fear had overwhelmed them stepped forward, the Chieftain commanded: "Separate yourselves from us, and return to your homes without shame, that you might not cause the hearts of your brothers to melt even as your own heart has melted."

When the ritual was concluded, the Chiefs of Thousands chose their Chiefs of Hundreds and Chiefs of Tens, and the army was organized into its contingents. The middle of the afternoon had passed before all were divided and prepared for the upcoming march. Then all of the Chieftains assembled before Samuel, who stood atop the wall of Mizpah near the gatehouse.

The sea of faces staring up at him beamed with adoration and pride. Their confidence in him was both a burden and a joy. "When the sun rises over the hills of Gilead tomorrow, some will see a great army of men marching from this fortress toward the sea.

"But that is not what I will see.

"Some will see lines of wagons drawn by horses and mules.

"But that is not what I will see.

"Some will see a forest of spears and hear the tromp of sandaled feet on the dusty road.

"But that is not what I will see or hear.

"Let your eyes of faith be opened: It is not we, but Jehovah of Armies who marches against the Philistines tomorrow. We are but the sword in His mighty Hand. Do not let your hearts melt at the thought of our enemy. Some of us will die in the days to come. But though we are gathered to our forefathers, our names will survive in the hearts and minds of the children of Israel, and in our God's boundless memory. In His due time, we who have shown our trust in Him even to the death will return to live in a new Eden."

The next morning, darkness had only begun dreaming of the light of dawn when Samuel and Liora slipped from their bed and ran, with the furtiveness of misbehaving children, out of the city and into the dew-dampened fields of trampled grass. South of Mizpah a shepherd's trail wound over a scrub-covered knoll and spilled them onto a plateau that over-looked the army on the plain below.

They raced the last distance to the abrupt edge of the plateau, laughing and out of breath. "You let me win," Liora panted.

He smiled his admission. As the sky woke above them it began to send down feelers, gentle puffs of wind that spun across the tops of the field grass with a touch so light-fingered it left no trace of its passing. Liora walked a few paces away and turned to watch the first coals of dawn spreading across the rounded hills on the eastern horizon.

Samuel just stood and stared at her with the stillness of a man who has spotted some rare and timid creature and dare not breathe for fear of startling it. He watched the light glimmer off of the dowry coins that encircled her head like a crown, burnishing the red highlights in the locks that had come loose from her *tsa'iph* during their run.

He thought of the poetry he had written for her when first they had met, and in the first years of their marriage. He had not written those kinds of poems for a long time, but not because his feelings toward her had changed, or dimmed. It was because in those early attempts he had learned that he did not have the skill in his pen to capture what he loved about her. The gentle grace of her movement, the line of her jaw below her ears, the curve of her lower back or her hips—they were a song so sublime that it could be sung by no one but her. His heart ached as he watched her, ached with a hollow regret that he could not tell her at that moment what he was feeling.

"You are too beautiful even to be brushed by the claws of war," he whispered, and she turned toward him. "I would not have you touched by battle and fear."

Her lips curved in the subtlest of smiles. "I do not fear."

"How can you not? You yourself well know what will happen to us—to our home, our family, and our nation if this campaign fails!"

"Yes, I know," she said. "Philistia will spill over with anger and hatred, and that flood will not be stopped until the land is drowned in blood."

"And yet you say you do not fear?"

"If it comes to that," she said, taking a step toward him and trapping his eyes with her own, "then you will be there, Samuel. You will stand between our sons and the hordes of Philistia, and the power of God will be in your hands, and His light in your eyes. Danger cannot touch us as long as you are faithful. And you, Samuel, beloved of God, beloved of Liora, will ever be faithful."

Horns rang out, summoning the troops to form up. Samuel gathered Liora in his arms and she rested her flower-soft cheek on his chest. "I am caught up in something, my love," he said. "Something so momentous that it carries me along with it as a river would a thistle-down, and I am helpless to check its power. I have let it carry me this far, but even the Seer cannot see where this road is leading."

"To Jehovah the end is already clear," she whispered.

"I wish I knew how to explain to you…"

"I trust you," she said. "That is enough."

— — ■ — — — ■ — — — ■ — — — ■ — — — ■ — — — ■ — — — ■ — — — ■ — — — ■ — — — ■ — —

The armies of Israel marched from the standing stone Evenezer as though borne on the rays of the dawn. They descended into the broad valley, swarming amongst the sun-bleached stone and the ancient olive trees, massive trunks as gnarled as pillars of bundled roots. Stretching into a long, haphazard column they flooded down the valley, winding through terraced hills dotted with the deep greens of trees and lush grass amidst a galaxy of blossoming wildflowers.

Their route took them through fields of scattered Philistine corpses, bloated and reeking; hyenas and jackals slipped among them like spirits, sending ravens and eagles hopping angrily into the sky.

The first ridge that the road crested was high enough that the glimmering sea was visible in the distance over the rows of increasingly green hilltops. Atop ridges and peaks, the white buildings of towns and cities gleamed in the distance, as white as pearl in the light of the rising sun.

They descended the ridge and continued following the road's tortured path through hills brilliant with red poppies and yellow daisies, rainbows against the bone-white olive trunks. Over the next hill they could see in the distance the ruins of Ramathaim, charred buildings and skeletal structures, silent and dead in a smear of grey on the hilltop. At the first glimpse, Samuel felt his heart sink within him and realized that he was not as prepared to see his home as he had once thought.

Nearer the ruins, charred fields nestled the road; they could see it disappear in the distance over the hills. Samuel and those traveling nearest him stopped where the narrower path to Naioth and Ramathaim diverged from the trade road.

"Will you go and see, my lord?" Reuel asked.

Samuel just shook his head and continued on.

Their route descended more sharply, following the slope of the land through the thickening oak forests that filled much of the Plain of Sharon. The road on which they traveled crossed the north-south highway at the foot of the hills; there, the army was joined by additional troops from the tribes of Dan, Asher, Reuben, Gad, and Manasseh.

They were already underway again when Shemer, chieftain of the tribe of Reuben, found Samuel in the midst of the Beneh. "My apologies for our tardy arrival, my lord," he said, going down on one knee and bowing.

Samuel grasped his shoulder and raised him up. "Please—we are all just men."

Shemer stood and nodded, but Samuel could see the discomfort in his eyes. "The Amorite uprising near Aijalon has grown. They have captured the pass. My men and I—and many of the men of Judah—were forced to make our way through the mountains on either side."

"Do you know any more about this uprising?"

Shemer shook his head. "No one seems to—except the rumors that the Amorites are preparing to take vengeance for some insult to their prince. But they are, as I said, only rumors."

Samuel nodded. "Thank you for being my eyes and ears, Shemer. We will wait and see what Jehovah will bring."

The forests of Sharon were dark and cool beneath the branches of the cedars, pines, and spreading oaks. The marching soldiers stretched their column, unable now to walk easily anywhere but on the road itself. It was well-traveled and well-maintained, except for a single place they crossed in the mid-afternoon where a flash flood had left its trail of dark silt and debris across the packed earth.

When they broke clear of the trees, the clouds had lifted further and the snowy cap of Mount Hermon was visible far to the north, a brooding presence watching over the whole of the land. The Canaanites believed that the gods had their abode on the mountain, and that at its peak was one of the great castles of Ba'al.

Sunset was glowing crimson on the waters of the Great Sea by the time they neared Aphek. The countryside grew more open, forests giving way to broad fields filled with wildflowers and blooming mustard plants. The road took them gradually in the direction of the Torrent Valley of the river Sorek, and the nearer they got, the wetter the land became. Trees and scrub grew lush and green now on both sides of the road. Occasionally they passed pools under the shadows of sycamores or palms emerging elegantly from rushes, reeds, and cattails. Perfect reflections of trees, grass, and flowers posed in the still water.

More of the land was cultivated on the Plains of Sharon near Sorek. Shepherds tended to their flocks on hillsides to the west and north, and slopes were dressed with vines and groves. As the road navigated the final stretch of their journey to Aphek, steep hills rose around them, the final efforts of the mountains to maintain their hold upon the place. Twisted, tortured rock loomed or crouched on either side of the road as though the monsters and giants of Canaanite myth had been turned to stone in their final moments of agony.

When they passed again beneath the shadow of the forest's boughs and branches, the road was for a distance crisscrossed with paths of men and beasts, some of them bordered by short walls of stacked, white stone that stood in sharp contrast to the bright green undergrowth. On Ahlai's advice, Samuel set three hundred men to work cutting and gathering small logs and branches with which to build siege ladders.

The sun was settling below the distant horizon of the Sea when they finally reached the encampment of the remainder of Israel's forces, less than a quarter of a day's journey from Aphek's walls. Tents sprawled across the plain amidst the scattered trees. Hundreds of campfires, smelling of roasting meat, sent thin spirals of smoke skyward from between tethered horses, camels, and donkeys. The staccato hammering of weapons being repaired and sharpened and of siege equipment being built echoed from the nearby foothills.

As soon as the evening meal was eaten, the chieftains gathered in Samuel's expansive command tent erected near the center of the encampment. Old Ner of Benjamin was there, with Kish hovering over him like a protective mother hen, and Jedaiel standing quietly nearby. Manoah of Dan, Tahash and Dathan of Ephraim, and Baghadh of Manasseh sat cross-legged on the rugs that had been laid over the dry grass.

The appointed commanders of the other tribes were there, also. From Judah, the largest and wealthiest of the tribes, had come Prince Elhanan, dressed in a robe of cerulean linen with a scarlet sash and turban; gold rings gleamed from his fingers and a necklace of gold dangled a tear-shaped ruby over his chest. Strikingly handsome, he seemed to Samuel to always be looking down his hawk-nose at those around him. Samuel noticed that Elhanan had positioned himself next to Baghadh and Tahash.

Two paces from Prince Elhanan sat Shemer of the tribe of Reuben, a stolid, heavily-muscled man with a neck like a bull's. Intense blue eyes peered out at the group from a ruddy, freckled face framed by red hair and beard. Each movement of his massive arms, freckled and criss-crossed with slender white scars, sent muscles rippling and bunching along their length.

Standing in one corner near the door was Cosam the Asherite, swarthy-skinned and hawk-nosed, with black, deep-set eyes and long, dark lashes. Gold earrings and a gold nose ring matched the gold-accented scabbard that hung at his side, encasing a wicked-looking sword with a broad, curved blade.

Shaga of the tribe of Gad sat cross-legged near Samuel, shoveling handfuls of cereal from a bowl on his lap into his mouth with one hand. From the ratted condition of his hair and beard, and the twigs Samuel spotted trapped in their tangles it looked as though he had just crawled through the underbrush of some dense forest. A well-worn, round shield rested against his back like a turtle's shell.

Barzel the Simeonite stood behind Shaga, hard eyes staring out from his scarred, weathered face as though he was mentally testing the mettle of every man in the room. A double-bladed bronze axe was strapped across his back, and a battered, Philistine-forged iron sword hung from his left hip.

Lodan the Issacharian was there as well, an elderly man who had served as the head of Israel's intelligence forces since Samuel's childhood, since the days of Jephthah and the battles of Aphek. Trim and fit, he seemed not to have aged in ten years.

From Zebulun came Bocheru, a full head shorter than Samuel, whose wrinkled, leathery skin had seen more than six decades of war on the coastlands of the Great Sea. He had been Elon-tohr's teacher many, many years before. Now he supported himself on a gnarled stick and stared calmly at the group around him from beneath wisps of white hair and bushy white eyebrows. The oldest battle-commander in the nation, he nonetheless carried himself with a stern confidence and a grace that belied his thin, wrinkled limbs.

Last in the group was a pair of men standing close together: Avith and Zattu, of the tribe of Naphtali. Avith was lithe, narrow-eyed and dark-skinned, always ready with a laugh or joke. The stump of his left arm, little more than a hand span long, protruded uselessly from his sleeveless shirt. Zattu, towering over him, appeared his opposite in every way: massive and broad-shouldered, pale-skinned, his eyes wide and serious—almost somber in his quiet way.

Samuel knew the story of the bond between the two men—nearly everyone in Israel did. Many years before, when Avith was a celebrated young commander in Jephthah's army, Zattu's daughter was killed by an Israelite man who was attempting to rape her. Zattu went to search for the perpetrator and execute vengeance against him. In his rage, he mistook Avith for the man. Avith was unarmed when they met, and Zattu drew his sword and cut off Avith's arm before he realized that he was not the murderer.

As soon as he realized what he had done, Zattu surrendered himself to the Elders of Naphtali, offering even his life in recompense for his error.

The local judges had, of course, enforced the terms of the Torah: for severing Avith's arm, Zattu must lose his own. Zattu willingly submitted to their judgment, but before the sentence could be executed, Avith begged that the punishment be delayed. He asked that Zattu instead be allowed to travel with him, and to serve and protect him in battle—to, in effect, have the opportunity to lose his arm in protecting the man who did not have one.

The judges agreed to the unusual request, and Avith and Zattu became inseparable companions. In the years that followed the two men developed a unique fighting style, battling shoulder to shoulder, the huge Zattu protecting Avith's defenseless left side with his own sword and shield. They had become renowned for their skill—it was said that the combination of Avith's skill and Zattu's strength made them the equal of a dozen men. Samuel had heard Avith joke that he had gained two arms in exchange for the one he had lost. He had also heard that the real secret of their effectiveness in battle was the fearlessness with which Zattu fought, heedless of his own life or safety, entering every conflict with an unhesitating willingness to give his own life protecting his friend. Others said that Avith was more deadly with one arm than most men were with two.

"My brothers!" Samuel said loudly, and the tent quieted. "Our strategy is simple. Tomorrow we go up against the walled city of Aphek, a city that was wholly Israelite in the days of my youth, and which will be wholly Israelite again. We will bring ladders against its walls, rams to its gates, and sappers beneath its walls. Benjaminite skill with bow and sling will cover our advance. Lodan?"

The dignified Issacharian bowed. "Two of my men are in the city as we speak; others have been and returned. The men who remain are dressed as Philistine archers. They will shoot arrows to a pre-arranged location before and during the battle—arrows bearing scrolls around their shafts. We will know exactly what is happening within the walls at all times."

"And the numbers?" Prince Elhanan of Judah asked.

Lodan's brow wrinkled. "It appears that a significant portion of the Philistine soldiers in Aphek were sent south shortly before my spies arrived in the city. The number that remains are enough to defend the city effectively, but no more."

"Rephaim?" asked Manoah.

Lodan shook his head. "None."

"What of troop movements from the south?" Cosam of Asher asked, twisting his moustache. "Philistia could be sending men even now by land or sea."

Manoah shook his head. "The men who have come from Danite land report no troop movement northward. Unless they have sent ships far out into the Sea—beyond sight of our watchtowers—then no more Philistine troops are forthcoming."

"It is not like the Philistines to give up a city without a fight," observed Elhanan.

"They are well-trained and well-armed warriors in a city with walls that are both high and thick," said Bocheru. Samuel liked listening to him— he spoke with a slow, easy confidence. "There will be a fight."

"They could have done more to defend Aphek, though," Samuel mused. "The Axis Lords know the importance of the city to their control of the trade routes."

"The Philistines in Aphek may have been in Mizpah a few days ago," said Jedaiel. "They will have learned to fear the name of Samuel."

Samuel let the observation go without comment. "I leave it to you men to organize your troops. I do not claim to have any skill in strategy."

Samuel saw looks of consternation on the faces around him. "I will say this," he added. "For centuries Zebulunites have served as our vanguard, Danites as our rearguard. Benjaminites have been our missile warriors, Gadites our mobile flanks, Issacharians our spies and runners, Judeans the core of our spear-and-shield men. Until the men of Judah can join us, those of the other tribes will have to make up the bulk of our core force. Other than that, I see no reason to change our ancient ways."

"Is this the strategy that will win this battle?" Shaga asked, bits of grain still stuck in his beard and moustache.

"No," said Samuel. "It will not be any strategy that will deliver victory into our hands. Truly the sons of Korah wrote:

'For my trust was not in my bow,
and well I knew that my sword could not save me.
Prepare your horse for the day of battle,
but know that salvation belongs to Jehovah.'"

Prince Elhanan shifted uncomfortably. "As most of you know, the thousands of Judah are still far to the south; my tribe could not assemble in time to follow me here. They will meet up with us as soon as they can.

"But there is something else...I do not know how this relates to our conflict with Philistia, but as many of you know the Amorites throughout Israel have been rising up against us in city after city—especially in the territory of Judah. The revolt apparently started as a result of a prince of the Amorites being betrayed and captured. Now the discontent has spread, and Beth-shemesh, Sha'albim, and Mount Heres are all threatened. My messengers who arrived from the region yesterday report that an army is gathering near Aijalon; they fear the Amorites may try to capture the pass."

"Will this prevent the men of Judah from joining us?" asked old Bocheru.

Prince Elhanan shook his head. "I have summoned them to me, but if they must choose between chasing Samuel's army across the Samarian highlands and defending their homes and families..."

The room fell silent and all eyes turned toward Samuel. He acknowledged a fleeting moment of anxiety, and then banished the emotion behind the wall he had built within himself. "We will leave that in Jehovah's hands. We cannot fight a threat before it takes form in front of us."

"Should I send men to keep us informed regarding what is happening at Aijalon, my lord?" Lodan asked.

Samuel shook his head. "When something happens, we will hear it."

"How, my lord?" Lodan asked.

"I am the Prophet," Samuel said. "The wind will whisper in my ears."

52

That night a half-moon and stars as numerous as the grains of sand on the shore of the Sea turned everything between the charcoal shadows a deep sapphire. Pools of orange light wavered, like reflections on the water, around each of the countless fires burning amidst the encampment.

Samuel wandered alone through the paths of shadow, letting the sounds of the assembled troops wash over him. Men were gathered in loose circles around fires of twigs or dung tossing dice, sharpening blades, laughing and talking to drown out their fears about the coming of the dawn. In the distance the booming, lonely cry of the bittern echoed desolately.

Sometime during the middle night watch he came to the encampment of the tribe of Naphtali. He passed a few paces from one of the circles of firelight, and the men gathered around it spotted him. "My lord Samuel! Join us, if you will!"

He stepped over to the fire and took a seat on the dry, flattened grass beside them. A young man, a son of fewer than twenty-five years, offered him a bowl of red lentils; he waved it away.

"They say that Jehovah will fight for us tomorrow, as He did at Mizpah," the young man said.

Samuel smiled. "He will fight for us, although we do not know what form that help will take. The arrows in His quiver are many—lightning and storm, earthquake and pestilence. But the courage of men is yet one of them."

The man nodded solemnly. "Avith has always told us that Jehovah does not sharpen the dull blade, nor move the sluggish hand."

"Avith is a wise man," Samuel said.

"He is the greatest commander Naphtali has ever seen," another man answered, a grizzled soldier with grey hair and a black beard. "Not one of his men doubts that Avith would risk his life for them—or Zattu either. He is a leader men will follow into the darkest night."

"I know only a little of his reputation," Samuel said.

"Ahhh," the man said, nodding and settling into his seat. "How about a story, then?"

Samuel shrugged his shoulders. "A story."

The man took a long drink of sour milk from a bowl and set it aside, wiping the white from his moustache. "You may have heard that, after the Ammonite Wars, Avith and Zattu were chosen by Judge Jephthah for his personal bodyguard."

"I had heard that—yes," Samuel said.

"Well the story of why they were chosen is the more interesting part. When Jephthah's army was besieging the city of Jogbehah, sappers from the tribe of Manasseh undermined the wall. But Judeans aboveground had brought in brush and set fire to the base of the bulwarks, and it had spread across the wall until it raged directly over the tunnel. The wall collapsed, dumping tons of rubble and blazing deadwood onto the sappers' heads.

"Avith and Zattu were moving the instant the wall collapsed, sprinting into the open end of the tunnel—the two of them plowing forward while dust, flame, and smoke were belching out at them like spume from a whale. They disappeared inside and we were all sure they were dead men. But before anyone could muster a real response, out they came, covered head to toe in ash and soot. Avith was dragging three sappers behind him—one of them he was practically carrying. Right behind him Zattu walked out of the dust with one sapper slung over his shoulders, herding four more in front of him." The man paused and shook his head. "Bravest thing I have ever seen."

"You served with them back then?" Samuel asked, surprised.

The soldier nodded once, curtly. "I did, my lord. And I have not left their service since that day. Nor will I, I hope, until they lay me down with my fathers."

"It is an honor to serve under such men," Samuel acknowledged.

"And more than an honor," the grizzled soldier said. "He—or I should say, they—are brilliant in battle, inventing new forms of the martial art with every move. I was with them once, just a few years ago, during a time of Girgashite raids. We were escorting our tribe's firstfruits to the Tabernacle at Nob, and stopped on the banks of the Jordan to water the animals.

"There were six of us, including Avith and Zattu. None of us saw it—the mules didn't even smell it. A behemoth burst out of the muddy water directly below them. In the first lunge, it tore the head off of one of the mules and vanished below the roiling water, turning it instantly crimson. Even as we stumbled backward, it thundered out of the river onto the muddy bank, plowing into the wagon and the men. Avith shouted for us to get the wagon clear and leapt toward the beast, Zattu right behind him.

"The monster swallowed Avith's sword in an instant, nearly taking his one remaining arm with it. Then Zattu hurtled into it, sword raised over his head, bringing it down on the beast's skull right between its beady eyes. Blood spurted from the wound, but the blade bounced off of the thick skull and the animal shrugged it off almost as though it had not felt it.

"It's mouth gaped—I swear, standing a few paces in front of me, it looked as though it could swallow the wagon whole. I could smell the fetid breath rushing from between its yellow teeth.

"Then Avith leapt forward again, left foot on the behemoth's bottom jaw, right foot on its nose, vaulting onto its head before the huge trap could close on his leg. In the very moment that his foot planted between the creature's ears, he raised one hand as though he was about to plunge a sword through its head. But his hand held no sword.

"And then—it did. Before Avith had even reached his destination on the animal's head, Zattu was tossing his sword. It spun toward Avith's empty hand and landed perfectly in his palm, blade downward—just in time for him to thrust it between his legs.

"From where I stood I saw the blade emerge inside of the behemoth's mouth. It thrashed, tossing its huge head like a dog shaking a rabbit between its jaws. Avith clung to the hilt of the sword, swung back and forth with such force I was sure his limbs would be ripped from his body.

"A moment later, the thrashing stopped, and the monster sank below the roiling, reddening waters of the Jordan. I watched Avith disappear into the murk and turned anxiously toward Zattu, expecting him to rush in and save his friend.

"He just looked at me and smiled. 'He will be alright,' he said in that deep, quiet voice. And, sure enough, before I had taken half a dozen breaths, Avith emerged from the water, sword still held in one hand."

The old soldier paused, taking another swig of milk from the bowl. "That would have been enough to cement their reputation in my mind. But it was just the beginning. Dripping river water, we clambered up the bank and through the undergrowth to rejoin the wagon.

"It was gone. Blood and camel tracks told the tale: Girgashite raiders had come while we were gone and captured the wagon and the rest of our men. The only thing that gave us hope was that we found no bodies. We knew that they had taken them alive.

"You would never have known Avith and Zattu had just fought a battle. They loped off across the grassy hills, heads scanning for the divots torn from the turf by the camels' hooves. The rest of us kept up us as well as we could, but Avith and Zattu—they seemed to be possessed by some inexhaustible power.

"We ran for—well, it felt like half a day. The trail led us to the Girgashite camp—about thirty of them. They had staked their camels and sat down to enjoy their booty. The rest of our men were bound and gagged in a circle, back to back, and four men armed with spears and swords stood guard over them. The Girgashites were eating the firstfruits from the wagon, laughing and congratulating themselves over their accomplishment.

"Avith and Zattu didn't even hesitate. Drawing their weapons, they roared into the middle of the camp. They must have killed half a dozen before the Girgashites even made it to their feet. The rest of us followed as quickly as we could, but by the time I caught up Avith and Zattu stood back to back in the center of a ring of men. They were attacked from every direction, but nothing could get past their whirling blades and Zattu's shield. Bodies just piled up at their feet. They were like a whirlwind—each seeming to anticipate the other's movements, defending where the other was vulnerable, attacking while the other distracted. The rest of the men and I, we ran to our brotheres and made short work of the four guards. When the captives were freed and armed, we turned back to the bulk of the raiders, still surrounding Avith and Zattu.

"Only there were no more raiders. The two of them stood, still back to back, chests heaving, covered in the blood of their enemies. In a circle around them bodies lay in heaps, crumpled and unmoving."

The old soldier took a last swig of the milk. "In all my days as a soldier, I have never seen anything like it."

Samuel shook his head and smiled. "It is a story worthy of a song."

The old soldier nodded. "May I live to hear it sung, my lord."

Samuel bade them goodbye and wandered back toward his tent, thinking about the pair of heroes called Avith and Zattu.

53

"Without fail I will bless you and multiply your offspring
until they are like the stars of the heavens and like the
grains of sand on the seashore; and they will capture the
gates of their enemies." – The Scroll of Bereshith

At first light the armies of Israel, arranged by tribe and divided into commands of thousands, hundreds, and tens, assembled on the plain outside the city of Aphek. They stood silent and still on the dew-jeweled grass, while Samuel marched forward alone toward the gates of the city.

He stopped half an arrow shot from the walls. "I am Samuel the Prophet," he shouted at the battlements. "Who commands those who have dared defy the will of God by claiming this city as their own?"

He saw movement atop the wall near the gate, shifting bodies making way for one man to step forward to the battlements. "So, we meet again, Sorcerer!" a familiar voice shouted back at him.

"Glaucus?" he asked.

"The same," the commander responded. "I see you have traded in your sandals for a much bigger pair."

"Awaken your ears, Glaucus—and all you men with him!" Samuel shouted. "The children of Israel reflect the mercy of the True God. Lay down your arms, open the city gates and we will allow you to live and to serve us as we teach you the ways of the Torah."

The soldiers on the wall murmured angrily; some clashed their spears to their shields.

Samuel ignored them. "But if you will not, Jehovah will cause the bars of these gates to wither and the stones of these walls to crumble, and we will break down these fortifications and enter into this city. And we will strike every man in it with the edge of the sword."

"Enjoy your dream while it lasts, Samuel!" Glaucus shouted back at him. "But do not try to frighten me with hollow words!"

"So be it!" Samuel answered. "When I return, it will not be with words."

He turned and marched back toward the waiting Israelites, forcing himself to walk slowly and not turn, although he half-expected at any moment to feel the stab of an arrow piercing his back.

The tribal commanders and chiefs of thousands were waiting for him atop a flat-topped conical hill where the standard of the House of Levi had been planted. Their eyes were flat and hard.

"'Blood pollutes the land,'" Samuel said. "'And no expiation can be made for the land for the blood that is shed in it, except by the blood of him who shed it.'"

He stared at them for a moment, and then raised *Mish'eneth* over his head. "For Jehovah!" he yelled.

"For Jehovah and Samuel!" Manoah roared, and the army took up the cry.

Samuel nodded toward the commanders. "Take the city," he said simply.

Horns echoed off of the hills and the walls; a forest of spears swept forward to the tromping of tens of thousands of feet. Arrows hissed from the battlements, but they were few and scattered and the Benjaminites answered them with a hail of stones and darts that sent the Philistines scurrying for cover behind their fortifications.

Zebulunites under the direction of old Bocheru carried hastily constructed ladders over their heads, planting the ladders' feet in the rocky soil at the wall's base and using long, cedar poles, still half-covered in bark, to tip them against the crenellations. Before their rails even touched the rock of the battlements Zebulunite warriors were scurrying up them like ants.

While the Zebulunites and the Benjaminite hail of missiles occupied the defenders, Barzel and the men of the tribe of Simeon raised their shields over their heads and rushed toward the gate in two parallel rows. Each man held one end of a span of rope, its other end grasped by the soldier opposite him. These ropes formed a cradle between the two rows in which rested a thick oak log cut from the ancient forests to the east. Even as they surged forward the log's momentum swung it into the gate's planks with a deep *crack*.

The Philistines threw stones and dumped burning vats of oil over the wall onto their attackers. The area in front of the gate disappeared in flame and clouds of thick, black smoke. Samuel waited anxiously for Barzel and his men to emerge from the holocaust, but they did not do so. He had begun to think that all had perished in the flames when several rhythmic *thuds* echoed out from the conflagration. It took him several moments to realize that somewhere within the smoke the indomitable Simeonites had taken up the battering ram and were again hammering on the gates.

Judean infantrymen dragged water-soaked skins and wool cloths and tossed them on the flames or on the Simeonites who were rolling on the ground trying to extinguish their burning clothes. The ram's bearers clustered tightly against the gate, still battering. The Philistines dared not drop oil on them lest they burn down their own defenses.

Israelites were swarming up the ladders like madmen. The battlements were covered in a sea of battling figures. Over the screams, the raging fire and the clash of weapons, Samuel could hear their chant: "Sam-u-el! Sam-u-el! Sam-u-el!"

"Forgive them, Jehovah," he whispered.

The flames around the gate had subsided; Prince Elhanan had the Judeans dumping buckets of water all over the area, including on the soldiers clustered around the ram. From thirty paces distant the Benjamininites under Jedaiel and Ner launched a constant volley of missiles at the area above the gate, keeping the Philistine defenders pinned down behind the crenellations on the wall.

The ground was a morass of mud, but the ram continued pounding. Several large cracks had appeared in the scorched and blackened oak planks, but it gave no sign of collapsing. Even from his place on the distant hill, Samuel could tell from the sound of the ram's blows that the men wielding it were tiring.

Others saw it as well. Kish loped toward the gate, ignoring the missiles that fell all around him, his battleaxe clutched in his hands. Stepping in behind him was Barzel the Simeonite, his own battered, bloodied axe resting on his right shoulder. Pushing through the struggling figures and corpses, they reached the gate itself, the huge Benjaminite to the left and the burly Simeonite to the right of the ram.

"Swing!" Samuel heard Kish bellow, and as the ram once again thudded against the planks, Kish and Barzel swung their axes in unison. Samuel could not see the results, but a cheer went up from the attackers near the gate.

"Swing!" Kish shouted again, and he and Barzel continued hewing at the planks with every crash of the ram.

More Philistines appeared on the battlements on either side of the gate, shields overlapping as they dropped rocks and shot arrows down on the attackers. Stones and arrows from the Benjaminites ricocheted off the defenses and spun away with whining cries. Men supporting the ram fell amongst their companions' feet, but fresh warriors, shields held over their heads, rushed in to replace them.

Samuel watched as one stone, the size of a man's head, fell on Kish's shoulder. He was sure the man would collapse, but the huge Benjaminite shrugged off the blow. Scowling up at the top of the wall, he reached down and picked up a fist-sized stone from the ground. He hurled it toward the battlements; it lifted a Philistine defender off of his feet and sent him tumbling backward off of the wall.

The ram swung again, but this time the gate's center caved inward with a mighty crack. Kish, Barzel, and a dozen other men threw their shoulders against the oak planks.

The gate burst open, swinging wide, its massive bars splintering. Simeonites rushed into the gap, but the Philistines were ready for them. Rows of archers were atop the buildings raked the foremost attackers with hundreds of arrows. Dozens died in the first volley; dozens more in the second. The gateway was choked with bodies lying atop one another.

The Simeonites could not withdraw; behind them Judean spearmen and Manassites continued to push forward into the city, unaware of what their countrymen faced. More men were squeezed through the gate into the square; more men fell victim to the hail of missiles.

Then Jedaiel appeared as if from nowhere, running toward the wall at the head of a string of Benjaminite slingers. They scrambled up the ladders and, drawing their short swords and knives, tried to cut themselves a place on the battlements overlooking the square. Gadites under Shaga saw what was happening and threw grappling hooks over the wall, ascending hand over hand to join their brothers and push the Philistines back enough to make room for the slingers.

At the first opportunity, Jedaiel loaded his sling and began launching stones, faster than the eye could follow, down into the Philistine archers in the square defending the gate. Other Benjaminites followed his example, and as they picked off soldiers one by one, gaps opened in the Philistine defense; within moments, the Simeonite and Zebulunite vanguard broke through the phalanx and burst into the city like water from a dam.

The Philistines fled, sluicing through the narrow streets toward the city's rear wall, leaping from the walls to rooftops, from rooftops to the ground. They melted into the alleys and through posterns and fled across the green fields with the Israelites on their heels.

It was only after most had disappeared into the surrounding countryside, relentlessly pursued by the Gadites, that Samuel made his way into the city and heard the first reports from the front lines of the battle.

The square was still crowded, but crowded by the aura of death as much as by the soldiers and silent corpses. Samuel tried not to look at the bodies of the slain, sprawled around him in pools of bright blood. He tried not to see the vacant, half-confused looks in the fixed eyes of the young Philistine soldiers that stared questioningly up at him. He clenched his teeth to force his stomach to settle as injured Israelite men were carried from the field on stretchers, weeping as they stared down at the ruined stump of what had been a limb. He forced himself to smile at the soldiers who passed by and glanced at him for approval.

"There was not a sound man among them," Manoah grumbled. "The Philistine dogs left their injured here to slow us down."

"Injured or not, they are still the enemies of God," Samuel said, as much for the benefit of the soldiers gathered around them as for Manoah's.

"And they will pay the ultimate price," Manoah said. "Few will escape Shaga and the Gadites."

Manoah was still talking when the scent of burning tar drifted past Samuel's nostrils. Something about the smell bothered him in a way he could not put his finger on. He scanned the gateway and the wall. Smoke hung in the air from the burning oil outside the gate, and he told himself he must simply be smelling its residue. But he knew it wasn't true. He could not explain it, but the scent of the smoke was wrong somehow—too much of the sharp, bitter smell of bitumen and not enough of the nutty scents of olive oil.

"Samuel?" Manoah had realized the Prophet's attention was abruptly elsewhere.

Then Samuel saw it—oily, black smoke that seemed to be oozing out from the base of the wall...

"Get the people out of here!" he snapped, turning toward Manoah and pushing him backward toward the buildings of Aphek.

"What...?"

"Go!" Samuel began urging everyone in the square back into the city's streets. "Back! All of you! Back!"

His face and voice must have conveyed the urgency he felt. The soldiers hurried away from him, stumbling over the bodies of comrades and enemies as they abandoned the open square for Aphek's narrow streets and alleys, glancing over their shoulders in confusion.

Samuel was still moving forward but had his back to the gate when a thunderous roar shook the ground under his feet. Hot wind, like a giant hand, shoved him from behind as dust and debris blasted all around him, whipping his robes and hair forward. He nearly stumbled to his knees, but managed to keep his feet even as stones that had once been the wall of Aphek tumbled past him.

Incredibly, he was not struck by any of them. When he looked up again, the eyes of all the soldiers who had been in the square were staring out at him from between the buildings of Aphek. There was awe in their faces.

He turned around to discover that almost the entire front wall of the city had collapsed, filling the square with rubble and debris piled over half-crushed bodies. In a glance he could see what had happened: the Philistines had tunneled under the foundations of the wall from the inside, shored up their tunnel with wooden bracing painted with tar, then set fire to it. Obviously they had done it just before they fled the city, knowing that the square would be filled with Israelites for some time after they broke through the gate.

They had planned to collapse the wall onto the waiting soldiers.

Men were still staring out at him through the swirling dust. He could read their wide-eyed expressions as easily as if they were inscribed in stone: *Prophet of God! Seer of the future!*

For a moment he thought of telling them that he had not foreknown anything, simply noticed the smoke and drew the logical conclusion from it. But it would not matter, he knew. To them, he was more than human.

They needed a hero.

They had chosen him.

Men began picking their way across the rubble, but their eyes kept drifting back to Samuel. Manoah approached, wiping dust and grime from his face. "Well prophesied."

Samuel shook his head. "It was no act of prophecy."

Manoah shrugged his indifference. "Many of the commanders want to know if they should follow Shaga and the Gadites."

Samuel shook his head. "No. I would have told Shaga not to go, if he had asked. We will see them again soon enough."

Manoah's brow furrowed. "What do you mean?"

"They will travel south," Samuel said. "They will rejoin their brothers who await us in the Pentapolis."

"Then you are determined to go forward with your plan?" Manoah asked.

Samuel nodded. "Before the next Sabbath, Philistia will feel the keen yearning of our blades." He took a deep breath, watching for a moment as the soldiers shuffled through the debris looking for the bodies of their dead comrades. "Send word to the commanders, Manoah. Tell them that as soon as the moon rises we will meet again in the courtyard of Aphek's meeting hall, built against the western gate of the city."

Manoah bowed. "As you say, my lord."

It did not take long for the commanders to make their way to the assembly hall; in fact, it took longer for soldiers to clear the floor and tables of the filth that had been left behind by the Philistines. Even afterward, the room stank of mold and wet dog, and Manoah commanded men to burn lamps filled with scented oil.

When Samuel walked to the front of the assembly, Baghadh was close on his heels. Before the eyes of all those gathered, he bowed low to Samuel's feet. "May Jehovah continue to bless our leader, Samuel, and may his words to us prove to be as the words of the True God Himself!"

The commanders clapped their approval while Samuel tried to think of a way to send the wretched Manassite away without appearing churlish or ungrateful.

Instead, he ignored him. "Lodan—what are the latest reports from your spies?"

Lodan took a step forward, bowing smartly, clothing clean and un-wrinkled, white hair and beard neatly trimmed. "As you suspected, my lord," he answered. "The Philistines travel south, amassing on the plain between Ekron and Gath."

"In the heart of the Pentapolis," Ner growled.

Samuel nodded. He had known it would be so.

"And the Amorites?" Samuel asked.

"An army of many thousands has assembled in the valley plain of Aijalon, my lord," Lodan said. "They are well-armed and have stolen every horse, mule, or camel they can get their hands on. They are preparing for war."

"They are," Samuel agreed, nodding. "But where?"

Lodan shook his head. "I have not been able to determine that, my lord. I have spies that have heard the Amorites talking of their plans, but it appears that none of the soldiers know where they intend to attack first. Their commander is keeping his plans secret."

"What do you say, Bocheru?" Samuel asked, turning to face the old Zebulunite who sat cross-legged near one wall.

"I think the Philistines let us take Aphek without putting up much of a fight," Bocheru said. "I think that we should ask ourselves why."

Samuel nodded. "And there is only one answer I can think of to that question: they are preparing a more elaborate reception for us in the south."

"Then we are walking into a trap," said Prince Elhanan.

Samuel nodded.

"What, then, shall we do?" asked Jedaiel.

"We shall brave its jaws," Samuel said.

The room went silent but for the uncomfortable shuffling of feet.

"And Aphek?" Manoah asked.

"We shall leave a token force here," Samuel said. "I am sure that all of you share my view that it is no longer a priority for the sons of Philistia. The Axis Lords have turned their eyes away from Aphek. They are gathering all their strength to bring down their full might upon us."

"But, my lord, surely this is madness!" said Dathan. "To march into Philistia? They will be waiting for us! They will confront us on the plains, where they can best use their chariots and cavalry against us!"

"They will be waiting for the armies of Israel," Samuel said. "What we shall bring to them is the wrath of God."

54

The following morning the armies of Israel marched south out of Aphek, leaving behind a token force to hold the city against the unlikely event of an attempt by the Philistines to retake it. They left with with the rising of the sun over the distant hills of Gilead, following the broad, smooth path of the trade route that paralleled the shore.

Samuel had only traveled the road once before, and he was struck by the way his view had changed. As de facto commander of Israel's armies, he took every step keenly aware of the safety of the men who had put their lives in their hands to follow him. The Sea now felt as though it were a vast, unprotectable flank. To most Israelites, the Great Sea was a barrier, an endless unknown that they did not dare venture out upon. But to the Philistines, he knew, it was a highway and a route to all places in the world. His eyes continually drifted to the west, scanning the glimmering water for any sign of swan-prowed ships nearing the shore.

They encountered fewer merchants and travelers than Samuel expected, and those they did meet looked upon them with eyes that shone with a tenuous hope and an intractable fear. The rumors of war had spread from Dan to Be'ersheba by now.

From the solemn greetings the merchants gave to the Israelites as they passed, Samuel did not think they expected to ever see him and the soldiers again.

A bank of fog that hovered along the beach dissipated as the day heated, and Samuel allowed himself to enjoy the sensation of a sea breeze on his face, cooling and refreshing in the warmth of the baking sun. Distant Egyptian ships plied the glistening waters on their way to Caphtor or Phoenicia, carrying incense, myrrh, gum, ivory, and antimony. On the road itself, camel caravans and donkey-pulled wagons hauled wool or grain north toward Cyprus, where they would exchange it for copper and tin, or south to Egypt where they would use it to buy weapons, house wares, ivory and sandalwood. Swarthy-skinned southerners with gold nose-rings brought camels from Ophir, burdened with precious stones, spices, and ivory. Atop one donkey-pulled wagon perched a set of barred, wooden cages holding baboons and apes who sat listlessly in their prisons, staring out at the passing soldiers with eyes that seemed knowing and sad.

In another wagon, Samuel caught a glimpse of a cage filled with tiny, ebon-skinned people—at first he thought they were children. Polished pegs of bone pierced their wide, flat noses and ears, and intricate patterns of raised dots decorated their faces and arms. He remembered hearing stories of such a people, from the distant headwaters of the Nile, but it was the first time he had seen them. He realized that it was only to be expected that, just as giant Rephaim inhabited Bashan and now parts of Philistia, somewhere else on the surface of the ground there would be an opposite people. He wondered if in some far corner of the world there waited, yet to be discovered, a people tinier still.

Samuel had ordered the commanders to push their men hard, and they reached the city of Lod, in a fertile valley at the southern edge of the Plain of Sharon, shortly after midday. The Philistines had abandoned it, leaving behind only mementos of their presence: a dozen Israelite corpses hanging from the walls on either side of the city gate. Ravens gripped their tattered clothing and tore their flesh, and Samuel ordered them cut down and buried in the field outside the city.

"They are trying to provoke you, my lord," Barzel said, his eyes narrow.

"They have succeeded," answered Samuel.

Barzel led a group of his warriors in a quick sweep of the city to make sure none of their enemy remained within. One of his men returned to report that Barzel had proclaimed the city taken in the name of Samuel and Jehovah.

"If we leave it empty behind us," old Bocheru warned, "Philistines or Canaanites will fill it. We must keep control of our route south, or risk facing armies on two fronts when we reach Philistia."

Samuel left two hundred men to hold Lod against any such attempt and they pressed on southward. The mid-afternoon heat hung sweltering over the coastal plain when they arrived at Gibbethon. The city had been held by the Philistines since before the first battle of Aphek, when Manoah and Na'amah had been saved from its destruction by Elon-tohr. Once again it was empty but for a few mutilated corpses hung by their necks from the battlements.

"Will we stop here for the night, my lord?" asked Shaga.

Samuel stared at the Gadites clambering up the wall to cut the corpses free. "I had hoped to," he said quietly. "But no more. The sons of Philistia wait for us to the south. Let us keep our appointment with them."

The road was straight and broad from Gibbethon into Philistia, but where it forded the River Sorek Samuel led the armies of Israel to the east, across the cultivated plains towards the Shephelah. They marched over the broad, swampy fields, their formation loosening as the day became evening and as carts and wagons stretched out behind unburdened infantry on the rough ground.

Sunset was burning at their backs, painting the lip of the Sea with its palette of fire, when they arrived at the camp of the great army of Judah. Thousands of tents sprawled over the trampled grasslands; a forest of smoke rose from hundreds of campfires. Samuel dismissed the tribal chieftains to arrange their own camps for the night and went in search of Prince Elhanan.

A command tent of goat's-hair cloth had been set up near the edge of the Judean encampment; from a tall pole emerging through the center of the tent's peaked roof fluttered a banner with Judah's lion embroidered in gold on a white background. Samuel nodded a greeting to the guards who stood at its door as he ducked to enter, but to his shock the men crossed their spears in front of him.

"My lord—the Prince has asked not to be disturbed," one of them said.

Samuel scowled. "He will want to see me, I think."

The guard would not meet his eyes. "He mentioned your name specifically, my lord Prophet. We were to allow no one to enter."

Samuel felt his face flush. He clasped *Mish'eneth* in front of him and glowered at the guards; he felt a perverse sense of satisfaction at seeing them squirming under the heat of his stare. The other tribal commanders filtered in and joined him in waiting: old Bocheru leaning on his stick, Manoah and Samson (his ankle now recovered from his fall), Ner and Kish, Shemer of Reuben, Cosam of Asher, Shaga of Gad, Dathan, Lodan the Issacharian, Barzel the Simeonite, and Avith and Zattu.

Finally someone inside the tent spoke, but in tones so low that Samuel could not make out the words. The guards leaned close to the tent cloth to listen, then nodded and looked up at Samuel. "You may enter, my lord."

"At long last!" snapped Manoah, stepping toward the door.

The guard put himself in Manoah's way. "The Prophet only, my lord."

Manoah put his hand on his sword hilt and stepped forward until his nose was a handbreadth from the guard's. "You are a single swallow of saliva from feeding this soil with your blood, man!"

The guard did not flinch. "I answer to Prince Elhanan of Judah. And Elhanan alone decides who enters Elhanan's tent."

Samuel held out his hand. "Peace, Manoah." He glanced back once at the commanders waiting behind him, then ducked through the flap into the tent.

He was not surprised to find Baghadh and Tahash inside with Prince Elhanan; a servant of the Prince stood behind Baghadh with a smoking censer to mask the diseased man's rank smell. He was, however, disappointed to see Elishama of Bethel in one corner of the tent.

"Ah, Samuel," Elhanan said, embracing him. "May you have peace."

"An inappropriate greeting for our time," Samuel said, looking from one face to another.

"Have no fear," Elhanan said. "We work only for the safety and welfare of the children of Israel."

"As do the men who you have left standing in the darkening night outside of your tent," Samuel said.

Elhanan's lips curled in the hint of a smile. "Their wait will soon be over, I hope."

"Let us come to the point, "interrupted Baghadh.

"I am waiting," said Samuel.

Elhanan sat heavily in an upholstered chair and rested his hands on the polished algum-wood arms, skillfully carved to look like the arching necks of swans. "My scouts have just returned. The sons of Philistia are waiting for us between Ekron and Gath. They have assembled a mighty army there: hundreds of scythe-wheeled chariots, hundreds of thousands of men, war hounds, the remaining Gedhudhra, and more than three hundred Rephaim. They wait for us on the plain, where their chariots can be used to best advantage. They are fresh, well-trained, and armed with iron."

Samuel kept his face impassive. "We have expected this since leaving Evenezer."

"There is more," Elhanan said. "The Amorite uprising—they have formed an army. They are on the move. The left Aijalon yesterday, headed west. Headed toward us."

"Even you cannot desire a war on two fronts," said Baghadh.

"I do not desire war at all," said Samuel. "But if it is Jehovah's will, I will march against Egypt herself."

Prince Elhanan frowned, lips tightening. "Do not allow stubbornness to make you a fool, Samuel. Look at your people. They are divided, split down the middle between following you and following Tahash ben Avdon."

Samuel glanced over at the young man, but Tahash was staring at the rugs beneath his feet and did not even acknowledge his name being spoken.

"If the people are divided, it is because you have made them so," Samuel said, turning toward Baghadh.

"Nonsense," said Baghadh. "The men of Ephraim expected a son of Avdon to become the next Judge of Israel—they want to follow Tahash. Manasseh looks to me for guidance, and I must direct them as my heart tells me to. It seems clear to me that Tahash is Jehovah's choice to lead the nation. And now Judah..."

Samuel looked from Baghadh to Elhanan and back again. "Ah. And now Judah is throwing her support behind Baghadh as well."

"You can end this schism now!" Elhanan rose to his feet again. "All that you have to do is speak a single word, and the rest of the tribes will do as you bid. You can unite the nation under a single leader, and give us our only—albeit slim—chance of defeating this foe."

"And what word would that be?" Samuel asked. "To lie to my people—our people!—and tell them that Jehovah has appointed Tahash to lead them? To tell them to follow Baghadh's puppet into battle?"

Baghadh sneered. "Tahash is his own man! Who are you to speak of puppets—you, who pulled Avdon's strings all his life!"

"Enough wrangling!" said Prince Elhanan, scowling at Baghadh. "The choice that lies before you is simple, Prophet. Accept Tahash as the commander of Israel's forces, or…"

"Or what?" Samuel asked, although he knew the answer.

"Or the tens of thousands of Judah, and the tens of thousands of Manasseh, and half the men of Ephraim, will not be marching into battle tomorrow," Elhanan said.

Samuel shook his head in disbelief. "And what do you say, Tahash? I called you friend once. Is this your wish?"

Tahash answered with the precise monotony of one who speaks another's words. "I must follow the instructions that Jehovah has given me. This battle is your folly and pride. I will not support it."

Samuel took a deep breath. "You do not know what you are doing. You are abandoning one fight only to take up another—but this time it is the Will of God that is your enemy."

Baghadh seemed not to have heard him. "If you want to see your dream fulfilled—if you want to have any chance at defeating the forces of Philistia, then you must let go of your pride, Samuel."

Samuel smiled. "You are—all of you—doomed to failure. I will pray that you come to your senses before it is too late."

He ducked out the tent door and faced the waiting commanders. "The tribes of Ephraim, Manasseh, and Judah are abandoning us. Speak it in the ears of your men, but do not fear. Neither with sword nor with spear does Jehovah save, but by His might. Tomorrow, we march into battle."

55

No sunrise was visible in the morning through the haze of grey that hung over the Philistine plain. The clouds oozed from charcoal grey to a washed-out blue-grey, lightening but not brightening the sullen sky. A cold wind curled off of the sea, fluttering and flapping the standards of the army of Israel as their commanders assembled around Samuel at the front of the muster.

Trampled grass, blackened rings from campfires, and scattered animal dung were all that remained of their encampment the night before. The warriors of the nine tribes waited in anxious silence, wrapped in woolen cloaks against the chill of the wind, white-knuckled hands gripping spears and shields, eyes narrowed with intensity and the unique introspection of men who go to greet death face to face.

Baghadh, Tahash, Elishama and Prince Elhanan had led the soldiers of Manasseh, Ephraim, and Judah north and east during the night. Samuel had not sent scouts after them, but he assumed they waited now in the cover of the low hills. What they waited for, however, he could not guess. For him to fail? For some vindication of their rebellion? For some more mercenary or opportunistic purpose?

He forced himself to put those concerns out of his mind and turned to Ahimelech, standing stoically beside him on the low rise that provided all the elevation that was available on the plain. He nodded and Ahimelech raised both hands and his dispassionate face toward the sullen sky.

"To You, O Jehovah, we turn our faces. We are in Your hands. Shelter us in Your palm, O our God, for there is neither victory, nor any defeat but by Your allowance. Grant our arms to be strong; make our hearts firm, make the edges of our swords keen against our enemies. To Your promise to our forefathers Abraham, Isaac, and Jacob we appeal: grant us to take possession of the Land of Promise, even as You have commanded us. By Your mighty arm, we stand or fall."

Ahimelech lowered his eyes and faced the people, arms still spread wide. "May Jehovah bless you and keep you. May Jehovah make His face shine toward you, and may He favor you. May Jehovah lift up His face toward you, and assign peace to you."

"Jehovah our God is one!" the soldiers responded in a muffled roar.

Samuel turned and nodded to the trumpeter standing at his left. Red beard bristling, the man puffed his cheeks and blew a clarion call across the valley. The commanders strode from the hill to their respective tribes and contingents. Drums pounded; within a few moments the army was in motion. Birds, feasting on the scraps of dinner and breakfast, scattered into the grey sky, screeching their protest.

Bocheru himself, astride a long-legged ass, led the perfectly ordered Zebulunite vanguard, vaguely reptilian in their oiled leather armor, bristling with weapons of all kinds under the snapping banner of a sailing ship. Behind them the bulk of the army marched, tens of thousands strong: Avith and Zattu leading the Napthalians, half-hidden behind their tall shields, beneath a flag emblazoned with a leaping hind; Shemer and the Reubenites under the sign of a shining sun; richly armed and armored Asherites, long, curved knives already clutched in their gloved hands, marching behind Cosam (black beard and moustache neatly oiled) and the banner of a spreading sycamore; Barzel and the Simeonites scattered among the other tribes.

On either flank were the Gadites, wild-haired and wild-eyed, oiled-leather bucklers strapped to their hairy left arms, bronze-headed spears in their right hands; they moved unevenly, as though impatient at having to wait for the rest of the army. Shaga marched next to their banner, a tattered flag embroidered with an open tent.

Behind each Gadite flank was half of the Benjaminite force, led on one side by Kish, and on the other by his father, Ner. Shieldless and only lightly armored or not at all, they bore bows and slings in their hands and short swords strapped to their sides; donkeys laden with sling stones in stiff, leather saddlebags walked among them, and the backs of the archers sprouted clusters of brown-fletched arrows in quivers of goat skin, the stiff, mottled hair still attached. A narrow wagon, almost chariot-sized, pulled by a pair of goats carried additional arrows and stones; a tall shaft of polished oak was attached to one corner of the wagon, its tip lurching this way and that with every jolting movement, ceaselessly whipping the Benjaminite banner of a ravening wolf.

The Danite rearguard followed Manoah and Samson, who himself bore their wind-snapped standard of a coiled snake. Comprised of equal numbers of missile and shock troops, they were the only contingent that bore any quantity of iron weapons; some of the wealthier warriors rattled in Philistine-style bronze scale mail hauberks and bronze greaves, dull now in the subdued light. Behind the rearguard Samuel, Ahimelech, and the Beneh walked, along with the Issacharian Lodan and his runners.

The valley was broad and flat, and they moved swiftly across it, eyes straining at the horizon for their first glimpse of their enemy.

They did not have to wait long. The Philistines appeared as a black line in the distance, the sound of their thundering approach carried to the Israelites in fits by the building wind. The line became a low, moving wall, then coalesced into a ragged black outline of infantry, cavalry, chariots, and, scattered among them, Rephaim towering over their cohorts.

The armies closed on one another; Samuel felt tension building in the air, as thick as smoke in a poorly-vented room and, like smoke, it gripped the army in an invisible choke-hold of fear. They were still a hundred reeds apart, but it was already obvious that the children of Israel were outnumbered two, three, even four to one.

Both armies ground slowly to a halt, facing each other across the empty plain. Lodan led Samuel and his companions a little west of the Danite rearguard to the best vantage point: a hillock, not even the height of a man, bare but for a single, worn, lichen-covered boulder. Mosquitoes buzzed irritatingly around them. The Tabernacle Guard who had accompanied Ahimelech from Nob surrounded them in a ring several layers deep, grim-

grim-faced, spears braced against the ground and protruding in all directions like the spines of a giant porcupine.

The Benjaminites were scrabbling to find any cover available; some of the Danite rearguard moved forward with tall shields to aid them. Bocheru galloped on his donkey past the vanguard, his slender arm holding aloft a sword more slender still, rallying them for the charge. Samuel looked for the Philistine command, for a small group of men upon a raised vantage point, as he was. He saw none. Phicol commanded the army now, and Samuel had no doubt that the noseless one led from a chariot in the middle of his Gedhudhra.

Samuel gripped *Mish'eneth* until his knuckles whitened. The wind gusted over the plain, rippling grass, tearing at clothing, snapping standards overhead. He thought suddenly of a passage from the Book of the Wars of Jehovah, a record of what had taken place at Rephidim in the Wilderness of Sinai: *And whenever Moses lifted his staff, the Israelites were victorious, but when he let his staff down, the Amalekites were the victors. Thus when the hands of Moses had become heavy, Aaron and Hur made for him a seat of stone, and he sat on it; and they supported his hands, one on either side. In this way they kept his hands raised until the setting of the sun. And Joshua vanquished the Amalekites with the edge of the sword.*

If only it were that easy, he thought, and chastised himself for his self-indulgence.

He felt that he should say something to his people, build them up or rouse them for the charge, but whatever words he spoke would be carried away by the wind before they reached any other than perhaps a few of the Danite rearguard. Instead he turned to the Issacharian bugler at Lodan's side and nodded once.

The horn cut through the wind: three short blasts and one long. With a roar of tens of thousands of voices, the Israelite army surged forward, building speed, running across the field with their weapons raised.

The Philistines met their movement, and dust rose from the hooves of the horses and the wheels of the chariots. The two forces swept toward each other, opposing waves meeting in a dry, yellow sea.

The *crunch* of their collision was punctuated by the screams of men and horses, ripping like lightning bolts of agony through the howl of the wind. For a moment—less than a moment—Israel held, and then the Philistine juggernaut washed them backwards in a deluge of savagery and blood.

Samuel stood in stunned surprise, disbelief clouding his mind. Israel was routed almost instantly; by the thousands they fled west, toward the slight cover of the Shephelah's hills and trees. Commands and contingents were shattered; battle lines disintegrated into pockets of resistance, islands of battling Israelites swallowed by a sea of men and chariots. Like a flood the Philistines washed over the field of battle; like a flood they covered the islands until they were no more; like a flood they swept all before them in a black wave of destruction.

Lodan was pulling at Samuel's arm, dragging him away as the conflict raged nearer. The Levite guards hurried him and Ahimelech from the field, but Samuel could smell the fear of the armed men around him, as potent as the rank of death.

They fled, stumbling over the grass as behind them men died, died by the hundreds under iron swords, huge battleaxes, and scythe-wheeled chariots. Samuel wept as they fled, tears blurring his vision as he was pulled by one arm across the field.

He glimpsed faces around him, but he did not know them, whether because they were men he had not met or because his mind failed him, he was not sure.

"Samuel!" they cried through their weeping.

Some stared in disbelief at wounds from which their lifeblood poured; one man held his severed arm in his other hand, staring at it in quiet confusion.

Arrows fell thick among them and several of the Levite guards went down, clawing at the dark shafts that sprouted from their anguished bodies.

"Samuel!" someone screamed; a man whose face was smeared with blood. He looked at the glowering clouds. "Where is Jehovah?" he asked, pleading desperation cracking his voice.

More arrows fell. The Levites raised their shields above their heads to form a roof of protection over Samuel, and striking missiles thrummed on the leather-covered wood like hail. Some found their way through; Samuel saw one of the guards whose shield and forearm were both transfixed by a bloodied shaft.

Gradually Samuel became aware that the riot of battle was growing more distant and lessening in intensity. *The Philistines will not give chase when they can hunt us at their leisure. They would rather gather us as slaves than spill our blood needlessly on the field of battle.*

He turned and saw Ahimelech beside him, his young face shadowed by the roof of shields. The High Priest's eyes were wet with tears, his face slack with sorrow. But there was no fear, nor anger in his features. He looked, to Samuel, resigned to what had happened, almost as though he had expected it.

No arrows had fallen for some time, and the Levites lowered their aching shield-arms and picked up their pace. They were at the outskirts of a forest of oak and sycamore, slipping through the sparse trunks that increased in number and density as they moved east. Samuel glanced over his shoulder. Only scattered Israelites were fleeing the same direction that they were. Even at a distance, he could see that many of the forms were splashed with crimson.

"God save us!" he heard one of the Levites whisper through his panting breath.

But He did not, Samuel thought, and a chill wracked his frame that did not come from the bitter wind. *He did not.*

56

Samuel would not credit it to Divine aid, but it was nothing short of a miracle that the scattered bands of fleeing soldiers eventually found one another. Slowly, defeated and broken, they filtered into the dense forest of cedars, sycamores, and oaks and collected, like pooling water, in a shadowed valley in the foothills to the southeast of the Kenite copper mines at Timnah.

Samuel told the Levite guards to make certain that no one disturbed him and clambered up a chalky rock face to a bare outcrop that jutted skyward almost to the tops of the trees. There he sat, cross-legged on the lichen-covered basalt, the wind whipping his long hair about his face with stinging strokes.

Below him, the battle commanders took stock of their situation. The Zebulunites had borne the brunt of the attack; of their number less than one in four remained alive. Old Bocheru had survived, suffering only a nasty gash across one cheekbone, bound now with a browning strip of linen. Of the remainder of the army, most still lived. The rout had been so complete that few besides the Zebulunites had stood their ground, and that quick flight had saved many lives. That and the sacrifice of the men of Zebulun.

Manoah did nothing constructive, storming around the makeshift camp with his bare sword still in his hand, his face a mask of such fury that his own men scattered when he approached.

In the end, it was Samson who began the task or re-organizing the survivors and establishing communication between the tribal contingents. Old Bocheru worked alongside him—Samson had trained under the Weapons Master in his teen-age years.

Samson quickly discovered that finding men skilled with the sword was easy compared to finding those that could put aside their emotions and opinions and continue to follow their commander after such a defeat. Avith and Zattu took the situation in stride, regathering the men of Naphtali a short distance down the valley.

"We await the Prophet's instructions," Avith said simply before he left to join his men.

Barzel of Simeon was outspoken in his lack of confidence in Samuel's leadership, and Shemer of Reuben was emboldened by Barzel's words to join him in his complaining. For a time Samson was afraid two more tribes were going to abandon the armies of Israel. But in the end the two chieftains, grumbling, went along with the remainder of the nation.

Cosam of Asher sat in bitter silence, picking his nails with his long, curved knife. "I am with you," he hissed at Samson when approached, "but only because I will not stop until I have brought vengeance down upon those dogs!"

Fair enough, thought Samson. *If vengeance drives you back to the battlefield, nurse your vengeance.*

Shaga of Gad was sucking the marrow out of a bone of some kind when Samson found him. His wild hair was matted even more than usual, this time with dried blood. Before Samson could speak, the Gadite looked up at him and swallowed. "When do we go back?"

"I was hoping you, and the other chieftains, could decide that," Samson said.

Shaga pushed himself to his feet; Samson abruptly realized Shaga's shield was still strapped to his back and his sword at his hip. "I say now," the Gadite said. He paused, gesturing vaguely at the forest around him. "Or whenever the rest of these are ready."

"I will carry your words to the other commanders," Samson said.

In reality, there was no one to carry anything to; everyone waited to be told what to do. Samson returned to Bocheru and sat down heavily beside him.

"What now?" the young man asked.

Bocheru poked Samson in the ribs with his gnarled walking stick. "What would you do, were you in command?" he asked.

Samson laughed. "Run screaming back to Zorah."

Bocheru's expression did not change; he stared and waited for another answer.

Samson sighed. "I suppose…We have to do something to counter their greater numbers. Phalanxes of men on the open plain favor their chariot warriors."

Bocheru nodded slowly. "And how do you propose we deal with that?"

"You are the Weapons Master!" Samson said, only half in jest. "You tell me!"

Bocheru continued to stare silently, waiting.

Samson threw up his hands. "I would divide our forces."

"Will that not weaken your line?" Bocheru asked.

"Our line is worthless against their numbers," Samson said. "We have to find an approach that keeps them from bringing their cavalry against us so powerfully."

Bocheru nodded. "Good. How would you accomplish this?"

Samson picked up a stick and scratched a diagram on a patch of chalky soil. "Divide our forces into four sections: heavy lancers in the center, led by the men of Zebulun. If we could hide men in the grass here, and here…" he marked the wide flanks of the battlefield; "…then they could come in from either side unexpectedly—dividing the Philistine vanguard in three directions. The Philistines will not be concerned about such a tactic on the morrow—their confidence now can be used against them."

"The Gadites from the sides?" Bocheru asked.

"The Gadites," Samson agreed, still staring at his diagram. "Probably the Asherite knife men as well."

"You said four divisions."

Samson nodded. "The Benjaminites and every man who can fire sling or arrow with accuracy must provide cover for the Gadite flanks—a constant shower of missiles, to slow the Philistine pursuit."

"Pursuit?"

"Pursuit." Samson scratched at the drawing again. "The central phalanx charges against the Philistine center—like so. As soon as they meet, our men allow themselves to be pushed backward—pretend to flee again, as the enemy will expect us to do. When the Philistine van pursues, stretching out after us, the Gadite flanks will rush in, closing like pincers and snipping off the head of the enemy. But they cannot make a stand. As quickly as they fall upon the Philistines, so quickly must they flee. Benjaminites positioned all around here..." he marked flanking positions on either side of the rearguard, "...will need to provide cover fire, to allow the Gadites to make their escape."

"So." Bocheru examined the drawing. "You have snipped off their nose. Is that all you hope to accomplish?"

Samson shook his head. "As soon as the Gadites flee, the Philistines will go in pursuit, splitting their army in half to rush east and west after them."

"Are you certain?" asked Bocheru.

"They do not fear us, and that is our strength. At that moment, when they sacrifice the solidarity of their line in order to pursue the hornets that have stung them, our central phalanx will turn and plunge into the unprotected heart of the army."

He looked up at Bocheru for approval. The old man was smiling. "You are a student to make his teacher proud," he said softly.

Encouraged, Samson continued: "The beauty of this plan is that it can be repeated again and again. When the central phalanx is overwhelmed, they turn and flee and the Gadites attack from either side. When the Philistines divide their forces again to pursue the Gadites, back comes the central phalanx."

"Nibble them to death," Bocheru said.

"We have a small mouth, my lord," Samson said.

Bocheru tapped his staff on the hard ground. "So does the termite, but by its jaws great trees are felled. Gather the commanders. Tell them of your plan."

Samson rose from his crouch, dropping his stick. "Me? I am no commander, my lord!"

Bocheru began to walk away through the trees. "I think you are," he said.

That evening, after Samson had addressed the commanders and told them of his plan, Manoah found Samuel still sitting at the top of the basalt outcropping. The cooling air brought a warm breeze down from the hills to the east, redolent with the resinous scent of cedar and juniper. The sky over the water, just visible through the branches of the surrounding trees, ignited in smoldering streaks of oranges and purples.

Manoah lowered himself, cross-legged, to the ground next to Samuel. "You have heard about Samson?"

Samuel turned; the wind tossed his hair across his face. "What about him?"

Manoah studied the colors on the western horizon. "It is his battle plan that will guide the commanders of Israel tomorrow."

"Ah." Samuel nodded. "That I did hear."

Manoah turned abruptly to face him, bright eyes reflecting the amber light of the sky. "Am I the only one who recognizes what this means? Tell me that you, too, see it!"

Samuel frowned. "I am sorry…I do not understand…"

"The prophecy, man! The prophecy! 'He it is who will take the lead in delivering Israel from the sons of Philistia.' He is taking the lead, Samuel! It is happening now, here, on the plains between Zorah and Eshtaol!"

Samuel thought about the Danite's words. Once again he had to admit to himself that his initial resistance to the idea could be nothing more than a reflection of his egotistical assumption that Jehovah would have informed him that He was anointing Samson. But Judges were called in different ways. Some, like Shamgar of centuries before, were only recognized as Judges after they had taken action, and the people had seen undeniable evidence of Jehovah's Hand acting through them. There was no reason this could not be the case with Samson.

"The day we have long waited for has come at last," Manoah continued. "Tomorrow, my son will become a leader of men."

"I pray that it is so," Samuel said. "The light of the new day will bring us, one way or another, into a new world. May Samson be the daystar that announces that dawn."

57

D awn the following morning saw the armies of Israel assembled once again on the broad, fertile plain between Ekron and Gath, far fewer in number than had gathered there the day before. They seemed smaller than a single company of the Philistine horde that faced them, merely a tightly clustered knot of heavily armored spear and shield men in phalanx formation. The Danite rearguard and Benjaminite slingers spread behind them in a wide arc, just close enough to shoot over their own warrior's heads.

Their arrival had driven most of the wolves, jackals, and hyenas from the field, but they still paced at the edge of the grass, eyeing the torn and bloated corpses from the day before, muzzles lifted as though smelling the blood that was about to be spilled.

Samuel had been informed of their plan by Bocheru and had given it his formal approval. He doubted if anyone believed that his approval meant anything anymore.

He found that he did not care. The night had carried his mind down many paths, but in the end he had found his way back.

He was the Prophet.

He was the gauntlet on the Hand of the Most High God.

He was the Judge of Israel.

He did not know what their defeat the day before meant. Already rumors were flying around the camp that he had known the defeat would happen—that it was all part of the Prophet's inscrutable plan. The story was just believable enough to be grasped at by every desperate warrior, clinging to their belief that following Samuel ben Elkanah could only lead them to victory.

And Samuel knew in his heart, beyond his own misgivings, that they were right in their belief. He was under no illusions that this was because of any qualities he possessed. But victory they would find under his leadership, although he knew not how or when. Perhaps his victory was for a future day. Perhaps it would be a spiritual victory, paid for with the blood of tens of thousands of the children of Israel spilled on the dark soil of Philistia. Maybe Jehovah would once again step in, as He had at Mizpah.

For some reason, Samuel doubted that He would. He could not explain why, but he felt as though the divine aid at Mizpah had been enough, as though Jehovah expected the faith of His chosen people, bolstered by what they had seen and experienced, to carry them now.

And Ahitub had chosen him. Whatever other doubts or fears haunted his soul, Samuel trusted Ahitub above all men he had ever known. No man had seen more clearly the will of God than his mentor.

An Issacharian runner informed Samuel that the men were assembled. He was about to signal the advance when Lodan galloped up to him on a silver-grey mule. The Issacharian swung to the ground, wincing.

"My lord," he said breathlessly, bowing.

Samuel had seen as soon as the man had dismounted that he bore bad news. "What is it?"

Still panting, Lodan said, "The Philistines have brought, or assembled, huge catapults that they now keep hidden in their rearguard."

Samuel frowned. "For what purpose?"

Lodan shook his head. "I do not know, my lord. They can lob stones into our midst, but those are easily dodged. Even a hail of small stones is hardly deadly to armored men, and the catapults are so inaccurate they would hit as many of their own men as they would ours."

"Larger catapults could have a greater range," Samuel mused.

"But without accuracy..." Lodan trailed off, shrugging. "I do not know, my lord."

"Phicol is no fool," Samuel muttered.

"But he may be mad," Lodan said.

Samuel took a deep breath. "I cannot argue with that." He turned to the bugler. "Sound the advance."

The red-bearded man raised the horn to his lips and blew two blasts, a short and a long. Swiftly and smoothly the Israelite phalanxes moved forward, the Zebulunites arranged in a spearhead formation in the vanguard.

Across the broad field, horns blared in response, and the Philistines surged forward. Samuel saw immediately that their charge was ragged; Cavalry and charioteers surged past infantry, driving forward with no concern for formation in their eagerness to reach their pitiful foe. All semblance of a line vanished as warriors raced in pursuit of the glory of amassing their own tally of corpses.

"Now!" Samuel shouted, and the bugler sounded the charge.

The Israelite phalanxes did not lumber; they shot forward like a hurled spear, racing across the plain toward the scattered Philistine cavalry. Too late the Philistines realized their mistake. Drawn out and scattered in their reckless charge, unable to mount an organized defense, one by one mounted warriors and chariots were crushed by the deadly Zebulunites. In moments the Zebulunite spearhead reached the first orderly lines of Philistines, and the force of their charge plunged through the Philistine shield line with unbelievable efficacy and grace.

Almost they cut too deeply into the enemy, but the Zebulunites were too wily to be caught in that trap. Leaving a path of broken bodies behind them, they reformed their phalanx, shield beside shield, bristling with spears. One flank gave way under a determined onslaught of the Gedhudhra, but suddenly Avith and Zattu were there, back to back, thrusting into the gap with blades whirling. They moved as one body, parrying, riposting, and slashing with greater speed than a single man could ever hope to. The Gedhudhra refused to fall back, and died beneath their blades.

It took the Philistines only moments to recover. Trampling their dead, they rushed in fury against this tiny enemy who dared to defy them, and the two forces met with a brutal *crunch*.

Immediately, the Israelites gave way. Their hasty retreat was just disorderly enough to be believable, but not enough to leave them truly vulnerable. The indomitable Zebulunites became the rearguard, and even the deadly Gedhudhra could not get past their defenses.

As Samson had predicted, the Philistines gave chase. Howling chants of victory they rushed heedlessly after their fleeing enemy, foreseeing a repetition of the previous day's slaughter.

"Now!" Samuel yelled. The bugler blew a single, long blast.

To either side of the Philistine vanguard hundreds of warriors rose from the tall grass and hurtled toward them, led from the east by Cosam and from the west by Shaga. The Gadites were like lions loping through the grass. Samuel glimpsed Shaga for a moment, his red tongue hanging out of his open mouth as he bounded toward his foe.

The Philistines did not see the attack from their flanks until it was far, far too late. The Gadites and Asherites fell upon them, swift and agile, vaulting over horses and chariots, rolling under rows of leveled spears, savage and fearless, the sky's grey light reflected in their cold eyes.

Shaga wielded his spear as though it had a head at each end, thrusting with sharpened tip and blunted butt cap, whirling it over his head like a performer in some exotic dance.

For a moment, Samuel glimpsed Cosam in the middle of a knot of heavily armed Philistine swordsmen. He looked small and vulnerable in his leather tunic amidst their bronze scale-mail hauberks, and his curved knife seemed a plaything beside their long, iron blades. But then the men charged, there was a whirl of leaping, lunging bodies, and Cosam emerged from the maelstrom as the last two of his attackers fell, their hands clutching their necks. Stepping lightly over the bodies of his foes, he strode toward the nearest conflict.

In moments, the Philistine vanguard was cut off from the rest of the army; just as quickly they were cut down and left dying on the field.

It took longer than Samuel expected for the Philistines to regroup, but regroup they did, tightening their ranks, strengthening them with chariots on the flanks and Rephaim giants moving in to bolster the middle. As soon as they had done so, the Gadites turned and raced back the way they had come.

Furious, the Philistines surged after them, dividing just as Samson had planned, a forked tongue of rage and deadly force. But in the midst of the melee even chariots and horsemen were no match for the swiftness of the Gadites. Like lions they had cut through their enemies' ranks, and like lions they sped back across the dry grass, scattering as they went. A few Philistines were unfortunate enough to catch up to them, and they met their ends on the unerring tips of Gadite spears.

Bocheru wasted no time taking advantage of the Philistine disorder. Turning on their heels, the army's main phalanxes abandoned their feigned retreat and rushed into the middle of the serpent's tongue.

The Philistine vanguard broke once again, shattered by the savagery of the Israelite charge; in moments hundreds of Philistines lay dead on the blood soaked grass.

The pattern repeated itself: the Zebulunites retreated, drawing the Philistines after them; the Gadites rushed in from either side and cut off the outstretched vanguard, isolating and crushing it, then fleeing with their enemy in infuriated pursuit.

Perhaps Israel could have kept up the tactic all day, each time biting off a few hundred more of their enemy. But neither Samuel nor Samson had accurately assessed Phicol's cruelty.

For the third time the Gadites had rushed in, cutting off the forefront of the Philistine attack. The spear and shield men of the phalanxes had turned back to their grisly work when the grey sky lit up abruptly with orange light.

From behind the Philistine army huge orbs of fire arced skyward, streaming thick black smoke and a trail of spiraling sparks. Samuel stared in disbelief.

Beside him, he heard Lodan murmur, "Sons of Belial!"

The fireballs were, as Lodan had predicted, poorly aimed. They crashed to the ground in the middle of the Philistine vanguard, hemmed now on all sides by Israelite soldiers. As Philistines dove in every direction, the globes exploded on contact, splashing what appeared to be liquid fire in every direction.

Before Samuel even had time to register what had happened, a second round of fireballs followed the first. Some landed outside the area of fighting completely; others fell among the Danite rearguard. But wherever they landed, they turned everything around them into a maelstrom of flame.

The Gadites were fleeing again, but this time in earnest. Many could not; Samuel heard their screams as they became living torches in the midst of the battlefield. Zebulunites and the other men of the phalanxes fled as well, but some were trapped in the blazing grass and fell in unspeakable agony. Others ran with clothing afire, or rolled in the brittle grass in a futile effort to extinguish the flames.

The Philistine vanguard was destroyed by the flames and, as they spread, they threatened the main body of the Philistine army as well.

But still the fireballs fell, a rain of tortuous death that only Phicol could have sanctioned, equally deadly to Israelite and Philistine.

Amazingly, this time the Israelite retreat did not descend into chaos. Swiftly the Danites moved forward, Manoah and Samson at their head. The bugler sounded the retreat unnecessarily; the entire Israelite force was fleeing, slipping through the Danite rearguard and scattering again to the northeast.

The Philistines saw their enemy escaping once again, and the Gedhudhra led a charge around the inferno, hurtling on horse and chariot toward the Danite line.

The rearguard numbered fewer than three thousand; three times that many streamed around the flames and into their ranks. Amazingly, the Danites threw them back. More Philistines arrived, and again they charged. Again, the Danites threw them back. At the center of the Danite line Manoah, Samson, and his brothers raged like winter storms sweeping in from the sea.

The Gedhudhra pulled back and reorganized. Now they outnumbered the rearguard by at least five to one. Again they charged, a thundering wall of scythe-wheeled chariots, Rephaim, and armored horses.

Again the Danites hurled them back. This time, though, the Philistines punched through the Danite line not far from its center. Roaring, Manoah hurtled into the breach, Samson at his heels. Side by side they fought, iron blades swinging with blinding speed. On that day, not even the Gedhudhra were a match for the sons of Dan. The strength of God was in their arms, and His light was in their eyes, and they fell upon their enemies in a blinding wave of unstoppable death.

At last the retreat was accomplished: the last of the Israelites were making their swift way toward the cover of the forested hills.

"Retreat!" Manoah roared. "Orderly, as men!"

The Danites fell back, slowly at first, walking backwards with their spears pointed at their enemies who were even then assembling for another charge.

But the savagery of Phicol caught him in his own cruel net. At the moment that the Gedhudhra charged forward once again, another fireball hit the ground between them and the retreating Danites. A wall of flame burst up, dividing them and spreading across the dry grass of the plain with the speed of a summer wind blowing off the desert plain.

"Go!" Manoah shouted. "Go!"

JUDGE OF ISRAEL

The Danites raced away from the flames. Heads down, they ran toward the east and the cover of the trees.

Manoah ran as well, but his eyes followed the movements of his son and despite their ignominious rout, his face was alight with a keen and shining joy.

58

The Israelite flight did not stop until early in the afternoon. The Philistines pursued them this time, abandoning horses and chariots to follow their lean hunting hounds into the forested foothills. The soldiers of Israel scattered, vanishing into the caves and defiles that cut through the Shephelah, following forest trails known only to those who lived there.

Eventually, though, the Philistines were forced to abandon the pursuit. Unable to catch their elusive quarry, they began to fall prey to ambushes and the attacks of archers and slingers hidden among the rocks. Some of the Gadites deliberately led them into hollows and bogs where the wily hill-men could vanish into the underbrush and, unseen, attack their pursuers with spears and rocks.

By the time the sun had made its way halfway to the western horizon, the Israelites were slowly gathering again, this time in a broad valley between the towns of Zorah and Eshtaol.

Manoah found Samuel as soon as he was able, wild with anger and joy. "The prophecy is fulfilled!" he said, almost shouting, so that eyes turned toward them from every direction.

Samuel smiled back at him, but his mind was too full of the horrors of the battlefield to concentrate on the Danite's words.

Samuel once again went off on his own to think and pray. In spite of the rout, no one was complaining against his leadership now, at least not that he had heard. Everyone was still in stunned disbelief at Phicol's cruelty; they knew that no one could have predicted that the young commander would sacrifice so many of his own soldiers so callously. As he walked, he began to hear, murmured all around him, echoes of Manoah's pronouncement: "Samson has received his appointment!" "Samson has become the Deliverer!"

Samuel picked his way slowly along the northern side of the valley, where the Danites had begun setting up a temporary camp. He ignored them, leaning on *Mish'eneth*, winding among the slender pines and the sprawling sycamores and oaks. The forest was still—even the gathering forces below him were quiet, subdued by their losses and by the burden of uncertainty.

He could not get out of his mind the horrors he had seen and heard that day: the burned faces and bodies, some dying slowly and in agony; others lying in anguished disbelief, staring at charred, mangled flesh and trying to comprehend that it was their own. And the smell...

He stopped a moment, leaning against a pine trunk. Its rough bark was cool against his palm and he tried to draw from it some of its serene stability. Movement to his left caught his eye, and below him he saw that he was no longer alone: trailing at a distance were Samson and the inseparable Avith and Zattu. They made no attempt to approach, and he allowed himself a smile at their obvious concern.

I am the Prophet and Judge of Israel, he said to them in his mind, wondering if his thoughts were sarcasm or truth. *Do you not know that I am overshadowed by the Hand of God?*

He began walking again, trying to formulate the words of a prayer. But he did not know what to pray for. Two days they had implored Jehovah for victory over their enemies, and two days they had been denied. Samuel could not claim to understand what Jehovah's purpose was anymore. Deep in his heart, his trust in God was still there, unshakeable and sure. He had accepted on some level that there might be a way for God's will to be done that did not involve a victory for Israel against their enemies, although he did not know what form that would take.

Jehovah will not leave his loyal ones, he heard Tirzah's voice saying, a memory from his childhood that had shaped the man he had become. But the passing years had taught him that his initial, childish understanding of that statement did not fit the complex reality of Jehovah's interaction with his people. To truly understand it, he now knew, one must grasp and accept that the accomplishment of Jehovah's will was what mattered, and that the sacrifices made by His followers in pursuit of that accomplishment were the soil in which would grow the blessings of future generations.

And at times, that soil was fertilized with the spilled blood of the faithful.

He wondered abruptly if—

Something slammed into his head and shoulders, a huge, black form descending like a giant bat from somewhere above him, crushing him to the ground. For a confused instant he glimpsed tar-black skin, lines and whorls of tattooed dots, white teeth filed into sharp triangles...

The Hunter shifted, and Samuel felt a painful pressure against his chest and left hip. His mind could not seem to catch up to the reality of what was happening. He heard the Hunter's growl of frustration as the huge, cadaverous figure leapt back from him.

Samuel glanced down and saw that *Mish'eneth* lay across his body; in its center, the tip of the Hunter's cruel knife was embedded. The staff of Ahitub had stopped the deadly thrust from entering Samuel's stomach.

In the same instant he realized that the Hunter was trying to withdraw the blade from where it had become stuck. Samuel had just enough presence of mind to twist the staff as violently as he could, breaking the Hunter's grip on the hilt.

At the same time another form, this one a young man, long braids streaming behind him, hurtled into the Hunter with savage force, roaring with the fury of a cornered lion. Both men tumbled to the forest floor.

The came to their feet a few paces from Samuel, and he crab-crawled backwards as the Hunter faced off against Samson. Samson's sword hung at his hip, but he did not draw it; arms hanging wide, like wrestlers, the two men circled each other.

Avith and Zattu were shouting somewhere to Samuel's left, their voices getting nearer as they rushed to Samson's aid.

The Hunter closed on Samson in a rush, and for a moment Samuel could see only the twisting of two forms, black skin on white, grappling with the animal intensity of mortal combat.

Then, somehow the Hunter got a foot behind Samson's leg and threw him backwards. Samuel winced as Samson's head snapped against a sycamore trunk with an audible *crack* and, eyes rolling back in his head, the young man slid to the dry leaves carpeting the forest floor.

The Hunter had only an instant's respite, though, for at that moment Avith and Zattu closed on him, howling the battle cry of the tribe of Naphtali. Avith's sickle sword slashed savagely at the dark form even as Zattu, protecting his friend with a tall shield in his left hand, lunged at the Hunter with a bronze-headed spear.

The two men fought in perfect synchronization, as swift and coordinated as if they shared a single mind. But as fast as they were, the Hunter was faster. He ducked Avith's blow—the bronze blade hissed past the black head, missing by a hairsbreadth—and caught Zattu's spear shaft between his wiry arm and chest. Spinning left like an acrobat, he swung the arch of his left foot against the shaft just past where Zattu gripped it.

Samuel saw a look of puzzlement cross Zattu's face as he realized that he was suddenly weaponless and that the Hunter now held his spear. He and Zattu turned together, Avith slashing downward before Zattu slipped into his place, shield held out to block the Hunter's riposte.

Unexpectedly, the Hunter rammed his spear into the shield with all of his weight behind it, pushing toward his opponent and downward at the same time. Zattu's shield arm was dragged down until the bottom of the shield hit the ground, exposing the big man's head and shoulders.

The Hunter plucked a brown, grape-sized bead from his necklace with his left hand, crushed it into white powder and flung it into Zattu's face.

The big man stumbled backward, eyes squeezed shut in pain, gasping and choking.

Avith turned so quickly his sickle-sword's blade struck the Hunter's side before Samuel even saw it move, sliding along his ribs and leaving a slender line of crimson in its wake.

Blood ran down the black ribs, but the Hunter seemed not to notice. He released his hold on the spear shaft and leapt to one side. Zattu was two steps away from Avith, and for an instant after his slashing blow, the one-armed man's left side was unprotected.

The Hunter's long, bony leg shot out in a savage kick to Avith's ribs and the Napthalite fell backwards, grunting with pain, legs buckling.

Still blinded, Zattu charged forward, shield held out in front of him like a weapon, the spear shaft jutting out from it like a smooth, white branch.

The Hunter grabbed the butt of the shaft just as it reached him and fell on it, shoving it into the rocky soil at his feet.

The spear stopped abruptly, but Zattu did not. The big man's momentum carried him forward with such force that the spear's tip punched the rest of the way through the split shield and sank into his abdomen below his ribs.

It had happened so quickly, Samuel was still trying to clamber to his feet. He watched Zattu blinking and wiping his eyes with the back of one hand, leaning forward just a little, the big man's weight borne by the spear buried in his stomach. Then he fell sideways and crashed to the ground in silence.

Avith was still on his knees trying to get to his feet, gasping for breath, his open hand spread over the spot where the Hunter's kick had landed against his ribs. The strange, black warrior jerked the spear from Zattu's body and kicked the shattered remnants of the shield off of it. Turning almost slowly, he grinned, showing his pointed white teeth. Then he hurled the spear at the fallen Naphtalian.

It might have finished him, but at the last moment the Hunter's aim was spoiled by a fist-sized rock colliding with the side of his black head. The spear struck Avith's side.

Samuel grabbed a second stone as the Hunter turned toward him, pointed teeth bared in rage.

"Samuel?" Samson's voice startled both the Prophet and the black warrior. Something in his voice sounded so strange, so otherworldly, that even in the midst of their battle both men turned toward the sound of it.

Samson was on his feet again, his shield abandoned on the ground behind him, his sword still sheathed at his side. His eyes were wide in an expression somewhere between fear and wonder.

"Samuel?" He said again, looking not at the Prophet but through him. "It is happening."

59

When Samson had awakened, lying against a tree trunk, for a moment he had had no idea where he was—or even, at first, who he was. He was surprised to find words coming from his lips, a murmured prayer that his mouth seemed to be making without him.

"Help them, Jehovah," he whispered, "Save Your people."

As his identity and his situation came rushing back into his mind, the first thing he noticed was not the fallen forms of Avith and Zattu on the ground nearby; nor was it the skeletal, black form of the Hunter towering angrily over Samuel, who stood in obvious terror with a rock in one hand and his staff in the other.

What he noticed was that everything was happening so slowly.

As though in a dream—at first he thought it was a dream, and that he had not yet awakened from the blow that had rendered him senseless— he saw a horsefly buzzing past his face, but it moved so slowly he could see each beat of its tiny, transparent wings. When he reached for it, he found that he could move at the same speed as always and, effortlessly, plucked it from the air between thumb and forefinger. Its wings continued to beat as it struggled to free itself; Samson could feel each stroke against his fingertips, like the brush of an eyelash on a cheek.

He was on his feet before he even realized it. The Hunter was turning toward Samuel, turning so slowly that he looked as though he were suspended in water, or clear oil.

In that instant Samson *knew*—knew without a doubt that he could pull the oak tree behind him out of the ground by the roots if he wanted to. He did not know how he knew, but he did. Power seemed to throb through him, a tingling force that made him quiver with energy, as though every muscle in his body were about to explode into motion.

"Samuel?" he said, and saw the Prophet's head turn toward him, ever so slowly.

"Samuel—it is happening," he said.

Now the Hunter was moving, plucking the spear from Avith's form. Samson watched with curious detachment as the man turned toward him, his tattooed face a black mask of hatred and rage. He watched as the Hunter lifted the spear, smoothly, expertly, and threw it at him.

The spear slid slowly through the air, spiraling as it came. When it was within reach Samson reached out with his left hand and slapped it away.

As soon as he touched it, the spear's speed changed. Like an arrow released from a Benjaminite's bow, the spear flew high into the grey sky to the west, vanishing from sight above the Plains of Philistia.

Samson laughed, letting the power flow through him. The Hunter was staring at him, his expression changed to one of awe and fear. He reached down—so slowly!—and lifted Avith's sword from the fallen man's hand. Yelling something that Samson could not make out, the Hunter leapt toward Samson, sword raised over his head.

JUDGE OF ISRAEL

60

S amuel only had time to cringe as the Hunter threw Zattu's spear at
Samson. Like everything else he did, the Hunter's throw was perfect, and the polished shaft flew unerringly toward the young man's
chest.

Then Samson moved. Samuel did not see how he moved; it was as
though he *blurred* for a second, the way a hummingbird's wings blur as it
hovers before your eyes. A loud *crack* echoed from the hills around them,
and the spear shot into the western sky so fast Samuel's eye could not follow
it, so far that it vanished in the dull grey of the clouds.

By the time Samuel looked again, the Hunter was flying through the
air toward Samson, Avith's sword clutched in both hands over his head.

Samuel tried to call out a warning, but his voice caught in his dry
throat.

But then Samson *blurred* again, and this time Samuel could make out
a hint, like a vague, translucent outline, of his movements. As the sickle-
sword descended with deadly force toward his head, effortlessly, Samson
reached up and crushed the Hunter's massive hands in his own fist. The
Hunter howled with shock and pain, but his hands, their bones shattered, let

go of the hilt. Somehow, in the same instant, the sword ended up in Samson's hands, its point aimed toward the huge black figure towering over him.

Then Samson *blurred* again and the Hunter's body was lying in three pieces, twitching on the dusty ground.

Samson stood over him, fire smoldering in his eyes, just a hint of his familiar mocking smile curling his lips.

From six paces away, Samuel could *feel* the energy coming off of the young man, washing over him like heat from a fire.

"'And he is the one,'" Samuel whispered, breathless, "'that will deliver the children of Israel out of the hands of the Philistines.'"

Samson's smile broadened and he spun in a circle like a child, his long, black braids swinging. "My father will be glad," he said. His voice sounded as though he were speaking from inside a cave.

Samuel nodded. He saw his friend Samson before him, but he felt as though he was looking at a stranger.

"You are the Hero of Israel," he said.

Then, without warning Samson's face went white and he fell to his knees. Samuel ran over to him, catching him as he began to topple forward onto his face.

"Samson!"

"Water!" Samson croaked, his face still white.

Samuel looked uselessly at the hillside around him. "In camp—I will get you water…"

Samson nodded once, and then his eyes closed and he collapsed in Samuel's arms.

61

"And your offspring will bring blessings to every nation on earth, because you listened to the voice of God."
– The Scroll of Bereshith

The *Beneh* carried Samson down the hillside to his tent. He remained limp and did not wake during the trip; had it not been for his soft, steady breath, he might have been dead.

Samuel discovered to his surprise that Avith was also still alive. The spear had pierced his side, but miraculously appeared to have missed any internal organs. He woke as the *Beneh* began to move him, at first yelping at their every movement. When he saw the still body of Zattu, though, his cries turned to silent tears and he seemed to have forgotten his own pain.

When Samuel returned to the camp, Manoah demanded to speak with him in private. Ducking into Manoah's tent, the big Danite grabbed

Samuel by both shoulders, his eyes bright. "What happened? Did he...what happened with Samson? Avith wounded, Zattu dead, and that big black monster cut to pieces—and my son returns without a scratch on him."

"I cannot say what happened, beyond what you have just described," answered Samuel, deliberately cryptic.

"He was empowered by Jehovah, was he not?" Manoah asked.

"I think that is a question you should ask him when he wakes," Samuel said.

Manoah would have pushed the matter further but Samuel ducked out of the tent to find a scowling Reuel waiting for him. "The diseased one has returned," he said through clenched teeth. "And is demanding an audience with you."

Samuel sighed. "Lead on."

He followed Reuel through the milling soldiers in the valley, moving towards the northwest. Near the edge of the makeshift encampment he found Baghadh waiting for him, flanked by Tahash, Prince Elhanan, and Elishama of Bethel.

There were no formalities. "You will not survive another day's battle," Baghadh said.

"You did not believe we would survive a single day's battle, and after two, still we stand before you," Samuel responded.

"You did not survive—you escaped, and by the skin of your teeth," Baghadh sneered. "And then only by running from the enemy and hiding in the hills. The next time you appear on the field of battle you may not be so fortunate."

"I will put my life in my palm as many times as Jehovah wishes it," said Samuel. "If it is His will to save us, He will do so."

"The Amorites are coming, Samuel," Tahash said. Samuel heard the genuine concern in the young man's voice and saw the corners of Baghadh's mouth curl derisively in response. "They have left Aijalon as a might army and may be here before nightfall."

"Even your faithful followers are beginning to desert you," Baghadh said. "Ask your commanders if you do not believe me—men are slipping away to conceal themselves in the caves of the hills. At least two tribes are ready to leave you in their entirety."

Samuel kept his face still, his body relaxed. He did not want Baghadh to see the anxiety that the diseased man's words engendered in him. He knew that Baghadh would not make such a claim if it were not true. And

And Samuel had no trouble believing it. Walking through the camp, hearing the moans of the burned and seeing their tortured skin, a part of him had wanted to run and hide. He had seen the same unreasoning fear in the eyes of men all around him.

"What do you want, Baghadh?" he said at last.

"We—the armies of Judah, Manasseh, and Ephraim—wish to fight alongside our brothers against our common foe. We wish to join you on the battlefield tomorrow."

"The dead who even now are being eaten by the ravens would say that your timing is poor," Samuel said.

Baghadh stepped closer, pushing his lesioned face to within a handbreadth of Samuel's; the man's spoiled-meat smell filled Samuel's nostrils. "You brought this down on yourself, and on the children of Israel! You and your pride! It did not have to be this way. Now humble yourself, and Jehovah may yet spare you and our people."

Samuel glanced toward Elishama, Tahash, and Prince Elhanan, then back to Baghadh, understanding finally dawning. "You wish to be given command of the army."

"Show the people that you trust in Jehovah's choice as leader!" Baghadh said.

"I have never given Tahash anything but friendship and support," Samuel said.

"Then," said Baghadh, "Demonstrate that support before the people. Give the staff *Mish'eneth* to Tahash and all the tribes of Israel will unite under his leadership."

Mish'eneth. So that is what this is about, though Samuel. Reuel muttered something under his breath, but did not attempt to interject himself into the conversation.

Samuel sent his silent prayer heavenward. *Grant me wisdom, Jehovah. Show me what to do.*

He felt that he received his answer immediately: his thoughts crystallized, and doubt fell away. To give the staff into the hands of Tahash broke no dictate of the Torah; Samuel could give it to anyone he chose. This simple act had the power to heal the schism that divided the children of Israel. It would put tens of thousands more soldiers on the field of battle—and whether or not Jehovah gave them the victory tomorrow, those additional swords could save many lives. More importantly, those men had become unwitting tools in Baghadh's hands. It was not their fault that they had not been there for their brothers. Uniting the tribes would be good for the people, and for their confidence in Jehovah. Stroking Baghadh's and Tahash's egos was a small price to pay for such a victory.

Smiling, he held out the staff to Tahash. "Take it, Tahash. *Mish'eneth* is yours. Remember its history, and try to bear it worthily."

Samuel enjoyed seeing the looks of surprise and glee on the faces of Baghadh, Elishama, and proud Elhanan as Tahash took the staff from his hand. "I will see you tomorrow on the field of battle," Samuel said, and turning on his heel went to check on Samson.

After the cooking fires had died down and the camp was enshrouded in darkness, Baghadh was awakened by a hand on his shoulder. Kicking free of his blanket, he rolled to his feet, casting about in the darkness for a weapon.

"My lord—it is I!" a voice hissed.

Baghadh crawled backwards, still shaking the sleep from his eyes.

"I must talk to you, my lord," said the whispering voice, and Baghadh woke enough to recognize the voice as Tahash's.

"What is going on?" he demanded, as irritated by his own fear as he was by the unexpected visit.

"I must talk to you," Tahash repeated. "Away from the camp."

"Surely this can wait until the light of the day!" Baghadh snapped.

"It cannot, my lord." Tahash paused, sighing heavily in the darkness. "If you will not come with me, then I shall speak of the matter here, in the dark." He shifted a moment, and Baghadh pulled himself to his feet.

"I must return this to the Prophet Samuel," Tahash said, so intensely it sounded almost like anger. He shifted again, and pushed something toward Baghadh. "I cannot keep it."

The light in the tent was more than dim, but it was sufficient for Baghadh to see that the young man held the staff *Mish'eneth* in his hand.

He came fully awake. "You are right, Tahash—we must talk away from the camp!"

He grabbed a cloak and wrapped it around his shoulders. "Follow me—and be silent! Let no one see us leaving."

Baghadh ducked out the tent flap and Tahash followed him. They crept through the silent tents and smoldering remnants of campfires, picking their way through the maze of cords that extended from each tent in a dozen directions.

They managed to get clear of the encampment without being seen and walked by moonlight up the hillside to the north, their footfalls silent in the dew-dampened sandy soil. Baca bushes gave way to sparse forests of oak and sycamore, and their pace slowed as the darkness grew more impenetrable under the cover of the trees.

Tahash finally stopped walking. "I can wait no longer," he said, still speaking quietly, although no longer in a whisper.

Baghadh stopped and turned. "So be it. Let me first tell you—."

"No! Let me speak!" Tahash's voice was sharp. Once again he held out the staff *Mish'eneth*. "I do not know anymore whether or not I have been called by God. I do not know if I have any purpose beyond being yet another of the many sons of my father. But this I do know—I have no right to bear this staff."

Baghadh was silent for a moment. "My dear boy—do not make this decision hastily. Think of the turmoil this will cause now. How will it benefit our people to face this uncertainty...?"

"The truth can do nothing but benefit them!" Tahash said. "How can it not? Samuel is Prophet and Judge, the anointed one of God!"

Baghadh walked a slow circle around the young man. "Perhaps...perhaps you are right."

He heard rather than saw Tahash relax. "Yes, my lord."

Baghadh continued walking. "If Jehovah is behind Samuel, what can we do but support him?"

Tahash's voice pitched higher. "Yes! Think of what we can do united—."

His voice was abruptly stopped by Baghadh's had clamping over his mouth. In the same movement, Baghadh slid his slender dagger into the young man's side, between his ribs.

Tahash bit down on the Manassite's hand and Baghadh nearly screamed. But the young man struggled for only a moment more before sliding to the ground, moaning quietly.

Baghadh let him fall. Tahash landed on his face and Baghadh rolled him over so that he could look the young man in the eyes. Debris from the forest floor was stuck to his cheek, caught in the blood that trickled from the corner of his mouth. "Die in peace, boy. Know that you have fulfilled the purpose for which you were born."

Tahash's eyes looked at him in confusion for a moment, then they went still and flat.

Baghadh knelt and took the staff *Mish'eneth* from Tahash's limp hand. Smiling so broadly that the sores on the corners of his mouth hurt, he shuffled back down the hill toward the dark camp.

62

The news that the tens of thousands of Judah, Ephraim, and Manasseh would join them sent waves of hope through the Israelite army. The following morning Lodan's spies returned with more good news: Phicol had used up all of his supplies of the liquid fire the day before. He had not expected Israel to return to the field of battle.

The clouds were beginning to break up over the Great Sea when the cold, suffused light of dawn filled the grey of the thick haze still hanging heavily over the great desert to the east. For a third time the armies of Israel assembled on the blood-soaked plain between Ekron and Gath, now in their classic tribal battle formation: Judean and Manassite phalanxes of heavy infantry in the center behind the Zebulunite vanguard, mobile Gadite flanks, missile support from the Benjaminites on either rear flank, and the Danite rearguard.

Samson had still not woken when they marched. Samuel had entered his tent in the morning to find Manoah shaking the young man by the shoulders so violently that Samuel had thought he heard Samson's teeth rattling. But his eyes had remained closed, his breath steady and even. Manoah had stormed out of the tent silently, scowling.

The big Danite had taken up his commander's post in the rearguard now, refusing even to talk to Samuel. As he had strode away his dark eyes said that he went to quench the rage in his heart with a deluge of Philistine blood.

"My lord." Reuel had come up behind him and Samuel turned. Reuel stood with a group of the *Beneh*, brow knitted.

"Here I am," said Samuel.

Reuel pointed across the field of battle. "Look, my lord."

Samuel followed his finger to the contingent of Manassites and Ephraimites in the center phalanxes with Judah. It took him only a moment to realize what Reuel was pointing at.

Baghadh sat in an open litter supported by two poles resting on the shoulders of four soldiers. But it was not the rich scarlet cloth or the gold-plated wood of the litter that caught Samuel's eye.

Baghadh was carrying the staff *Mish'eneth*.

"Where is Tahash?" Samuel asked.

Reuel shook his head. "I do not know."

"I do," said Lodan, striding up to them, his weathered face grim. "His body was found this morning on a hill outside Eshtaol."

"He was murdered," Samuel said. It was not a question.

"Stabbed in the back," Lodan confirmed.

What have I done? Samuel thought. *Baghadh may have used Tahash for his twisted purposes, but he also used me. I might as well have put the staff into his hands myself, and the knife into Tahash.*

A runner dressed in shepherd's clothing loped over to Samuel across the matted grass. "My lord? I bring a message from Manoah of Dan."

"Speak your message," Samuel said.

The messenger bowed. "He told me to ask the Prophet: Why the delay? The children of Israel await only your word, and the enemy does not grow smaller nor less prepared with the passing of the day."

Samuel huffed through his nose. "That, indeed, sounds like Manoah." He straightened his shoulders. "Tell your commander that I value his experience in these matters. Tell him also that the army marches on my timetable, not his."

The messenger bowed. "Even as you have said, my lord." He turned and loped back across the field.

After a moment's pause, Lodan murmured, "Manoah is not wrong, my lord."

Samuel turned to face the Issacharian. "No, he is not." He turned to the leader of his Levite guard, a hard-bitten veteran named Ochran. "Take whatever men you need and take Baghadh away from the battle. Bind his hands and leave a trustworthy guard to watch over him."

Ochran nodded sharply. "Even as you have said, my lord."

The Levite turned to leave but Samuel called after him: "Ochran!"

He looked back. "My lord?"

"Be careful. Do not underestimate him."

Ochran nodded and smiled. "I will not, my lord."

As he left, Samuel forced Tahash's death and Baghadh's betrayal out of his mind and turned to face Lodan. "Sound the trumpets."

The horns rang out, stark and brazen in the quiet of morning. The army surged forward to the thundering of countless footfalls, the rattling of harness and scale mail, and the thrum of swords and spears drumming on taut leather shields. The battle-cries of the twelve tribes burst from thousands of mouths, a cacophony of courage and determination beneath standards fluttering in a fresh sea breeze.

Their cries were answered. On the other side of the field of battle the Philistine army also began to move, a wave of armored bodies, horses, and chariots riding on the crest of its own rage.

Both armies built speed; the vanguards rushed across the bloodsoaked field toward one another, weapons glinting in the red light of dawn. Then the sky went dark again with myriads of arrows and stones, raining indiscriminate death onto both sides.

Samuel saw Israelites falling as they charged, collapsing to the ground in stunned surprise as hundreds of rushing feet passed them by or trampled them, unable to give thought or care to the fallen.

The lines closed, the roar built to a crescendo, and the two vanguards threw their spears. Almost as fast as the deadly shafts spiraled through the air, the men who had thrown them followed.

They collided with a muffled crunch. The men of Zebulun, their thinned ranks reinforced now with the best Judean and Ephraimite soldiers, took the brunt of the collision, and for a moment the mass of both armies ground to a halt in a tangle of limbs and weapons.

The Philistine force still outnumbered the Israelites by at least two to one, but somehow the Israelites threw the enemy back onto their own dead. Both sides regrouped, more Judeans moving forward to take the places of the felled Zebulunites, and the Philistines charged again

The Zebulunites fought back with uncanny skill and bravery, but even those who refused to retreat were simply carried from their feet by the onrush of Philistines and pushed inexorably backwards. The savage battle cry of the Gadites rang out over the other sounds of battle and Shaga and Cosam led charges in from either side, bolstering their brothers. Again, they threw the Philistines back. Gadites and Asherites threw themselves nearly under the whirling scythe-wheels of the chariots to hamstring the horses. Chariots toppled or ground to a halt, forming a sharp-edged blockade in the midst of the Philistine charge.

The Philistines retreated then, for a moment, and both sides took the opportunity to drag away the bodies and weapons of the fallen, but not out of respect. They had no choice but to move them as quickly as possible or risk tripping over them in the heat of battle.

Then the Philistine frontlines coalesced again, and this time they took a new shape, a fell and fearful shape that carried with it a terror that Samuel could feel even from his position behind the rearguard.

Three rows of scythe-wheeled chariots moved forward until they formed the center of the vanguard. Each was pulled by a pair of stallions, their black leather harnesses studded with spikes jutting out in every direction. In each chariot rode a well-armored driver and two Gedhudhra, armed with spears, swords, and shields.

On either flank towered companies of Rephaim in coats of scale mail, bronze helmets, and bronze greaves; they cradled axes in their gnarled fists and thick-shafted javelins sprouted from quivers on their backs.

A Philistine horn blew, and Samuel saw the Israelite front lines compress, bracing for the charge. It was not enough. The chariot-horses reared, hooves flailing. Judeans threw their spears, but the horse's necks, chests, and underbellies were encased in boiled leather and bronze armor and few missiles found their marks. The Israelite infantry could do nothing but flee from the whirling scythes on the chariots. And when they fled, right or left, they met the advancing Rephaim, their massive axes swinging. Mighty warriors leapt to meet the giants, shields held out before them, but were swept away as if they were children and their weapons playthings.

The rest of the Philistine army surged forward behind the Gedhudhra, armored shock troops carrying swords of iron that bit deeply into the Israelites' bronze blades and clove their leather armor. Their sheer mass built a momentum that drove their enemies before them like foam before the crest of a wave.

Samuel saw Gadites slashing wildly at the legs of the chariot-steeds as they passed, but more often than not they were caught by the whirling scythes before they could leap clear. Dozens died beneath the wheels.

The Israelite line broke in several places at once and Samuel had the call to fall back sounded. The Danite rearguard moved forward even as the rest of the army slipped through their ranks to try to reform a little farther to the north. For a few moments, the Danites held back the wave, but then the ferocity of the Gedhudhra and the power of the Rephaim overwhelmed them, and the Danites, too, fell back in a hurried retreat. Zebulunites and Gadites rushed to their aid, pulling together the shattered remnants of the army into a semblance of a defensive line again.

From his position, Samuel could just see the front lines: Manoah, roaring, his iron sword swinging furiously; Shaga as savage as a wild animal, tangled hair flying; Cosam the Asherite spinning, curved knives in both hands; Jedaiel launching sling stones faster than the eye could follow, felling men with every shot.

It was not enough. Mighty as the heroes of Israel were, they were surrounded on all sides by the unstoppable sweep of Rephaim axes and the deadly skill of the Gedhudhra. No one could withstand the furious charge of the chariot stallions, their wild eyes flashing white over their blood-spattered noses.

Samuel was so engrossed that he failed to hear the galloping of a horse behind him. He did not turn until Lodan's voice at his shouldered startled him into jumping back.

Lodan's face was white, and not just with exhaustion. "My lord...the Amorites..."

Samuel felt his heart sink within him, but kept his face impassive. *I am a tree. I cannot be moved.*

"They will ride onto the field of battle in less time than it takes to eat a good meal," the Issacharian said. Samuel could see the man's pulse beating in a vein on his throat. "They come swiftly, well-armed and provisioned, from the northeast."

Another roar went up from the army and both Samuel and Lodan turned to see its cause. Once again, the Philistines were steadily pushing the Israelites back. Cosam fell to a Rephaim axe, and did not rise again. The Israelite flanks curled back, farther and farther.

The Benjaminites released an endless hail of arrows and stones into the attackers, and many fell. But for each Philistine that lay silent on the grass, two moved to take his place. Even as they watched, two companies comprised of hundreds upon hundreds of Philistine infantrymen broke away from the main body of the battle and raced, broad shields held ahead of them, toward the archers and slingers. Countless soldiers fell to the skill of the Benjaminites, but they seemed willing to sacrifice themselves heedlessly to accomplish their goal.

Only moments had passed when the first of the Philistine infantrymen reached the Benjaminites in their defensive positions. The slingers and archers dropped their missile weapons and took up their swords and spears to grapple with their attackers at short range.

Without the cover of the Benjaminite missiles, the number of Philistines driving against Israel grew rapidly, in strength and in numbers. The Israelite line buckled, stretched, but held.

Then from the Philistine's eastern flank Phicol appeared, standing behind the driver in a massive scythe-wheeled chariot pulled by four black stallions. On either side of him crowded black-clad Gedhudhra on foot, snarling hunting hounds straining at their leashes, and a half a dozen Rephaim. Avoiding the carnage at the center of the battle lines, Phicol led the group to the eastern flank.

Samuel saw immediately what he was doing. The mightiest warriors had moved toward the center of the line, reinforcing their brothers where the attack was strongest. Phicol's contingent slammed into the eastern flank and instantly smashed it into oblivion.

Again, Samuel had the call to fall back sounded. He fought feelings of frantic desperation that seemed to be clawing at the back of his neck. Inexplicably, his father's face suddenly appeared in his mind: silent, white, and cold.

Manoah, Shaga, and Jedaiel fought desperately to hold some semblance of order as the Israelite forces retreated, dodging scythe-wheeled chariots, pounding hooves, and the fangs of dozens of unleashed hounds. The defensive lines broke apart; men ran for their lives, heedless of anything but escaping the machine of death that threatened to consume them.

The Philistines built momentum as the Israelites began their flight in earnest. The Levite guards were beginning to urge Samuel from the field, arranging their own defenses to usher him safely to cover.

Then, above the raging cacophony of battle, Samuel heard another sound: the drumming of hundreds of hooves, the piercing notes of battle cries hurled defiantly into the morning air.

He turned, back toward the northeast, in the direction toward which the Israelites were fleeing.

Over a low rise came another army, a motley group of farmers, herders, and miners, half of them mounted, sickles, pruning hooks, bills, axes, and knives in their hands. They raged down the low rise toward the fleeing Israelites.

The Amorites had come.

The Israelites were pinned between two enemies.

There was no escape.

63

Reuel was beside Samuel now, pulling at his *me'il*, urging him away with panicked words that reached Samuel's ears but not his mind. He felt no fear, only confusion, only a sense that the world had suddenly become a place that he did not understand.

He watched with curious detachment as the army of the Amorites rushed toward the battle. The Israelites begin to mill in the plain before him, turning this way and that, some fleeing to the east and west, others standing in defeat, or laying down their weapons and getting on their knees in a plea for a mercy they knew would not be shown.

The Philistine juggernaut plowed forward and, as the heart went out of their opponents, more Israelite bodies cluttered the bloodied plain.

The Amorites poured onto the battlefield, weapons held high, screaming their battle cries. In moments they closed on the rear of the Israelite force.

But they did not attack.

Rushing through the fleeing and surrendering Israelites, they ignored the sons of Israel who parted for them in terror, piercing their ranks in dozens of places, like a flood let loose over a plain divides into rivulets between islands of dry soil.

In moments they had reached the line between Israel and Philistia. Battle cries ringing out, they threw themselves savagely at the Philistines.

Samuel barely had time to wonder at what was happening. Even as the first Amorite soldiers engaged the enemy, a richly dressed young man galloped up to Samuel and his guards on a white horse, flanked by four well armed guards.

The Levites formed a tight circle around Samuel, spear-butts braced against the ground, muscles taut.

The young man held up his right hand, palm forward. "Hold! I mean the Prophet Samuel no harm."

To Samuel's shock, Reuel pushed through the Levite guard and ran forward toward the young man, arms spread in greeting. "Jiram!"

The richly dressed Amorite prince that Reuel had called Jiram smiled down at him. "Reuel. I am glad to see you made it safely back to your master—and that you survive still."

"And I you," Reuel said, grasping Jiram's hand in both of his own. He gestured toward the Prince's guard and the army still rushing behind him. "But what is the meaning of this?"

Jiram smiled and turned back to Samuel. "I am, as you have heard, Jiram, Prince and heir to the kingdom of the Amorites."

Reuel took three stumbling steps backward, mouth and eyes opened wide.

"Your servant once came to my aid in a time of dire need," Jiram continued. "He rescued me from certain and torturous death. Today I bring men loyal to me to pay back the debt I owe him."

Samuel turned to Reuel. "You did not tell me you had saved the life of a prince of the Amorites."

Reuel threw up his hands, looking as though he had been caught in some sin. "By the life of my soul, my lord—until this very moment, I did not know who he was!"

Prince Jiram laughed. "We will talk again after the battle, if we survive." He glanced over his shoulder at the melee. "Our numbers will help, but we will need to break the might of the Rephaim and the cursed Gedhudhra. And that no one has ever been able to do."

"No one except for my master," Reuel said.

"Except for the Judge of Israel," Lodan added.

Jiram looked over his shoulder at the melee. "May he do so again. I must return to my men. Whatever plan you have to defeat these deadly foes, show it soon!"

He turned and galloped off, flanked by his four guards.

The arrival of the Amorites had driven the Philistines away from the Benjaminite slingers and archers, and the latter had once again begun raining missiles down on the heads of their enemies. The size of the Philistine army worked against them—their own archers were, for the most part, kept out of range by the presence of the infantry and cavalry.

Rallying his men to him, Shaga the Gadite raged into the middle of the battle once again, his spear whirling and thrusting in every direction. The Zebulunites fell in behind him, forming a tight triangle that pushed deep into the enemy lines. Into the void left behind them rushed the Asherite knife-men and the newly-arrived Amorite cavalry.

The Philistines tried to close the gap but could not. The Gedhudhra found themselves face to face with Shaga's wild Gadites, fighting alongside the Zebulunites, Manoah, and Kish who had come down from the Benjaminite positions to join the front lines. The battle raged north, then south, each side fighting with the heedless fury that is born only from the primal urge to survive. One, then two of the Rephaim were felled by teams of Gadite spearmen working together, but then the giants gathered into pairs that proved a match for even a dozen of the wild hill-men.

But with each passing moment more Amorites rushed onto the field, and slowly, inexorably, the Philistines were pushed back, only to regroup and be pushed back further still.

"What is he doing?" Lodan said, and Samuel followed his gaze to a section of the front lines.

Phicol drove his chariot toward the far eastern edge of the battling troops. Samuel heard complex combinations of horn blasts over the din of battle, and men among the Philistines responded. The Gedhudhra fell back and allowed regular infantry to take their place. Slipping through their own men, they moved to join the noseless commander.

The Rephaim did the same, followed closely by the chariot teams, the Philistines parting to allow the whirling scythes room to pass. The Gedhudhra charioteers did not always wait for their path to be clear—Samuel saw more than one Philistine soldier cut down. The hounds, too, were summoned.

Lodan was the first to realize what was happening. "Call the Danite rearguard to us! To us!" he shouted at one of his runners. The young man sped away.

Samuel turned to him in confusion. Lodan did not have time to respond. "Move us toward the rearguard!" he ordered the Levite spearmen. "Keep your formation!"

"Closer to the fighting?" one of the Levites asked.

"Just do as I command!" Lodan roared.

It was only then that Samuel saw what the Issacharian feared. While the mass of Philistine soldiers at the front lines continued to engage the Israelites, keeping them distracted and unaware of what was happening on their eastern flank, Phicol swiftly assembled a deadly series of phalanxes: charioteers, Gedhudhra foot, Rephaim, hounds and houndsmen. The most powerful and fell warriors of his army gathered into a tight knot and, with the swiftness of the wind over the tops of the grass, rushed west and north, toward the rear of the Israelite army.

Towards Samuel.

Lodan's sword hissed from its scabbard; Samuel heard him whispering a desperate prayer. Reuel and the *Beneh* clutched what few weapons they had and got behind the Levite guard, who waited with braced spears for the Philistines to arrive.

But they were too few, too weak. Samuel knew with no shadow of a doubt that Phicol's death squad could effortlessly smash not only the Levite guard, but virtually any defense that could be mustered against them. Phicol had seen what was happening and made the desperate decision of the defeated: to risk all to kill the enemy's leader.

He glanced back toward the front lines as Lodan sent another runner after the first. Even if they could get a message to the commanders on the front lines, there was no way those commanders could fight their way back to Samuel, not without losing hundreds or even thousands of their own men in the process. The Gadite flanks had been absorbed into the body of the army now, as well, and the Benjaminites could not withdraw from the protected positions from which they fired upon the enemy.

That left only the Danite rearguard. They were nearly as far away now as the rapidly approaching Philistines, and they were just beginning to realize the danger. But Samuel could see by their hesitancy that they were unable to form a unified response. Their commander, Manoah, was at the front lines, his own rage and hunger for vengeance having driven him to abandon his tribe and position.

Some of the Danites began rushing to intercept Phicol's attack, but halfheartedly. Even had the entire tribe's warriors gathered in a well-organized, well-planned defense, they would have likely been unable to stop the savage charge that hurtled toward Samuel. Fragmented and lacking direction, Phicol would scatter them like sheep.

Samuel turned toward Reuel. The young man was looking at him with hopeful wonder in his eyes. He did not speak, but he did not have to. Samuel heard the words that he, and all the others gathered around him, were thinking as loudly as if they had shouted them in unison.

How will you save us, Prophet of Israel?

He turned away, unable to face their confidence. For the first moment since the days following his father's death, he experienced a moment of serious doubt. Had he deluded himself? Had he misread the meaning of the salvation which Jehovah had granted to His people at Mizpah? Had he been, all this time, following not the will of God, but his own pride?

The Philistines rushed closer; the hollow thunder of hooves on the ground seemed to travel up Samuel's legs to his spine. At last, other commanders in the Israelite army had seen what was happening and were trying to come to Samuel's defense. But the tens of thousands of Israel were bound up with their enemy on three sides. In some cases, disengaging meant dying; in others, there was no way for the soldiers to make their way back through their brothers in time to reach Samuel and his companions.

"We must flee!" Lodan said, herding the *Beneh* backwards as if they were wayward children.

Samuel did not move. "No, Lodan. We cannot flee. How long will we elude mounted warriors and chariots on flat ground?"

"Longer than if we stand here!" Lodan said.

Samuel ignored him. He heard the murmured prayers of the Levites; some of them were looking skyward now. Samuel did not know if it was simply a turning of their faces to Jehovah, or if they were searching for a divine lightning storm coming to destroy their enemies.

There will be no storm, Samuel thought. *There will be no splitting of the earth to swallow up those who ride against us.* He did not know how he knew, but he felt it with certainty, as though the truth of it were written in his bones.

A few dozen Gadites were racing across the plains toward them, moving so swiftly it looked as though they would beat Phicol and his death squad to Samuel's position. But it did not matter, Samuel knew. The Gadites were unequalled warriors, but even hundreds of them could not hope to stop a charge of chariots, Rephaim, and Gedhudhra. Even if the Zebulunite weapons masters could somehow have broken free from the middle of the fiercest fighting and come to their aid, it would not have been enough.

The dark warriors who descended on Samuel and his companions were among the most deadly ever to walk the land of Canaan. And they had nothing to lose.

Samuel wanted to pray, but he could not think of the words.

At last he raised his arms and face heavenward. All eyes turned toward him in silence.

"May our deaths support Your great Purpose, O Jehovah," he said. "And Remember all who on this field offered up the greatest sacrifice."

He did not dare look at the faces around him now. He knew what he would find: Terror. Disbelief. Shock.

"Do you want a sword, my lord?" Lodan asked him, and Samuel just shook his head, smiling. They were beyond the help of swords.

He could see the faces of the Gedhudhra now, and of the Rephaim: blood-spattered, masked in rage—faces that reflected the endless hunger of the grave. The Gadites arrived, breathless and filthy with gore, and took up positions alongside the Levites, a pitiful fraction of what was needed to stop the coming charge.

Phicol raised his sword and roared, and the rest of the Philistines roared alongside him.

Samuel realized that he was not afraid to die. In some ways it was a relief to know that his struggles, his fears and worry, were over forever.

The Gadites and Levite guard began to scream, bracing for impact.

Then, from the corner of his eye, Samuel saw a figure streak toward them from the north, a single man running faster than Samuel had ever seen a man run before, faster than a horse at gallop, faster than a storm wind from the heights of Ammon and Moab.

The man seemed almost to appear rather than arrive, stopping on the dry, matted grass between the Levite guard and the oncoming Philistines, a lone figure standing unafraid before the hundreds of warriors descending furiously down on him.

TIMOTHY WILKINSON

He tossed his head and Samuel saw his long braids shaken across his broad back.

It was Samson.

64

The first of the enemy to reach Samson were a dozen hunting hounds, snarling, lean bodies leaping through the air with drooling mouths open. Samson caught the two nearest by their lithe throats, one in each hand, and swung their bodies like flails so furiously he sent the rest flying, crushed and broken.

Close behind them was a two-horse chariot bearing three Gedhudhra. The horses reared and their flailing hooves descended on the young man.

Moving so fast he seemed to blur before their eyes, Samson caught the front hooves of the horses, one in each hand. The horses screamed in terror, and Samuel could see the great muscles in their chests knotting as they tried to free themselves from Samson's grip. It was useless. Shoulder muscles bulging, Samson heaved upward and away.

The horses flew backward into the air, rotating on their yoke around the chariot wheels, spinning upward like a giant spoke, flipping the vehicle and then crashing, horses upside-down, atop three more approaching chariots.

The Philistine charge broke, men and horses scrambling clear of the shattered wood and broken bodies that lay in a confused tangle on the field. Samson did not hesitate. Iron sword now clutched in one hand, in two bounds he leapt the overturned chariot and the still-thrashing horses and landed in the middle of the Gedhudhra.

Howling, they raised their weapons and came for him.

Howling, he transformed into a bladed whirlwind before their eyes.

In the length of a breath a dozen Gedhudhra fell, dying. Spinning, Samson backhanded three others and the men hurtled into their companions as though they had been kicked by an aurochs. Battle-hardened warriors did not even have time to swing their blades at him before the found themselves falling, staring in stunned disbelief at fatal wounds that seemed to have appeared spontaneously on their bodies. A knot of the deadly warriors locked shields and rushed at Samson as one; the Danite pulled a wheel from one of the chariots, snapping the axle as though it were a twig, and hurled the disc at them. It collided with the wall of shields and they and their bearers crumpled like a wasp's nest struck by a slung stone.

Then one of the Rephaim descended on him, huge axe swinging, its handle as tall as Samson himself. The Danite caught the axe mid-swing, grabbing its thick haft in his left hand just below the blade. Roaring, the giant tried to jerk it away only to find himself staring in confusion at his abruptly empty hands. Samson held the axe for only an instant before flipping it in the air, catching it by the far end of the handle, and hurling it at the approaching horsemen. Whirling sideways, it smashed half a dozen warriors from their mounts before landing with crushing force in the middle of a group of infantrymen.

In the same movement, he wrenched a spear from one of the crushed charioteers and threw it completely through the Rephaim.

Desperation drove the death squad now. Two more chariots galloped furiously at the Danite, having worked their way around the wreckage. At the same time two more Rephaim giants closed, axes already swinging.

Samson tore a spear from the hands of a dead Philistine lying at his feet and hurled it toward one of the Rephaim. It pierced his chest and the giant had time only to blink once before he crashed to the ground.

The Danite turned and sprang like a lion, landing between the two horses of one of the approaching chariots. Grabbing the yoke, he lifted it as though it were a flagpole and the chariot its lofted flag, and brought it crashing down on the other Rephaim's head. That giant, too, collapsed amidst an explosion of splintering wood and smashed bodies.

The second chariot closed. Samson crouched and leapt into the air, clearing horses, chariot, and all and landing like a cat behind the vehicle. The three Philistine warriors inside were dead before they had time to turn around.

Half a dozen Gedhudhra threw their spears in unison, the shafts hissing towards Samson from every direction. Samuel did not see what the Danite did—it was too fast for the eye to follow. But an instant later spear fragments were shattering away from him and toward the throwers.

Now even the Gedhudhra approached warily, shields raised, using their chariots as cover, keeping in the long shadows of the Rephaim.

It made no difference. Samson hurtled toward them, hardly seeming to touch the ground. Stretched like a leopard in mid-leap, sword extended before him, he was swinging even before he landed. Wood-and-leather shields were shredded, layered bronze armor pierced as though it were made of linen. Samuel watched in stunned disbelief as men fell, and flew, tossed through the air like twigs. Samson stepped under the downward stroke of a Rephaim axe, raising one fist so that the thigh-thick haft collided against his knuckles; the handle shattered like kindling broken over a man's knee. Samson caught the head end as it fell and buried it in the giant's chest, then whirled in time to step between a team of charging horses and, placing one hand on each of their manes, shove them to the ground with such force that their front legs snapped beneath them. The chariot came to an abrupt stop and its two occupants flew over the front of the vehicle toward the harness. Samson batted them aside as though they were moths. The men flew, broken, through the air and crumpled to the ground twenty paces away.

In their dispassionate way, the Rephaim turned and left the battlefield, striding silently off toward the west. Abandoned by the giants, the Gedhudhra drew their ranks closer together and began easing away from the unstoppable madman that they faced.

Samuel could see Phicol's face. Even through the inflamed scar tissue that twisted and marred his features, through the blood and dirt and sweat that streaked his skin, the Prophet could see the young man's anger.

Phicol wheeled his chariot around and led the Philistines rushing away from Samson and the heaps of shattered bodies lying silently in a circle around him.

Samson watched them go for only an instant, shoulders and chest heaving. Then he picked up a spear and ran, head down, toward the front lines of the battle.

The Danite rearguard had seen what he had done; they parted and let him pass through their ranks, and the rest of the army followed their example.

Still standing in shocked awe, Samuel could not see Samson himself when he disappeared into the horde of battling warriors. Instead he saw a convulsion in the middle of the front lines when the Hero of Israel arrived, followed by the sight of bodies hurtling through the air. The Philistine line broke; the soldiers turned and ran in abject terror back toward the south. Their battle cries ringing out once again, the tribes of Israel followed Samson in the pursuit, sweeping their enemies from the field until all had fallen or disappeared from the plain into the horizon to the south.

The tremors of the battle faded into the distance. Samuel and those around him stood now in a field of silence but for the sound of the flies and the carrion birds flapping their wings and cawing raucously over the dead.

Samuel looked across the bloodied field, covered in unmoving shapes that, if he squinted just a little, could have been nothing more than stones scattered haphazardly among the reddened grass.

65

When the last of the Philistines had disappeared into the south, Samson once again collapsed into death-like sleep. He was borne on a litter on the shoulders of his brothers back to the site of the battle, where the armies of Israel gathered once again at Samuel's summons.

The sun's last rays were still clinging to the horizon and the stars were opening in the east when the chieftains were finally assembled. Of those who had marched from Mizpah and Aphek many had survived. Old Bocheru's body was embalmed in linen and spices, to be borne to his city of Kitron for burial. Avith likewise had prepared the body of Zattu and seemed anxious only to return home to Naphtali.

Shemer of Reuben still lived. Cosam's body, hacked almost beyond recognition, was recovered from the mounded dead. Barzel the Simeonite was still on his feet, alongside Prince Elhanan of Judah, Dathan of Ephraim, and Baghadh from Manasseh.

Both Kish and Ner had survived. Kish's nearly bare torso was criss-crossed with a web of red cuts that he seemed not to notice. Lodan and Manoah, too, joined the gathering beneath the light of the rising moon.

Jiram, Prince of the Amorites, stood off to the side, deliberately separating himself from the tribal commanders. A bloodied bandage wrapped the upper part of his left arm.

Before Samuel could even speak Baghadh stepped forward. "Praise Samson, who has delivered us from our enemies with a strong arm!"

The commanders began to cheer, but Samuel roared so loudly that he cut them short: "No! Praise Jehovah, for it is He who appointed Samson, and God alone who gave this victory into our hands."

Nodding, the men shouted toward the lights of heaven: "Praise Jehovah of Armies! Praise Him with great praise!"

Baghadh waited for the cheering to stop. Holding the staff *Mish'eneth* prominently in front of him, he raised his nose. "Perhaps now Samuel will see fit to tell us who will lead Israel when he returns to his duties in Ramathaim."

"Samuel is our Judge," someone shouted.

"There is some truth in Baghadh's words," Samuel said, raising his voice. "Let it be known that from this day there will be two Judges in Israel."

Baghadh was stepping forward and beginning to bow as Samuel finished his announcement: "Samuel ben Elkanah of the tribe of Levi, and Samson ben Manoah of the sons of Dan!"

The crowd erupted in cheers, but Baghadh's face went white beneath the red lesions. His eyes blazed. "Do not toy with me, Samuel!" he snarled. Turning to address the crowd, he held up the staff. "I am the bearer of *Mish'eneth*, the staff of the High Priest! It is I who united the tribes of Israel again—a unity that bought us this victory as much as did the heroism of the boy Samson!"

Samuel glared. "Have I not said to you, Baghadh: It is Jehovah who chooses the Judges in Israel? Jehovah—not you, nor I! I think that not a man here honestly doubts that Samson has been chosen by God. But as for you—I do not think there is a man here who does *not* doubt it."

"Be careful, Samuel!" Baghadh snapped. "No man, be he Prophet, Priest, or Judge, can besmirch the name of Baghadh with impunity!"

Samuel felt his anger like heat behind his eyes, tickling his nose. He took a step toward Baghadh. "And what would Tahash, the son of Avdon, have to say about Baghadh's name? What would he say, if he was not brought to silence by a traitor into whose hands he foolishly put his life?"

"You cannot be suggesting that I had anything to do with that young man's death!" Baghadh's eyes narrowed and his head began to bob faster. "Everyone is well aware that I treated him like a son!"

"No doubt. And do you have any living sons?" Samuel asked.

Baghadh gathered his robes about him. "I will not stay here to be slandered by this upstart! Men of Israel! I am Baghadh, Elder of the tribe of Manasseh, trusted advisor to our fallen commander, uniter of the fractured tribes, bearer of the High Priest's staff of office! I do not willingly leave your company. But I will show forbearance to you, until you come to appreciate what I have done for you here today. But I leave you with this: beware Samuel!"

Ahimelech stepped forward and faced the lesioned Elder, their faces only a pace apart. "You may hold my father's staff in your hands," he said. "But history will remember this victory as belonging to Samuel, the Judge of Israel."

Baghadh whirled in a rage and strode away from the circle, disappearing in moments into the darkening night.

Samuel waited until the sound of his footfalls had faded, then turned to Jiram. "Prince of the Amorites—come forward."

Jiram took two steps forward and bowed. "I congratulate you on your victory over our common foe."

Samuel nodded. "The grievances between our two peoples are ancient; they flow through our blood. Though every man here appreciates what you have done for us this day, I cannot declare the conflict between our nations ended. But let it be proclaimed again among the sons of the Amorites: to any man who chooses to turn away from the gods of Canaan, and to serve Jehovah whole souled, he will become our brother. His cause will be our cause, and our Law his Law."

Jiram bowed again. "And for my part—I do hereby decree that for as long as I am ruler of my people, there will be peace between us, unless the sons of Israel break that peace."

"So be it," said Samuel. "Farewell, Prince Jiram. Be assured that no act of kindness toward His people goes unnoticed by our God. May His blessings overtake you."

Jiram turned and vanished into the shadows. His voice seemed to float on the darkness, calling to his commanders to prepare to leave.

Samuel turned back to the leaders of the tribes of Israel. "As for us—tomorrow we will bury our dead, and offer sacrifices to Jehovah in gratitude for this victory. Lodan—let runners be sent from Dan to Beersheba and from the desert to the sea , proclaiming to our people and to any others who will listen that Jehovah has once again given victory into the hands of His people."

Lodan nodded. "Even so, my lord."

"As for the rest of us," Samuel continued. "Sleep, if you can. The power of the sons of Philistia has been broken. The sun rises tomorrow on a new Israel."

Judge of IsraeL

66

As soon as dawn's light had chased the deepest shadows from the road, Baghadh and his entourage headed north toward his home. He left as quickly as possible, afraid of having to face another confrontation with Samuel when the Prophet's position was so strong and his own, for some inexplicable reason, had become so weak.

He sat inside his litter, its linen curtains hanging all around him to shield him from the sun and heat. Clutched tightly in both hands was *Mish'eneth*. He found comfort in the presence of the staff. Even though it had thus far not bought him the respect he deserved, he felt confident that in the near future, when the memory of the battle was not so raw in people's minds, that they would recognize the true significance of his possessing it.

After all, he reflected, the High Priest was the most powerful man in Israel. Next to him in authority were the Judges. And he had been given the High Priest's sign of power from the hands of a Judge.

He sighed and leaned back in his litter, thinking about the comforts of home that awaited him: wine, good food, and his women; perhaps a hot bath in rose water. Samuel might think that he had won, but Baghadh knew differently. He was smarter than the Prophet, and always had been. His plans were deep, rooted in the most primal fears and hopes of the people around him. And, unlike Samuel, he had the gold and silver needed to put any of those plans into action.

It was unfortunate that he had lost his position of strength with the Philistines. As far as he knew, all of his contacts were dead. Then again, he mused, he was not sure if he really wanted to be in bed with Phicol. The young commander seemed little more than a madman with a sword. Baghadh suffered no illusions that Phicol would not just as soon kill him as look at him.

But there were many powerful men in Israel who still owed him for money loaned, for favors granted, for dark secrets kept. When he was ready to challenge Samuel, he had no doubts that he would find all the support that he needed to do so.

Shouts from outside the litter startled him, and the bearers jolted to a halt. "What is it?" Baghadh shouted.

There was no response, except for further shouting that quickly transformed into screams of terror. Baghadh grabbed the curtains to push them aside and look for himself when his litter was abruptly dropped and he crashed to the rocky ground of the road.

Pain lanced through his right foot and he screamed. He had landed on his toes, folding them in half under the crushing weight of his body, snapping all five bones in his foot simultaneously.

Fighting waves of claustrophobia and nausea, he clawed his way free of the tangle of linen that clung to his head and limbs as though it were a living thing intent on strangling him.

He emerged into the light and saw his blood smeared on the rocks where he had skinned his knees, hands, and elbows when he fell.

People were fleeing past him—his people, his servants and the soldiers he had hired to escort him home. He turned this way and that, searching for the source of their fear.

Steadily, deliberately, a lion loped down the opposite bank of the road toward him. It was a huge creature, the biggest lion he had ever seen, grizzled and black-maned and marked with a long scar that ran down one side of its tawny muzzle. The scar gave the beast a sinister look, as though its only purpose was indiscriminate slaughter.

Baghadh got halfway to his feet and collapsed again, scrambling backwards on hands and knees away from the beast, his vision misting red with the pain of every movement. He heard himself yelling words, but was not aware what they were. The men around him who were not fleeing stood in mute terror, some with weapons clutched in white-knuckled hands.

"Stop him, you fools!" he screamed, finally getting his feet under him. He hopped backwards, leaning heavily on *Mish'eneth*, working back through the frozen soldiers. Every movement was a jolt of agony, pain lancing through his leg and body so intensely it threatened to render him unconscious.

The lion sauntered across the road and sniffed at the ruined litter. The crowd of people shifted away from the beast, deeper into the undergrowth, some overcoming their fear enough to run heedlessly up or down the road.

The lion looked up from the litter, opened its mouth and roared.

The sound shook the world. Hardened soldiers fled like frightened children. Baghadh clawed at the string of amulets around his neck, hands shaking. "Pidray, daughter of lightning—save me!"

The lion turned from the litter and sauntered toward him.

"Tallay, daughter of the dew! Arsay, goddess of the soil—aid me now, I beg you!"

The string holding the amulets broke, spilling jeweled idols and charms across his lap and into the undergrowth at his feet. He bent to pick them up, feeling hopelessly confused, then let them lie and continued lurching backwards.

At least a dozen people now stood between Baghadh and the monstrous cat. Some of them were young men, almost children, their legs frozen by fear.

Somewhere beneath Baghadh's terror a tiny hope blossomed. If he just kept moving backwards, the lion would be occupied with those who stood between them. He just had to get as many people as possible between himself and...

The lion looked up from the ground, its golden eyes lazy and sad, as though its predatory life was an exhausting burden.

Those eyes fixed on Baghadh.

He told himself that it could not be, that it was only a trick of his mind in the cold clutch of fear. But the lion's gaze did not break. It blinked once, languorously, and then padded his direction.

Baghadh tried to run, stumbling backwards, lurching with pain and terror. He heard the sound of a child's shrill screaming and then realized it was his own voice.

"Ugar, goddess of fields! Protect me, your faithful servant!"

The lion wove harmlessly through the quivering people standing between Baghadh and the road. The great beast moved past some of them so nearly they could have reached out quivering hands and brushed his black mane as he passed.

"No! No! No!" Baghadh shouted. "Ba'al! Dagon, father of all! Please, help me!" He fell over backwards and almost vomited at the pain that shook him. Something hot and wet irritated his thighs and he looked down in confusion to discover that he had urinated all over himself.

He heard himself calling out to Jehovah, but the words sounded foreign in his mouth, as empty and meaningless as he knew they were.

He crab-crawled backward, entering a grove of young trees growing from a moist, green patch of ground. The lion was moving more quickly now, loping past the last of Baghadh's servants, guards, and bearers, its cold eyes still fixed on a single goal.

Baghadh's unbroken foot caught on a root and he went down in a heap, rolling onto his back as quickly as he could and clawing at the ground on either side with his hands and elbows.

Then his vision seemed to collapse until he saw only the massive head of the lion looming over him and smelled its fetid breath. He shook so badly he could no longer move and the air seemed trapped in his lungs.

The lion stretched out its neck and, almost effortlessly, with a sickening crunch, bit off the lower half of Baghadh's left leg.

In his final moments, somewhere beneath the sound of his own screams of agony, Baghadh wondered that terror could wrack him even more than the pain that was suddenly the whole of his world. The lion shook what he held in his bloodied mouth, spattering blood on leaves and trunks, and then casually dropped it. Baghadh could hear nothing but the piercing shriek of his own screams, could taste nothing but blood in his mouth, could see nothing but the gaping maw and dagger teeth that descended toward his head...

67

In the western side of the hill upon which the city of Nob was built Israelites had, centuries before, carved a tomb. The tool marks of the workers had long since been erased by the grating hand of time, so that it now appeared to be a cave formed by some natural process with an inexplicable concern for symmetry. Though the tomb itself was dark, its mouth was framed by the lush green of early summer plants, dotted with the gentle pinks and whites of lily, asphodel, poppies, and delicate cyclamen. The blossoms lent their comforting perfume as an accompaniment to the eager singing of birds gathering seeds in the tall grass, and the breeze carried not only their scents and sounds but an undeniable sense of newfound hope.

Only the dove seemed to understand that the group gathered at the tomb's mouth stood in the shadow of death; his mournful call stirred Samuel's heart and sent goose-pimples down the back of his neck.

Ahitub lay upon a folded linen cloth just outside the tomb's mouth. His kind face seemed not to have found peace even in death: his lips curled in a slight frown and his pale brow between his dark lashes was wrinkled as though in frustration.

It was a look Samuel knew well. How often it had provided all the motivation he had needed to return to a poorly done task with renewed determination to improve his work.

How often it had reminded him of the burden borne every day by his mentor, the High Priest of Israel.

The memorial tomb's entrance was decorated with lamp stands of gold and silver that whispered slender ribbons of smoke into the clear skies; the Levites and guards gathered were clothed and armed in the most expensive and well-crafted garments, armor, and weapons: spoils of their recent victory. In the end the army had taken a mountain of treasure from the abandoned Philistine camp, and Samuel had dedicated it to be used for the maintenance of the Tabernacle.

The stirring of a breeze carried the scent of myrrh, aloes, and incense to Samuel's nostrils and he breathed deeply. *How carefully we perfume death*, he thought. *As though by clothing her in beauty we can convince ourselves that she is not the heartless reaper we know her to be.*

Ahimelech was arrayed now in the ceremonial garments of the High Priest, having at last undergone the installation ceremony he had for so long avoided. He looked, Samuel thought, as uncomfortable in the role as his father had in the days of Samuel's childhood.

Perhaps that discomfort was part of what made a High Priest successful.

Perhaps it was the most important qualification for the role.

His thoughts, bearing him inexorably to memories past, carried his gaze over his shoulder to where Liora stood quietly in the shade of a gnarled olive tree, her hands resting on Joel and Abijah's shoulders. She met his gaze and he allowed himself to drink of her stillness, to borrow from her some of the steady confidence that he seemed always to lack. At her side Tirzah stood with her hands clasped in front of her. Ichabod waited in the shadow of the trees, his glance jumping from Tirzah to Ahimelech and back again.

Behind her stood Manoah and Samson, the former beaming with undisguised pride, the latter unable to hide his rascally grin even on a day of memorial.

At last Ahimelech stepped forward. "To You, O Jehovah, we entrust the spirit of this, Your son," he said. "May he be at peace in Your boundless memory until You call him forth again."

The singing of swallows filled a moment's silence.

"And for the sake of Your people, grant me Your strength and wisdom, and the faith of my father," Ahimelech whispered.

He nodded to the waiting Levites and they lifted Ahitub's body and bore it into the tomb, emerging moments later to roll a flat cylinder of stone across its entrance.

The gathered crowd waited for Ahimelech to speak again, but he did not.

"What, then, happens now?" Manoah asked at last.

"Now, we enjoy peace for as long as it lasts," Ahimelech said. "Let that be enough."

He turned and began making his way along the path that led back toward the Tabernacle.

Samuel nodded. "Let it be enough," he said, and taking Liora's hand in his own, he slowly led the gathering back toward the city.

67

Samuel took three full days to return to Naioth, keeping a leisurely pace and stopping along the way at Gibeah, Bethel, and Mizpah to bid farewell to his friends and companions of the previous weeks.

Samson and Manoah did not accompany them, choosing instead to travel west to the tribal territory of Dan and their family there. Not far from the site of their great victory, they said their farewells.

Samuel embraced Manoah. "Now is, at last, Jehovah's time," the big Danite said.

Samuel nodded. "As always, His timing is perfect. May He continue to bless you and your household, Manoah of Dan."

"And you, Prophet," Manoah said.

Samuel hugged Samson and kissed him on both cheeks. "Do not fear, my friend. Jehovah will be with you like a terrible, mighty One."

Samson gave him a crooked smile, narrowed one eye, and pushed his thick shoulders forward. "Fear? Me?" He glanced over at his father. "Perhaps that is one emotion I need never feel again."

Samuel stared at him a moment. "Perhaps."

Samson nodded and gripped Samuel's forearm. "Farewell, my friend. Listen for word of my exploits in Philistia."

"I will listen," Samuel said, nodding. "The whole nation will listen."

Samson turned away then, but not before Samuel saw that there were tears in his dark eyes.

— —

The first part of their journey home took them up the north-south road along the coast. The weather was fair and bright, and a gentle breeze carried the fresh scents of the sea across the ripening fields and scattered swamplands. Traffic had increased on the road, as though everyone from Egypt to Anatolia had already learned of Israel's victory over the Philistines and returned to the trade routes to make up for the business they had lost.

They had barely begun their travel on the first day when they came upon the ruined litter of Baghadh, abandoned in a heap in the middle of the road.

Samuel examined it in surprise. "How is it that no one has taken these embroidered curtains, or these bronze fittings?" he wondered aloud.

"Or at the very least moved it from the middle of the road!" Reuel said. He was stooping at the margin, squinting into the dry soil.

"What do you see?" Samuel asked.

Reuel stood and pointed. "Lion tracks."

Samuel joined him, studying the markings in the soft earth. "A few days old already." He looked up and pointed into the trees to the west. "They lead off in that direction."

Both men slipped quietly from the road, following the remains of the tracks, leaving Liora and Samuel's sons in the care of the rest of the *Beneh* still on the road.

The tracks led to a patch of blood-soaked ground, still swarming with flies. Nothing else remained: neither bone fragments nor scraps of clothing nor flesh. After staring at it a moment, they turned away, sickened and sad.

They had not gone two steps back toward the road when Reuel made a noise of exclamation and leaned down to lift something from the tall grass.

It was the vermilion staff, *Mish'eneth*.

He held it out to Samuel. "Ahitub's gift finds its way home at last."

When Samuel, Tirzah, Joel, Abijah, Reuel, and the *Beneh* finally arrived at Naioth, the sun had reached its zenith in the cloudless sky above them. It was one of those days when the air seemed somehow more clear and the light more vivid than usual. Shadows melted away and colors shone more brilliantly. Forgotten details of familiar scenes revealed themselves and brightness found its way into the darkest corners of homes and hearts.

They found the School just as it had been left by the Philistines: a charred skeleton emerging from a skin of damp ashes. On the hill to the northwest, the people of Ramathaim had already repaired much of the damage to the city itself. But no one had touched Naioth or the destroyed School. Cattle, sheep, and goats wandered at the edge of the ashes, trying to find a little grass and seeming resigned to the fact that their paddocks and barns had vanished.

Samuel and his companions stood for a long time at the edge of the ruins. The task of rebuilding seemed so overwhelming Samuel could not get clearly in his mind where he might even begin. The *Beneh* began to pick their way across the rubble, looking for anything salvageable.

He took his son's hands, one on each side, and strode slowly through the untended grass at the edge of the settlement. They had not taken many steps before their eyes were simultaneously drawn to the same spot on the charred ground.

Emerging from the blackened soil and stubble was a single stem of bright green, a tiny trunk branching out into seven tinier branches, each finished by a pair of delicately veined leaves. Between three of the pairs of leaves a fingertip-sized white flower blossomed, a burst of insistent life.

"Our tree!" Joel cried, falling to his knees in the black soil.

Samuel smiled, realizing as he did so that it had been a long time since he had smiled with abandon.

"It growed!" Abijah said, clapping his hands.

Joel was running his hand over the ground around the tiny tree. "Where is the wheel…?" He could not think of the word, and instead gestured sharply with his hand, tracing an invisible cut through the soil.

Samuel knelt beside him on the charcoal and scorched earth. There was no sign of the chariot track that had cut the little tree down.

"The hurt and harm caused by the wicked are temporary," Samuel whispered, gathering his sons to him. "They cannot stop the Hand of our God. Life rises from the ashes."

He stood, wanting abruptly to laugh. "Do you hear that?" he shouted at the sky. "Let all men give ear to this: God's purpose cannot be thwarted! You cannot check His Hand! Dare to defy the God of Israel and be brought to silence!"

Joel and Abijah laughed at his shouting. "Jehovah wins!" Joel yelled at the fluffy clouds.

Samuel and Liora laughed as well. "Yes, Joel," Samuel said. "Jehovah wins."

An approaching hubbub of voices drew his attention to the road from Ramathaim. Turning, he saw that a group of robed men were descending ceremoniously toward the School: the Elders of the city. Samuel walked over to Liora's side and waited for them.

"Welcome back, Samuel ben Elkanah, Prophet and Judge of Israel," one of the men panted, trying to catch his breath.

"Why have you not begun repairs on the School?" Samuel asked.

The Elder glanced back at his companions nervously. "Many have suggested that you would...It was believed that now that you are the Judge of Israel, you might return to Nob and take the *Beneh* with you there."

"Indeed?" Samuel looked at the gathered Elders, trying to take the measure of their faces.

"All saw you offer a sacrifice outside of Mizpah," another Elder said. "We believed...some believed that you will begin serving at the Tabernacle as a Priest."

Samuel smiled again, knowing already what he would do. He called the *Beneh* to him. "Gather as many stones as you can," he told them. "Anything larger than your two fists together—the flatter the better."

They obeyed without question. As they brought the stones, Samuel began to stack them not far from where the courtyard of his home had once been. Slowly, with the Elders watching in confusion, the stack took shape: about the length of a man, the width of an arm's length, and rising to hip height.

Samuel enjoyed watching the looks of stunned disbelief settling over the faces of the Elders as it gradually dawned on them what he was doing.

When the altar—for altar it was—was finished, Samuel stood in front of it, *Mish'eneth* held before him in both hands. "I, Samuel ben Elkanah, do hereby proclaim this to be a holy site, and do sanctify this altar for the offering of sacrifices to our God. From here, too, pleasing smoke shall rise to Him."

"An altar? Here?" sputtered one of the Elders.

"Are you, then, a Priest?" another asked.

"I am not a Priest," Samuel responded. "I am the Prophet Samuel ben Elkanah. And I am the Judge of Israel."

JUDGE OF ISRAEL

Timothy Wilkinson

The Appendices

APPENDIX A:
GLOSSARY OF PEOPLE, PLACES, AND THINGS

Aaron	*A-run*	The brother of Moses and the first High Priest of Israel
Abiel	*a-BY-el*	Patriarch of the clan of the Matrites in Gibeah; father to Ner
Abijah	*a-BY-jah*	Second son of the Prophet Samuel
Abimelech	*a-BIM-eh-lek*	Son of Judge Gideon who proclaimed himself king of Israel
Abinadab	*a-BIN-eh-dab*	A holy man of Kiriath-jearim in whose home the Ark of the Covenant was kept following its return from Philistia; his sons were Eleazar, Uzzah, and Ahio
Abraham	*AYB-rah-ham*	Patriarch and forefather of the Arab and Semitic peoples
Abraham, Mountain of		Mountain near the city of Bethel from which God showed Abraham the land of Promise
Ahimelech	*a-HIM-eh-lek*	Firstborn son of High Priest Ahitub, and grandson of Chief Priest Phinehas
Ahio ben Abiel	*Ah-HY-oh*	Of the clan of the Matrites; brother to Ner, Uncle to Kish
Ahio ben Abinadab	*Ah-HY-oh*	One of the sons of Abimelech who assisted in caring for the Ark of the Covenant
Ahitub	*Ah-HY-tub*	Firstborn son of Phinehas and High Priest of Israel following the death of Eli
Ahlai	*AH-lye*	Chief of the Elders of the city of Mizpah
Ai	*AY-i*	Canaanite royal city east of Bethel captured by Joshua during the Conquest
Aijalon	*I-ja-lawn*	Valley pass and fortified city in the mountains of Judah; site of Joshua's famous victory during which the sun stood still over Gibeon
Allen-bacuth	*AL-len-BAK-kooth*	"Massive Tree of Weeping" near Bethel under which Jacob buried Rebekah's nursing woman, Deborah
Amorites	*AM-or-ite*	Hamitic people inhabiting the land of Canaan east of the Jordan prior to the Israelite conquest
Anat	*AN-at*	Canaanite goddess of war, the hunt, and savagery, Baal's sister, daughter of El/Dagon; known for her cruelty and bloodlust
Aphek	*AY-fek*	Fortified city in Ephraim along the major north-south coastal trade route; site of several battles with the Philistines and the

TIMOTHY WILKINSON

Term	Pronunciation	Definition
		capture of the Ark of the Covenant
Ark of the Covenant		The sacred, gold-plated acacia chest once located within the Holy of Holies in the Tabernacle and associated with Jehovah's presence; it contained the tablets upon which were written the ten commandments, Aaron's staff that miraculously blossomed, and a golden container of the supernaturally-provided food, manna
Arsay	*AR-say*	Canaanite goddess of soil; one of the daughters of Ba'al
Asher/Asherite	*ASH-er*	One of the Twelve Tribes of Israel
Asherah	*ASH-er-ah*	A Canaanite fertility goddess often represented by a phallic sacred pole
Ashipu priests	*Ash-EE-poo*	Canaanite priests who served as prophets and leaders in sex-worship
Ashkelon	*ASH-kel-lawn*	One of the five cities of the Philistine Pentapolis and their only major seaport
assinu priest	*Ass-SEEN-noo*	Homosexual priests of Canaan who performed or presided over aspects of sex worship in the rituals of Canaanite religion
Avdon, Judge	*AV-don*	Eleventh Judge of Israel (in order of their appearance in the Book of Judges)
Avith	*AV-ith*	Naphtalian chieftain who, along with his friend Zattu, forms part of a deadly pair of warriors of renown
Axis Lord	*AX-iss*	From the Hebrew *seranim*, a Philistine loanword with the same consonants as the word for "axle"; one of the five Philistine leaders who shared power and ruled a city of the Pentapolis
Azariah	*Az-ah-RYE-ah*	An ancient Kohathite Levite
Ba'al	*BAY-al*	Primary god of the Canaanites; god of thunder, rainstorms, and the renewal of growth brought by the rains
Baghadh	*BAG-had*	An Elder of Manasseh
Barak, Judge	*BAY-rak*	Fourth-listed Judge of Israel who defeated the Canaanites under General Sisera
baru-priest	*BAY-roo*	Canaanite diviner, seer, and interpreter of omens and signs, including oil on water, smoke of incense, casting of dice, livers of sacrificial animals, flight of birds, stars
Barzel	*Bar-ZEL*	A chieftain of the tribe of Simeon
Bashan	*BAY-shan*	Region east of the Jordan known for its mighty oak forests and cattle
Be'ersheba	*BEE-er-SHEE-bah*	Southernmost city of Israel, and gateway to the great desert to the south
behemoth	*Be-HEE-moth*	Hippopotamus

- 434 -

Belial (sons of Belial)	*BEE-lee-al*	The quality or state of being useless or good-for-nothing; a son or daughter of Belial is a person without value
Beneh Hannevi'im	*BEN-eh HAV'-er-im*	"The Sons of the Prophets." A term used by several Bible writers to refer to members of prophetic schools first established by Samuel
Benjamin/Benjaminite	*Ben-JAY-min*	One of the Twelve Tribes of Israel
Bethel	*BETH-el*	A prominent city located at the southernmost portion of Ephraim's territory
Beth-shemesh	*Beth-SHEE-mesh*	A city on the northern border of Judah's territory, to which the Ark was returned after its capture by the Philistines
Black Sea		The modern Black Sea
Book of the Wars of Jehovah		An ancient record (now lost) of the victories in battle of the nation of Israel
Canaan/Canaanite	*KAY-nun*	A Hamitic race that once occupied a major portion of the land to which they gave their name; also the name of the territory of modern-day Palestine
Caphtor	*KAF-tohr*	The island of Crete, from which the Philistines emigrated
Carmel, Mount	*KAR-mell*	A ridge of mountains jutting out from Israel's central mountain range to the northwest
Cheran	*KEE-ran*	Ephraimite from Gath-Rimmon whose son, Gavriel, was called as a prophet when still a child
Chilian	*KILL-ee-an*	A Philistine battle chieftain under Sarnam
Chousor	*KhOO-sor*	Canaanite craftsman/smith god also called Kothar-and-Khasis (skillful and clever); identified with Ea or Ptah of Egytp and with the city of Mempthis
Cosam	*KOS-am*	A military chieftain of the tribe of Asher
Cushan	*KOO-shan*	Mesopotamian king defeated by Judge Othniel shortly after Joshua's day
Dagon	*DAY-gawn*	Philistine name for El, highest and father-god of the Canaanite pantheon. He was represented as having a man's head and body and a fish's tail
Dan (city)	*DAN*	A city (formerly Laish) captured by Dan and representing the northernmost border of Israel
Dan/Danite	*DAN*	One of the Twelve Tribes of Israel
Dathan	*DAY-than*	Eldest of Judge Avdon's sons and the presumptive heir to his position as family head
Dead Sea		Also known as the Salt Sea

Deborah	*DEB-oh-rah*	Prophetess of Israel during the days of Judge Barak
Devarim, book of	*DEV-ah-rim*	Fifth book of the Pentateuch, now known as Deuteronomy. The name means "words."
Dor	*DOHR*	A Manassehite city on the coastal plain
Ebal, Mount	*EE-ball*	A mountain in Samaria opposite Mount Gerizim across the Vale of Shechem
Evenezer (town)	*Ev-en-EEZ-er*	Site on Plain of Sharon near Aphek where Israel was twice defeated by the Philistines in Eli's day
Evenezer, Stone of Help		Standing stone (dolmen) raised by Samuel to commemorate Israel's victory over the Philistines at Mizpah
Edom/Edomite	*EE-dum*	A land east of Canaan inhabited by the descendants of Esau, Jacob ben Isaac's brother; enemies of Israel
Eglon	*EGG-lawn*	An obese Moabite king who oppressed Israel and was killed by Judge Ehud
Ehud, Judge	*EE-hud*	Second listed Judge of Israel, killer of Moabite king Eglon
Ekron	*EK-rawn*	The northernmost city of the Canaanite Pentapolis
Elda'ah	*EL-day-ah*	Servant of Judge Avdon
Eleazar	*El-ee-AY-zar*	An elderly man of noted faith in whose home the Ark of the Covenant was kept after it was returned to Israel by the Philistines
Eleazar, (son of Abinadab)	*el-ee-AY-zar*	Firstborn son of Abinadab of Kiriath-jearim, appointed to watch over the Ark after it was moved to that city
Elhanan	*El-HAY-nan*	A prince (or highest-ranking chieftain) of the tribe of Judah
Eli	*EE-lye*	A High Priest of Israel; father of Phinehas and grandfather of Ahitub
Elishama	*El-LY-shah-mah*	Grandson of Judge Tola and one of the chief Elders of the city of Bethel
Elkanah	*El-KAY-nah*	Father of the Prophet Samuel and the husband of Hannah and Peninnah
Elon, Judge	*EE-lawn*	A Zebulunite judge, listed tenth in the order of appearance in the book of Judges
Elon-tohr	*EE-lawn-TOHR*	Zebulunite warrior reputed to be more skilled in battle than any man living at the time of the Battle of Aphek
Endor	*EN-dor*	A Manassehite city on the plains south of Mount Tabor; home of the Ghost-wife Yiddishah
ephod	*EE-fod*	An apron-like priestly garment with a belt, or girdle
Ephraim/Ephraimite	*EE-fray-im*	One of the twelve tribes of Israel

Eshtaol	*ESH-tay-all*	A Danite city in the Shephelah
Gabbai	*GAB-bye*	Levite inhabitant of Ramathaim-zophim whose house was taken over by Baghadh
Gad/Gadite	*GAD*	One of the twelve tribes of Israel
Galilee	*GAL-ih-lee*	A mountainous region of Naphtali and including the territory of Zebulun, known for its abundant springs, fertile soil, and variety of crops and trees
Galilee, Sea of	*GAL-ih-lee*	The modern Sea of Galilee
Gath	*GATH*	One of the cities of the Philistine Pentapolis, located east of the Philistine plain
Gath-Rimmon	*GATH-RIM-mon*	A Levite city in the territory of the tribe of Dan
Gavriel	*GAV-ree-el*	Son of Cheran, called to be a prophet at a young age
Gedhudhra	*Ged-DTHU-drah*	The death-troops of Sarnam, Lord of Ashkelon; trained in the long war against Egypt and chosen for their unquestioning loyalty and fierceness in battle
Gedor	*GEE-dor*	Benjaminite son of Abiel, brother of Ner, of the family of the Matrites
Gerizim, Mount	*GAYR-iz-im*	Mountain in Samaria across the Vale of Shechem from Mount Ebal
Ghost-wife of Endor	*EN-dor*	The witch, or spirit-medium, of the city of En-dor. *See also Appendix C* .
Gibbethon	*GIB-beh-thon*	A Levite city in the territory of Dan, located on the edge of Philistia
Gibeah	*GIB-ee-ah*	Benjaminite city that served as a lookout point in times of war; home of the family of the Matrites
Gideon, Judge	*GID-ee-on*	Judge of Israel who, with 300 men, defeated an army of 165,000 Midianites, Amalekites, and Easterners and whose son Abimelech attempted to make himself the first king of Israel
Gilboah, Mount	*Gil-BOH-ah*	A mountain east of the Plain of Jezre'el; site of one of Judge Gideon's great victories
Gilead	*GIL-lee-ad*	Mountainous region of Israel located east of the Jordan and north of the river Jabbok
Gilgal	*GIL-gal*	An important city east of Jericho where the tribal heads under Joshua set up twelve standing stones to commemorate their miraculous crossing of the Jordan and where all those born in the wilderness were circumcised before conquering the Promised Land under Joshua
Girgashites	*GIR-gah-shite*	Canaanite people from West of the Jordan

Glaucus	GLOCK-us	Philistine garrison commander stationed near Ramathaim
Great Desert		The Arabian desert to the east and southeast of Palestine
Great Sea		The Mediterranean
Guni	GOO-nee	Elder of the city of Lebonah
halil reed-pipes	HAL-leel	Pipes similar to pan pipes or reed flutes
Hannah	HAN-nah	Mother of the Prophet Samuel and wife of Elkanah of Ramathaim
Heber	HEE-ber	Kenite husband of Jael, the Israelite woman who killed Sisera, army chieftain of Jabin, after his defeat by Judge Barak
Heres, Mount	HEE-rez	Mountain on the border of Judah and Dan where Amorites continued to dwell after the conquest by Joshua
Hermon, Mount	HER-mawn	Highest peak in Canaan located on the border between Israel and Lebanon; its snow-covered slopes provide water to the land all year round
Hophni	HOF-nee	Second son of High Priest Eli and brother of Phinehas; killed at the second Battle of Aphek
Horeb, Mount	HOH-reb	Also called Mount Sinai; where Moses saw the burning bush and where he struck a crag and miraculously produced water for the Israelites in the wilderness
Hunter, the		A Masai warrior in servitude to Sarnam; a warrior and hunter of almost super-human skill
Ibzan, Judge	IB-zan	Zebulunite Judge of Israel after Jephthah, known for his large family rather than for any action taken by him on Israel's behalf
Ichabod	IK-ah-bod	Youngest son of Phinehas and his wife Mara
Isaac	EYE-zak	Son of Abraham and a patriarch of the nation of Israel; father of Jacob who was renamed Israel
Ishipu priests	Ish-EE-poo	Cross-dressing Canaanite priests who led sex-worship rituals
Israel	IZ-ray-ell	The name given to Jacob ben Isaac and the name of the nation born from his twelve sons
Issachar/Issacharian	ISS-ak-ahr	One of the twelve tribes of Israel
Jacob	JAY-kob	Also known as Israel; patriarch of Israel, son of Isaac and grandson of Abraham
Jael	JAY-ell	Wife of the Kenite Heber; she killed the Canaanite king Jabin's army chieftain, Sisera after his defeat by Judge Barak by driving a tent stake through his head

JUDGE OF ISRAEL

Jedaiel	*Jed-DYE-ell*	Benjaminite warrior and slinger extraordinaire
Jephthah, Judge	*JEF-thah*	A Manassehite; eighth-named Judge of Israel who dedicated his daughter to a life of Tabernacle service after Jehovah gave him victory over the Ammonites
Jericho	*JER-ik-oh*	One of the most ancient Canaanite cities and the first to be conquered by Joshua after crossing the Jordan
Jerusalem	*Jer-OO-say-lem*	An important and ancient city of Israel built atop Mount Zion and inhabited by the Jebusites
Jezre'el	*JEZ-ree-ehl*	A plain in Samaria between Mount Gerizim and Mount Ebal
Jiram	*JY-ram*	A fellow captive befriended by Reuel during their march toward the slave markets
Joel	*JOH-ell*	Firstborn son of the Prophet Samuel and his wife, Liora
Jogbehah	*Jog-BEE-hah*	City east of the Jordan conquered by Judge Jephthah in his campaign against Ammon
Joppa	*JOP-pah*	An ancient Canaanite seaport located in the northern portion of the territory of Dan
Jordan River	*JOR-dan*	The main river of Canaan and the natural division of east and west Canaan; it drains Hula lake, flows through the Sea of Galilee and terminates in the Dead Sea
Joseph	*JOH-sef*	Favored son of Jacob/Israel; his two sons, Ephraim and Manasseh, founded two of the Twelve Tribes of Israel
Joshua	*JOSH-oo-ah*	The leader of Israel and Commander of its armies during the conquest of Canaan
Judah/Judean	*JOO-dah*	One of the twelve tribes of Israel
Karnack	*KAR-nak*	Also known as Thebes; Egyptian capital city under Pharaoh Akhenaton
Kenath	*KEE-nath*	One of the many sons of Judge Avdon
Kenites	*KEN-ites*	A semi-nomadic people known for their metal-working skills; often hired by the Egyptians to work their mines
khopesh	*KHO-pesh*	A sickle-sword; the most common sword design in Canaan and Egypt, it was originally made from a modified sickle that could be re-converted back into a farm implement during times of peace
kinnor lyres	*KIN-nohr*	A small harp with a hollow wooden frame
Kish	*KISH*	A warrior of the House of the Matrites in Gibeah; son of Ner and father of Saul
Kishon River	*KY-shawn*	A small river that flows through the Plain of Jezre'el

Kohathite	KOH-*hath-ite*	Descendants of Kohath, one of the sons of Levi. They were assigned to Tabernacle service with the responsibility to transport the Ark of the Covenant, the screen that shielded the Holy of Holies from view, the Table of Showbread, the Menorah, the Altar, and the utensils
Korah, Sons of	KOH-*rah*	Descendants of the rebellious Israelite prince, Korah, who did not follow their father in his rebellion and later became known for their Psalms and musical compositions
Lake Hula	HOO-*lah*	Northernmost body of water in Israel; source of the Jordan River. It is surrounded by swampland and largely comprised of runoff from the slopes of nearby Mount Hermon
Lanak, Mount	LAY-*nak*	Mountain outside Pirathon; site of many ancient tombs, including the tomb of Judge Avdon
Lebanon	LEB-*ah-non*	Region bordering the land of Canaan to the north, famous for its lush forests and mountains
leben	LEB-*en*	A dish made from sweetened yoghurt
Lebonah	Leh-BOHN-*ah*	A village along the N-S highway that followed the Jordan, not far from the city of Shiloh
Levi/Levite	LEE-*rye*	One of the tribes of Israel; Assigned as the Priestly tribe and therefore not counted among the Twelve; also not given their own allotment of land in Canaan
Liora	Lee-OHR-*ah*	Wife of Samuel the Prophet
Lod	LOD	City on the southern edge of the Plain of Sharon and on the main N-S trade route along the coastal region of Palestine
Lodan	LOW-*dan*	A Chieftain of the tribe of Issachar, specializing in military intelligence
lugal	LOO-*gal*	Ancient Canaanite board game
Luz	LUZ	Canaanite city which Joshua burned and on which the city of Bethel was built
malchia	Mal-KEE-*ah*	Ancient Mycenaean game involving the casting of lots in order to advance the players toward being crowned *malchia*, or king
Manasseh/Manassite	Man-ASS-*eh*	One of the twelve tribes of Israel
Manoah	Man-OH-*ah*	A prince of the tribe of Dan; hero of the wars of Aphek, husband of the beautiful Na'amah, and father to Samson
Mara	MAH-*rah*	Wife of Priest Phinehas, who died giving birth to Ichabod after the second Battle of

Aphek

Matrites	*MAT-ryte*	Benjaminite family to which Abiel, Kish, Ner, and Saul belonged
Mehanaim, Forest of	*Meh-hah-NAY-im*	Forest east of the Jordan where Jacob anciently met a company of angels while traveling
me'il	*MEE-ill*	A distinctive garment worn by Priests and prophets during Samuel's day; a sleeveless coat or robe, often tied like an apron
metsilloth bells	*Met-SILL-oth*	Finger bells shaped like tiny cymbals
Midian/Midianite	*MID-ee-an*	Descendants of Abraham's son Midian and the land they inhabited northwest of Arabia and east of the Gulf of 'Aqaba. They were notably defeated by Judge Gideon
Mikloth	*MIK-loth*	A Benjaminite of the clan of the Matrites, father of Shimeah
Mish'eneth	*MISH-en-eth*	The name given to the traditional staff of the High Priest of Israel
Mizpah	*MIZ-pah*	A fortified city in Benjamin's territory
Moab/Moabite	*MOH-ab*	Descendants of Lot by his eldest daughter and the land they inhabited between the Dead Sea and the Arabian Desert
Moriah, Mount	*MOH-rye-ah*	Along with Mount Zion, on this rounded peak is the city of Jerusalem, although in Samuel's day it was not built upon. Famously the site of Abraham's attempt to sacrifice his son, Isaac
Moses	*MOH-zess*	Greatest leader of the Israelites who led them out of Egypt and to whom was transmitted the Torah
Mot	*MAWT*	Canaanite god of death, often represented with a wide-opened (insatiable) mouth; believed to be responsible for darkness and drought
Mount of Olives		A chain of rounded limestone hills east of Jerusalem comprised of Mount Scopus, the Mount of Ruination, and the Mount of Olives
Mount of Ruination		One of the rounded peaks of the Mount of Olives, east of Jerusalem
Mycenae	*MICE-in-ay*	The territory of ancient Greece and home of the peoples from whom the Philistines descended
Na'amah	*NAY-ah-mah*	Wife of Manoah of Dan and mother of Samson
Nadab	*NAY-dab*	Brother of Ner and son of Abiel of the clan of the Matrites
Naioth	*NY-oth*	A village on the outskirts of Ramathaim where Samuel built the School of the Prophets

Naphtali/Naphtalite	*NAF-tal-lie*	One of the twelve tribes of Israel
Nazirite	*NAZ-ir-ite*	Group of Israelites living under a sacred vow; they are forbidden from eating any products made from grapes or touching anything unclean. Except for Nazirites for Life, they are also forbidden from touching dead bodies
nebels	*Neb-ells*	Small cymbals or bells
Ner	*NER*	A Benjaminite son of Abiel, father of Abner and Kish and grandfather of Saul
Noah	*NOH-ah*	Patriarch of human family who survived the Great Flood
Nob	*NAWB*	A city of Benjamin near Jerusalem and the Mount of Olives; where the Tabernacle was rebuilt after Shiloh's destruction
Olives, Mount of		Primary peak of a group of limestone hills east of Jerusalem, and a common name for the hills as a group
Ophir	*OH-fur*	A (currently unidentified) place from which much high-quality gold was mined
Ophrah	*OH-frah*	Judge Gideon's hometown and the site of his tomb
Othniel, Judge	*OTH-nee-el*	First listed Judge of Israel. Nephew of Caleb, son of Jephunneh, he led Israel's defeat of Cushan-rishathaim, king of Syria
Pentapolis	*Pen-TAP-oh-liss*	The five primary cities of the Philistines: Ekron, Gath, Ashkelon, Ashdod, and Gath
Phicol	*FY-cawl*	Sarnam's battle commander; a savage warlord without a nose
Philistine	*Fil-LIS-teen*	A tribe of Bronze Age Mycenaean Greeks who emigrated from Crete and the surrounding region to Palestine and Egypt
Phinehas	*FIN-ee-ahs*	Son of High Priest Eli who died at the second Battle of Aphek
Phoenicia/Phoenician	*Fo-NEE-shah*	Narrow coastal country between the mountains of Lebanon and the Great Sea; north of Israel. Its people were renowned as seafarers
Pidray	*PID-ray*	One of the daughters of Baal, she is the goddess of lightning
Pirathon	*PEER-ah-thon*	City in the mountains of Ephraim; site of Judge Avdon's grave
Ramah	*RAY-mah*	Benjaminite city on a hill north of Jerusalem
Ramathaim	*Ray-mah-THAY-im*	Small village in the mountainous territory of Ephraim and hometown of the Prophet Samuel and his family
Rameses	*RAM-ess-eez*	Dynastic name of a family of Pharoahs
Rebekah	*Reh-BEK-ah*	Wife of Isaac; daughter-in-law of Abraham; a matriarch of the Israelites

Rephaim	*REF-ay-im*	Race of giants originally from Bashan but who allied themselves with the Philistines at the time of the first battle of Aphek
Reuben/Reubenite	*ROO-ben*	One of the twelve tribes of Israel
Reuel	*ROO-el*	Young prophet of the School and self-appointed personal assistant to Samuel
Rohgah	*ROW-gah*	Prophet of Israel who lived in the days of Samuel's youth
Ruination, Mount of		One of the rounded peaks of the Mount of Olives, east of Jerusalem
Samaria	*Suh-MAYR-ee-ah*	District in Israel north of Judea, west of the Jordan, and east of the coastal plain and mountains
Samson	*SAM-sun*	Danite son of Manoah and Na'amah, prophesied by an angel to take the lead in delivering Israel from the Philistines
Samuel	*SAM-yoo-el*	Son of Elkanah and Hannah given by them to Tabernacle service as a small child; appointed prophet at 12; founder of the School of the Prophets in Ramathaim
Saphold	*SAFF-old*	A Rephaim warrior who fought alongside the Israelites in the first and second battles of Aphek
Sarnam	*SAR-nam*	Military commander and sometime Axis Lord of Philistia and the city of Ashkelon
School of the Prophets		A community founded by Samuel outside Ramathaim where prophets could receive training and support
Scopus, Mount	*SKOH-pus*	One of the rounded peaks of the Mount of Olives, east of Jerusalem
Scroll of Bereshith	*Bay-rah-SHITH*	The Bible book of Genesis
sennet	*SEN-net*	An ancient Egyptian board game
Sha'albim	*Shay-AL-bim*	City on the eastern border of Dan's territory where Amorites were used as slaves by the Israelites after Joshua's conquest
Shaga	*SHAH-gah*	Gadite chieftain
Shamgar, Judge	*SHAM-gar*	Judge of Israel after Ehud and before Barak. He delivered Israel by killing 300 Philistines with a cattle goad; Josephus records that he died in his first year of judgeship
Shaphash	*SHAY-pash*	Canaanite goddess of the water and sea life
Sharon	*SHAY-ron*	Fertile plain along the northern portion of Israel's Mediterranean coast; filled with cultivated land, pasture grounds, and oak forests
Shataqat	*SHAT-uh-kat*	A Canaanite demoness accredited with healing powers
Shechem	*SHEE-kem*	A major city at the east end of the valley

that runs between Mount Gerizim and Mount Ebal in Samaria, it controlled trade in both North-South and East-West directions

Shemer	*SHEE-mer*	Chieftain of the Tribe of Reuben
Shephelah	*She-FEE-lah*	The hill country between the coastal plains of Philistia and the mountains of Judah
Shiloh	*SHY-low*	City that once housed the Tabernacle and Ark; destroyed by the Philistines following the battles of Aphek
shofar	*SHOW-far*	Traditional ram's horn instrument, used for ceremonial and military purposes
Sihphil	*SIH-fill*	A Canaanite sorcerer-priest who serves as advisor and aid to Sarnam
Simeon/Simeonite	*SIMM-ee-on*	One of the twelve tribes of Israel
Sinai, Mount	*SY-ny*	A mountain in Arabia which Moses ascended to receive the Ten Commandments and the Torah
Sisera	*SIS-er-ah*	Army chief of Canaanite king Jabin; defeated by Judge Barak and killed by Jael, the wife of Heber the Kenite
Sons of the Prophets		*See* Beneh Haveriim
Aram	*AY-ram*	Syria
Tabernacle		The portable temple built under Moses' leadership not far from Mount Zion. It was established more permanently in Shiloh after Joshua's conquest, then moved to Nob following the defeat at Aphek. It contained the Ark of the Covenant.
Tabor, Mount	*TAY-bore*	A prominent mountain at the end of the Valley of Jezreel and the site of Judge Barak's victory over the Canaanites
Tahash	*TAY-hash*	One of the sons of Judge Avdon
Tallay	*TAL-lay*	Canaanite goddess of dew, and one of the daughters of Baal
Tammuz	*TAM-mooz*	Sumerian god and consort of the fertility goddess Ishtar/Inanna. His sign was the cross.
terebinth	*TAYR-ah-binth*	The turpentine tree (pistachia palaestina); incisions in the bark yield a perfumed resin which can be distilled into turpentine
Thebez	*THEE-bez*	A fortified city with a tower from which a woman threw a stone upon Abimelech, son of Judge Gideon, during his attempt to establish a monarchy with himself as king
threquet	*Thruh-KET*	Magical ritual designed to increase a warrior's strength, speed, and bloodlust and make him near-invincible in battle
Tirzah	*TEER-zah*	Only daughter of Judge Jephthah; given by

		him to Tabernacle service following his victory against the Ammonites
Tiy, Queen	*TYE*	Wife of Pharoah Rameses who attempted to have her husband killed and take over the throne
tof drums	*TOF*	Large, free-standing drums played by two men at the same time
Torah, the	*TOH-rah*	The Law of Moses, comprised of the first five books of the Bible (the Pentateuch)
Tsa'iph	*TSAY-iff*	The headdress or scarflike covering worn by all Israelite women over their hair when they are in public
Tyre	*TIRE*	The principal Phoenician seaport, located just outside Asher's territory on Israel's northern coast
Ugar	*OO-gar*	One of the daughters of Baal, goddess of cultivated fields
Urim and Thummim	*YOOrim, THUM-mim*	Sacred lots kept in the High Priest's ceremonial breastplate and used to determine the divine will on important matters
Uzzah (son of Abinadab)		One of the sons of Abinadab, assigned to watch over the Ark of the Covenant when it was placed in Abinadab's home after it was returned to Israel by the Philistines
wadi	*WAH-dee*	A riverbed which remains dry for much of the year, filling during heavy rains
White Cliffs of Gibeah		Limestone and chalk cliffs located near the trade road outside the city of Gibeah
Yarkon River	*YAR-kawn*	A river that flows from the city of Aphek west, across the plain to the Great Sea
Yarmuk River	*YAR-mook*	Torrent valley and tributary of the Jordan flowing in from the east just south of the Sea of Galilee
Yiddishah	*Yid-DEE-shaw*	Name of the Ghost-wife (witch) of Endor, a spirit medium
Yotan	*YOH-tan*	A seven-headed dragon in Canaanite mythology, defeated and slain by Ba'al
Zabbad	*ZAB-bad*	One of the many sons of Judge Avdon
Zattu	*ZAT-too*	One of a pair of celebrated warriors from the tribe of Naphtali who always fought as a pair
Zebulun/Zebulunite		One of the twelve tribes of Israel
Zechariah	*Zek-ah-RY-ah*	A son of Abiel of the Benjaminite clan of the Matrites, brother of Ner and uncle to Kish
Zephon, Mount	*ZEE-fawn*	Mountain on which the Canaanites believed that the gods maintained one of their palaces
Zimri	*ZIM-rye*	A young prophet of the School found murdered shortly after the arrival of Cheran and Gavriel

Zion, Mount	*ZY-awn*	The mountain upon which Jerusalem is built
Zorah	*ZOH-rah*	A Juedean city in the Shephelah on the border of Dan's territory; here Samson was born and raised
Zur	*ZUR*	A Matrite Benjaminite brother of Ner and son of Ahiel

APPENDIX B:
BIBLIOGRAPHY

Alter, R. (1999). *The David Story: A Translation with Commentary of 1 and 2 Samuel.* New York: W. W. Norton & Company, Inc.

Achtemeier, P. J. (Ed). (1985). *Harper's Bible Dictionary.* New York: Harper & Row.

Aharoni, Y. (1979). *The Land of the Bible, 2nd Revised Edition.* Philadelphia: Westminster Press.

Albright, W. (1932). *The Archaeology of Palestine.* New Jersey: Fleming H. Revell.

Anderson, B. W. (1978). *The Living World of the Old Testament, 3rd Edition.* London: Longman.

Bray, W., & Trump, D. (1970). *The American Heritage Guide to Archaeology.* New York: American Heritage Press.

Comay, J. (1971). *Who's Who in the Old Testament.* New York: Rinehart & Winston.

Cornfeld, G. (1976). *Archaeology of the Bible: Book by Book.* (D. N. Freedman, Ed.) New York: Harper & Row.

Davis, J. D. (1944). *The Westminster Dictionary of the Bible* (Revised ed.). (H. S. Gehman, Ed.) Philadelphia: The Westminster Press.

Dothan, T. (1982). *The Philistines and their Material Culture.* New Haven and London: Yale University Press.

Douek, N., James, P., Oliphant, M., Rollin, S., Ferguson, J., Campbell, W. S., et al. (1987). *Great Events of Bible Times: New Perspectives on the People, Places, and History of the Biblical World.* (J. Harpur, Ed.) Garden City, New York: Doubleday & Company, Inc.

Edersheim, A. (1994). *The Temple: Its Ministry and Services.* Peabody: Hendrickson Publishers, Inc.

Edwards, I. E. (1972). *The Treasures of Tutankhamun.* Middlesex: Penguin Books, Ltd.

Finkelstein, I. & Shanks, H. (May/June 2010). The Devil Is Not So Blackas He Is Painted. *Biblical Archaology Review,* pp. 23-25.

Frank, H. T. (1972). *An Archaeological Companion to the Bible.* London: SCM Press.

Gordon, C. (1953). *The World of the Old Testament.* New York: Doubleday.

Gower, R. (1987). *The New Manners and Customs of Bible Times.* Chicago: Moody Press.

Gray, J. (1964). *The Canaanites.* London: Thames & Hudson.

Halley, H. H. (1965). *Halley's Bible Handbook.* Grand Rapids: Zondervan Publishing House.

Hamilton, E. (1969). *Mythology.* New York: The New American Library.

Harris, R. L. (1995). *The World of the Bible.* New York: Thames and Hudson Inc.

Heaton, E. W. (1956). *Everyday Life in Old Testament Times.* New York: Charles Scribner.

Herzog, C., & Gichon, M. (1997). *Battles of the Bible.* Mechanicsburg: Greenhill Books, Lionel Leventhal Limited.

Hyslop, A. (1959). *The Two Babylons.* Neptune: Loizeaux Brothers, Inc.

Jenkins, S. (1985). *Nelson's 3-D Bible Mapbook.* Nashville: Lion Publishing plc.

Joseph, F. (1991). *The Works of Josephus: Complete and Unabridged* (New Updated Edition ed.). (W. Whiston, Trans.) Peabody, Massachusetts: Hendrickson Publishers, Inc.

Keller, W. (1958). *The Bible As History: A Confirmation of the Book of Books.* (W. Neil, Trans.) New york: William Morrow and Company.

Kenyon, K. M. (1970). *Archaeology in the Holy Land, 3rd Edition.* Atlanta: John Knox Press.

Koninklijke Brill NV. (1999). *Dictionary of Deities and Demons in the Bible* (2nd Extensively Revised Edition). Grand Rapids: William B. Eerdmans Publishing Company.

Leith, M. J. (2008, November/December). Of Philistines and Phalluses. *Biblical Archaeology Review* , pp. 34, 82.

Levene, D. (2009, March/April). Rare Magic Inscription On Human Skull. *Biblical Archaeology Review,* pp. 46-50.

Mazar, A., & Panitz-Cohen, N. (2008, July/August). To What God? Altars and a House Shrine from Tel Rehov Puzzle Archaeologists. *Biblical Archaeology Review* , pp. 40-47.

Mazar, E. (2009, March/April). The Wall that Nehemiah Built. *Biblical Archaeology Review,* pp. 24-33.

Mazar, E. (June 2010). Did I Find King David's Palace? *Biblical Archaeology Review E-feature.* www.bib-arch.org/e-features/king-davids-palace.asp

Miller, M. S., & Miller, J. L. (1996). *Harper's Encyclopedia of Bible Life.* (B. M. Bennett, & D. H. Scott, Eds.) Edison: Castle Books.

Na'aman, N. (2009, January/February). The Trowel vs. the Text: How the Amarna Letters Challenge Archaeology. *Biblical Archaeology Review* , pp. 52-56, 70-71.

Old Time Gospel Hour. (1980). *The Bible Almanac.* (J. I. Packer, M. C. Tenney, & W. White, Eds.) Nashville: Thomas Nelson, Inc.

Overschelde, V. A. (1961). *Illustrated New Testament.* Collegeville: The Order of St. Benedict, Inc.

Oxford University Press. (1974). *Oxford Bible Atlas.* (H. G. May, G. N. Hunt, & R. W. Hamilton, Eds.) Oxford: Oxford Univeristy Press.

Oxford University Press. (1993). *The Oxford Companion to the Bible.* (B. M. Metzger, & M. D. Coogan, Eds.) New York: Oxford University Press.

Pearlman, M. (1980). *Digging Up the Bible.* New York: Morrow.

Rainey, A. (2008, November/December). Inside Outside: Where Did the Early Israelites Come From? *Biblical Archaeology Review* , pp. 45-50.

Rainey, A. (2008, November/December). Shasu or Habiru: Who Were the Early Israelites? *Biblical Archaeology Review* , pp. 51-55.

ROHR Productions. (1999). *The Holy Land Satellite Atlas, Volumes I and II.* (R. L. Cleave, Ed.) Nicosia, Cyprus: ROHR Productions, Ltd.

Schoville, K. N. (2008, September/October). The Necessary Partnership of the Bible and Archaeology. *Biblical Archaeology Review,* pp. 30, 74.

Shanks, H. (2009, January/February). A Fortified City from King David's Time. *Biblical Archaology Review* , pp. 38-43.

Shanks, H. (2009, March/April). The Palace of Solomon's Daughter? *Biblical Archaeology Review,* pp. 4, 70.

Smith, G. A. (1966). *The Historical Geography of the Holy Land.* New

York: Harper & Row.

Soggin, J. A. (1985). *A History of Israel.* London: SCM Press.

Sudilovsky, J. (2009, March/April). "Apples of Gold." *Biblical Archaeology Review,* pp. 14.

The National Geographic Book Service. (1967). *Everyday Life in Bible Times.* London: The National Geographic Society.

The Press and Information Office, The Embassy of the Arab Republic of Egypt. (1977). *Background to Egypt: Five Thousand Years of Civilization.* London: The Press and Information Office, The Embassy of the Arab Republic of Egypt.

The Reader's Digest Association, Inc. (1979). *Great People of the Bible and How They Lived.* Pleasantville: The Reader's Digest Association, Inc.

Times Books Limited. (1987). *The Harper Atlas of the Bible.* (J. B. Pritchard, Ed.) New York: Harper & Row, Publishers Inc.

Watch Tower Bible and Tract Society of Pennsylvania. (1979). *All Scripture is Inspired of God and Beneficial.* New York: Watchtower Bible and Tract Society of New York.

Watch Tower Bible and Tract Society of Pennsylvania and International Bible Students Association. (1988). *Insight on the Scriptures.* Brooklyn: Watchtower Bible and Tract Society of New York, Inc.

Watch Tower Bible and Tract Society of Pennsylvania. (2003). *See the Good Land.* New York: Watchtower Bible and Tract Society of New York, Inc.

Wiseman, D. J. (1973). *People of Old Testament Times.* Clarendon: Oxford University Press.

WM. B. Eerdmans Publishing Company. (1979). *The New Bible Dictionary.* (J. D. Douglas, F. F. Bruce, J. I. Packer, R. V. Tasker, & D. J. Wiseman, Eds.) Grand Rapids, Michigan: Wm. B. Eerdmans Publishing Company.

Yadin, Y. (1963). *The Art of Warfare in Biblical Lands: In the Light of Arc haeological Study.* New York: McGraw-Hill.

Zohary, M. (1982). *Plants of the Bible.* London and New York: Cambridge University Press.

APPENDIX C:
IN DEFENSE OF ARTISTIC LICENSE:
POINTS OF CONTENTION OR INTERPRETATION

On the Use of the Divine Name, Jehovah[1]

"One of the most fundamental and essential features of the biblical revelation is the fact that God is not without a name; he has a personal name, by which he can, and is to be, invoked."—*The New International Dictionary of New Testament Theology* (Volume 2, page 649)

God's personal name in Hebrew is written יהוה. These four letters are called the Tetragrammaton, and are transliterated into English as YHWH or JHVH. This name appears more often in the Scriptures than any other—almost seven thousand times in the Hebrew and Aramaic texts of the so-called "Old Testament." The name is a form of the Hebrew verb *hawah*, which means "to become." The name itself signifies "He Causes to Become"—a designation of the One who fulfills all his promises and unfailingly realizes his purposes.

There can be no doubt that the divine name was commonly used in ancient times. Many archaeological discoveries bear this out. For instance, in a burial cave southwest of Jerusalem, a Hebrew inscription from the second half of the eighth century B.C.E.[2] contains statements such as "Jehovah is the God of the whole earth."[3] Pottery fragments discovered in Arad from the second half of the seventh century B.C.E. included a private letter that began, "To my lord Eliashib: May Jehovah ask for your peace" and ends, "He dwells in the house of Jehovah."[4] In 1975-6, a collection of Hebrew and Phoenician inscriptions were discovered in the Negeb that included the Tetragrammaton in Hebrew letters. Just outside Jerusalem's walls, a small,

---

[1] Edited and reprinted from Appendix B of *Prophet of Israel*, Lulu Press Inc., 2008.

[2] Throughout this text, I use the abbreviation B.C.E. "Before our Common Era" rather than B.C. "Before Christ." Primarily this is because it has by now been well established that Christ was not born in the "zero" year. Similarly, the designation C.E. "Common Era" is a more accurate reflection of our times than A.D. "Anno Domini."

[3] *Israel Exploration Journal*, Volume 13, No. 2.

[4] *Ibid*, Volume 16, No.1.

rolled-up strip of silver was excavated and dated to before the Babylonian exile. It had the name of Jehovah written on it in Hebrew.[5] The Lachish Letters, written on potsherds and found in the ruins of Lachish, appear to be communications from an officer at a Judean outpost to his superior during the war between Israel and Babylon toward the end of the seventh century B.C.E. Seven of the legible letters begin their message with a salutation that uses the Tetragrammaton; it appears in the messages eleven times.

No one today knows how the name of God was originally pronounced in Hebrew. Superstition caused the Jews to stop speaking the name in the 1st or 2nd centuries, and eventually its proper pronunciation was forgotten. (As an example of this change, in Jerusalem's Israel Museum one fragment of the Greek *Septuagint* that has been dated to the first century C.E. has God's name four times in Zechariah 8:19-21 and 8:23-9:4. Four hundred years later, the Alexandrine Manuscript was written, and in this copy of the *Septuagint* God's name had been replaced in those same verses by abbreviations of the word *Kyrios*, or "Lord").

When the name was written by superstitious Jewish scribes, the consonants were marked with the vowel points for the word *Adhonai*, or "Lord." (They apparently deemed it too holy to write accurately, although Moses clearly would not have agreed with them). From this came the spelling Iehouah, which eventually became Jehovah in English. Most modern scholars feel that "Yahweh" (or some variation thereof) is a more accurate representation of the ancient pronunciation.

Should we, therefore, abandon the pronunciation "Jehovah" because we know that it is not the ancient Hebrew pronunciation? Of course not. If we did, we would have to abandon "Jesus" in favor of "Yeshua" or "Yehoshua"; Jeremiah in favor of "Yirmeya'hu"; Timothy in favor of "Timotheus". In fact, we would have to change the pronunciation of virtually every name in the Bible. But we do not. Even when we are sure of the pronunciation of an ancient name, we typically replace it with the recognized, English version. After all, we do not fault the Italians for calling Jesus *Gesù*, or the Greeks for calling him *Iesous*. This is the nature of translation—we use the most commonly recognized version of a particular word in our own language. To abandon the name entirely—to, in fact, replace it with less meaningful titles like "Lord" or "God" is an absurd notion with absolutely no grounds in scripture or logic.

---

[5] *Biblical Archaeology Review*, March/April 1983, page 18.

In the words of John W. Davis, a missionary in China during the 19th century: "If the Holy Ghost says Jehovah in any given place in the Hebrew, why does the translator not say Jehovah in English or Chinese? What right has he to say, *I will use Jehovah in this place and a substitute for it in that?* . . . If any one should say that there are cases in which the use of Jehovah would be wrong, let him show the reason why; the onus probandi rests upon him. He will find the task a hard one, for he must answer this simple question,— *If in any given case it is wrong to use Jehovah in the translation then why did the inspired writer use it in the original?*"—*The Chinese Recorder and Missionary Journal*, Volume VII, Shanghai, 1876, italics added.

Many translators and scholars have recognized this truth:

- "From this point onward I use the word Jehovah, because, as a matter of fact, this name has now become more naturalized in our vocabulary and cannot be supplanted."—*Theologie des Alten Testaments* (Theology of the Old Testament) by Gustav Friedrich Oehler, second edition, published in 1882, page 143.

- "In our translations, instead of the (hypothetical) form *Yahweh*, we have used the form *Jehovah*...which is the conventional literary form used in French."—*Grammaire de l'hebreu biblique* (Grammar of Biblical Hebrew), by Paul Jouon, 1923 edition, page 49.

- "That they [the Jews] now allege the name Jehovah to be unpronounceable, they do not know what they are talking about...If it can be written with pen and ink, why should it not be spoken, which is much better than being written with pen and ink? Why do they not also call it unwriteable, unreadable, or unthinkable? All things considered, there is something foul."—Martin Luther, 1534

Strangely, however, most modern Bible translators still choose to remove the name wholesale, or nearly so, replacing it with the title "LORD" or "GOD" in all capitals. Most of them cite reasons identical or similar to the following:

- "In this translation we have followed the orthodox Jewish tradition and substituted 'the LORD' for the name 'Yahweh' and the phrase 'the LORD God' for the phrase 'the Lord Yahweh.' In all cases where 'Lord' or 'God' represents an original 'Yahweh' small capitals are employed."—J.M. Powis Smith and Edgar J. Goodspeed, 1934 edition.

- "For two reasons the Committee has returned to the more familiar usage of the King James Version [that is, omitting the name of God]: (1) the word 'Jehovah' does not accurately represent any form of the Name ever used in Hebrew; and (2) the use of any proper name for the one and only God, as though there were other gods from whom he had to be distinguished, was discontinued in Judaism before the Christian era and is entirely inappropriate for the universal faith of the Christian Church."—Preface to the *Revised Standard Version.*

No other gods from whom Jehovah had to be distinguished? There are millions of gods! The Bible itself attests to this fact. (1 Corinthians 8:5; Philippians 3:19). The Old Testament is filled with references to gods; the Hebrew word *'elohim* is even used by Bible writers to refer to Israelite men in positions of authority. (Psalms 82:1, 6; Exodus 4:16; 7:1). The fact that Jehovah is the *almighty* God does not alleviate the need to distinguish Him from the thousands—millions today—of other gods. If there was truly no need to 'distinguish' Him, then why would these same translators use small capitals to designate these instances in which they have chosen to overrule the judgment of the original writers?

It is astonishing to me that Bible translators, supposedly men who revere the book that they are translating, would decide that a name that the Bible itself uses nearly 7,000 times is "entirely inappropriate" for Christians! It should be noted that they do not raise these issues as regards any other name in the Scriptures, including that of Jesus Christ himself, although many of them consider him Almighty God incarnate.

Interestingly, the same translators that insist on removing the divine name from their works do so only when the name stands alone. The name of God is one of the most common elements of Biblical Hebrew names, appearing prominently in Ahijah, Elijah, Irijah, Isshijah, Jahzeiah, and many, many others—not to mention the oft-quoted "Hallelujah". Almost every Biblical name that ends in "-ah" or "-iah" is, in fact, derived from the name "Jehovah." None of these translators has changed Elijah's name to Eliyahu, or some other "more accurate" Hebrew equivalent. Nor have they replaced the "Jah" in his name with "Lord" or "God", capitalized or otherwise.

Thankfully, many modern translators have recognized that their responsibility lies, not in amending the divine text in accordance with Jewish tradition or their own opinions, but in reproducing the words of the original writers as accurately as possible. Thus the translators of the *American Standard Version* of 1901 wrote in their preface: "[The translators] were brought to the unanimous conviction that a Jewish superstition, which regarded the Divine Name as too sacred to be uttered, ought no longer to dominate in the English or any other version of the Old Testament . . . This Memorial Name, explained in Ex. iii. 14, 15, and emphasized as such over and over in the original text of the Old Testament, designates God as the personal God, as the covenant God, the God of revelation, the Deliverer, the Friend of his people . . . This personal name, with its wealth of sacred associations, is now restored to the place in the sacred text to which it has an unquestionable claim." Similarly, Steven T. Byington wrote regarding *The Bible in Living English*, "The spelling and the pronunciation are not highly important. What is highly important is to keep it clear that this is a personal name. There are several texts that cannot be properly understood if we translate this name by a common noun like 'Lord,' or, much worse, by a substantivized adjective." J. B. Rotherham wrote of his *Studies in the Psalms* (1911): "The employment of this English form of the Memorial name (Exo. 3:18) in the present version of the Psalter does not arise from any misgiving as to the more correct pronunciation, as being Yahwéh; but solely from practical evidence personally selected of the desirability of keeping in touch with the public ear and eye in a matter of this kind, in which the principal thing is the easy recognition of the Divine name intended."

I have chosen, therefore, to use the name "Jehovah" in this novel, the common English translation of the Hebrew name that would have been used in Samuel's day. If by this usage readers become aware of the bizarre and unjustified removal of the divine name from so many versions of the Bible, it would be for me a great reward for my efforts in taking on this project.

On the Making of Images

Certain scholars, some strict Muslims, and modern Hasidic Jews have interpreted the second of the Ten Commandments as forbidding the making of any representation of a natural (created) object, whether such an object was used in worship or not. The Scriptures do not justify such a narrow interpretation of the Law. The Copper Sea which stood in the Courtyard of the Temple was supported by cast bronze bulls. The steps approaching King Solomon's dais were flanked by figures of lions. Archaeology has also provided us with countless other examples of everyday Israelite objects from as early as the tenth century B.C.E. which were clearly made as representations of natural figures. (A well-known example is the "ivory pomegranate" inscribed "Belonging to the temple of Yahweh, holy to the priests" purchased by the Israel Museum in 1988). For this reason, I have included such representations in this story, including the use of heraldic banners which use symbols to represent individual tribes (see the heading "Israelite Tribal Heraldry" below).

Anachronistic Proverbs

The books of Proverbs and Ecclesiastes are generally believed to have been written and/or compiled by Solomon. (This has become a matter of some contention in recent years based on (what I feel are) highly controversial linguistic and semantic grounds. I have yet to see any critic provide hard evidence to dispute the Bible's claim and Jewish tradition in this regard). I have made reference to several of these Proverbs in this work, on the grounds that Solomon admitted to being, not only a writer, but a compiler of these sayings. (Ecclesiastes 12:9) It seems reasonable to me that some of them could have predated Solomon by many years. In some cases, these may have been wise sayings that had been passed down from as far back as Joshua's day, and were already in common use in the tenth century B.C.E.

Standing Stones

Considering the attention garnered by the megaliths, menhirs, sarsens, and dolmens of Europe, I find it fascinating (and a little disappointing) how little attention has been paid to the ancient stone monuments of Palestine. Standing stones have been an element of the culture of the Levant from the earliest times (from at least as early as Jacob's day, in the 17th century B.C.E., according to Genesis 28). They played an important role as remembrancers for the people of Israel both before and after the conquest.

Interestingly, symbolic stone constructions were also built by other cultures in Palestine before the arrival of Joshua and the nation of Israel. As one example, in the West Bank region there is a set of giant concentric rings of stacked stone known as Gilgal of the Rephaim. Ancient Jewish tradition says that it was constructed by the race of giants sometime before the 16th century B.C.E.

In any case, the standing stones referred to in this story are specifically mentioned in scripture and, in some cases, still visible to tourist visiting the land of Israel today. They are every bit as significant and fascinating as the various henges and dolmens of Europe, and often illustrate turning points in the history of the Israelites.

I have included them in this story not only to call attention to these interesting structures of the Levant, but because they provided a metaphor of the culture's connection with the land that I felt was too opportune to miss.

The Staff and its Significance in Scripture

Modern western cultures have relegated the staff or rod to a "walking stick," a device whose function is limited to aiding weekend adventurers or the infirm. For the agrarian peoples of ancient Palestine, though, a staff was much more—and especially so in the case of the nation of Israel.

The staff was a symbol of authority to the nomadic herders. It was a vital tool in caring for and protecting the sheep. While it could and did serve as a support device while traveling, it could also be used as a weapon, for discipline, for rescue, for communication, or for the construction of temporary shelter from the elements.

It is not therefore totally surprising to see the staff take on almost mythic proportions in the history of Israel by the time of Samuel's appointment. Jacob refers to his staff as a symbol of his presence or his arrival (Genesis 32:10), Judah provides it as valuable identification and collateral (Genesis 38:18), Messianic prophecies regarding the tribe of Judah use it as a symbol of kingly authority (Genesis 49:10), Jehovah gives one to Moses as a symbol of his appointment as the leader of the nation (Exodus 4:17), and Aaron's is transformed into a serpent to demonstrate Jehovah's power over the Egyptian priests (Exodus 7:9). Moses 'stretches out his rod' to turn the Nile to blood, to call forth a plague of frogs, a plague of gnats, a plague of locusts, and thunder and hail. The same rod is used to part the Red Sea and to gain supernatural victory in battle (Exodus 17). A rod is used by Jehovah to indicate his choice of High Priest (Numbers 17), and Moses uses it to miraculously bring forth water from a crag.

In light of these and other facts, I have made the staff a symbol of authority and a metaphor in this story as well, even going so far as to having it play a role in the performance of Samuel's miracles.

TIMOTHY WILKINSON

The Climate and Ecology of Ancient Palestine

The Palestine I present in the Eternal Throne Chronicles is obviously a far lusher, more forested, and climatically milder place than we find it to be at present. As with all things ancient, there is an ongoing debate as to the ecological and meteorological conditions of Israel three millennia ago.

One thing is certain—even modern-day Israel has a remarkably diverse ecology. From the snow-covered slopes of Mount Hermon it is possible to view, in one glance, broad and barren deserts of yellow sand, lush green jungles, fertile valleys of checkered fields, plateaus and steppes of garigue, sandy Mediterranean beaches, majestic forests of oak and cedar, and more. There are few places on earth with such variety of geography and climate within so small an area.

Many researchers believe that the dawn of the Iron Age in the tenth century resulted in a dramatic increase in the harvesting of timber, since the production and forging of iron require enormous amounts of fuel. Archaeology seems, to a greater or lesser degree, to back up this assumption. Certainly the land of Israel was once a place of great forests, the remnants of which can still be glimpsed in a handful of preserves. At some time the entire Plain of Sharon was a mighty, sprawling forest of oaks; the forests of Hereth, Mehanaim, Ephraim, and Bashan are all celebrated in Scripture for their majesty and density. When forests are referred to by Bible writers, they are generally connected to an element of danger or mystery (David's hiding place in 1 Samuel 22:5, the site (and cause) of Absalom's death in 2 Samuel 18).

I have chosen to portray the climate of Palestine as more temperate and less arid. Partly this is because it serves the purposes of the story. Partly it is because the Bible record seems to describe it so. Partly it is because when the land was still covered in trees, especially the hills and mountains of the Shephelah and Judah (which would have been taller three thousand years ago), clouds traveling inland from the Mediterranean would have been more likely to drop their precipitation before evaporating over the Arabian Desert.[6] This increase in rainfall, added to the fertility of a soil that had not

---

[6] A fascinating article by Bill Mollison published in Issue No. 28 (FebApril 1988) of the *Permaculture Journal* discusses some of the ways in which trees increase precipitation even in a local area. Trees provide surfaces on which moisture-rich air blowing in from the sea can condense (both because of the cool surface of the leaves and the slowing effect of forests on onshore breezes). Roughly 25% of the condensed water re-evaporates from the leaves and is added to clouds; these are blown inland and drop the

been depleted by millennia of farming, erosion, and irrigation, add up to considerably more lush Israel.

The science I have used to come to these conclusions may be considered suspect by some. They may comfort themselves with the acknowledgement that the decisions were primarily made to serve the purposes of the story, and are not intended to represent historical fact. To the best of my knowledge, however, they do match the depictions and descriptions of the Bible writers.

Samson

Of all the artistic decisions I made in this volume, I expect that none will be more controversial than my portrayal of Samson's empowerment.

In the Book of Judges chapter 13 verse 25, Samuel writes: "In time Jehovah's spirit started to impel him [Samson] at Mahanedan between Zorah and Eshtaol." This statement is given no further explanation, and the next episode recorded is his pursuit of a Philistine wife in Timnah.

Mahanedan may be the name of a town (no literary or archaeological record of one has ever been found), but its literal meaning, "Camp of Dan," could as easily refer to an encampment of the army of Samson's tribe. Its location, between Zorah and Eshtaol, is a prime location for the battles between the Philistines and the Israelites under Samuel that are referred to in 1 Samuel 7:14.

What form Samson's empowerment took is not explained, either by Samuel or by Josephus. Every other Judge in the Bible (with the possible exception of Shamgar) when empowered became a divinely-appointed commander of the armies of Israel, leading them to victory against their enemies. Samson is unique: not once in the Scriptural account is he described as leading an army. He operates alone, an unstoppable, one-man force.

The only possible clue to the nature of Samson's empowerment is found at Judges 14:10 where, upon his arrival in Timnah, the Philistines assign thirty groomsmen to "keep with him." Was this simply some Philistine marriage ritual? Or did the Philistines already know something about Sam-

---

moisture as rain. Eckman spirals caused by the tree line add 40% to rainfall along those lines. The forest also provides particulate matter in the air on which raindrops can form.

son that motivated them to keep him under guard by thirty soldiers while he was in Philistine territory?

We cannot know the answer, but I am inclined to believe the latter. Samson began to be impelled by Jehovah's spirit at the (military) "camp of Dan," the site of great battles between Israel and Philistia; the next time he enters Philistia (peaceably, to marry a Philistine woman) they assign a guard of thirty men to keep an eye on him. Others will come to different conclusions, but to me, it seems likely that they already feared this young hero. They express no surprise at his supernatural abilities when they are next demonstrated.

It is left to the reader to decide if Samson's empowerment was his supernaturally-aided defeat of the Hunter or his unofficially becoming the director and tactician of Israel's forces in the battles that conclude this story.

The Ghost-Wife of Endor

Bible readers will recognize the "Witch of Endor" from King Saul's infamous encounter with her in 1 Samuel 28. There are many indications that the decades leading up to King Saul's reign were a time when such spirit mediums were common—not the least of which is Saul's campaign against them as described in 1 Samuel 28:3. These mediums apparently used Canaanite magic to summon the ghosts of the dead, very much as spirit mediums continue to (claim) to do today.

That such summoning of the dead is impossible is obvious from the Bible's own testimony that "the dead are conscious of nothing" (Ecclesiastes 9:5), they no longer have thoughts (Psalm 146:4), and that the soul, rather than going on to a further existence in another realm, is mortal (Ezekiel 18:4, 20).

It is also highly improbably that, even if Samuel were alive in some other realm, he or his God would allow him to be summoned by a woman whose practices were condemned in the Torah. Are we to believe that spirit mediums were so powerful that they were able to summon the "souls" of anyone they wished, good or bad, from "heaven" or "hell," in spite of Jehovah's condemnation of the practice? Even putting doctrinal considerations aside, such a belief defies reason and common sense.

The account in 1 Samuel 28 indicates that only the medium herself actually "saw" the "ghost" of Samuel. Saul, desperate to believe, accepted the medium's (rather vague) description as being of Samuel. Whatever image or voice the medium heard was either the product of some other maleficent power with sufficient insight or knowledge to predict Saul's approaching death, or (and I do not believe this to be the case) the work of a medium whose cold-reading abilities paralleled those of the supposed mediums of our day.

The term "Ghost Wife" I have taken from Robert Alter's excellent literal translation, referred to in the Bibliography. I felt that it vividly captured the role of the medium.

Israelite Tribal Heraldry

Our wide-range view of the history of Israel, taken with the perspective of passing millennia, gives us a picture of a single, united nation. That concept has become a prominent political theme since the Second World War. But when we narrow our focus to the ninth and tenth centuries B.C.E., a different picture emerges.

It was at Mount Sinai in the year 1513 B.C.E. that Israel became a nation. It was comprised of an amalgamation of thirteen related tribes and countless foreigners who joined themselves to those tribes (including entire peoples, such as the Gibeonites of Joshua chapter 9). It would be many centuries before Israel viewed itself as a single people. Tribal loyalty remained stronger than national until after Saul's day, perhaps reinforced by divine edicts forbidding intermarrying between tribes and strict delineation of unalterable tribal territories.

Under these circumstances, over a period of over 700 years of tribal intermarriage, each tribe would have no doubt developed distinct genetic traits and characteristics. It was possible for an Israelite to identify a man of another tribe by his looks or by his accent (Judges 12:1-6).

I have combined this knowledge with Jacob's death-bed prophecy in Genesis chapter 49. There, Jacob foretells specific characteristics that would apply to each tribe. All of them come true in various ways, applying sometimes to the actions of the tribe as a whole, and other times to events connected with specific persons in the tribe.

While Israel was traveling in the wilderness, their camps were organized by tribes, and each tribal encampment was marked with a 'sign' or 'banner' (Numbers 2:2). While the Bible does not give descriptions of these signs, it seems that they were some kind of tribal and family ensigns. Such designations would be very useful in organizing a camp of upwards of three million people.

I have therefore assigned to each tribe a heraldic sign that would be used as a rallying point in battle, and have at times emphasized the unique nature of individual tribes.

The Nature of the Revelations of the Sons of the Prophets

The term "Sons of the Prophets" as used in the Scriptures is widely accepted to be referring to some sort of school or commune set up by Samuel to serve the unique needs of the community of prophets and to provide training and mutual support.

Samuel's writings explicitly describe three types of prognosticators: seers, whose abilities seemed to involve the perception of things not visible to common men; prophets, whose primary assignment was the proclamation of Divine statements; and Visionaries, who apparently were able to see future, past, or distant events by means of visions. (During Samuel's day, the term Seer was also used as a generic term for all three types—see 1 Samuel 5:9).

It seems unlikely that Jehovah would have given a vision like the one I have described to a child like Gavriel. Although many times in the Scriptures God does give his prophets messages that they themselves do not understand, to do so to a small child seems unnecessarily frightening—especially if the message took the form of a vision.

This poetic license was taken only because it better served the purposes of the storyteller, and is in no way supported by any research I have done.

Baghadh

Some anthropologists believe that Bronze Age Palestine and other areas of the Middle East must have been rife with sexually transmitted disease, an unavoidable side effect of their licentious religious and cultural practices. I have chosen to afflict Baghadh with syphilis. This disease was not identified until many centuries later, but it is certainly possible that it existed. The symptoms I describe, while typical only of the worst outbreaks, are entirely realistic.

Malchia

This game is known to have been played in the first century—I have indulged in a little anachronism here on the basis that it *could* have been played earlier. The games is known in Greek as *Basileus* or "king." Markings for this game can be seen on the paving stones at Gabbatha in Jerusalem to this day.

TIMOTHY WILKINSON

APPENDIX D:
CHRONOLOGY

"Anyone approaching the study of ancient history for the first time must be impressed by the positive way modern historians date events which took place thousands of years ago. In the course of further study this wonder will, if anything, increase. For as we examine the sources of ancient history we see how scanty, inaccurate, or downright false, the records were even at the time they were first written. And poor as they originally were, they are poorer still as they have come down to us: half destroyed by the tooth of time or by the carelessness and rough usage of men." (*The Secret of the Hittites*, by C. W. Ceram, 1956, pp. 133, 134).

"The purpose of this book is to present, in series, the chronologies of various contiguous areas as they appear in 1964 to the eyes of regional specialists. Despite the new information, the over-all situation is still fluid, and forthcoming data will render some conclusions obsolete, possibly even before this volume appears in print." (The Foreward (p.vii) to *Chronologies in Old World Archaeology*, edited by Robert Ehrich, 1965).

Bilblical chronology is a subject to which many volumes have been devoted, all of them written by sharper minds than mine. Unfortunately, these volumes tend to be consistent in only one thing: their disagreement with one another. The reality is that, while the overall framework of Biblical chronology has been firmly established for some time, the details of certain time periods (i.e., the book of Judges) are still unclear. There is simply not enough information given in the Scriptures to be definitive on the subject. This has required the author to make certain decisions, not on what I believe to be true, but on what I believe could possibly be true. My conclusions are conjectural and, as such, will be (appropriately) contested by some, roundly denounced by others.

The following is an effort on my part to provide the barest outline of Biblical chronology that may help to inform the novice of the reasoning that has informed my choices in this story. For those who desire more information, I refer them to the excellent article on "Chronology" in the encyclopedia *Insight on the Scriptures*, listed in Appendix B.

The following chart gives the basic scriptural foundation upon which the chronology I have used in this story is based.

	Event	Date B.C.E.	Years between events
The 1,656 years of this period are clearly described in The Scroll of Bereshith 5:1-29 and 7:6. The figures given are based on the Masoretic text, well established as more accurate than the Greek *Septuagint*.	From Adam's creation	4026	
	to the birth of Seth		130
	to the birth of Enosh		105
	to the birth of Kenan		90
	to the birth of Mahalalel		70
	to the birth of Jared		65
	to the birth of Enoch		162
	to the birth of Methuselah		65
	to the birth of Lamech		187
	to the birth of Noah		182
	to the Flood	2370	600
This era is described in The Scroll of Bereshith 11:10-12:4. The year that Terah died was also the year in which the Abrahamic covenant was validated, and Abraham entered into Canaan.	to Arpachshad's birth		2
	to the birth of Shelah		35
	to the birth of Eber		30
	to the birth of Peleg		34
	to the birth of Reu		30
	to the birth of Serug		32
	to the birth of Nahor		30
	to the birth of Terah		29
	to the death of Terah	1943	205
These figures are based on The Scroll of Bereshith 12:4, 21:5, 25:26, 47:9, and Gal 3:16, 17.	to the birth of Isaac		25
	to the birth of Jacob		60
	Jacob's entry into Egypt		70
	to the Exodus	1513	215
1 Ki 6:1 gives 480 yrs from the Exodus to temple construction. Deut 2:7, 29:5, Ac 13:21, 2 Sam 5:4, 1 Ki 11:42, 43, and 12:1-20 give the basis for these calculations.	to Israel's entry into Canaan	1473	40
	to Saul's reign	1117	356
	to David's reign	1077	40
	to Solomon's reign	1037	40

In the midst of this tidy timeline we must insert the problematic period of the Judges.

Judge	Term of office	Reference
Othniel	40 years	Judges 3:9-11
	18 years of oppression by Moabites	Judges 3:14
Ehud	80 years	Judges 3:12-30
Shamgar		Judges 3:31
	20 years of oppression by Canaanites	Judges 4:3
Deborah/Barak	40 years	Judges 4:1-5:31
	7 years of oppression by Midianites	Judges 6:1
Gideon		Judges 6:2-8:32
	Abimelech and Jotham	Judges 9:1-57
Tola	23 years	Judges 10:1-2
Jair	22 years	Judges 10:3-4
	18 years of oppression by Philistines, Ammonites	
Jephthah	6 years	Judges 10:6-12:7
Ibzan	7 years	Judges 12:8-10
Elon	10 years	Judges 12:11, 12
Abdon	8 years	Judges 12:13-15
	Forty years of oppression by Philistines	Judges 13:1
Samson	20 years	Judges 13:2-16:31

We can establish the overall length of this period, even though it is not directly apportioned in Scripture: We have several periods of known length (the time spent wandering in the wilderness, the rules of Saul and David, and the years of Solomon's reign leading up to the building of the Temple) that total to 123 years. Subtract that from the 479 years between the Exodus and the beginning of Solomon's fourth year, and we are left with 356 years from Israel's entry into Canaan in 1473 B.C.E. until the start of Saul's reign in 1117 B.C.E.

But totaling all of the terms of office of the Judges and the periods of foreign oppression gives us a sum of 410 years! Obviously, then, some of these terms of office were served concurrently, rather than successively. Indeed, the descriptions of Judges Ibzan, Elon, and Abdon give no indication of their taking any military action at all during their terms. Did they judge Israel during the 40 years of Philistine occupation (Judges 13:1)? We must make educated guesses, but the Scriptures provide no basis for any degree of certainty. It is noteworthy that Judges 13:2 does not begin "After him..." as does 12:8, 12:11, and 12:13. Samuel, the author of the book, deliberately wrote "Meanwhile.." This seems to me to indicate that the events of chapter 13 are happening sometime during the 40 year occupation. This wording also allows for the possibility that the reigns of Judges Ibzan, Elon, and Abdon took place during this 40 years. Having this kind of overlap provides one explanation for the chronological difficulties of the book of Judges. It also places the reigns of Ibzan, Elon, Abdon, and Samson during the lifetime of Samuel—which, in turn, matches the political situation between Israel and the Philistines during this time.

We can establish the date of one specific event during the period of the Judges. At Judges 11:26 Jephthah, at the start of his term of office, refers to a period of "three hundred years" during which Israel had controlled lands east of the Jordan. Using the year 1473 B.C.E. as the date of Israel's crossing of the Jordan and the conquest of Jericho (as established above), the start of Jephthah's six-year term would begin at around the year 1173 B.C.E. Samuel's birth and death can be approximately placed using contextual information (such as the date of Saul's and David's coronations, etc.). Since Josephus (*Antiquities*, Book 5, 10:4) tells us that Samuel became a prophet at twelve years of age, reasonable inferences as to the date of his death place his time of service at Shiloh concurrent with the Judgeship of Jephthah. Certainly other conclusions can be arrived at; this is the one I have adopted for the purposes of this story. (See also *Insight on the Scriptures, Volume II*, p. 26, published by Jehovah's Witnesses).

The language in Judges 12 through 16 seems to suggest a chronology much more definitive (and successive) than other portions of that book. After mentioning Jephthah's death in 12:7, verse 8 reads, "*After him*, Ibzan of Bethlehem led Israel." Verse 11 follows with, "*After him*, Abdon son of Hillel, from Pirathon, led Israel." After Abdon's death in verse 15, Chapter 13 verse 1 begins, "Again the Israelites did evil…" and proceeds to introduce the Judgeship of Samson. (All italics mine). The use of the phrase "after him" which is not used in introducing the terms of office of the previous judges, seems to indicate a continuous chronology, rather than an overlap or simultaneity of Judgeship.

Using this (admittedly suppositional) logic, Samson's 20 year time as Judge would have taken place sometime between Samuel's childhood at the Tabernacle but after the 25 years served by Ibzan, Elon, and Abdon and before Samuel's appointment of Saul as the first king of Israel.

Using the information of these two tables, however, it is not difficult to extrapolate many other dates, often to a precise degree, and sometimes (as in the case of the periods of the various Judges) to an approximate degree. A timeline can be constructed, then, that might look something like this:

DATE	EVENT
4026	Adam's creation
3896	Cain slays Abel, Birth of Seth (Gen 4:8, 25)
3791	Brith of Enosh (Gen 5:6)
3701	Birth of Kenan (Gen 5:9)
3631	Birth of Mahalalel (Gen 5:12)
3566	Brith of Jared (Gen 5:15)
3404	Birth of Enoch (Gen 5:18)
3339	Birth of Methuselah (Gen 5:21)
3152	Birth of Lamech (Gen 5:25)
3096	Death of Adam (Gen 5:5)
3039	Enoch taken (Gen 5:24)
2984	Seth dies (Gen 5:8)
2970	Birth of Noah (Gen 5:28)
2886	Enosh dies (Gen 5:11)
2791	Kenan dies (Gen 5:14)
2736	Mahalalel dies (Gen 5:17)
2604	Jared dies (Gen 5:20)
2490	120 year pronouncement by God (Gen 6:3)
2470	Birth of Japheth
2468	Birth of Shem
2375	Lamech dies (Gen 5:31)
2370	Death of Methuselah, **The Great Flood** (Gen 7:11)
2369	Rainbow covenant (Gen 9:12, 13)
2368	Birth of Arpachshad (Gen 11:10)
c.2335	Birth of Sargon the Great
2333	Birth of Shelah (Gen 11:12)
2303	Birth of Eber (Gen 11:14)
2269	Tower of Babel; Birth of Peleg (Gen 11:1-9, 16)
2258	Egypt enters First Intermediate Period
2239	Reu born (Gen 11:18)
2207	Serug born (Gen 11:20)
2177	Birth of Nahor (Gen 11:22)
2148	Birth of Terah (Gen 11:24)
2134	Beginning of Middle Kingdom of Egypt
c.2100	Ur-Nammu founds final Sumerian dynasty
2030	Death of Peleg (Gen 11:17)
2029	Death of Nahor (Gen 11:25)
2020	Death of Noah (Gen 9:29)
2018	Birth of Abraham (Gen 11:26)
2008	Birth of Sarai
2000	Gilgamesh epic written; Hittites settle Anatolia; Mycenaeans conquer Greece
1977	Serug dies (Gen 11:23)

1950	Elamites destroy Ur
1943	Abraham crosses Euphrates; beg. of 430 years to Law (Gen 12:4, 7; Ex 12:40; Gal 3:17
1933	Lot rescued, Abram and Melchizedek (Gen 14:16, 18; 16:3)
1932	Ishmael born (Gen 16:15, 16)
1930	Arpachshad dies (Gen 11:5)
1919	Covenant of Circumcision; Judgment of Sodom & Gomorrah (Gen 17; 19:24)
1918	Birth of Isaac; Beginning of "450 years" (Gen 21:2, 5; Acts 13:17-20)
1913	Weaning of Isaac, Ishmael banished; beginning of 400 year affliction (Gen 21:8; 15:13; Acts 7:6)
1900	Shelah dies
1893	Abraham attempts to sacrifice Isaac
1881	Death of Sarah (Gen 17:17; 23:1)
1878	Isaac and Rebekah married (Gen 25:20)
1868	Death of Shem (Gen 11:11)
1858	Birth of Esau and Jacob (Gen 25:26)
1843	Death of Abraham (Gen 25:7)
1839	Eber dies
1830	First great Babylonian Dynasty
1818	Esau marries Hittite wives (Gen 26:34)
1800	Hammurabi rules in Babylon--end of Sumerians; Stonehenge built
1795	Death of Ishmael (Gen 25:17)
1781	Jacob flees to Haran (Gen 28:2)
1774	Jacob marries Leah and Rachel (Gen 29:23-30)
1767	Birth of Joseph (Gen 30:23, 24)
1761	Jacob returns to Canaan; wrestles angel, renamed Israel (Gen 32:24-28)
1750	Joseph sold into slavery (Gen 37:2, 28)
1738	Death of Isaac (Gen 35:28, 29)
1737	Joseph made Prime Minister (Gen 41:40, 60)
1728	Jacob's family enters Egypt (Gen 45-47)
1711	Death of Jacob (Gen 47:28)
1700	Hittites form old kingdom with capital at Hattusas
1668	Hyksos invasion ends Middle Kingdom of Egypt
1657	Death of Joseph (Gen 50:26)
b.1613	Some time before this date was Job's trial
c. 1600	Egypt becomes first world power (Exo 1:8)
1597	Birth of Aaron
1593	Birth of Moses (Ex 2:2, 10)
1570	Start of New Kingdom in Egypt
1560	Birth of Joshua
1553	Moses kills Egyptian, flees (Exo 2:11, 14, 15; Acts 7:23)
1531	Hittites destroy Babylon, Hammurabi dynasty ends
1514	Moses at the burning bush (Exo 3:2)
1513	1st Passover, Exodus, Red Sea; end of 400 year affliction, 430 years period; Law covenant made; Bible writing begun by Moses (Gen 15:13, 14;

Exo 12, 14, 24; Gal 3:17; John 5:46)

1512   Tabernacle completed; priesthood installed; Exodus, Leviticus completed (Exo 40:17; Lev 8:34-36; Lev 27:34; Num 1:1)

1500   Aryans conquer Dravidians in India; Hinduism originates in Indus

1474   Death of Aaron

1473   Job, Numbers, Dueteronomy written; Moses dies; Israel enters Canaan (Num 35:1; 36:13; Deut 29:1; Deut 1:1, 3; Deut 34:1, 5, 7; Josh 4:19)

1467   Major conquest completed; End of 450 yrs (Josh 11:23; 14:7, 10-15; Acts 13:17-20)

1450   Book of Joshua completed; Death of Joshua; Hittites conquer Asia Minor (Josh 1:1; 24:26, 29)

1447   Benjaminites mass sex sin

1437   New generation of Israel subjected to Canaanites

1436   Othniel raised as Judge, subdues Canaan; 40 years of peace

1424   First Jubilee celebrated

1396   Israel subject to King Eglon 18 years

1395   Judge Ehud raised up, delivers Israel; 80 years of peace

1365   Amenhotep IV and Nefertiti rule Egypt

1348   Tutankhamen rules Egypt

1316   Judge Shamgar kills 100 Philistines

1317   Israel subjugated to King Jabin of Hazor

1318   Judge Barak, Deborah defeat Sisera; 40 years of peacce

1279   Judge Gideon defeates Midianites with 300 men; 40 years of peace

1278   Midianites devastate Israel

1274   Hittites battle Egypt at Battle of Kadesh

1239   Gideon dies, Abimelech usurps power

1238   Judge Tola judges 23 years

1215   Judge Jair judges 22 years

1200   Sea Peoples devastate Hittite empire; Archaic period of Greece begins

1185   Fall of Troy at the hand of the Mycenaean Greeks

1181   Jephthah driven out; Hannah makes vow at Tabernacle

1180   Samuel born

1179   Rameses III conquers the coalition of Sea Peoples under Sarnam

1177   Samuel brought to Tabernacle, registered as a Levite & Nazirite

1176   Ahimelech born; Libyans and allies invade Egypt

1174   Israel repents of false worship due to oppression by enemies

1173   Jephthah becomes Judge and Leader of Israel

1172   Jephthah battles Ammon; Tirzah sent to Shiloh

1171   Jephthah defeats the tribe of Ephraim

1168   Samuel becomes Prophet; Defeat at Aphek; Death of Eli & his sons; Sacking of Shiloh and move of Tabernacle to Nob

1167   Ark returned to Israel; Ibzan becomes Judge; Angel visits Manoah

1166   Samson is born

1162   Samuel marries

1161   Judge Ibzan dies

1160   Elon becomes Judge

1158   Egyptian workers strike when Rameses III fails to pay them

1157	Saul born; Harem conspiracy in Egypt, Queen Tiy attempts assassination
1156	Rameses III dies of injuries during trial of conspirators
1155	Rameses IV sends expedition to gold mines in south of Egypt
1151	Joel born to Samuel; Judge Elon dies and is buried at Aijalon
1150	Abdon becomes Judge; Rameses IV dies of smallpox
1149	Abijah born
1142	Abner born; Judge Abdon dies; High Priest Ahitub dies; Battle of Mizpah; Samuel becomes Judge of Israel
1141	Samuel's circuit begins
1138	Samson begins judging Israel
1137	Jonathan born to Saul
1133	Ishvi born to Saul
1131	Malchishua born to Saul
1130	Doeg the Edomite born
1128	Abinadab born to Saul
1127	Nathan the Prophet born?
1126	Merab born to Saul;
1125	Armoni born to Saul
1124	JUBILEE YEAR
1123	Mephibosheth born to Saul
1121	Ish-bosheth born to Saul; Samson captured?
1120	Joel and Abijah sent south with wives
1119	Samson killed
1117	Saul anointed; Samuel's sons corrupt (1 Sam 10:24; Acts 13:21)
1116	Attack by Nahash
1115	Defeat of Nahash--confirmation
1114	Army grows-Philistines ally with Rephaim
1113	Battles of Michmash and Migron
1112	Ishvi, son of Saul, dies accidentally; Michal born
1110	Kish dies
1107	David born (1 Sam 16:1)
1100	Book of Judges completed; Phoenician traders settle on Iberian Peninsula (Judg 21:25)
1095	Saul defeats Agag--Condemned!
1092	David anointed by Samuel; plays for Saul
1091	Battle of Elah; David made war chief
1090	Book of Ruth completed (Ruth 4:18-22)
1089	David marries Michal
1088	David and Samuel at Naioth
1087	Mephibosheth born to Jonathan; David in Nob, Achish
1086	Doeg kills priests
1085	David saves Keilah--is pursued
1084	Samuel dies; Nabal; David's flight to Philistia
1083	David in Philistia
1082	Battle of Mt. Gilboah-Death of Saul, sons
1078	1 Samuel completed (1 Sam 31:6)

1077	David becomes king of Judah (2 Sam 2:4)
1076	Ishbosheth installed as king by Abner
1075	Battle of Helkath-hazzurim; Death of Asahel
1074	Absalom born to David
1073	Abner defects to David; Joab kills him
1072	Ishbosheth killed
1071	Zion taken by David
1070	David King of Israel & Judah; conquest Jerusalem; moves Ark (2 Sam 5:3-7; 6:15; 7:12-16)
1069	David builds house with Hiram
1067	Battle at Ba'al-perazim
1066	Battle of Rephaim
1065	David brings Ark; plans temple; gets covenant
1064	David conquers Philistia, Moab
1063	David conquers Zobah, Aram; Edom
1062	David honors Mephibosheth; conquers Ammon/Aram
1061	Seige of Rabbah-sin with Bathsheba
1059	Child David and Bathsheba dies.
1058	Solomon born; Rabbah taken.
1057	Rape of Tamar
1055	Absalom kills Amnon, flees
1052	Absalom recalled; Revolts! David flees
1051	Hushai; Athitophel's suicide
1050	Civil War! Absalom killed and mourned
1049	David returns to Jerusalem
1048	Sheba's revolt; Amasa killed
1047	Three year famine
1045	Sons of Saul exposed by Gibeonites
1044	Wars with Philistia--Mighty men
1040	Book of 2 Samuel completed (2 Sam 24:18)
1037	Solomon becomes king (1 Ki 1:39; 2:12)
1034	Temple construction begun (1 Ki 6:1)
1027	First Temple completed (1 Ki 6:38)
1026	Temple dedicated by Solomon
1020	Song of Solomon written (Cant 1:1)
1000	Ecclesiastes completed (Eccl 1:1)

Obviously, the apportioning of events between the years of 1450 B.C.E. and 1117 B.C.E. are supposition on the part of the author. This is also true of most of the events between 1117 B.C.E. and 1037 B.C.E. This timeline is one way in which the information in Judges and the books of Samuel and Kings can be rectified. It is by no means the only way. Many readers will no doubt recoil in horror at the suggestion that Samson was alive in Saul's day, or that Samuel could have been serving as a Judge at the same time that Samson was. I do not assert that this outline is accurate, or even highly plausible. It is one possibility, one which seemed to me to fit the information available in the Scriptures and to serve the story I was attempting to tell. Perhaps by the time the next volume of this Chronicle is published (deo volente!), I will have re-written this timeline to reflect discoveries uncovered in my continued research on the subject.

TIMOTHY WILKINSON

Appendix E:
The Two Eternal Thrones

It is unquestionably one of the most celebrated and retold stories in human history. Its heroes are among the most widely recognized characters in the western world. It has not only survived, but remained popular for over a thousand years, and an unceasing stream of books, films, and art still flow from this seemingly inexhaustible reservoir.

It is the story of King Arthur and the Knights of the Round Table.

In spite of all of its incarnations, there are elements of the story that remain fairly constant and have become part of popular culture: the otherworldly origin and supernatural powers of the wizard Merlin. King Uther's lust for Queen Igraine and the unforeseen importance of the offspring of that union. Arthur's training by Merlin. Arthur's selection as king by his pulling of the sword from the stone. The new king's unification of the squabbling tribes of Britain under a powerful, central monarchy. Arthur's magical sword Excalibur. His gathering of the Knights of the Round Table, including a valiant trinity of brothers from Orkney: Gawain, Gaheris, and Agravayne. The quest for the Holy Grail. The disastrous love triangle between Arthur, his queen Guinevere, and one of his knights, Lancelot. Arthur's battle against his rebellious son, Modred, at Badon Hill that leads to the downfall of the kingdom. Arthur's disappearance, and the promise that he will one day return to lead his people to an era of peace and prosperity.

Where did it all come from? Who really was King Arthur, and what is the origin of this enduring, extraordinary story?

The question has been hotly debated for centuries. To some degree, it is a question of what one means by "origin." The historical origin of a king *named* Arthur? There is no shortage of candidates to choose from; from the 5th century Brythonic king Riothamus, to the 7th century king Anwyn, to the Penine king Arthwys, to another Arthwys, King of Elmet, to a Scottish prince named Artur (Ford, 2007). One of the leading theories is that he was a "heroic British cavalry general named Arturius" who "halted the pagan

Saxon invaders with their Pictish and Anglian allies...and in 517 won a decisive victory at Mount Badon...He fell in 538, at the Battle of Camlan, near Glastonbury, which was both the seat of an ancient pagan cult and a Christian shrine associated with St. Joseph of Arimathea. There his knights secretly buried him" (Graves, 1962).

But there is more to origin than the source of a name. Perhaps the more important question is: Where did the *stories* come from? It has been clearly established that, by and large, the events in the Arthurian saga are not historical. So who was the king, and whose the kingdom, on which the legends were based?

I believe that the answer to that question can be found in yet another widely known story, this time an historical account written in the tenth century B.C.E.: the story of King David of Israel.

The Earliest Sources

Let us trace the development of the Arthurian legend to put this theory to the test. The earliest sources that refer to the famous king share almost nothing with the modern legend save the name. Some see references to Arthur in ancient Welsh bardic tales about the hero Bran the Blessed. Bran bore the title *Arddu* (pronounced *Arthu*) and possessed a magic cornucopia called *Cor Benoit*, which appears to have become one of the sources for both the Holy Grail and the name of the Grail castle, Corbenic.[7]

A series of elegies supposedly composed by the bard Aneirin around the year 638 called *Y Goddodin* contains one of the first known references to the famous monarch by name when, in discussing the valor of a particular warrior in the tale, the author mentions that he 'was no Arthur.' Similarly, the *Death Song of Cynddylan* (circa 655) metaphorically describes valiant warriors as 'whelps of Arthur' (King Arthur in Literature).

Sometime around the year 730, in his *Ecclesiastical History of the English People*, St. Bede the Venerable records details of the Battle of Badon Hill and names Ambrosius Aurelianus and Vortigern (but not Arthur) as participants (King Arthur in Literature).

A century later, the *Historia Brittonum* (attributed to the Welsh monk Nennius) includes tales of the wizard Merlin (called by Nennius "Ambrosius" and based on the Welsh folk-hero Merddyn Wyllt) and the Battle of

---

[7] (*Cor* may have been mistranslated as *cors*, or body, and become a reference to the Body of Christ).

Badon Hill. (Matthews, 1989) In this account, Arthur is there, but not as king—he leads the army as the *dux bellorum*, or military commander.

A Latin collection of Welsh history, *The Annales Cambriae* was written sometime around 970. It also mentions the "Battle of Badon, in which Arthur carried the cross of our Lord Jesus Christ on his shoulders for three days and three nights and the Britons were victors." It also includes a reference to "the strife of Camlann in which Arthur and Medraut fell." The *Annales* also mentions the battle of Arfderydd and says that following the battle "Myrddin (Merlin) went mad" (Green, 2007).

Arthur next appears in the tenth century Welsh tale *The Spoils of Annwfyn*, leading his war band (including a knight named Llwch Lleminiawg, considered by many to be the original Lancelot) on a series of expeditions into the underworld (Matthews, 1989). It is generally accepted that this story summarizes a number of Arthurian tales that already existed when it was written. This tradition continues with the stories *Culhwch and Olwen* and *The Dream of Rhonabwy* in the famous medieval collection *The Mabinogion* (probably written between 1060 and 1200). Interestingly, several of these tales contain references to the Cauldron of Annwfyn, a bowl that has the power to heal and/or return life to the dead. Some scholars believe that this may be another root of the legend of the Holy Grail, although that is by no means a consensus view (Matthews, 1989).

In the *Mabinogion* "the magnetic figure of Arthur drew to him a vast panoply of Celtic heroes, whose honour it became to serve at his court." (Matthews, 1989) This is, of course, echoed in every following version of the story—the assemblage of the Knights of the Round Table. The *Mabinogion* details the superhuman exploits of these warriors that brought them to Arthur's attention.

Here we see the early appearance of Biblical parallels—although taken on their own they would seem nothing more than a literary commonality. Nathan the Prophet, author of the Bible book of 2 Samuel follows the same pattern as the author of the *Mabinogion*. King David gathers his *gibborim*, his "Mighty Men," and 2 Samuel chapter 23 gives us the backstories of these knights and their feats of valor.

The History of the Kings of Britain

But the origin of the story as it has come down to us today really begins with the pseudo-historical work of a Bishop of St. Asaph named Geoffrey of Monmouth. Claiming that he was translating a "certain very ancient book written in the British language" given him by one Walter, Archdeacon of Oxford, in around 1135 he wrote *Historia Regum Britanniae* (Matthews, 1989). In his writings, Geoffrey specifically stated that he intended to portray Arthur as the one who would make Britain "a new Israel."

Merlin the Enchanter appears early in *Historia*. He is a prophet from a very young age with supernatural powers who serves as an advisor to Arthur throughout his reign. When he dies, Arthur's kingdom begins to fall into decline. He corresponds to the Biblical prophet Samuel, who likewise manifests supernatural powers as a child (1 Samuel 7:10, 1 Samuel 12:18) and serves as an advisor to David. After Samuel's death, David's kingdom begins to fail.

In Geoffrey's account, Vortigern is threatened by Saxon invaders and unwisely shows them mercy, leading to years of warfare. In the Bible book of 1 Samuel, Israelite King Saul is likewise threatened by foreign invaders and shows mercy to their king, Agag (1 Samuel chapter 15). For this he is condemned by the prophet Samuel and told that his kingship will not last (1 Samuel 15:22, 23).

As the story continues, Vortigern's successor, Uther Pendragon, sees the wife of the Duke of Tintagil, the Lady Igraine, and immediately lusts after her. With the help of Merlin, Uther lures the Duke to his death so that Uther can bed his wife, a union that results in the birth of a child named Arthur, who is destined to become king. This episode appears to be a clear reference to another event in 1 Samuel. King David sees Bathsheba, the wife of one of his knights, Uriah the Hittite. With the help of his military commander, Joab, David has Uriah sent to his death while the king takes Bathsheba to his bed (2 Samuel 11). Although the child of this union dies, the son that is born afterward is named Solomon, another prince destined to be king.

In Geoffrey's account, Arthur follows up his inauguration by defeating the Saxons and his other enemies throughout Europe, eventually uniting "the various petty kings and chieftains who had reasserted their claims to the land after the last vestiges of Roman rule came to an end." (Matthews, 1989) Arthur's leadership produces a united monarchy that ushers in a period of peace. According to the Bible writer Samuel, David also welds the feuding (Judges 8:1, 9:1-57, 12:1, 15:11, 20:1-48) tribes into a united monarchy, and then begins expanding the empire's borders in every direction.

Near the time of his coronation, Geoffrey's Arthur learns that a giant from a foreign land is terrorizing Britain. The local knights are all too afraid to challenge this champion. Arthur travels to the scene with his knights Sir Kay and Sir Bedivere (probably rooted in the Celtic fire god Cai and the war-god Bedwyr) but, after seeing the giant, decides to face the monster on his own. The king kills his enemy with a single blow to its brow, and then has its head cut off and carried as a trophy back to their camp. From this and later exploits, Arthur gains the reputation as a giant-killer and eventually rids the kingdom of these monsters. (Green, 2007)

In all likelihood, parts of this story originated in ancient stories of the Welsh hero Lugh who, in *Cath Miage Tuired,* slays a giant with a sling-stone. (Green) It is easy, though, to recognize in this account the famous Biblical story of David and Goliath. Once again, a giant from a foreign land (in this case one of the Rephaim who have settled in the Philistine city of Gath) is terrorizing Israel, and the local knights are too afraid to answer Goliath's challenge to single combat. David kills Goliath with a single slingstone to the forehead, then cuts off his head and carries it as a trophy back into the Israelite camp. During later years of his reign, he and his knights defeat a number of other giants (1 Samuel chapter 17) until all mention of the Rephaim disappears from the Bible.

In Geoffrey's account, while Arthur is gone fighting the Romans under Ceaser Tiberius his son Modred steals the king's throne. Arthur returns to a civil war against his own son which culminates in Modred's death and Arthur's mortal wounding. King David faces a similar insurrection when his son, Absalom, steals the throne of Jerusalem and drives the kingdom into civil war. (2 Samuel chapters 15 through 17) In the ensuing battle Absalom is killed and David—and his kingdom—never recover from the tragedy. (2 Samuel 18:33)

Wace, the Canon of Bayeaux

We know little about the Anglo-Norman writer Wace, other than that his work, *Roman de Brut,* written around 1155, is primarily a translation of Geoffrey of Monmouth's *Historia Regum Britanniae.* In the "translation" process, however, he does add the idea of the Round Table and gives Arthur's sword the name Excalibur (from Caledfwlch in Welsh, Latinized to Caliburnus by Geoffrey of Monmouth).

Chrétien de Troyes

The French poet Chrétien de Troyes composed a series of narrative poems between c.1170 and c.1185 supposedly based on an unnamed source book given him by his patron, Count Philip of Flanders. Chrétien gives us the stories of Arthur's greatest knights. (Matthews, 1989) In *Perceval, le Conte du Graal* the knight Perceval sees a *graal*—in this account a wide, deep dish or bowl containing a single Mass wafer which is all that sustains a quasi-Christian character known as The Fisher King. (Loomis, The Grail: From Celtic Myth to Christian Symbol, 1991) Chrétien also introduces Camelot and the tragic love triangle between King Arthur, Queen Guinevere, and one of Arthur's knights, Lancelot.

Of course, as already mentioned, the love triangles in the Arthurian story mirror David's illicit relationship with Bathsheba, the wife of Uriah, one of David's greatest knights.

Gerald of Wales

The famous churchman Gerald of Wales authored seventeen popular and well-respected books of British history between 1156 and 1223. In one of them, he writes that he was at Glastonbury Abbey in 1190 or 1191 when the monks there exhumed the body of King Arthur from his grave. It is now widely accepted that the monks of Glastonbury invented the "exhumation" as a publicity stunt to draw pilgrims to the abbey. I mention the account only to demonstrate that it was not uncommon for churchmen of the time to use the legend of King Arthur for their own agendas—be it by inventing his grave or inventing events in his life.

Robert de Borron

It is to the Burgundian knight and poet Robert de Borron that we owe some of the latest additions to the legend. His work *Le Roman du Graal* was comprised of three poems: *Joseph d'Arimathea, Merlin,* and *Perceval.* I write *was* because all but one and a half of the poems are lost to history; we know of their contents from prose versions that are also believed to have been written by de Borron between 1191 and 1202.

He also Christianized the legend, explaining Merlin's supernatural powers by presenting him as the offspring of the devil and a nun, and adding some detail to the story of Joseph of Arimathea's possession of the Grail. *Le Roman du Graal* is filled with Christian symbology: a fish that represents Christ, the punishment of false disciples, sin as the source of want among the people, a "godhead" of three Grail-keepers. (Matthews, 1989)

But it is from his poem *Merlin* that de Borron's most memorable contribution comes. Here we first find mention of the Sword in the Stone, a symbol by which the true king of Britain can be identified. Merlin brings the kings and leaders of the land to his test of their right to rule: a sword plunged through an anvil which sits atop a block of stone, which can only be withdrawn by the rightful heir to the throne. The various tribal leaders of the country are gathered around the stone, and each of them tries his hand at removing it. But it is the youngest one present who is successful and is proclaimed by Merlin to be the rightful king.

De Borron's drawing of a sword through an anvil from a stone is, of course, a fairly straightforward metaphor for the production of weapons-grade metal from raw ore, a fitting subject for the story of a leader who may have seen his people through a part of the transition from bronze to iron. King David found himself in the same position. In the days of his predecessor, Saul, the Philistines had established such a monopoly on the production and repair of iron that Samuel reports "there was not a smith to be found in Israel...and all the Israelites would go down to the Philistines to get each one his plowshare or his mattock or his axe or his sickle sharpened." (1 Samuel 13: 19, 20) The Philistines (believed to be one of the "Sea Peoples" who were driven from Mycenae) had conquered Anatolia not long before this and archaeology indicates that they carried the Hittite secrets of iron-making with them into Palestine, where it remained their secret for many years. The Bible is not specific on the subject, but when David returns to Israel after spending time as a vassal lord in Philistia, he begins to consistently win battles against the Philistine army. Did he bring with him the carefully guarded metallurgical secret of the Hittites? It is at around this time that iron tools and weapons begin to show up with regularity in the Israelite archaeological record.

In any case, the drawing of the sword from the stone also reflects two accounts from the Bible, both of which cooperate to make David the undisputed King of Israel. The first is the gathering of the sons of Jesse in 1 Samuel chapter 16. As with the lords assembled around the Sword in the Stone, one by one Samuel presents the men to God, and one by one they are found unworthy. Then the youngest son is summoned from the field; David, still a boy, is selected and anointed as king.

The second account is David's confrontation with the giant Goliath. Just as with King Arthur, the confirmation of David's destiny involves a giant, a unique sword, a stone, and a young, unknown contender for a disputed throne.

The swords of both kings deserve additional mention. As we have already seen, Arthur's sword is the magical Excalibur, received from the quasi-religious figure the Lady of the Lake. David takes Goliath's sword for his own. Nowhere is it suggested that the sword has magical powers, but imagine the size of a sword forged for a nine-and-a-half foot tall national champion! Not only would it have been huge, but also made of the finest quality metal that the Philistines had available to them—perhaps even steel forged from meteor-ore.[8] Only twice in the entire canon of the Hebrew Scriptures are any real details given about a specific weapon. One is the description of Judge Ehud's custom dagger in Judges Chapter 3 verse 16. The other is David's comment regarding Goliath's sword, a statement that finds no parallel anywhere else in the Bible. When it is returned to him at the hands of the religious figure, High Priest Ahimelech, the future king says, "There is no other like it." (1 Samuel 21:9) In both Arthur and David's cases the possession of an extraordinary sword is one of the indications of a divinely-approved ruler. What would David have looked like as he charged into battle with an enormous (possibly two-handed for him) sword against enemies who typically carried blades less than twenty-four inches long? (Herzog, 1997)

The Vulgate Cycle

The next significant development in the Arthurian saga was a series of five volumes of prose written by Cistercian monks under the direction of the famous clergyman Bernard of Clairvaux sometime between 1220 and 1240. (Matthews, 1989)

This religiose retelling adds a number of important elements now considered vital parts of the story. Bernard writes that in the king's old age Arthur decides that he wants to be remembered for something more than his military exploits. He seeks a mission of spiritual value, and thus is conceived the Quest for the Holy Grail. The Cistercian monks provide a brief history of the Grail, explaining that Joseph of Arimathea carried the sacred cup, used by Christ at the Last Super, to Britain. The Grail can be found only by a knight who is pure in heart, and the character of Galahad (a son of

---

[8] Two centuries earlier, Egyptian Pharaoh Tutankhamen was buried with a very fine steel dagger lying on his chest. Archaeologists have concluded that the dagger was made of meteor-steel, likely forged by Hittite smiths (Shawn, 1995).

Lancelot's adulterous affair with the lady Elain of Carbonek) is invented for this purpose. Galahad is the model of warrior-asceticism, an example for the Knights Templar that Bernard so fervently endorsed. (In fact in the Vulgate Cycle Galahad's coat of arms is a white shield with a vermilion cross, the same symbol assigned to the Templars by Pope Euguene III, a disciple of Bernard's). Galahad's name is a Biblical one—a corruption of Gilead, meaning *Witness Heap*, suggesting Galahad's inextricable connection to the "heap" of testimony provided in the Hebrew Scriptures to point toward the coming of the Christ. (Loomis, The Development of the Arthurian Romance, 2000) He it is who finds the Grail, proving himself more 'pure in heart' (as the Tennyson poem, *Sir Galahad*, expresses it) than Arthur and Lancelot.

During the Grail quest Galahad, Perceval, and Bors all board a boat upon which wait a "strange sword" and a crown. A maiden tells them that the boat had been built by King Solomon in anticipation of a descendent of his who would become the greatest knight in the world and achieve the Grail Quest. She also informs them that the crown was Solomon's and the sword was King David's own (taken from the giant Goliath).

Once again the affair between Lancelot and Guinevere is highlighted and to the sinful nature of Arthur and his knights is ascribed the downfall of Camelot. Mordred is introduced as Arthur's son and nephew, the result of the king's unwitting incest with his sister Morgaine, or Morgan le Fay.

When the relationship between Lancelot and Guinevere is uncovered, Lancelot escapes and Guinevere is sentenced to death. Lancelot returns to rescue her but in the process accidentally kills Gaheris and Gareth, the sons of Lot. Driven by the implacable vengeance of their brother Gawain (originally Gwalchmai, a Welsh solar deity), Arthur travels to France to attack Lancelot. While he is there, Arthur's illegitimate son Mordred takes over the kingdom of Britain, claims that Arthur is dead, and commands Guinevere to marry him. When Arthur learns of Mordred's treachery, he returns from France and meets his son in the Battle of Badon Hill. Arthur kills Mordred, and Mordred gives Arthur a mortal wound. At the end of the tale, Arthur is borne away by Morgan le Fay[9], the Lady of the Lake, to Avalon, with the promise that he will one day return.

---

[9] Morgan le Fay who had, until this point in history, been portrayed as a healer or as the Celtic battle-goddess Morgana, is now transformed into Arthur's evil, enchantress half-sister. Apparently this was a result of further

Once again, the Vulgate Cycle's version of events parallels those of King David's reign. In David's later years, he desired to be remembered for something more than his military exploits. He sought a mission of spiritual value, and determined to build a Temple for his God, Jehovah, in Jerusalem. (2 Samuel 7:1, 2) Like Arthur, he is found unworthy to do so ("because of the warfare with which they surrounded him" according to 1 Kings 5:3) and the task is given to one more pure in heart—his son, Solomon. (2 Samuel 7:12, 13)

John Matthews (1989) writes that "the grail represents not just a spiritual quest in place of the violent physical, but a connection between the mundane and the spiritual, as well as a means of healing the people and the land, the means to ultimate good. It is only a representation of a more potent reality: the sacrificial blood of Christ which it contains."

In all of this it is a potent parallel to the Temple of Solomon, for which this entire description also holds true.

Lancelot's killing of Gaheris and the ensuing feud echoes an episode early in David's rule. In 2 Samuel chapter 2 Abner, Saul's uncle and military commander, is pursued by a young Asahel, one of the famous sons of Zeruiah who are among David's greatest knights. The veteran Abner begs Asahel to give off the chase because he did not desire to kill the lad. When Asahel refused, "Abner got to strike him in the abdomen with the butt end of the spear, so that the spear came out from his back; and he fell there and died where he was." (2 Samuel 2:20-23) From that day forward, Asahel's brothers, Joab and Abishai, driven by their desire for vengeance, murder and manipulate their way through the kingdom (see 2 Samuel 3:22-27, 11:14-25, 18:1-17, 20:8-33, 1 Kings 1:18, 19) until Joab is finally executed by Solomon after David's death.

As the sons of Lot were key players in the civil war that divided Arthur's kingdom, Joab was indirectly responsible for the success of David's son Absalom's insurrection against David, although in the end it is he who slaughters Absalom against David's direct orders. (2 Samuel 18: 9-17) And just as Mordred tried to force Guinevere to marry him to give legitimacy to his rule, one of Absalom's first acts on taking the city of Jerusalem is to

---

religious influence on the story—the Cistercians believed that attributing the powers of healing or prophecy, even in literature, to a woman who was not a member of a religious order was blasphemy.

"have relations with the concubines of his father" on the roof of the palace "under the eyes of all Israel." (2 Samuel 16:20-22)

Mordred gave Arthur a wound that would not heal; Absalom's rebellion and death cast a pall on David from which the king never fully recovers.

Le Morte d'Arthur

In around 1470 a former Member of Parliament was languishing in Newgate prison after a string of bizarre crimes: the ambush and attempted murder of the Duke of Buckingham, robbing Coombe Abbey and insulting the abbot, the rape of one Henry Smyth's wife, large scale cattle theft, and highway robbery. He had already escaped incarceration twice—once by swimming the moat of Coleshill prison and once by making an armed breakout from Colchester Castle.[10]

The accused was Sir Thomas Malory, King Arthur's most famous biographer. During his years in Newgate, Malory assembled the work of previous chroniclers into the first "coherent history of Arthur from his curious birth to his dramatic death." (Graves, 1962) Malory called it *The hoole booke of kyng Arthur & of his noble knyghtes of the round table*. William Caxton published the work for Malory—posthumously and anonymously (apparently for fear the author's reputation would decrease sales). He called it *Le Morte d'Arthur*.

Malory did not add much that was new to the core of the legend (his work seems to be based almost entirely on the *Vulgate Cycle*), but his decisions as to what to include shaped *Le Morte d'Arthur* into the most Davidic version of the story that had been published up to that time. His language and pacing is Biblical. (Matthews, 1989) As an example, note the description of Galahad's arrival at court, "redolent with New Testament detail" (Matthews, 1989): "In the Meanwhile came in a good old man, and an ancient, clothed all in white, and there was no knight knew from whence he came. And with him he brought a young knight, both on foot, in red arms, without sword or shield, save a scabbard hanging by his side. And these words he said: 'Peace be with you, fair lords.'" (Malory, 1962)

---

[10] It should be acknowledged that some modern historians believe that the Sir Thomas Malory responsible for these crimes is, in fact, a different person than the writer of *Le Morte d'Arthur*. This is not, however, the predominant view.

JUDGE OF ISRAEL

Of course, the stories are outspokenly "Christian," but in name only: they are thick with fornication, adultery, pedophilia, brutality, incest, and vengeance. Robert Graves, in his introduction to Keith Baines' 1962 translation of the work, observes that Mallory had turned Arthur into "a counter-Christ, with twelve knights of the Round Table to suggest Twelve Apostles, and with a Second Coming." The intended audience of the work were a people for whom the "ascetic morality preached by Jesus" was completely foreign. Their behavior, much like that of the Knights of the Round Table, was largely shaped by their determination to protect their personal and national honor at all costs. It was difficult to reconcile this attitude with Jesus' admonitions to humility and 'turning the other cheek.' The seigniorial class of the time identified more with their interpretation of the morality of the ancient Israelite warrior who "fought ruthlessly: thrusting women through the belly with his javelin, dashing the little ones against stones, and smiting noncombatants with the edge of his sword." (Graves, 1962)

But in Malory's version it is particularly easy to identify the Davidic parallels. Here we find Merlin/Samuel (whose birth is the result of supernatural intervention) becoming a prophet at a young age and manifesting supernatural abilities, responsible for the enthronement of Vortigern/Saul and Arthur/David. Vortigern/Saul unwisely shows mercy to their foreign enemies and is condemned for it. Uther/David falls in lust with Igraine/Bathsheba and beds her while arranging the death of her husband the Duke of Tintagel/Uriah the Hittite. A child of this union, Arthur/Solomon, becomes the next king when his father, Uther/David, on his deathbed, throws his support behind him.

Here we see the leaders of Britain/the sons of Jesse gathered before Merlin/Samuel, one by one rejected until the youngest and humblest among them, Arthur/David, is chosen. Confirmation of the new king involves a unique sword, a battle with a giant, and a stone. Arthur/David takes up his exceptional weapon: Excalibur/the sword of Goliath.

We watch as Arthur/David assembles his knights/mighty men, and we wonder at the supernatural skill and strength they demonstrate as the litany of their achievements is set before us. We note the significance of the sons of Lot/Zeruiah: Gawain, Gaheris and Gareth/Joab, Abishai, and Asahel.

After a life of unparalleled success in battle against his enemies, Arthur/David determines to pursue a more spiritual goal, the Grail Quest/construction of the Temple. But Arthur/David is found unworthy to do so, and the privilege is enjoyed by one more pure in heart, Gala-had/Solomon.

Central to *Le Morte d'Arthur* is the tragic love triangle of Ar-thur/David, Guinevere/Bathsheba, and Lancelot/Uriah (both foreigners). This transgression in combination with crimes committed by Lance-lot/Abner against one of the sons of Lot/Zeruiah plunges the nation into civil war. After driving his father away, Arthur/David's son, Mor-dred/Absalom propositions/beds Arthur/David's wife/concubines. In the ensuing battle, Mordred/Absalom is killed and Arthur/David receives a wound from which he never fully recovers.

Conclusions

As has been clearly documented, the "final" version of the legend of King Arthur is an amalgam of the work of many biographers, historians, and spinners of legend. Its roots are sunk all the way down to pre-Roman times, to Celtic, Welsh, and Irish mythologies. Does not this cumulative origin ar-gue strongly against the idea that the story is based on the Biblical King Da-vid?

The Bible is no more (and, arguably, no less) a source than is *Y Goddodin, Historia Brittonum, The Mabinogion, Historia Regum Britanniae, Le Ro-man du Graal*, the Vulgate Cycle, or *Le Morte d'Arthur*. All of the contributors to the medieval Arthurian literary tradition built fresh constructs on the wea-thered structures left by their predecessors. The real question is: from where did they get their new material? Not from history—that much is sure. It is easy to assume that they were simply the compilers of the work of previous chroniclers, as so many of them claim to be, but that does not put the question to rest. For if Geoffrey did not, in fact, invent the story of the se-duction of Igraine, but received it from the author of some "very ancient book", then whence did *that* author get the account? The story of Arthur is an amalgam, of course, but the amalgamators threw in additional material of their own as they worked. Certainly, some of the ideas came from their imaginations, but consider two facts that make it extremely unlikely that all, or even most, of it did so.

First: who were these "compilers?" Geoffrey was a Bishop, Wace was a canon, Chrétien de Troyes was writing for a devout Cathari, Robert de Borron blatantly Christianized the work, Bernard of Clairvaux was an abbot promoting the ideas of the Knights Templar. As has already been noted, several of them admitted to religious aspirations for their writing. To what would they turn when seeking to flesh out the story of Britain's greatest king? To the greatest king of the Bible, of course—a hero with the human frailties they needed to make him an accessible model for Christian knights.

Second: there are simply too many parallels between the Arthurian story as it has come down to us and the Biblical account of David's life to be coincidental. It would be a different matter if the Bible (or some other ancient source) were filled with stories of prophet-advised, giant-slaying kings with extraordinary swords who gather knights of superhuman ability, are condemned for their involvement in an illicit love triangle, fail to achieve their loftiest goal due to impurity in their hearts, and battle their own sons in a civil war that ends in the son's death and the father's ultimate destruction. But the Bible is not filled with such characters and events; nor is any other work of literature. This combination is unique to two tales: David, the greatest king of Israel, and Arthur, the greatest king of Britain.

To the medieval audience for whom these tales were originally written, Arthur represented a unique leader—one who was loved by his subjects, but had human weaknesses and faced human trials. Arthur was presented as a re-incarnation of the values that King David had always been known for. Although Arthur's life ended in disgrace, the author expresses confidence that he, like Jesus, son of David, will return and rule again with all the traits that made him extraordinary. In Malory's words: "In many parts of Britain it is believed that King Arthur did not die and that he will return to us and win fresh glory and the Holy Cross of our Lord Jesu Christ…And inscribed on his tomb, men say, is this legend: Hic iacet Arthurus, rex quondam rexque futures." (Malory, 1962)

For these reasons, David is called by Jewish rabbis "the first and the last of the Jewish rulers." (Shitah Hadashah) Among British historians and bards, Arthur is named, as above, "the once and future king." (Malory, 1962)

Timothy Wilkinson

-Works Cited-

Ford, D. N. (2007). *King Arthur*. Retrieved June 28, 2009, from Britannia History: http://www.britannia.com/history/h12.html

Graves, R. (1962). *Introduction to Sir Thomas Malory's Le Morte d'Arthur*. Garden City: International Collector's Library.

Green, T. (2007). *Concepts of Arthur*. Chalford Stroud: Tempus Publishing.

Herzog, C. &. (1997). *Battles of the Bible*. London: Greenhill Books, Lionel Leventhal Limited.

King Arthur in Literature. (n.d.). Retrieved June 22, 2009, from Legend of King Arthur: http://www.legendofkingarthur.co.uk/literature-king-arthur.htm

Loomis, R. S. (1991). *The Grail: From Celtic Myth to Christian Symbol*. Princeton: Princeton.

Loomis, R. S. (2000). *The Development of Arthurian Romance*. Mineloa. Dover Publications.

Malory, S. T. (1962). *Le Morte d'Arthur*. (K. Baines, Trans.) Garden City: International Collector's Library.

Matthews, J. (1989). *The Elements of the Arthurian Tradition*. Rockport: Element, Inc.

Watchtower Bible and Tract Society, Inc. *The New World Translation of the Holy Scriptures*. New York.

Shawn, I. a. (1995). *The Dictionary of Ancient Egypt*. New York: Henry N. Adams, Inc.

Shitah Hadashah 2. . (Zohar I, 82b; III, 84a.).

JUDGE OF ISRAEL

TIMOTHY WILKINSON

-About the Author-

Although he has worked as a construction laborer, concrete mason, replica maker, retail clerk, store manager, mortgage broker, glazier, canoe-builder, journalist, film producer, musician, recording artist, educational consultant, web designer, professional sailor, tutor, and teacher, since the age of seven Timothy Wilkinson has been a writer of fictions. An avid sailor and a teacher of history and literature, author of volumes of poetry and plays for screen and stage, he spends his days on Washington State's Olympic Peninsula with his wife Chelsey and their dog, Bolt. His latest endeavor, the *Eternal Throne Chronicles*, of which *Judge of Israel* is the second installment, is the fruit of nearly a decade of re-writes, abandoned drafts and an ongoing pursuit of historical truth.

Judge of Israel